Praise for Andrew Vachss

"Vachss's reverence for storytelling is evident in the blunt beauty of his language." —*Chicago Sun-Times*

"Vachss's style is personal, laconic, shaded, and of course creepy. If you like hard-boiled . . . narrative, this is the read for you." —*Los Angeles Times Book Review*

"Vachss seems bottomlessly knowledgeable about the depth and variety of human twistedness."—*The New York Times*

"A contemporary master. . . . Decidedly hard-boiled, his prose is lean, tough-edged, and brittle." —*The Atlanta Journal-Constitution*

"Vachss's stories . . . burn with righteous rage and transfer a degree of that rage to the reader." —*The Washington Post Book World*

"Vachss's style is as compelling as his vision is unnerving. You'll get paper cuts from flipping the pages." —*Post and Courier* (Charleston, SC)

Andrew Vachss

Aftershock

Andrew Vachss is a lawyer who represents children and youths exclusively. His many books include the Burke novels and three collections of short stories. His books have been translated into twenty languages, and his work has appeared in *Parade*, *Antaeus*, *Esquire*, *Playboy*, and *The New York Times*, among other publications. He divides his time between his native New York City and the Pacific Northwest.

www.vachss.com

BOOKS BY ANDREW VACHSS

THE BURKE SERIES

Flood
Strega
Blue Belle
Hard Candy
Blossom
Sacrifice
Down in the Zero
Footsteps of the Hawk
False Allegations
Safe House
Choice of Evil
Dead and Gone
Pain Management
Only Child
Down Here
Mask Market
Terminal
Another Life

THE CROSS SERIES

Blackjack
Urban Renewal

OTHER NOVELS

Shella
The Getaway Man
Two Trains Running
Haiku
The Weight
That's How I Roll
A Bomb Built in Hell

SHORT STORY COLLECTIONS

Born Bad
Everybody Pays
Mortal Lock

THE AFTERSHOCK SERIES

Aftershock
Shockwave

Aftershock

Andrew Vachss

Vintage Crime/Black Lizard
Vintage Books
A Division of Random House LLC
New York

FIRST VINTAGE CRIME/BLACK LIZARD EDITION, MARCH 2014

The Library of Congress has cataloged the Pantheon edition as follows:
Vachss, Andrew H.
Aftershock / Andrew Vachss.
p. cm.
1. Psychopaths—Fiction. 2. School shootings—Fiction.
3. Mercenary troops—Fiction. 4. Murder—Investigation—Fiction.
5. Oregon—Fiction. I. Title.
PS3572.A33A67 2012 813'.54—dc23 2012018001
839.82'38—dc23 2012047015

Vintage Trade Paperback ISBN: 978-0-307-95088-8
eBook ISBN: 978-0-307-90775-2

www.weeklylizard.com

Printed in the United States of America
10 9 8 7 6 5 4 3 2 1

for . . .

Gale, who battled incoming her entire life, never took a backward step, and was cut down way too soon.

When I came to the place we always meet, you were already gone. I miss you, girl. You always knew I understood, without a word exchanged.

Keep watch, now!

I am most grateful to:

Lorraine Darrow

Without whose masterful command of *réaliser un film,* as well as every iteration of *la langue française* (including native Parisian, Corsican guttural, and Cajun-mix), this book could not have been crafted, nor this new series launched. Needless (but necessary) to say, any errors are mine and mine alone.

Aftershock

There's things we still don't talk about, not even to each other.

We'd been walking opposite paths when we first met. She knew there were people like me in her world; I never thought there could be anyone like her in mine.

Dolly must have known what I'd been doing in that slaughterhouse—my skin color alone would have told her that much. She probably thought she knew why I was there, too, but she would have been wrong.

I would have told her the truth—I *wanted* to tell her everything—but I didn't know how.

After a while, I decided Dolly must have been some kind of dream—the kind people say you have when you come close to death. The tremors that keep coming, even after the earthquake has passed.

If I'd had a childhood, it had been wiped from my mind before I woke up in that hospital so many years ago.

I'd run away from that hospital without knowing why, or even whatever I thought I'd been looking for. An old man found me while I was rooting in garbage bins every night just to stay alive—it was the best of the few choices a street boy like me had. Luc was long gone, too, but I can remember every minute I spent with him.

Even if ex-legionnaires had clubs, I knew I wouldn't be welcome—I was no good at pretending to be loyal, not to anything. And mercenaries don't have friends; that's the unspoken contract.

All those years, anytime a problem came up, I'd talk it over with myself. I'd had a lot of practice doing that.

But when Dolly happened again, I knew it couldn't be an accident. When she left *that* time, I chased the dream of being with her.

It was a long, hard time, but I never stopped, never lost faith. Whatever drove me, it was something I trusted. And that trust proved true. Finally, Dolly took my hand, giving up her past to join a man without one.

She found a way to keep to the path she had chosen. I'd never had choices before. And now the only path that matters to me is any one we can walk together.

Killing a deer—what they call "hunting" around here—is like fishing with sonar. Or climbing a mountain while a team of Sherpas walks ahead of you to build a base camp before you arrive. Time enough to take off your oxygen mask and warm yourself by the artificial heat before you have some champagne and turn in for the night.

All that's needed is money. Of course, *other* people with money sneer at them for doing it: "They wouldn't be hunting deer if the deer could shoot back."

They sound like they're on opposite sides, but they're really standing on one side or the other of a line that runs right through the center of their "circle"—the same circle that surrounds their club like a fortress wall.

People with money might disagree on how it should be used. There's only one rule: it can never be used *up*. If that happens, they kick you out of their club.

Whether members pay to go on a catered safari or watch wars on television makes no difference. "They're all cut from the same cloth," a guy I served with told me once. I thought he was Irish, but I never asked—that was one of the rules.

When he said "cut from the same cloth," he meant that people who watch violence from a safe distance can never know the reality of it. They only know what people like us tell them. And we never tell them the truth—why would we? So they read books, or watch television, or see a movie.

That's where some of them got the idea that taking body parts off enemies started in Vietnam. Like those ear necklaces. Some say those prove how war turns people into beasts. They're as stupid as those who believe they're looking at the work of a genuine hard man.

Those last kind, they're the buyers. They never think of what they buy as anything but the real thing. How would they tell?

The hardest men aren't soldiers—they're the ones who push the war buttons; they hire the soldiers, and tell them who to kill.

Men like us, we make a lot more money than soldiers who fight for a country. We know things, too. Taking body parts didn't start in Vietnam. And it was never about souvenirs.

I know this because I heard it from soldiers who heard it from other soldiers, all the way back. No matter where in the world, you always needed proof if you wanted to be paid in anything besides money.

Maybe you were forced to fight; maybe you were the aggressor—that doesn't matter. If you wanted to be paid in respect, the highest peak was to show a piece of the enemy, prove you were close enough to touch him.

You can still see this: rotting heads mounted high on stakes surrounding a village. That's a blood art. If you impale the heads skillfully enough, the weather will eventually reduce them to bleached skulls.

Those pieces have a story of their own. That's why they're more prized than gold. When you return with your proof, the whole village scatters the enemy's body parts all around their border, a warning to whoever thinks of being the next attacker.

In some places, this is the only kind of safety there ever is, or ever can be. And that spell only holds as long as the children of the village grow up to take the place of those who planted the stakes. And their children's children.

That's where "raising the stakes" came from. No matter how big the gambler, there's stakes only a very few will play for. Broke, you can always get some more money and play again. Broken, you're done playing.

I know this because I saw it happen. I watched jungle fighters carve still-beating hearts out of fresh-killed enemies and gnaw on them like starving leopards.

The men watching with me, they were older, more experienced. They told me I wasn't seeing savagery; I was seeing tradition. Been going on for centuries, they said. Eat your enemy's heart and you take his power for your own.

Like any belief, any religion, it started before anyone alive could actually remember. So it has to keep generating its own power to keep creating new believers.

So far, it has.

I saw some of my own kind chop off fingers from corpses to make amulet necklaces. But in the jungle, it's never what you did, it's always why you did it. If the finger-choppers ever showed off the trophies they took to the heart-eaters, it would make them suspicious.

In the jungle, suspicious is the same as scared.

If the heart-eaters got too suspicious, they might take some lives to calm themselves.

But they'd never eat *those* hearts.

There were two of them this time. Waiting inside one of those pre-fab deer blinds. Lightweight, easy to carry strapped to your back; you can snap one together on-site, using just hand tools.

Finished, the blinds stand about eight feet off the ground, with narrow openings that let in plenty of fresh air during the night. No glass in those windows—that would interfere with the mossy netting covering the protruding barrels of tripod-mounted zoom-scoped rifles.

The hunters get up before dawn, crawl out of their Gore-Tex sleeping bags, deposit their own urine in tight-capped plastic jugs so the smell won't conflict with the deer estrus they sprinkled all around. Then maybe chew quietly on an energy bar while they wait for the prey to show up.

I'd been there for three twenty-fours, waiting for them. It had taken them more than one trip to get everything in place. They hadn't been worried about leaving a trail—deer don't pick up human smells the way flesh-eating animals do.

I had to wait for dawn—they didn't have nightscopes or suppressors. I had both, but that was no guarantee I could finish both of them before they got off a few bursts.

Gunfire during the deer season wouldn't make the police nervous, so long as it was daylight hours. Jacking deer with a salt lick and a searchlight—now, that would be illegal.

People who called themselves real hunters would say it wasn't sportsmanlike, either.

The doe showed up right after the sky lightened. A good-sized one, but they weren't hunting for meat—it was heads they wanted. Heads with antlers, the kind that look good on a wall.

But I couldn't wait for a buck—there might be other hunters too close by then.

Their cheesy blind was on four legs, so it only took one crack from the hammer side of my tomahawk to topple the whole thing.

Like I said, the good thing about hunting season is that nobody spooks at rifle fire so long as it's during daylight. When the store-bought blind came crashing down, the two men were too busy cursing to pay attention to anything but themselves.

One thought his leg was broken. The other was just shaken up, but that didn't stop him from going on about suing whoever they'd bought that blind from.

I was so close I didn't even need the scope. They never saw me. I put a round into each of them. Head shots—I wasn't worried about spoiling a trophy.

It only took another few seconds to spray a bright-green "X" on each of their orange jackets.

That brought the total to seven. Two the first year, three the second, and now these two.

I hoped that would be enough. There's no rules of engagement in the only kind of war I'd been trained to fight. An enemy is an enemy, asleep or awake. They're all threats, some more immediate than others.

I watched the press conference on TV. The local politicians all had something to say. Even the dough-faced District Attorney weighed in with his standard little speech about how only "collaboration" between agencies was going to solve *any* crimes. He proudly announced that a statewide task force was already on the job.

One of the reporters asked why they didn't call in the FBI. How could they hope to catch a serial killer without a profile?

That's when a beefy guy in a dark suit stepped to the mike. He said he was going to release information previously withheld from the public, because the last two kills confirmed their earlier conclusions.

"We're dealing with terrorists. I don't mean the kind who blow up planes; I mean those 'animal rights' extremists who think hunting should be outlawed."

He went on to explain how the homicides were all "signature

kills." The green "X" sprayed on each victim. The NO MORE! posters scattered throughout the woods.

He told the audience there was an entire movement of such people out there, hunting the hunters. "They have the same mindset that believes torching a bunch of SUVs is going to save the planet. We know there's a significant underground of ecoterrorists in America, especially in this part of the country."

The man looked straight into the forest, as if he was daring those terrorists to come out and fight.

"There's no way a group like this is going to stay under the radar forever. Which is why we're appealing to you, the public. One or more of you may know one of the killers. If you have information, any information at all . . ."

A phone number kept scrolling across the bottom of the screen as he talked. Nothing about a reward, though. That would keep the calls down. And there was no missing baby to search for, so nobody would be walking the woods. You know how they do that: holding hands so they don't overlook a single inch of ground, all trying to stay within range of the TV cameras.

"Let me stress that we do not want any vigilante group trying to take matters into their own hands. We will have various . . . indicators planted throughout the area. Until further notice, this area is closed to all hunting. It is now under the control of the United States government. Anyone carrying a weapon of *any* type will be detained and questioned."

The way he said that would have scared off most people all by itself.

The FBI team never caught the killers. But even after they left, hunters avoided that horseshoe-shaped section of woodland like it was diseased. Maybe it was those notices posted all over the place that the sector was off-limits because of an investigation in progress. Maybe it was something else.

People who lived close to that horseshoe of forest didn't say it out loud, but you could tell they were relieved. In this state, you can get a hunting license just by filling out a form. No tests. And with the weapons some of them used, there should have been. Every once in a while, a wild shot would fly out of the woods.

Years ago, a little girl who had been playing in her own backyard had been crippled by a stray bullet. They never found who fired that shot. People knew something like that could always happen again. Not that they were against hunting, they made sure to tell you.

"Why" doesn't count, only "what." And what the hunters did was stay out of that section of the woods.

That's how I was trained. The best way to secure a perimeter is to raise the stakes. The more the enemy had to ante up, the fewer would even sit down at the table.

Dolly spent a lot of time behind our house. Gardening, fixing shelters for animals, always coming up with some new idea. The chances of a stray bullet hitting her weren't high, but I'm not a gambler.

I met Dolly when she was a nurse, working with a Médecins Sans Frontières team, deep inside a kill-zone they should never have entered. They believed that their *raison d'être*—to save lives without regard to ideology—was known throughout the world, and that their mission was respected by all. So it wouldn't matter if they were captured by the "wrong" side, especially in a war where people changed sides every day.

But once they were on the ground, it only took them a short while to realize that none of them were safe. Especially the women.

Still, they stood their ground. Some soldiers get "brave" and "stupid" mixed up, but no one with Dolly's team did.

I found that out when I came to. I'd been walking drag, so the land mine's explosion hadn't torn me up the way it had the column in front of me. But my right thigh took a shrapnel fragment that tunneled in like a metallic termite.

I knew I had to cut it out. I sterilized the blade with wooden matches. My hands were steady enough, but the damn thing was buried too deep for me to get at it without risking the femoral artery. So all I could do was squeeze a tube of antibiotic paste into the wound, gauze-wrap it down, tape it tightly in place, and start moving.

The leg wouldn't take any weight, and I knew that every movement would send blood pulsing even harder inside me. But anything was better than staying where I was—it's only in movies that people sneer at torture.

I was carrying what the guy who sold it to me had called a "Vietnam tomahawk." It made a crutch out of a tree limb so easily that I vowed never to work without one ever again.

After that, I could move pretty well, but not as quietly as I wanted to.

They'd issued us GPS units, promised all we had to do was tap the little screen and they'd send in an evac team. Even if I'd believed them—and I don't think any of us did—I knew what they'd do if they only got one signal, instead of at least half a dozen.

So I took off my GPS, set the alarm on my electronic watch for three hours, tapped "vibrate," and shoved it between the pulled pin and the contact point on the baseball grenade, so that only the unit's width kept it from exploding. With any luck, the "vibrate" alarm would pop the watch loose and set off the grenade.

That was for the people who'd sent us in. The people we'd been sent to kill couldn't know how many had been on our team. If the grenade did its work, anyone coming across the bodies would think the land mine had gotten us all.

And even if someone stationed behind us was also radio-signaling to the other side, a body count wouldn't help much, not with all that splatter.

That was all I could think to do. That, and get as deep into the brush as I could, following my compass to true north. For a man like me, true north was always away from the enemy.

I kept hearing the voice of my old *juteux,* playing like an endless loop in my head: *"Aujourd'hui, vous allez me haïr, et certains vont même prier pour que je casse ma pipe. Mais un jour, vous souviendrez de moi et vous me remercierez. Parce que ce jour-là, si vous êtes toujours en vie, ce sera grâce à moi."*

I remember that sadistic scum like it was yesterday. Smiling at our pain. I didn't bless him like he'd once promised I would. But I reluctantly acknowledged that, were it not for that training, I might not still be moving.

There's a reason why the finest credential any merc could carry back in those days was to have served in La Légion Étrangère. I'd only done the minimum—five years. Long enough to earn my citizenship, but not long enough to qualify for speciality instruction.

That last, it was only for lifers. Why would I want that? That whole "loyalty to France" they never stopped preaching was a one-way street down a blind alley. The citizenship you earned by war didn't make you French. All you really earned by signing on was the right to be expendable.

But the training *was* the finest—if you survived it. The Legion lost more recruits during training than any other fighting force in the world. Gave the survivors still another useless medal to show off.

Today, they say it's different. Now they ask questions. The Legion's image as a haven for those who wanted to leave their past behind is out of date. Now aspiring recruits are subjected to detailed Interpol background checks.

"We don't accept the hardened criminals anymore, the murderers or rapists," the paper quoted an officer, "so this makes our job easier."

I didn't need to be fluent in French to understand what the officer was saying: "We have no more colonies, so we have no need of disposable outlaws."

I don't know how much ground I actually covered. When I woke up, I was in some kind of medical tent, lying on a cot, an IV running into each arm. I twitched the toes on the leg that had taken the shrapnel, and gave thanks for the pain that followed.

I kept my eyes slitted so I could gather data. There was a lot of movement inside the tent, but I couldn't see any weapons, so I knew I wasn't a captive. Or a comrade.

Voices. Not frantic, but tight and clipped, the way medics talk in the field. English, French, Italian, Spanish. Couple more languages I couldn't recognize.

I made a little noise, opened my eyes just as she came over.

Dolly, I mean.

"Vous parlez le français?"

"Un peu," I lied.

"English, then? American?"

"Yes."

"Me, too. I'm a farm girl. Born and raised in Indiana."

I didn't say anything more. I didn't know if she was asking me where I was born and raised, but I did know that answering her by claiming I was a citizen of *any* country would brand me for what I really was—no armed white man had any business being where they found me.

"My name is Dolly. I'm a nurse. The surgeons took a little metal out of your leg. The IVs are an antibiotic feed and a saline solution. You won't be able to move for a while, but you should make a full recovery once you're evacuated."

"Where am I?"

"In the Triangle. Just north of the RBC."

"RBC" was what the French used to call the area that the Belgians held on to for such a long time. For us, it was just "the Congo."

Mercenaries might tell you all kinds of stories about why they're fighting, but the only truth is that they get paid to do it. Who the paymaster is, that's a question you don't ask. The money's always in hard currency, directly into your "home" account.

They *have* to pay good. Whether a merc claimed he signed on to fight Communism or liberate the downtrodden proletariat, it wouldn't matter if he was captured. There's a Geneva Convention for POWs, but fighting under a foreign flag meant you weren't entitled to that protection. Ask whoever's the current dictator of Equatorial Guinea.

Not so when I'd been a *légionnaire*. Every one of us—not officers, they weren't "us"—was fighting under a foreign flag. None of us were French. But the Legion was exempt. If any of us were ever captured, we'd be entitled to POW status.

Some said that this was only right. After all, why should we be regarded as mercenaries if we could only be called into action by one country?

They told us this POW business many times. What they didn't tell us was that guerrilla fighters didn't give a damn about any Geneva Convention.

Some of us, you could see they didn't care if they lived or died.

Such feelings were permitted, but only if they accepted that the enemy had to die before they did.

None of that ever mattered to me. I knew how the French regarded all of us. We might be citizens on paper, but none of us could ever be one of them.

And I knew that any merc claiming to be a former *légionnaire* wouldn't buy himself mercy from anyone, anywhere.

"The Triangle" could mean Chad or the Sudan. My money was on Chad. Even if Qaddafi had another aneurysm and again proclaimed that Chad was actually part of Libya, he wouldn't send troops this far south.

And even if that foaming-mouth psycho *did* send them, they wouldn't go all the way. You can order soldiers only so far. If it's a choice between jumping off a cliff or lobbing a grenade into an officer's foxhole, somebody's going to handle it. And nobody's going to talk about it.

I didn't say anything about Chad. I wasn't posing as a historian, and I didn't think telling her that La Légion had done some work there before I'd even enlisted would be a smart idea.

"How are you going to get out?" I asked her.

"There's a road. Not much of one, but good enough. It'll be a bumpy ride, but we'll get . . . we'll get to where there's a plane waiting. Probably in less than three hours. Unless we run across some hostiles."

"Who?"

"You mean, which side? It doesn't matter. Either they'll let us through or they won't," she said. A warrior's fatalism: You fight. You live or you die. There is nothing else.

"Where are my . . . my weapons?"

"The only weapons you had when we found you were a pistol and some sort of hatchet."

"Can I have them back?"

"No. I'm sorry, but we never carry weapons. If we're stopped, the only chance we have of being allowed to proceed is if they take our mission for what it really is. A weapon, that would make it seem as if—"

"I don't mean this minute; I mean, when you drop me off."

"Drop you off?"

"What else could you do?"

"Everyone goes back the same way. At the end of the truck road is where we have the plane waiting."

"To where?"

"This time? Switzerland."

I calculated my chances. Didn't take long. I'd have a better chance in Switzerland, even if they turned me over to the UN. The blue helmets would know what I'd been doing in the Congo, but they wouldn't do anything about it. Far as they were concerned, the Congo was a stable area.

Working as a mercenary was only a problem if I was captured by the wrong side. So, if I could get to a place that thought *all* sides were wrong, I'd be at true north.

Of course, I knew they wouldn't let me stay there long.

After I healed, I went back to work, but I wasn't going back to a jungle. Between surviving the land mine and not catching malaria, I figured I'd used up any luck I'd ever have down there.

In the haze of recovering from the wound, getting my hands on my money, and crossing the ocean, I was never sure if I had just fever-dreamed Dolly. But, years later, I saw her again. In an AIDS ward in San Francisco. I wasn't a patient; I was there for the same reason she was—to do a job.

My job was the opposite of hers. But no less merciful. The people who hired me loved the man who had to die. The man who *wanted* to die. But the doctors were keeping him alive—human guinea pigs were hard to come by, and who better to test the latest advances in pain management on?

Dolly remembered me. But all we had time for was a cup of coffee—she was moving on again. Some terminal-cancer-cure thing they were trying out. High up in the Chiricahua Mountains, where they could see anyone coming for miles around. Mercenaries work in America, too.

I wished she would stay, but that wish was buried inside a place I couldn't let show. So I was glad when she left—I couldn't do what I'd come there to do with her around. It wasn't that I thought she'd finger me or anything, it was that I . . . just couldn't stand the idea of her thinking of me as still doing the same work I'd been doing when we first met. And I couldn't back up my story by burning the people who hired me—that would be the same as breaking my word.

That cup of coffee was long enough for me to learn her whole name. I didn't trick it out of her.

I might have told her a bunch of lies, but, considering what I'd been doing when we met, that would have been stupid. Not stupid because she would have seen through them, but stupid because I didn't want her to think I would lie to her. Ever.

Just because I couldn't explain any of that to myself didn't mean it wasn't true. I somehow knew I needed her to trust me if there was ever to be a chance for . . . for things I couldn't allow myself to think about.

A few months passed. She never called the number I'd left with her, and I tried to make myself stop wishing she would.

It was as if trying so hard not to wish for something *made* it happen. When she called, I didn't waste the chance. I asked her if she would sit with me long enough for me to say what I wanted to say. She didn't bother with a bunch of questions, not even "Why?" She just told me where she was.

I didn't tell her a story. I told her the truth. Not just about what I'd been, but what I wanted to be.

We had plenty of time then. Almost a week. Mostly, I listened. I found out that Dolly had seen too much war—too much pain, suffering, death. The worst had been right in Switzerland, in a place where they treated torture victims. She told me she'd had to get out before she became like one of them. I didn't understand what she meant, not then.

Dolly's dream was to live somewhere on the Oregon coast. She loved the idea of being so near the ocean. One day, she was going to buy a little cottage there. She had scouted around for a long time before coming to that decision. But now she was sure—all she wanted was to be in a place where she could live in peace.

The only part of what she said that I felt inside myself was what she wanted. True north. That had always been my dream, too. I'd never had another one. Not until Dolly.

By the time we parted, I had my mission statement. For a man like me, there was nothing more. *"La mission est sacrée"* had been drilled into me long ago.

It took longer than I'd hoped to settle all accounts. But I knew impatience could turn fatal in a heartbeat. So I painstakingly erased my back-trail, then I waited alongside it like a wounded Cape buffalo. After a full year went by without anyone following, I was ready.

I held the phone in my hand for a long time. I still remember watching my hands tremble. I stared at them as if they belonged to a stranger. My hands don't tremble.

I managed to dial the number. The new one I'd memorized the

last time we met. She had been griping about her lousy cell phone, and I told her I could probably fix it, me being so handy with tools and all. Only took a few minutes.

"Please don't be afraid" is all I could think of saying when I heard her voice.

"I'm not," she said, very calm. "But there better be more to this call or I *will* be mad."

I didn't play around. I'm no good at it. I knew I had only a little slice of time. And only one round chambered, anyway. So I let it loose.

"I have the place," I told her. "The one you wanted. I want to show it to you. I could pick you up wherever you are. Or, if you didn't want me to do that, I could meet you at the airport. Eugene—Eugene, Oregon—that's the closest airport to the place I found."

"But—"

"I'll do anything you want." I stopped her from saying anything more. "Just tell me what it is, and I'll do it. On my life."

It took her a few more weeks, but she did take that flight. And even then she only stayed a couple of weeks at the cottage I'd found.

After that, it was almost six months before she could do the same thing with her last job that I'd done with mine.

"Before" doesn't matter anymore. Not to me, not to Dolly. We both gave up our opposite pasts. I mean, Dolly gave up being a healer; I gave up being a killer for hire.

I was honest with her about that from the beginning. She'd have to start over, so she couldn't transfer her credentials. She'd always be a nurse in her heart and with her hands, but she couldn't work as one.

Giving up my past—for me, that was nothing. I'd done it

before. It was no more than shoveling coal into a furnace, waiting, then shoveling out the ashes into a wheelbarrow. Finally, carrying them to a place where the wind would scatter them.

I'd had to do that before. This time, I *wanted* to. Still, that wasn't enough. It was Dolly who told me I could never really leave my past until I atoned for it. Otherwise, it would haunt me from inside—I could never be at peace.

I remembered those torture victims in Switzerland, so I knew what she said was true. I never wanted to go back. To my work, I mean. As it turned out, the price of leaving that work behind forever was to do one more job of it.

The man who created the paperwork for Dolly's new life was a genius. Not like some guy on TV who's good at answering questions—the real thing. He was the same caliber as the one who'd told me to put every penny I had stashed into gold back when it was under three hundred U.S. an ounce. I did that. When he told me it was time, I cashed it all out.

So, when he told me to put it all back into gold, and then pull it away again, I did that, too.

I would have been shocked at how much money I ended up with, except that the genius never said anything he didn't know. Which meant that most of the time he didn't say anything.

I'm the same way, except for the genius part.

The ID man, he was so smart that he even said to my face that he wouldn't want his daughter to be with anyone like me. And this was *after* I got her back from the man who had taken her.

It hadn't been a kidnap thing. Not a grab, I mean. She went with this guy willingly. That was what he did, get girls to go with him.

"I never paid any attention to her," the genius told me. "She was my . . . daughter, I suppose. But she was really only her mother's child, and her mother was too busy spending the money she extorted from me to spend time with her. It couldn't have been too difficult for that *fils de pute* to convince my daughter that she wasn't wanted. Not by me, not by anyone."

"Except him."

"*Oui,* except him. Except for that vulture. My Dominique was not . . . gifted in any way. She was not beautiful, she was not talented. She was just—and this I admit I could know only from reports—a good, decent girl. So when . . . ah, it must have been *so* easy for him."

"What is it you want me to do?"

"*Je veux la récupérer.*" Before I could ask him what "I want her back" meant to him, he switched to English, like he was downshifting to help him climb a steep hill: "No! Damn it! I don't want her 'back.' She was never with me. Truth? I don't want her at all. I just want her to have what she deserves. And no girl deserves . . ."

I switched to English, too. I was more comfortable saying certain things in that language—it must have been my native tongue. When I ran from that hospital, it was all I spoke.

I learned a few words of French on the street. More from Luc. And still more from La Légion. But now I use it only when I must reach back into my past.

"With all the information you have already gathered, I could . . . remove the vulture. But you have to know that your daughter will only return to the same—"

"Not if a message is left," the man said in response to my unspoken statement that any abandoned child will go to the foulest flesh-peddler if she believes she is wanted. This I knew to be true.

He wanted more than death for that vulture—he wanted his skull on a stake, for all those of his tribe to see.

"He does his work alone, you said?"

"Yes, I said that! And, yes, he deserves the fate I wish for him. Just tell me the price."

That's when I spoke with Dolly's voice. "There is only one price, payable on delivery."

"Yes, yes. Just name it and—"

"Penance, that is the price."

"Vous êtes dingue ou quoi?!"

"No, I'm not insane. I am saying this to you: If all you want is to remove an enemy, and perhaps leave behind a warning for others, I am no longer the man for such a job. But if you want to recover your daughter, if you want to atone for your abandonment that made her such easy prey, that I will attempt. And if you accept my terms, I will succeed or I will die."

"I asked those in my employ to inquire. And your name came up, again and again. *C'est un tueur que je veux engager, tu piges? Pas un prêtre.*"

I translated the words easily enough: "I want to hire a killer, not a damn priest." And I answered only: "I am no priest."

"Yet you demand—"

"I demand nothing. I ask, I plead for an opportunity. I have much to atone for myself. This would be my chance as well as yours."

He looked at me with the amoral measuring gaze of a buyer evaluating a blood diamond.

"Be clear" is all he said. "Be *very* clear, now."

"I will remove the vulture. And any of his comrades necessary for me to complete that task. I will leave behind a warning that any who approach your daughter again will meet the same fate. I will return your daughter to you. What you will do is provide all the identifications I need. For that, I will pay you. For returning your daughter, you will pay *her*. You will pay what you owe her."

"And you will succeed or you will die?"

"If you looked for me as you said you did, this you already know."

He closed his eyes for a long moment. Then he nodded.

The vulture wasn't hard to find. A young, light-skinned black man, not much older than the girls he pulled. I told him that I understood he had merchandise for sale, and that I represented a buyer. A wealthy buyer.

"Who told you where to find me, man?"

I broke into the rapid-fire, guttural Corsican French I had learned years before. I could see he didn't understand a word, but the foreign language convinced him that the buyer was the kind of internationalist he'd probably been trying to connect with since he went into business. Putting teenage girls on the street was a small-profit deal. Between the emotionally anesthetic drugs always tempting the girls, and predators who only wanted to use the goods once, he couldn't expect any of them to last long.

When he turned his head and yelled, "Neek, get your ass out here," he didn't know he had just closed his own coffin. By the time the girl stumbled into the room, struggling with the four-inch heels that were to be her working shoes, her "man" was under the same couch he'd been sitting on.

"Where's D-mand?"

"He had to run out," I said, holding up a pager to indicate that the dead man was taking care of business. "I'm the one who drives you to Seattle."

"Seattle?"

"I just do what I'm paid for. And D-man—"

"—D-*mand*," she corrected my error.

"I thought that was what I said. Anyway, you ready to go? He told me he had all new stuff for you waiting, so don't worry about packing."

"This isn't the way to Seattle."

"I know," I said, switching my voice to everything she hadn't been trained to expect: polite, educated, and respectful. "And I apologize for deceiving you. But it had to be done. D-mand sold you. To me, he thought. But, actually, it was your father who hired me to bring you home."

"Home? My *father*—"

"I understand. But now . . . at least, give him a chance. He took some big risks, and spent a lot of money to make this happen. A lot of money to make you see the truth about that vulture—the one who just sold you like a used car. Your father knows that nothing he could say would persuade you that he did all this because he loves you. He only wants the chance to try. If you don't like what you see, if you don't want to be treated as he intends, he won't stop you from leaving again."

I didn't have to immobilize her. The twin shocks of being sold like a piece of meat and her father actually wanting her were too much for her fragile system.

The new ID papers were waiting when I returned the girl. They were "start from scratch," so the genius probably thought I needed American citizenship—he already knew I was a legal citizen of France.

What he didn't know was that the ID he changed was itself legitimate. I'd been an American citizen for a long time. That was part of the price for some work I'd done in the Cambodia-Laos region.

I hadn't been the only ex-legionnaire in the area. For some of the older ones, the loss to the Viet Minh was still burning a hole in their guts. Some were just going back to familiar territory, drawing extra pay because they knew the terrain so well.

My job was different. The Americans wanted to know the truth of the "live sightings" of POWs being reported ever since a guy named Garwood walked up to a man in Hanoi and said he was a U.S. Marine who'd just escaped captivity.

Not many believed him—most thought he'd just gone over and the Viet Cong had kicked him loose when they had no more use for him. But his story had enough supporters to make the American government need "confirm or deny" info that would stand up if it was ever needed.

I understood that didn't mean they'd ever tell the truth, no matter what I turned up. And they understood my backstory—so they knew I'd never say anything. To anybody, ever.

Nobody under the name they'd given me was ever going to come to anyone's attention. I hadn't worked since then. I'd never work under that name or any other. I was done with all that.

Dominique is still with her father. Over the years, he's helped me in many ways, refusing payment as if I had insulted him.

And he's been true to his word. Never would he allow what is now the most precious part of his life to waste hers in a desperate search for love. Whether he ever believed anything else I'd told him made no difference. Not then, and certainly not now.

In the stretched-out moment when I heard the door open, I had plenty of time to make a decision before the first footstep creaked.

Time enough to slide the silenced pistol back into its compartment. Time enough not to push the button that would make the last five steps disappear. Any intruders who got this far might walk ninja-soft, but they wouldn't be weightless. Easier to make the whole stairway disappear in a soft explosion, but the last thing I wanted to do was attract attention. That's why the pistol was silenced. Even a fall from the stairs onto a concrete floor wouldn't necessarily kill, and I had to seize any chance to learn how anyone had gotten so close.

How they had gotten past the only person on earth whose life mattered to me.

Inside that rocket-blast of thought was another one—no one could ever get that far unless Dolly had betrayed me. And if she had done that, my life was over no matter how this played out.

"Dell?"

"I'm right here, Dolly," I called, leaving my voice to trail behind me as I backed away to the pool of blackness that formed the entire far wall of my basement "workshop."

My voice was still where I last used it, but I wasn't. And I had a new weapon trained on the staircase, its scope turning blackness to greenish light. A modified FAMAS bullpup auto that people in my old line of work had called *"un clarion."* If someone had forced Dolly to open the door and call my name, she was as good as dead anyway. The only job I'd have left would be to make sure that everyone else in the house followed her.

And find out who sent them.

And then take out the chain, link by link.

Her voice hadn't sounded afraid. That could have meant a lot of things, but it stopped mattering the second I heard her misbegotten mutt woof at whatever small animal was outside the house. If there had been a human intruder, Rascal would have been inside. Growling deep in his throat. Waiting, just like I was.

"Dell, I . . . I really didn't want to disturb you. And I'm not coming any further if you don't want me to. But sometimes you're down here for hours on end and I . . . I didn't think this should wait."

"Come on down, honey. It's okay," I said, watching through the scope so I could make sure Dolly was alone. When she was on the third step, hands held palms-up to tell me she was okay, I said, "Ah, never mind. Give me a second and I'll come upstairs."

Dolly didn't know anything about my way of keeping her safe from some deer-killer's bullets. And she'd never know what I'd been forced to do when something even more dangerous had wormed his way inside our home a couple of years ago.

I remember thinking, *Alfred Hitchcock is dead. He's lying there dead, and I don't know what to do about it.*

I wasn't surprised when I found him dead on the ground. The woods behind our house are state-owned but wild—a country where Darwin makes the rules. I've been in enough places like that to know how they work.

Alfred Hitchcock was one of those crow-raven hybrids you see around this piece of the coast all the time—too big for a crow, but without that classic thick raven's beak. You couldn't miss him, even at a distance. He had a white streak along one side of his head, like the fire-scar a bullet leaves when it just kisses you on the cheek as it goes by.

He hadn't shown up for a few days, but that didn't worry Dolly. Though she loves all her animals, she doesn't regard them as pets. "They have their own ways" is what she always says.

It was Dolly who named him Alfred Hitchcock. "Look how he walks," she said to me one day, pointing out behind the house. "See how dignified he is? Not raucous like the others. You never hear a peep out of him. He just paces back and forth, like he's deep in thought."

I realized he did kind of look like that famous profile of Alfred Hitchcock, especially the way his head wobbled when he walked. Dolly had names for all the creatures who came to visit, and you could tell she thought about each and every one before she finally decided what to call them.

Take Winston. He's a chipmunk, but not one of those little things they have on the East Coast; this one's damn near the size of a squirrel. Dolly named him because he had a stance like a bulldog. And he was fearless, too. Whenever he saw Dolly on the back deck, he'd rush right up and take a peanut out of her hand. Then he'd just sit on his haunches and strip away the shell casing, the way you'd sit and share a beer with a pal.

Winston had a mate—Dolly called her Mrs. Churchill—and a whole family of little ones. They lived under one of the sheds in the backyard. The entrance to their den was marked by two jagged pieces of granite I put there, leaving just enough room between them to form a portal. It looked like they'd hired an architect to build it that way.

And something was always going on back there. Like a couple of hummingbirds fighting it out over one particularly fine fuchsia bush. Those little guys are as territorial as wolverines, and they buzz-bomb each other almost too fast for the eye to follow. Or maybe a stray cat would come visiting. Big mistake. The mutt Dolly had rescued from the shelter spent a lot of time out there, too, in this little house I built for him. Any cat that padded into the yard would launch Rascal out of his doghouse door like a feline-seeking missile.

I think that's why we have so many birds around all the time—Rascal is hell-bent on turning the whole place into a cat-free zone. A dog is like a person: he needs a job and a family to be what he's meant to be. Rascal always came inside for supper, and he'd stay inside until daybreak. He slept on this sheepskin mat I cut for him. I tried putting it by the back door, but Rascal kept dragging it over until it was just outside our bedroom, and finally I just left it there.

Dolly also had herself a whole flock of jays. They were a lot larger than any I'd ever seen. Out here, they're called Steller's jays—big-bodied thugs with black heads and high crests. Every morning, if Dolly didn't get out there quick enough, they'd hammer on the back door with their beaks like a mob of crazed woodpeckers. And they'd keep it up until she went out with a little bucket of peanuts and just flung the whole thing into the yard.

"Slopping the jays" is what she calls it, and that's not being unfair to them; they do act like a pack of hogs. No manners at all, wings flailing, shrieking loud enough to empty a cemetery.

Dolly doesn't care how much noise they make, but she won't let them fight. I know it doesn't make sense, but the birds actually seem to mind her. Once, I saw a couple of the jays really get into it over a big fat peanut, leaping into the air and ripping at each other like spurred gamecocks. Dolly yelled, "You two just stop that!" and they did. Even looked a little ashamed of themselves.

Sometimes, one of the bolder chipmunks will charge right into the middle of a mob of jays and try to swipe a peanut for himself. But mostly they hang around by their portal, standing straight up like prairie dogs, waiting until I wind up and throw long-distance over their heads. The peanuts bounce off the shed, and the chipmunks have a private feast—the jays are too busy to take notice.

The roof of the chipmunks' shed is where Alfred Hitchcock always waited. He had a spot all to himself, and he seemed content just to watch all the ranting and raving without getting involved.

When things got quiet enough to suit him, Alfred Hitchcock would kind of float on down to the yard. He'd go right into his back-and-forth pacing until Dolly called his name. Then it would be my job to lob a peanut close enough for him to pick it up without acting all undignified, but not so close that he thought I was trying to hit him. I got real good at it.

One day, I was out on the deck by myself, testing some new optics I was putting together, when Alfred Hitchcock showed up. He watched me from his perch on the shed for a long time before he finally dropped into the yard and started his walk.

"Alfred!" I called to him, but he just ignored me.

When Dolly came out later, I told her what had happened. "I guess he only likes you," I said.

"It's not that, honey. It's what you said to him."

"I said the same thing you do. Called his name."

"His name is 'Alfred Hitchcock,' Dell. Not 'Alfred.' He's a very dignified bird."

When he came back, a few days later, we were both outside. "You try it," Dolly insisted.

"Alfred Hitchcock!" I called.

And damned if the bird didn't stop his walk and cock his head, like he was waiting. I tossed him a peanut. He slowly strolled over, picked it up, and lofted himself back to the shed's roof. Dolly and I watched him eat the peanut.

That had been a fine moment.

Now Alfred Hitchcock was done—lying dead on the ground. There's at least one bobcat working those woods. I'd seen the prints myself—way too big for a house cat, but no claws showing. If it'd been a bobcat that nailed him, I would have been okay with it. Maybe a little sad, but not all that worked up. Dolly doesn't feed the night hunters—they have to look out for themselves.

But I know a human kill when I see one. No flesh was missing from Alfred Hitchcock's body, and no animal could have wrapped one of his legs with a strand of wire. No animal uses gasoline. Or matches.

No animal kills for fun.

If he had fallen to a natural predator, I wouldn't have said a word to Dolly. I would have just given him a proper burial, and let her think he'd moved on. Maybe found himself a girl bird who wanted a dignified mate.

But I knew better than to bury him. I couldn't let whoever had tortured Alfred Hitchcock to death know anybody had seen their work. So I just slipped back the way I'd come.

I didn't leave tracks. I learned that the same way I learned that you don't always get to bury your dead.

The Legion had been all about its own traditions. *Tu n'abandonnes jamais ni tes morts, ni tes blessés, ni tes armes.*

Never abandon your dead, your wounded, or your arms. Maybe this was supposed to give us that *esprit de corps* they were always yammering about, but we all could do the math. Carrying your dead off the field of fire would slow you down and make you a better target, too. Why should that matter to the officers? To them, we were as disposable as bullets.

Once I left and started working freelance, I could feel the difference. Jungle or desert, I was never with a unit that even thought about carrying away their dead. The best you could do for some of the badly wounded was to finish them off. They were always grateful to go—none of us ever wanted to be taken alive.

And no weapon is sacred. Why carry a jammed or broken rifle with you when you're trying to put distance between yourself and the battle scene?

La Légion est toujours avec toi. Always with me. When I was their property, maybe. But when I became a soldier for money, their fine words left me as I'd left them. Forever.

When I finally got back to the house that day, it was full of kids, like it always is on afternoons during a school week. Teenagers. Dolly's just a magnet for them. Mostly girls, but anytime you've got that many girls, there's going to be some boys, too.

She knows how to have fun, my Dolly. And she can tell some stories, believe me. But what she's best at is listening; I know this for a fact.

There's a lot of stuff I never told Dolly, not out loud. Not because I wanted to keep it a secret. Dolly's got this . . . I don't know the word for it, exactly, but she feels things inside her that other people are feeling. I would never want Dolly to have some of the feelings I still have inside me.

Maybe that's why those kids are always talking to her. Not the phony way they'd talk to some school guidance counselor; more as if she was the kind of aunt you could trust, the kind who'd never rat you out to your folks, no matter what you told her. If you needed an abortion, she'd know where to go, and take you there herself. That last part, I knew for a fact, too.

She's always teaching those kids something, like how to stitch up those crazy costumes they're wearing out in public today. And they're always teaching her stuff, too. Like how to work her cell phone with her thumbs to send messages. She showed me one of those messages one time—it was like it was in a different language. When she tried to explain it to me, I told her I didn't care about stuff like that, stuff I'd never have a use for.

What I didn't tell her was that using any kind of code was for business only. I was out of business, and I didn't want any reminders of what I used to be.

I don't . . . I don't dislike kids, exactly, but I've really got nothing to say to them. I'm not interested in anything they've got to say, either. What could they know at their age? Well, maybe it isn't their age. When I was younger than any of them, I was already doing things that these kids only see in movies. Not things I'm proud of.

After a while, they got used to my staying in my workshop in the basement, and they never bother me when I'm down there. Dolly doesn't have a lot of rules in her house, but the ones she has you better follow, or you're eighty-sixed. Like bringing drugs or booze into her house. Try it once, it's two weeks. If there's a next time, it's your last.

No one can ever open that basement door, anyway. Even if they get past everything else, only Dolly knows the keypad code.

I've actually got two places of my own. The basement workshop, and what Dolly calls my den. She fixed it up real fine. It's got a big dark-red leather easy chair, and a flat-screen TV with earphones, so I can watch the BBC without the racket from all those kids bothering me. I like to read, too. I never read that "I was there" stuff. I tried it for a while, but it wasn't any different from what the library racked in the Fiction section.

One wall is nothing but bookshelves. The others hold my terrain maps. They're from different places I've been, but I never explain that to anyone.

There's this big porthole window, so I can see right out into the yard. Some days, I'd be sitting there and Alfred Hitchcock would pace right past that window, like he was making sure everything was okay.

Every once in a while, a couple of the boys wander back to the den. If the door's closed, they never knock. But if it's open, they know they can just walk right in. Sometimes girls come in there, too.

The boys always want to talk about Vietnam. I don't know where they got the idea that I'd been there. I guess they figure anyone my age must have—especially with all the liars running around VFW halls bragging about what heroes they'd been.

A town this size, especially nestled away in a cove of its own, word gets around. Even if the "word" is all wrong. I had been inside Vietnam, all right, but long after the last American soldier had pulled out.

"Did you ever kill anyone?" That's their favorite question.

I always tell them the truth and lie with the same words. "Yes," I would always tell them, "but that's what war is. I never killed anyone who wasn't trying to kill me."

That was true for a lot of places I've worked. But after La Légion, I never wore a uniform. Dog tags would have been nothing more than extra weight. I wouldn't have known what to put on them, anyway.

"Does it make you mad when people say they're against the war?" they'd want to know. They meant that mess in Iraq—the one that spilled back over from Afghanistan, and was on its way back there now. Some of their relatives had told them stories, about how it hurt them to come home after fighting for their country, only to be hated for doing it.

"No," I'd always tell them. "That's got nothing to do with me." And that part was the truth.

"My father says Jane Fonda was a traitor," one of them said once. I could see he was trying to get me going.

"I can see where he'd think that," I answered, calm and mild-voiced.

"But do *you* think that?" one of the girls asked. At that age, they're a lot sharper than boys.

"It's not people like me who matter," I told them. "It's people like you."

"How come?"

"Because the only way anyone listens to someone like Jane Fonda is when people treat them like they're important. If some-one's a big enough celebrity, journalists ask them questions about stuff they don't know anything about, because fans want to know what their . . . idol, or whatever they're called . . . what they think. About anything.

"Jane Fonda was never a soldier. She wasn't a political scientist, or a historian. And she sure was no expert on Southeast Asia. But if she calls a press conference, everybody shows up. That's all that happened."

"That's true!" one of the other girls said, backing me up. A tough-looking little freckle-face with big owl glasses, she looked like she was used to standing her ground. "Once I saw Britney Spears on TV. They were asking her about global warming. I'll bet her idea of global warming is when the air-conditioning breaks."

I'd caught a glimpse of Dolly smiling at me over the girl's shoulder. I still treasure how that made me feel.

The morning after the day I found Alfred Hitchcock, I told Dolly I was driving over to the city. There's always some different things I need for my projects, and she knows I'd never buy anything over the Internet. I asked her if she wanted me to bring back anything for her, and she said what she always does: "A surprise!"

So I'd stopped at the nursery first, picked up a whole mess of stuff for Dolly. A couple of gay guys own the place, Martin and Johnny. They're nuts about Dolly. I'm not sure how they feel about me, but that doesn't matter. Not to them; not to me.

I never ask for anything in particular; they just load up whatever they think Dolly might like. We've got all kinds of lilies growing in big tubs I made out of cut-down barrels. I put some PVC to work as a liner and drilled a few drainage holes—and Dolly did the rest. We've got purple and white lilacs, too—what Dolly calls a butterfly bush. The fuchsia is reserved for the hummingbirds. We even have some black bamboo—thin, strange-looking stalks, not the heavier ones I'd been so scared of falling into a long time ago.

I got Dolly some new orchids, for inside the house. Those were my own idea. I know I should have left the nursery stop for last, to keep everything fresh. But I had to get Dolly's surprise out of the way, because I wasn't sure how late I'd be out looking for what I needed. So I misted everything down real good, and covered it all with a dark mesh tarp.

As it turned out, I had to drive quite a distance until I found the place I wanted. They've got a lot of those places in any city, and they all look alike—either the glass in the windows is all blacked out, or there's no windows at all.

The guy at the desk didn't look up when I came in the door. That's part of what buyers count on—same reason they don't have security cameras.

They wouldn't need cameras for the usual reason, either. Every pro-level stickup man knows all the cash goes straight down a slot into a safe in the basement, and the clerk never knows the combination.

I found what I was looking for easy enough—there was a big selection.

I paid for what I bought the same way I paid for Dolly's plants. I don't have any credit cards, and I don't have a checking account.

Dolly didn't say a word about how long I'd been gone. And she loved everything I brought for her. I took the other stuff down to my workshop.

I knew who he was. Just like I knew Alfred Hitchcock hadn't been his first one.

I didn't need his name, because I had his path. His kind, they always move in straight lines. You may not know where they're going, but you can always track them from where they've been.

The local paper puts the crime reports on a separate page. Not big crimes, like an armed robbery or a murder. Around here, something like that's so rare it would make headlines. The "Crime Beat" page is just a printout of the entire police blotter. Drunk driving takes up most of it, with some domestic violence sprinkled in. Lately, a lot of minor-league meth busts, too. But you also see things like shoplifting, disorderly conduct, urinating in public . . . any petty little nonsense you could get arrested for.

The paper says they were all "found guilty," but I knew that was just code for "took a plea." That's why sentences for real crimes never seemed to match the charges. Who gets probation for sexual assault on a minor? I guess that's why they call them "bargains."

The library has a complete archive, going all the way back. I read three years' worth. Found seven little notices that quali-fied: five "animal cruelties"—no details; it wasn't that kind of newspaper—and two fires they called "arson, under investigation."

After I marked the locations of those crimes on my close-terrain map, I used my protractor and saw they were all within a 2.3-mile radius of where Alfred Hitchcock had been tortured to death. You wouldn't need a car to cover that much ground, no matter where you started from.

That's when I started leaving the door of my den open all the time, even when I wasn't around.

Under the bookshelves, there's a cabinet. It has a lock built into it, but I sometimes forget to use it. You can tell that by looking—the key would still be in the lock, sticking out.

The boys knew I kept magazines in there. All kinds, from *Soldier of Fortune* to *Playboy,* staying with the image they had for me. I'd added the stuff I bought on that last visit to the city.

It only took a couple of weeks for one of those to go missing. Whoever took it would never notice that I had removed the staples and replaced them with a pair of wire-thin transmitters.

Those transmitters were real short-range, but I was sure I wouldn't need much. I knew he was somewhere close. And that he would never imagine anyone hunting him.

Dolly was asleep when I slipped out that night. Rascal was awake, but he kept his mouth shut. He gave me a look, so I'd know he wasn't sleeping on the job.

When I picked up the signal, I didn't try to track it to the exact house—I wasn't dressed for that kind of risk. All I really needed was the general area, anyway. The library had a city directory, and every high school yearbook, going back more years than I'd need.

The school was closed for the summer. There was no security guard. The alarm system was probably older than me.

The guidance counselor's office wasn't even locked.

I could tell it was a woman's office without turning on my shrouded fiber-optic pencil flash. Whoever she was, she kept her file cabinets locked. And the key in her desk.

Jerrald had a thick file. He'd been evaluated a number of times. I kept seeing stuff like "attachment disorder." I skipped over the flabby labels and went right to the stone foundation they built those on—the boy had been torturing animals since he was in the second grade, starting with his own puppy.

The counselors wrote that Jerrald was "acting out." Or "crying for help." Some mentioned "conduct disorder." Some talked about medications.

To read what they wrote, you'd think they knew what they were talking about. Every one of his "misconducts" always had some explanation.

But I'd known men who'd once been boys like Jerrald. So I knew what he'd really been doing.

Practicing.

The counselors had done all kinds of things for Jerrald. Individual therapy. Group therapy. Pills that he probably never took.

The most recent report said he had been making real progress. Jerrald had a Facebook page. I knew what that was from those kids Dolly always had around—a kind of diary they write on their computers. Some put up stuff they wanted to show off: paintings, poetry, photography, short stories.

I read some of Jerrald's stuff that the counselor had printed out. All torture-rape-murder stories. The counselor said that they were a good outlet for Jerrald—a "safe place for him to vent."

Even Jerrald's English teacher said his writing showed real promise.

I knew the only promise Jerrald was ever going to keep.

I left the school the same way I'd left Alfred Hitchcock's body in the woods—nobody would ever be able to tell I'd visited either place. Two rules: You enter without breaking. And you remember that nobody misses what you don't take.

The best way to keep anger out of your blood is to go back to your training. Nothing personal. Always do it by the numbers.

The anger was all mine, all against myself. I'd thought I'd already done my job by stopping the deer-killers. But keeping them at a safe distance didn't matter when Dolly was letting even more dangerous people in the door. Just the *thought* of leaving my Dolly exposed dialed all the blood in my body to subzero. Blood doesn't have to flow if there's no heart for it to oxygenate—and if you do it "by the numbers," like I'd been trained to, there's no heart involved.

By mid-May, I'd found out that Jerrald's parents were going on vacation. To Hawaii. They were taking his little sister with them, but not Jerrald. He was eighteen, more than old enough to leave on his own for a couple of weeks.

I don't know whose idea that was. Or, I guess, whose idea they *thought* it was.

The newspapers speculated that Jerrald must have been building some kind of bomb in his room. One serious enough to blow out the whole back of his house, where his bedroom had been.

Anytime a high school kid gets caught with heavy explosives, it's a big deal, no matter where it is. The cops said the bomb was probably a crude, homemade device. "Very simplistic," their expert said. "You can get instructions on how to build one on the Internet."

They printed parts of Jerrald's Facebook page in the papers— he had more than nine hundred "friends," especially fans of his writings. But he was obviously a very disturbed young man, all the experts agreed on that. Probably been bullied, too, they said.

What they didn't say out loud was how relieved they all were that he'd never had a chance to bring the bomb to school.

The town had a big funeral for him. A lot of kids were crying. Dolly went, too; some of those kids really wanted her there.

I didn't go. I was out in the deep woods, giving Alfred Hitchcock a proper burial. Simple and dignified, the way he would have wanted it.

I thought that was the last of it. I'd pulled the perimeter in so tight that I was sure my Dolly was safe, even from another kid like Jerrald. It wasn't until I followed her upstairs that night that I learned how wrong I was.

I found Dolly sitting at the huge slab of butcher block she had fixed up like a kitchen table.

The lights were on.

Rascal ran over to me, like he'd been waiting days for the little strip of rawhide he always scored whenever I came out of my workshop.

As I handed over his prize, I checked Dolly's hands. They were still free enough to use any of the signals I'd taught her; but all she did was pick up a cup of that herbal tea she likes, and take a sip.

I sat across from her.

"I'm sorry, Dell. I'm probably just shook up. From the phone call," she said, pointing at the cell sitting on the tabletop.

"Don't worry about it. I wasn't doing anything important. Just killing time."

She gave me a look. "MaryLou's in jail," she said. If you didn't know Dolly, you'd think she was telling me about some little thing, just making conversation. But I could hear the threads tightening inside the calm of her voice.

Battlefield calm. Like when she was moving between beds in a field hospital, talking to the wounded men. All professionally sweet and cheerful, even though they'd just gotten a radio signal that "hostiles" were only a few klicks away. And on the move.

I made my mouth twitch, just enough to tell her that I didn't know who she was talking about.

"Oh, Dell! You remember her. The real tall girl with pale-blue eyes. Always wears her hair in a long ponytail. She was going to college in the fall; I don't remember exactly where. On a softball scholarship. She's a really good pitcher. That's why they call her Mighty Mary. Because she throws so hard. She had more strikeouts—"

I shook my head to cut her off. Whoever this girl was, she hadn't been one of those who came into my den sometimes. I never look close at those girls, even the ones that stay with Dolly all the time they're here, but I'd have remembered the one she'd just described. Anyway, I needed Dolly to get to whatever this big trouble was. Was Dolly just being herself, looking after another kid? Or was she in it deeper than that?

Dolly read my thoughts. Easy enough for her to do, I guess. My walls are thick and high, but Dolly's always been inside them, wearing them like some other woman would a mink coat.

"Yesterday was the last day of school. MaryLou was walking down the hall when, all of a sudden, she pulled a pistol out of her backpack and started shooting."

"How many?"

Dolly knew what I was asking. "One dead," she said. "Two others wounded, neither of them near critical. I guess it's a good thing she only had six bullets."

"Six bullets or six shots?"

"I don't know. All Kendra—she's the girl who called—all Kendra said was that MaryLou shot Cameron Taft. Then she fired a few more times and just threw down her gun."

"Did the cops come in shooting?"

"Why would they do that? Kendra said MaryLou was just sitting on the floor, like she'd finished her homework and was taking a break. She was the only one in the hall. Everyone else was in the classrooms, hiding under the desks or whatever. Kendra said 911 probably got a hundred cell-phone calls."

"What else?"

"Nothing else. All I know is, the police came and took her away. To jail, I mean."

"Straight to jail?"

"Dell, I don't understand. Where would they stop along the way?"

"At the hospital."

"You mean if—? Wait! I already told you, the police didn't do any shooting."

"Okay."

"Okay? What do you mean, 'okay'? MaryLou killed a boy. And we don't know why."

"I mean: 'Okay, you're not involved,' Dolly. That's all. You want to get her a lawyer, is that it?"

"We *have* to get her a lawyer. Her father's been on the Double D"—I guess I'd been paying more attention to those kids than I thought, because I knew she meant Drunk Disability—"for years, her mother's got a job packing groceries, and her little sister, Danielle, she's only . . . I mean, she goes to the same school. She's a sophomore. So what kind of money could that family have?"

"If they don't have money, the state has to—"

"No!"

"Ssssh, honey. It's okay. Find out who's a good lawyer around here, we'll take care of him, all right? They're not going to set bail on a murder charge, so you've got some time to ask around."

"I don't have to," she said, the steel back inside the core of her voice. "The best criminal lawyers are all far away from here."

"How could you know that?"

"I don't know that. What I do know is that the criminal lawyers around here, all they know is how to plead guilty. It's like a joke with some of the kids. They say the DA is as soft as warm custard. He's more afraid of trials than the plague. And he's been in office since forever, so I guess the local lawyers all got used to making deals. Now they're no good for anything else."

"You want me to . . . ask around?"

"No. What's the point? MaryLou did . . . what they said. There had to be fifty different witnesses, and they found the pistol where she dropped it in the hall. So it's either going to be a guilty plea or an insanity trial."

"Then . . . ?"

"She's going to be in court Monday. It's so terrible. That's the same day she was supposed to be leaving for summer camp—softball camp, I mean, at college. Now she's probably never going to play softball again."

"It's still early—"

"I have to make sure whatever lawyer they assign asks the judge to allow me in to see her."

"I don't know how that works."

"This is only Saturday. By the time they bring MaryLou to court, you could find out."

The way Dolly said it, I knew she wasn't talking about what I *could* do.

We were still talking when the early light started to crackle the darkness. Nobody saw me leave.

It took a little more than two hours to get to a city where I could ask around.

Actually, I didn't have to ask, just listen. I felt my way into a section of the city where the bars would open early. Plenty were talking about the shootings—I guess it had been on the news—but I never heard a single lawyer's name mentioned.

Most of the talk was about whether the trial would be on TV.

So I drifted back over to another part of town, where I could find coffeehouses, bookstores, outdoor-supply stores. Closest thing to intel I could pick up was a kind of general agreement that the girl must have been bullied at school.

Although nobody that far away from the scene claimed to have witnessed any bullying of MaryLou, I only had to listen to learn that there were other ways to bully schoolkids than by slapping them around. Bullies could write ugly things about the target on their Facebook pages, send nasty e-mails, even use Tweets—some kind of Internet darts. But it seemed those kind of kids ended up killing themselves instead of anyone else.

And no way a girl they called Mighty Mary was getting bullied, especially in a place where girls' softball was such a big thing.

So I took the shortest route in. Dolly asked MaryLou's best friend, Megan, to get one of her parents to put "Aunt Dolly" on the visiting list.

"They were kind of weird about it," Megan said when she got back, "but I took Franklin with me, so they didn't argue. You can visit today. Is that soon enough?"

"Sure it is, honey," Dolly told the girl. "You did a great job."

The girl smiled like she'd never heard those words before.

Nobody noticed me sitting in an easy chair in the living room. I knew that, if people aren't expecting anyone to be around, and you don't make sounds or move, you might as well be invisible.

I didn't learn that in La Légion—the Americans taught me. Well, one American. He was an Indian, which is what they call the people they took this country from. In Oregon, they pay restitution for that by allowing Indians to open all kinds of casinos. To preserve their culture.

"It is less than a second, that space where you have to decide if you have been detected," he told me. "If you can be completely calm *inside* that second, they will show themselves before they see you. There is no guesswork. This"—he tapped his nose—"must always match. If your own scent is the same as what surrounds you, you will not alert those who search only with their eyes."

All I knew about the Indian was that he was called Ira, and that he never made it back to wherever his home was.

The jail had a women's wing. A small one, but with conference rooms for the lawyers, and a much bigger one for visits.

"I don't see your name on the list," the guard said, nodding at me.

"This is my husband," Dolly told him. "I couldn't . . . handle this without him there. I just can't believe little MaryLou would . . ." Her voice went fluttery, showering tension like a glass butterfly in a brick cage.

I stayed silent and still, right hand grasping my left wrist, covering the scar, which was bigger than any wristwatch I'd ever wear. I put a dull look on my face, selling it as best I could. The guard had to think that if they let me in on the visit I'd just sit there like a lump, maybe go get some of whatever they were selling out of the vending machines.

But he never looked up, so he didn't see my eyes. He just waved his hand, like a prince allowing a commoner to cross his land.

MaryLou was sitting at one of the tables. As soon as I saw her, I remembered seeing her before, though she'd never been one of those who wandered back into my den. Her table was in the corner farthest away from the door where we walked in.

There's no magic to it. And it's not a movie script, this back-to-the-wall stuff. Your body naturally puts itself wherever it feels safest. MaryLou may have been scared, or just acting on instinct. For me, it was perfect: I sat facing her, so all anybody could see was the back of my head. Hard to make an ID from that, especially since I never took off the fisherman's cap I was wearing.

She stood up and hugged Dolly. Her pale eyes were clear and peaceful. I'd seen that look before, right after a firefight. *La mission est sacrée*. Whatever she'd wanted to do in that school, it was already done.

"Oh, sweetie, what happened?"

I shook my head as I pressed a thumb inside Dolly's hand.

"Don't say anything about this case," I told MaryLou. "Not to us, not to anybody."

She turned her head a few degrees. Made sure Dolly agreed with what I'd said. Then she nodded an okay at me.

"Especially not to anyone you meet in here. Some of them would trade you for a snort of meth. And that's not the biggest bullet you have to dodge. Some of the other women in here are facing heavy charges, and they'd be happy to swear you said anything that would help the DA, in return for some time off the years they're facing."

Another nod. Her eyes were that same pale blue, but I was checking for something else, and I found it. Now they were focused, hard, and sharp.

"Don't say anything to whatever lawyer they give you, either."

Her eyes widened a bit at that, but her posture didn't change; she stayed as relaxed as if I were talking about the weather.

"When you see me again, I'll be with a lawyer. Could be the same one they give you, or one you've never seen. Point is, you see me, you'll know it's all right to talk. Talk *then*, not before. Not even in court. Never volunteer anything."

"I got it." Her voice was firm, not annoyed.

Dolly took that as her cue to start talking. Did MaryLou have enough clothes? Was she on any special diet? And a hundred more, all wrapped around the "Did you need any medications brought over?" that would tell Dolly what we were dealing with.

"I don't know what I'm allowed to have," MaryLou told her. One answer, covering all the questions with the same blanket.

"I'll find out," Dolly promised her. "And I'll have everything ready for the lawyer tomorrow."

"When I go to court?"

"Yes, honey. But when it comes to medications, just tell me your doctor's name and I'll get them to you before that."

"Like what?" MaryLou asked, an edge to her voice that I could feel more than hear.

"Oh, like, if you were a diabetic. Insulin isn't something you can—"

"Nothing like that," MaryLou assured her, the edge gone from her voice.

"Honey, you know your friends are all behind you."

"Yeah. And they all just want to know *why*, right?"

"That's only natural," Dolly told her, as if defending the motives of MaryLou's friends. "And Megan was the one who got your parents to say I was your aunt Dolly."

"No way Megan went over there alone."

"She said she was with Franklin. I've never met him, but he must—"

"He's my friend," MaryLou said. "Maybe my *best* friend. If my father took one look at him, he'd give up whatever Megan asked him for."

I hadn't been planning to say anything more, but I could see this was starting to run off the rails. Too much talking. "Not now" is all I said.

I guess that was enough. They switched gears, but kept talking for another hour or so. I don't know what about—I wasn't there. Inside my head, I played out the little bit I knew: MaryLou wasn't crazy. Which meant she had some reason for doing what she did. Especially the way she did it.

Killing the enemy? Sure, that made sense. But you don't take them all out, throw away your weapon, then sit down and wait for their reinforcements to show up.

You don't waste time covering your trail, either. They'll know who killed their comrades. Your job is not being there when they find the bodies.

I ran through other things that might have explained what

happened, but I stopped when I realized MaryLou hadn't saved one of the bullets for herself.

So not a planned suicide, with dead bodies serving as the good-bye note. And she'd only had the one weapon, so not a kamikaze move, either. Back to where I'd started—whatever mission she'd been on was over the second she was done shooting.

Dolly had contacts all over the place at the hospital, so I already knew that MaryLou's tox screen had come back negative. They were probably looking for some sort of speed or hallucinogen, but the only unusual finding was her being way too over-percentage in red blood cells. That puzzled the hospital, so one of the ER nurses, a pal of Dolly's, called.

Dolly had told her there could be a hundred reasons for that, leaving the door open.

When I came back from wherever I'd gone to, MaryLou was telling Dolly, "Yes, I'm sure."

"I'll be there tomorrow," Dolly said, hugging her again. "And some of your friends, too. But I can pick one to sit with me. Do you care which?"

"No. But please tell Franklin—Megan has his cell—not to come. If he sees them take me away, he could get all . . . confused. Anyone else is okay, but I need you to make the pick, Dolly. Then nobody's feelings get hurt."

"I'll handle it," Dolly said. Nobody hearing her voice would have doubted that.

"**W**hat's with the red blood cells your nurse friend told you about?" I asked Dolly on the drive back.

"If MaryLou had an infection—and there's all kinds of infections women her age can pick up—you'd expect to see a high count on white cells, not red."

"Maybe they should have looked for EPO."

"I thought you never paid attention, Dell."

She was talking about that Tour de France bicycle race they show on TV every year. Dolly is addicted to it, never misses a single one. I only watch it to be with her. "Just enough to learn," I told her. "Not enough to say anything."

"But why would MaryLou have had EPO in her blood? She's not—"

"Big game coming up? College scouts? Scholarship?"

"Dell!"

We didn't say a word to each other the rest of the way.

That evening, Dolly finally let loose what was building inside her.

"Why did you tell MaryLou not to speak to a lawyer? Even if he was some sleaze the county assigned to her, he couldn't repeat anything she said. There's this lawyer-client privilege, right?"

"Right."

"And that whole EPO thing. You're thinking that maybe she overdosed, or mixed a bad cocktail? Or she was blood-doping on her own?"

I didn't say anything.

"When MaryLou did . . . what they say she did, it was on a Friday, the last day of school. The last day of that school *forever* for MaryLou. There's no way she was partying the night before, so it couldn't be the aftereffects of someone slipping a date-rape drug into a drink."

I knew she had more to say, so I just shifted my body enough to tell her I was listening.

"And she's not a violent girl. The only time I ever heard of her hitting anyone was when she beat up her little sister."

"How did you hear—?"

"Oh, *everybody* heard. It wasn't any big secret. Last year, Danielle showed up at school with raccoon eyes. So the nurse called the Child Protective people. Her parents said they had no idea what happened. Her father's a confirmed slug—he just watches his big-screen all day and night. And her mother, when she's not working, she stays drunk. So, with Danielle saying she fell down the stairs the night before, there was nothing they could do. But everyone knew MaryLou had really smacked her around."

"You know why?"

"I don't have a clue. I mean, teenage girls get into fights over nothing, but MaryLou is twice Danielle's size, and Danielle was only in middle school then. Some of the clique girls tried to rumor it as all about jealousy, but that never took root."

"Why would MaryLou be jealous of her kid sister?"

"Well, supposedly, it was because Danielle's so much smarter. I mean, she's already skipped two years in school. And she's very cute, too. Doesn't look anywhere near her age . . . but that happens a lot more now than it used to."

"Wait! What happens?"

"Puberty, Dell. It's not even a little bit surprising when a ten-year-old starts menstruating. And they . . . develop right along with it."

"Oh."

"And MaryLou, well, you've met her, Dell. She isn't what you'd call . . . pretty. She's bigger than most of the boys, too."

"Ever happen again? Her beating up her sister, I mean."

"No. I would have heard if it did."

I nodded agreement—I knew what Dolly was saying was true. It's not just that this is such a small town, it's that the pipeline runs right through our house.

"Dell, do you think . . . ? I mean, do you think MaryLou was on some kind of drug?"

"Me? No. A lawyer might, though. There's no other way to beat this case except some kind of temporary insanity, right?"

"Well, she must have been on *something*."

"No. She went in there with a job to do, and she did it."

"How can you possibly say that?"

"Dolly . . . Dolly, you know what I did. What I did my whole life, before I gave it all up."

"We don't talk about that."

"And we don't have to now, either. But you asked me— remember?—how could I know that she was on a mission, how could I know that once it was over nothing much else mattered to her?"

"But that's like saying she meant to do it."

"She did. And she got it done. That's why nothing else matters to her anymore."

"It matters to me, Dell. Maybe I don't know what actually happened. But, whatever it was, all that matters is what happens to MaryLou now. And what is that going to be?"

"I don't know. Not yet, anyway."

"Dell, you're scaring me."

"That's the opposite of what I'm trying to do. How would you expect me to help MaryLou? Go to law school?"

"You don't have to talk to me like that!"

"Dolly, you want me to try and do something, or you don't. If you do, I will. If you don't, I won't. But if you want me to help, you can't help *me,* understand?"

I couldn't help thinking how truly beautiful she was. From the moment I met her, Dolly's face was always surrounded by a soft, rose-colored kind of light. I thought that aura was her own kind of perimeter. I knew her grayish eyes could go from love's soft glow to laser strikes in a blink. But I'd never seen this kind of glow that was always around her change colors before. Now it looked like a darkening evening sky, the way it gets just before the thunderbolts come.

"I couldn't stand to lose you, Dell."

"You won't. If it gets ugly, I'll just walk away. And nobody will know I've ever been wherever I walk away from."

"But MaryLou—"

"She's yours, not mine."

Dolly just sat there for a few minutes. Then she reached out and took my hand.

"She *is* mine. But if there was any risk to you, I'd walk away, too, Dell. I'll do it right now, if you say so."

I squeezed her hand. Just hard enough so she'd know we had a deal.

Monday, the courtroom was like the last bus out of a town facing a hurricane. It wasn't big enough to hold all the people who were there when it opened, never mind those who kept trying to get in.

I scanned them quickly, but it looked like a cross section of the town. Nobody stood out. Nobody looked at MaryLou with what I'd been watching for.

Dolly squeezed my hand twice: "No." So MaryLou's parents weren't anywhere to be seen.

MaryLou herself was sitting at a table close to the judge's perch, a man I didn't know next to her. I could see him whispering to her, more and more urgently, but she never so much as turned her head in his direction.

A good soldier, I thought to myself. *Takes it in, acts it out.*

A bailiff told everyone to quiet down and stand up, but he was more asking than telling. And nobody was willing to give up their seat, anyway.

The judge came in. Sat down. Made an imperious little motion with his hand. The bailiff told everyone to be seated, as if they weren't doing that already.

I guess that second order didn't apply to MaryLou, or the man next to her. Or the guy I guessed was the DA at the other table.

He looked more nervous than anyone else. His fat face was already greasy with sweat.

The judge started talking. I tuned him out so I could focus on faces. But I refocused on him when I heard his tone change.

"Counsel," he said to the man standing next to MaryLou, "are you telling this court that your client refuses to enter a plea?"

"She refuses to speak at all, Your Honor."

"Is that correct, young lady?"

MaryLou didn't move.

"Are you dissatisfied with your representation?"

MaryLou stood like a statue.

"Counsel?"

"Your Honor, under the circumstances, I have no choice but to move for a—"

"I don't want to hear any motions until I hear a plea, counsel."

"Yes, Your Honor."

Silence took over. The judge broke it: "Very well, as defendant prefers to stand mute, the court will enter a not-guilty plea on her behalf. Additionally, in view of the gravity of the charges, the defendant will be remanded without bail."

A couple of female court officers bracketed MaryLou as they walked her out a side door. *Probably a tunnel straight into the jail,* I thought. I filed that away. I couldn't expect any of the guards to give me a tour, but maybe there were architectural blueprints still around—the jail itself looked as if it had been built fairly recently.

Outside, I watched from the parking lot. If there were any reporters around, I couldn't tell. I didn't see anyone asking questions.

I caught up with the man who'd been standing next to Mary-Lou as he walked out the same door I had. He was wearing "I'm from around here" clothes: some kind of corduroy jacket, a white shirt, and a red tie with white whales on it. Carrying something that looked like a canvas courier's bag on a strap over one shoulder. Maybe thirty-five years old.

"Excuse me," I said, coming at him from the side. "Could I have a couple of minutes of your time?"

"Who are you?"

"A friend of MaryLou's. I have some information that might be helpful to you."

"Well?" he said, hands on hips.

"She won't talk to you because you've been appointed by the state. And it's the state that's prosecuting her."

"How do you know this?"

"Like I said, I'm a friend."

"Well," he said, a little smirk on his face, "that's her choice. But unless she's prepared to hire private counsel, I'll be the one who—"

"She *is* prepared to hire private counsel. That's why I'm here."

"Fine. Then have her new—"

"She doesn't want new counsel."

"She hasn't got a choice about that. Unless she wants to represent herself," he said, doubling up on the smirk.

"I guess I'm not making myself clear," I said, ignoring the guy's posturing. "She wants you to be her lawyer, but she wants you to be working for her, not for the state."

"I don't work for the state," he lectured. "The state pays me to represent her because any person charged with a crime is entitled to counsel, even if they're indigent. Given the girl's age—she's legally an adult, but hardly expected to have any income—the court assumed indigence. That's why I was assigned."

"I'd feel better if you were hired, instead."

"Are you saying you want to hire me? I assure you, whoever you are, that I'll work just as hard no matter who pays me."

I liked him for saying that, but I didn't get all carried away with it.

"I'm sure that's absolutely true. But . . . well, you know how kids are."

"Yes. But the state pays—"

"I know what the state pays," I told him. "I wouldn't insult you by offering the same kind of slave wages."

"Are you saying—?"

"What I'm saying is"—I cut him off—"could we go to your office and talk?" As I spoke, I compressed the air between us, so I could walk him farther away from the courthouse but still let him think he was leading me.

His office was in a one-story building clad in fake-wood light-blue siding. There were the names of a few other lawyers as well as his own—Bradley L. Swift—on a sign that had a few empty slots below the filled ones.

He asked the piggish woman at the front desk if there had been any calls. She seemed to take some pleasure from telling him no. My guess was that she worked for the landlord, not the lawyer.

His personal office was decent-sized. Computer with a small flat screen, fax machine, two-line cordless phone sitting in a cradle. Small reddish cloth sofa against one wall, pair of wood chairs on the client side of his desk. His own chair was a match to the sofa.

I sat across from him. Before he could start talking, I put five thousand in hundreds on his desk. That shut his mouth quicker than a leveled pistol would have done.

"I don't know much about criminal law," I told him. "I know you don't get paid by the hour. The way I figure it, a case like this, it would have to cost at least twenty-five thousand. If I'm right, then there's your retainer. I'll pay you the rest as we go along, the same way as this."

He swept the cash into a drawer of his desk like he was hiding evidence of a crime he was guilty of. A serious one.

"That is a fair fee for a case this complex," he said, playing it like he pulled in that kind of cash all the time, but having a little trouble with his voice. "Who should I make the receipt out to?"

I waved my hand, showing him I didn't want one. That killed any interest he had in knowing my name.

"You're retained now?"

"Certainly. I'll notify the court and—"

"I don't care about that. I just wanted to make sure I understood how things work."

"Work?"

"I read somewhere that you don't need a private investigator's license so long as you're working for a lawyer. Is that true?"

"I . . . That's something I'd have to check for myself, frankly. Using private investigators is kind of rare around here."

"The state won't pay for them?"

"Well, in some cases, maybe. In fact, one like this, they might very well do so."

"Can you look it up?"

"Look what up?"

"Whether I could be your private investigator even though I don't have a license."

"Oh. Yes, I can do that. Just give me a minute."

I couldn't see what he called up on his computer screen, but I figured it wouldn't matter.

"Yes," he said, swinging back to face me. "I'll need your name, of course. In case you have to testify or—"

"I won't be testifying. But I will be with you when you go back and visit MaryLou this afternoon." I put an Oregon driver's license on his desk. "My name is Jackson. Adelbert B. Jackson. Okay?"

He looked at his watch, like he had a lot of pressing business to attend to.

"How about two o'clock? Would that work for you?"

"Yes. And after that visit, I could go back anytime and see MaryLou on my own, right? Working as your investigator, I mean."

"Certainly, if that's what you want."

"What I want is to know if they've got a special place for lawyers to meet with their clients. And if it's wired."

"There *are* attorney-client rooms. But this isn't some television show. No looking through one-way glass walls, no hidden cameras, nothing like that. Still, there *is* one thing you should know: if an inmate makes a call on one of the jail phones, those calls *are* recorded. That's no secret—there's a big sign right above the phones."

"You're sure? Bet-your-life sure?"

His complexion went white as he nodded agreement. I could see my question had spooked him, so I knew he'd have the correct-and-checked answers to my questions by two that afternoon.

"No comment," I said.

"What?"

"That's all you have to say about this case. To reporters, to anyone writing a book, to someone in a bar . . . to anyone at all."

"Of course," he assured me.

"And by the time we meet this afternoon, can you have your secretary type up something on your letterhead that says I'm working for you?"

"Absolutely," he said. If I was dumb enough to think he had a secretary, that was fine with him.

As I drove away from where I'd parked, I could see TV buses disgorging all kinds of equipment. One even had a big satellite dish assembled. The on-camera people were inside, getting their makeup straight. My guess was that their timing had been off—they thought that MaryLou's appearance wasn't going to happen until later, and that it would take a lot longer than it already had.

Dolly was there when I got home. I told her what I'd done.

"That's perfect, Dell. What did you think of her lawyer?"

"The only thing I couldn't understand about him was his haircut. What do you call it when women wear their hair down over their forehead? Like bangs, but there's a name for it."

"I think you mean a pageboy. It was a popular hairstyle years ago, but you don't see them much on girls anymore."

"On a man?"

"Well, actually, you'd see more of that style on men than women . . . at least in this part of the country."

"Huh."

"Well, what else? About the lawyer, I mean."

"There's nothing else. He's only got to be able to let me move around. Any problems, I'll be able to pull out a letter on his office stationery. If it turns out there's actually going to be a trial, we'll get someone else."

"All right, honey. So when do you start?"

"Two this afternoon. I'm meeting him at the jail, and he'll get me inside with him to talk to MaryLou."

"But you told her not to talk to anyone."

"I told her not to talk to anyone unless I gave her the okay. And she hasn't. I just have to get in there with this lawyer once. Then I can come back anytime I want. Without him, I mean."

"What do I do?"

"I don't know," I told Dolly. "But I will. And real soon."

"You're not going out like that." I knew Dolly wasn't asking a question, but I couldn't figure out what she meant. So I did what I always do when that happens—I just wait for whatever she's going to say next.

"You have a perfectly good suit, Dell. The one I bought you. The one that's been hanging in the cedar closet ever since."

"You want me to wear a suit?"

"Yes, I want you to wear a suit. You're not some visiting friend now, you're a private investigator."

"But the lawyer, his suit was like some corduroy crap. If I go in there looking like I make more money than him, maybe that wouldn't work so good?"

"You wear more than just a suit, Dell. Sure, it's a little fancy, but you want people to take you seriously. You don't need a tie, okay? Just one of those—"

"—nice silk shirts you bought for me? The ones that have been hanging in the cedar closet all this time?"

"Don't be such a smartass."

"I know. . . . Just go put on the suit, right?"

She sat there at the long butcher-block table, tapping her fingernails.

I went into our bedroom and changed.

When I came back down, Dolly's smile was a sunburst. She got up and walked over to me. Stood on her toes and kissed me on the side of my mouth.

"I didn't mean to act so . . . bossy, Dell. It's just that this is so important. The media, they're making it even *more* important already. And MaryLou's all alone."

"No, she's not," I told her, knowing it was a blood promise the second it came out of my mouth.

The lawyer would have been waiting for me if I'd shown up at two. But I'd been standing in front of the jail since one-thirty, waiting for him.

"Let's go" is all he said.

"Bradley Swift," he said to the guard. "Counsel for MaryLou McCoy. This is Mr. Jackson. He works for me as an investigator."

The guard gave him a "big fucking deal" look and buzzed us through.

The room they put us in was plenty big enough. Empty except for some chairs placed around a wood table.

MaryLou was brought in a few minutes later. Only one guard to escort her this time. And she wasn't cuffed.

As soon as the door closed, Swift said, "MaryLou, this is—"

"I know who he is," she cut him off. "And only my friends call me MaryLou. In here, I'm 'Ms. McCoy.'"

She shot me a "Was that all right?" look, and I nodded. Then I told her, "Mr. Swift here had to bring me through. I'm his private investigator. Which means I can come back on my own. You understand, MaryLou?"

"Sure," she said, flashing me just a little touch of smile, showing me she knew I got the "Ms. McCoy" bit.

"The Visiting Room, it's okay for some things," I went on. "But it's not a safe place to talk about this case."

"Got it."

"Ms. McCoy." Swift spoke up more to be part of the conversation than anything else—MaryLou had already made it clear where he stood with her. "Do you have any questions? Concerning the legal proceedings, I mean?"

"When will it happen?"

"When will what happen?"

"The trial. When will that get going?"

"Oh, not for a while. There are a number of options we have."

"Like what?"

"Well, the facts don't seem to be in dispute. You didn't make any statement, true enough. But . . ."

"Yeah, I get it. So?"

"Well, if you were . . . coerced in any way, or acting under the influence of some drug, or—"

"Forget that."

"Well, that still leaves us with some options, but if you're going to stand mute the way you did in the courtroom today, I can't really present much of a . . . psychological defense. The DA's Office would have the right to have one of their own experts examine you, and if you won't talk to them, it makes a very bad impression."

"You don't have to talk to anyone," I said.

Swift gave me a look like I was overstepping my bounds, but he dropped it quicker than he'd brought it up. I don't think he was smart enough to figure out who he was dealing with—not yet, anyway. But one thing he did know—I was a paying customer.

"The judge already put the not-guilty plea in for her, right?" I asked the lawyer, to let him save face.

"Yes. But if we're going to be using a . . . psychological defense, we have to give notice to the—"

"You can stop talking like I'm not in the room," MaryLou told him. "And I'm not telling anyone I'm crazy. Then or now."

"It's not necessarily—" Swift cut himself off, seeing MaryLou's face harden. She let it happen slowly, like plaster of Paris setting.

"I'll be back," I told MaryLou.

"I'll be here," she said, twisting her lips into something like a smile.

"Look, I understand you have some sort of prior friendship with the girl," Swift said once we were back outside. "But when you hired me, it was to be her lawyer. What did you think you were buying?"

"Time," I told him. "As much of it as possible."

"Oh, I can do that for sure. A case like this, there's no way the DA isn't going to farm it out."

"What does that mean?"

"It means they never try big cases down here. The DA's Office, I'm talking about. Unless there's going to be a plea, they'll go crying to the AG's Office, like they always do. That way, if there's a guilty verdict, they can take credit for it. And if it goes the other way, they blame it on whoever comes in to actually try the case."

"How would that work? Bringing someone else in, I mean."

"They get someone from the AG. Or even from another office. What they call a 'special prosecutor.'"

"And that takes time?"

"Sure. But that's not the only way to stall this thing. I've got all kinds of discovery motions I can make. Nobody on their side is going to be in a hurry to try this one, that much I can practically guarantee. And that's not even counting plea negotiations."

"Plea negotiations? What could they possibly offer MaryLou?"

"They could take the death penalty off the table, for openers."

"They execute kids here?"

"She's eighteen. An adult. But you're right—executing someone her age would be a political mistake."

"Political?"

"Plenty of people in this part of the state are opposed to the death penalty, especially in this county. And not just people—people who vote. That scares the DA to death. He spends all his time pleasing people. That's the only thing he knows how to do. Hell, they may not even farm this one out—the locals already feel too strongly about it, like it's *their* case, not one for an outsider to handle."

"So what *could* they offer her?"

"It depends on what excuse they could give."

"That's why you mentioned the psychological stuff?"

"Yes. The more we give them, the more they could live with a life sentence."

"If they're not going to kill her anyway, how's that such a great deal?"

"This is a Measure Eleven case. The judge doesn't have that much discretion. She'd have to go to prison, and, remember, it's not just one murder charge, it's a whole laundry list of felonies. Provided nobody else dies, that is. Under the best of circumstances, we could try for a manslaughter on top, with the rest to run concurrent. That would be the deal of the century. But, who knows, if it turns out she was an abused child or something . . ."

"You heard her."

"That she won't cooperate? Yes. But it's still my obligation as an attorney to thoroughly investigate any avenue that might—"

"You're not getting paid by the hour."

He gave me a long look. At least he was facing me: hard to see his eyes under that pageboy haircut.

"I assume you won't be turning in any written reports," he finally said.

"No."

"Okay," he said, like I'd asked him for permission.

Driving back, I was trying to make sense of it. Realized I couldn't, not without asking some questions.

I don't know how to do that, not really. The only time I'd seen men questioned, the only question was how much pain they could take.

I didn't like seeing that, but I knew I couldn't look away—the men I was with would take it as a sign of weakness. Some of those men chased weakness the way other men chased women.

The only thing I learned from watching was that, if you put a man in enough pain, he'll scream.

Actually, I learned something else. One man finally screamed. When they made the pain stop, he told them where his outfit's base camp was. Then they shot him.

When we hit where he'd said the base camp was, it was just a clearing hacked out of the jungle. Not big enough for a camp, but plenty of room for the trip wires surrounding it. The strike team got blown to chunks of flesh and bone. Nobody followed them. The man they'd tortured must have been laughing under all those screams.

I can do a lot of things, but most of them aren't much use to me now. Being with Dolly, that was all I wanted.

And whatever Dolly wanted, I wanted to get for her. I had learned some new things to be with her; if that's what it took to stay with her, I could learn some more.

"**H**ow far do you want to go with this?" I asked her late that same night.

"Far? You mean . . . what, Dell?"

"Break her out, that far."

"No."

I waited. I knew there was more to come; Dolly did this when she wanted to make sure I understood whatever she was going to say.

"She couldn't live underground," Dolly finally said, already accepting that I might be able to break her out. "Not MaryLou. She's not built for it."

"She looks like she is. She's in jail, and she's just a kid. But nobody's even so much as tried her."

"How do you know that?"

"Not a mark on her. Not on her face, not on her hands. That means either she rolled over or nobody pushed. And she's not the kind to roll over."

"Oh. Well, that's not what I meant. Even if she could get around her looks—I know there's ways to do that—she'd die of loneliness. She needs . . . people. Friends. Sports. She needs to be connected."

"There's places where she could make new friends."

"Overseas, you mean?"

"Yeah. She couldn't just disappear. Not in America, but there's places that'd take her."

"No," Dolly whispered, roadblocking the idea.

"MaryLou's not crazy. So she had a reason. But she's not telling—not so far, anyway. It's like all we have is this big chunk of granite. So you start boring your way in from one side, and I'll take the other."

"I can do that."

"It's not just boring in, baby. You and me, we have to cut a tunnel. *One* tunnel, so we meet in the middle, yes? And we have to make sure the stone doesn't crack while we're working through it."

"So—go slow?"

"It's not so much that as making sure we're headed toward the same light. The one in the middle."

"What's there, Dell? What's in the middle?"

"MaryLou," I said, real soft.

I held her until she drifted off. Drifted off for real. When Dolly thinks I'm going someplace after she goes to sleep, she stays tense, even asleep.

"They have to tell you what they've got, right?"

"They're supposed to," Swift told me. "There's a Supreme Court case that says, if they don't turn over everything that's exculpatory, any conviction gets thrown out."

"Exculpatory?"

"Anything that might prove her innocence. Or even what might make the case against her look weaker to a jury."

"What about the gun?"

"What about it?"

"Don't they have to match the ballistics?"

"Well . . . sure. But that's probably not going to help us. When the police got there, she was just sitting on the floor. The gun was right next to her."

"Couldn't we get the gun itself, too? Not to take away or anything, but to have our own ballistics guy run tests?"

"I suppose so. You don't see a lot of expert testimony in cases around here."

"Too expensive?"

"That's probably part of it. But challenging experts is a tricky business. It could backfire easily enough."

What you mean is, you've never had your own expert. On any case, ever. Probably never even asked for one, I thought. But all I said out loud was "So who's their expert? Some cop?"

"Probably."

"And they're never wrong?"

"I know, that doesn't mean they *couldn't* be, but . . ."

"The fee we agreed on? I understand that doesn't include whatever you'd have to spend on experts, okay?"

Little clots of red popped up on his round face. Bull's-eye.

"And no matter what, they *have* to tell you everything about the gun they found?"

"Certainly," he said, back to where he felt safe. "In fact, that's one of the motions I'm going to file."

"When?"

"Uh . . . today, in fact."

"And they can't refuse?"

"No. Not for something like that."

"Okay. I'll see you later, then."

"You could just call, if you want."

"I don't like talking on phones," I said, "but sometimes speed is more important than safety. So here's my cell-phone number, in case something comes up." I handed over the number of the pre-paid on the back of an index card.

The writing for the phone number wasn't mine. It wasn't anybody's. Nobody uses pantographs much anymore, I guess, but they were perfect if you wanted untraceable "handwriting."

Since I was already dressed for the part, I went over to the jail. They put MaryLou and me in that same lawyer's room, so I guessed there weren't going to be any arguments over that in the future.

When the guard brought MaryLou in, there was something about the way she handled the job that made me think. I'd have to run it past Dolly.

MaryLou sat down. I put my finger to my lips. Then I took out a pad and wrote, "Why them?" in soft pencil.

I pushed the pad over to her side of the table. She looked at what I'd written for a long time. Then she shook her head and pushed the pad back over to me.

"Not trust me?" I wrote.

She shook her head again.

I pointed at my temple, made a gesture as if smacking myself in the head, sighed. It brought a little smile to her face.

She reached for the pad. Wrote, "I trust Dolly."

"But even if she asked you . . . ?"

"No. This isn't about trust."

"OK," I wrote. "The cops took the gun. Did they take anything else?"

"Everything else. I had to strip. They kept it all. Gave me some sweats. People dropped off other clothes for me. I guess they searched those clothes, too. Before they gave them to me."

She pushed the pad back to me. I took out a match. She pointed to the big NO SMOKING sign. I held the match to the paper I'd torn from the pad I'd been writing on. It went *poof!* and disappeared. I blew out the match and pocketed it.

"Cool!" MaryLou said, sounding like a little kid for a second.

It was just flash paper. A guy in Marseilles gave me a few pads of it a long time ago. Guess it still worked.

I wrote, "I'm going to come around and sit next to you, so you can whisper. Cup your hands around your mouth, then open them just a slit. I'll do the same. Is that OK?"

She nodded. *No stranger to secrets,* I thought.

I got up, crossed around, and whispered into her left ear, "Do you give a damn about what happens next?"

She nodded her head vigorously.

"You didn't expect to get away with it, did you?"

"You mean, like escape or something?" she whispered back.

It was my turn to nod.

And hers to shake her head.

"Your parents?" I whispered.

She made a push-away motion with one hand, shook her head.

"Useless?" I whispered, to be sure.

"At their best," she whispered back.

I sat there for a few minutes. MaryLou tapped the back of my right hand. The crude stitches they'd put in a long time ago had left bluish, lumpy lines. I never even noticed them myself anymore.

I copied her "useless" gesture.

She smiled.

I cupped my hands, said, "MaryLou, I'm blundering around here. Dolly wants me to do . . . she wants me to do whatever I can. But she also doesn't want me doing anything *you* don't want. So—now's the time to tell me, understand?"

"I don't want to spend my life in prison," she whispered back. "But don't ask me any 'Why did you do it?' questions. I wouldn't answer them even if I could walk out of here today."

"You said 'life.' One of the women you're locked up with told you the DA would never ask for the death penalty."

She gave me a puzzled look. Then whispered, "How could you know that?"

"Same way I can make paper disappear. Be careful of people who act like they're schooling you."

She looked at me a long time. Eye to eye. Then she said, "Whatever I have to do."

"I need a close-terrain map."

"For right around here?" Dolly asked.

"No. For the school. All those kids you're always having over, it sounds like they never stop talking."

"Oh." She kind of giggled. "I guess that's what it would sound like to you, honey. But I still don't know what you're asking for."

"I guess I don't, either. You know I wasn't born here, so—"

"I don't know where you were born, Dell. Neither do you. Why does it matter, all of a sudden?"

"One thing I *do* know is that it wasn't here. And you're right—it doesn't matter, not anymore. What I'm trying to say is, I don't know how school . . . works here. How it breaks down."

"Ah! You mean, like jocks and nerds, stuff like that."

"More like a . . . chain of command, I guess. The pyramids.

Who's on top, who's on the bottom. For all the clubs and cliques. And the outsiders."

"I know what you mean. And I already have that much. But what I don't have is what I guess you really want to know. Specific names, right?"

"Yeah. Like . . . Okay, her best friend is Megan. And this Franklin guy. For all I know, MaryLou was the big boss of some clique herself."

"Not MaryLou. She was a star athlete, all right. But 'Mighty Mary' was just something the papers started calling her. Around school, it wasn't really a compliment. More like saying she was standoffish. Even snobby. But the *real* snobby ones—especially the girls—they're always in groups."

"Boys, too?"

"Oh yes! Maybe even worse for them. There's a fraternity. Kind of like they have in college. You don't have to be an athlete to get in, I don't think. But I can find out."

"Good. Any of those boys in that group have some outsider they single out? Put down? Talk about like he's some kind of freak?"

"There is one. I don't remember his name. But what he does is tape girls fighting. Fighting with each other. Then he puts them on the Internet. It's a kind of porno—you know, like girls in negligees having pillow fights. But this is the real thing, the fighting. They don't just pull hair, they punch and kick. Even bite. You can hear the crowd cheering on the tapes, but you only see the girls.

"And they *do* talk about this guy like he's this real degenerate. But that doesn't stop them from watching the tapes. Even egging some of the girls on themselves."

"Good! This fight-film guy, he ever get one of MaryLou?"

"I don't think so. But I can find that out, too."

"So he doesn't *get* the girls to fight, he just shows up when they do?"

"It has to be that. There's no way *this* guy could get girls to fight."

"Why not him?"

"The boys who get girls fighting, it's fighting over them, you see? This film guy—and I will find out his name for you—the way the girls talk about him, it's like he's real creepy, so I can't see any of them fighting over him."

"Then I need a bigger map. If you had a close-up map of this town, would you be able to point out places where kids hang out?"

"I can download a map like that easy enough. But hang out for what, Dell? Some places, they . . . socialize, I guess. Others, it's more like Lovers' Lane. Or getting high. Or skateboarding. You see what I mean?"

"Yeah. And if you could mark which places are for which things, that would help a lot."

"I'll start now," Dolly told me, as she booted up her laptop.

❚ don't ride my motorcycle much anymore. But it's got plates and insurance, and I keep it fresh-tuned. I store it off the ground, so the tires don't flat-spot.

A 1995 Honda VT600C isn't much for speed, and it doesn't come close to the handling of the ones they make now. But it also doesn't look like anything. Actually, it kind of looks like it could be all kinds of different bikes—especially in battleship gray with extra-quiet pipes.

Another good thing about using a bike is that the cops *expect* to see you with a helmet and face shield, wearing gloves. So you can be damn near invisible if you stay off the main roads. Even more so after dark.

I keep the bike behind the false back wall of the garage. That part's vented, so I can fire the bike up indoors if I ever have to. But this time I planned to walk it far enough so I could pull the clutch in and coast downhill. Anyone who heard it after that wasn't going to connect it with our house.

I made sure everything was tight, including the HID boat light I have taped to the front of the tank. It's not for seeing; it's for blinding. Anyone hit in the face with that on full beam isn't going anywhere. Unless he's driving—then he'll probably crash.

But they're not illegal, and neither is the Glock 23 I carry. For this part of what I wanted to do, having a registered handgun with me made more sense.

I did a before-battle check, point by point. Then I went back inside.

I wasn't surprised to see Dolly using a bunch of different-colored markers on a map.

"The colors are codes," she told me. "Like, see the ones in red? Those are danger zones."

"Danger?"

"Dangerous to kids, I mean."

"Because . . . ?"

"Because of a lot of different reasons. See, here?" she said, touching a red dot on the map with a black line drawn through it. "That's a skateboard park. It's fine in the daytime, but a different crowd takes over at night."

"And they're dangerous because . . . ?"

"You know. Drugs, liquor—"

"Dolly, I'm not interested in places where kids shouldn't be hanging out. I don't know how much time we'll have, so I want to start with the worst. But it has to be someplace you could hide and use a videocam."

"Here," she said. "The only reason anyone would go there is to park and make out, or have sex."

"I still don't get it."

"There's talk about someone who doesn't have a car."

I was on her wavelength instantly. "Who's doing the talking?"

"Everyone, it seems like. All of the girls, at least."

"For how long?"

"I don't— Wait! You mean, how long has this story been going around, yes?"

I just nodded.

"Three, four years, minimum."

"Good enough."

"Good enough for what?"

"Good enough place to start," I said, thinking of the kind of guy who liked to video girls fighting. A guy who none of the girls would ever be fighting over.

I laid the bike down just a few feet in from the road, and pulled some loose brush over it. Nobody would see it in the dark. And even if they did, there was no way to hot-wire it. Or even wheel it away—I had it locked in gear.

But none of that would stop somebody who stumbled over it and cell-phoned his pals to bring a pickup truck. That's why I had it fixed so if anyone lifted it off the ground a flare would go off. That should be enough. Still, liquor makes people stupid, and meth makes them crazy, so it wasn't an absolute guarantee that some amateurs wouldn't try and haul it away.

But if the flare went off, I'd see it. And the GPS unit I was carrying would tell me where they took it to, even if I didn't get back over there myself in time to stop them.

It only took me a few minutes to find him. Whoever he was, he wasn't short of cash. An infrared videocam outfit wouldn't come cheap. Maybe that full-cover ninja outfit cost some serious money, too—I couldn't tell from a distance.

The red dot on the videocam popped whenever he activated it. No way to see that dot if the camera was aimed your way. But if you came up behind it, it was a lighthouse beacon.

He was on a rise, overlooking the Lovers' Lane on Dolly's map. Not even thirty meters from the action.

I didn't like that ninja suit. No way for me to tell if it was a uni-body, so I had to take him in two moves instead of one. A one-arm choke is a sentry-killer. We called it a "scorpion." The natural reaction is to use both hands to pull the pressure off your throat. That leaves the killer the chance to use his free hand, the one with the blade.

The problem with any snap-choke is the tiny distance between going too far and not going far enough. I had better equipment for handling this, but I didn't have time to go back and get it, and I didn't want to waste another twenty-four—no way a guy like him would come back in daylight.

He was in the middle of filming something when I took him down. Even though I was sure he wouldn't want anyone to know he was there, I couldn't risk his making panic noise, so I snapped the choke instead of squeezing it. I was trained in both styles, but neither was designed to leave a sentry alive.

As I dropped to the ground, I pulled him with me. I dropped the hold, slid my left hand across his throat, found the Velcro closure at his neck, and ripped it open. My right hand snapped open my black-bladed Tanto—I had its serrated edge just below his Adam's apple before he got his breath back.

"Don't make a sound," I whispered, moving the serrated edge just slightly so he'd understand his situation.

He smelled so foul I was grateful it was a windless night.

"I'm not going to hurt you." I spoke *very* softly, because I didn't want to reassure him, I wanted to keep him paralyzed with fear. "There's only two outcomes here. You can be calm, let yourself relax, and we can talk. Or I can rip your throat out."

He couldn't make himself relax—he was just a little short of rigor. But he could keep quiet. The only noise was his ragged breathing.

"I've been watching you for a long time," I whispered. "You've got something I need. If you help me, we can be friends. If you don't want to be my friend, that makes you my enemy. And then I have to leave you here. Understand?"

He started to nod, but the blade stopped him in the middle of trying.

"Good," I said, as if he'd agreed to be my friend. "That's real good. Who knows? Maybe, someday, you'll need a friend like me."

He didn't make a sound, but I could feel his tightened muscles loosen a bit.

"Good," I said again. "Now I have to put a bandage around your eyes. It won't hurt, but I can't let you see my face. You understand that, don't you?"

I slowly slid the knife off his throat. He didn't move. I had the precut slab of heavy gauze duct-taped around his eyes and the knife back in place before he could think about moving, even if he hadn't been too frozen to try.

"See how easy this works?" I whispered. "Now I can stop holding on to you, and we can have a conversation. All right?"

I slipped around from underneath him, and pulled him into a sitting position. Gently. Like a friend would.

"You have to answer me, so I know this is okay," I said.

His voice was a whisper almost as serrated as the Tanto's edge. Fear does that. "I . . . I wasn't doing—"

"That doesn't matter. You understand? It doesn't matter. It's not my business what you do. Once you answer my questions, I'll just go away. Fair enough?"

"Okay," he whispered. I couldn't sense whether he was just cooperating out of terror, or if he realized he'd never really had a choice.

"You've got a lot of DVDs," I whispered. "I don't want any of them. I don't even want to see them. If I did, I would have just gone to where you live and taken them. What I need from you is your skills."

"My . . . skills?"

"Who knows better than you what goes on down there? You see everything, but nobody ever sees you. A true master of your craft."

I could feel him tremble. I didn't have to be a psychologist to know what that meant.

"Every night, kids park down there. What I want to know—*all* I want to know—is if you ever saw this kind of scene. Listen close: a particular car pulls in; then, soon as all the other cars see that one, they pull right out."

"Not a car," he whispered. "A truck. A purple-and-white truck. The school colors."

"I knew that wouldn't get past you," I praised him. Felt the trembling again. "How was it purple and white? The cab and bed in different colors?"

"No, no. It's stripes. Thick stripes, all over. Wavy ones, like on a flag in the wind."

"You're doing real good. Now, after that truck comes in, after all the other cars pull out, do *other* cars pull in?"

"Just one car. But it's always full of boys. No more than five, never less than three."

"Is it the same car all the time?"

"No. Sometimes they—"

"You don't film that part, do you? But you have to stay in place to keep from getting spotted. So you *hear* what happens, yes?"

"Yes. They pull the girl into . . ."

When he finally came around, he'd have to convince himself the man he never saw was gone before he'd dare to rip the bandage off his eyes. His camera would be right next to him, but his heart would be hammering so hard he wouldn't notice for a few seconds. And he wouldn't notice the chloroform burns on his nostrils until he got to wherever he lived and looked in a mirror.

Or maybe he didn't like mirrors much.

I guessed he'd probably stay away for a while. But not for that long—there's things inside of some people much stronger than any fear.

It would be nice to fool myself and think the *rouge-ou-noir* choice I'd let my stack ride on had come up. Yes, I had some intel, but it was all negative—I couldn't see Mighty Mary waiting for a train to arrive. But that "school colors" thing, that could be worth something.

That's our school," Dolly said when I got back. "I mean, the school the kids go to."

"High school?"

"Sure."

"Can you find out who drives a truck painted in those colors?"

"Probably more than one."

"In thick stripes? Wavy ones, like the bars on a flag?"

"Oh. That I could probably find out in a few minutes."

"Not tonight, tomorrow. And, Dolly . . ."

"What, Dell?"

"Back your way into it. Let them tell you. Get the conversation around to weird paint jobs you've seen around and—"

"Ah, baby. You think I'd—what?—call one of the girls up and ask who owns that truck?"

"I was just—"

"Go get some sleep, honey."

"I've already got some info for you," he announced, the thinnest vein of pride in his voice, as if he was trying on a new suit to see if it really fit.

I made one of those universally understood gestures. Or universally misunderstood. People see what they expect to see.

"The gun was a—" He paused to check his notes, making sure. "—a Charter Arms Pathfinder."

"They'd have to tell you more than that."

"I'm coming to it, okay?" He sounded peeved that I hadn't fully appreciated all his hard work. "A Charter Arms Pathfinder, model 72224. I did some research on it"—meaning he'd spent a couple of minutes with a search engine—"and you'll never believe what I came up with. That pistol was only a .22!"

"Let me see what you printed out."

He was still a little sulky, but he handed over the single page from the website. It had what I needed: MaryLou's weapon had been a snub-nose revolver, full grip, six shots.

With that one page, I knew why MaryLou had gotten so close to the first kid, why only that one shot had been fatal, and how she missed completely with the last three. "This is real good," I told

Swift. "I don't know how this legal stuff works. Do they have to give you the rest, or do you have to get it on your own?"

"I'm not sure I understand what you're saying."

"Did the pistol have a serial number? It would have, unless it was removed."

"You can't just peel off a—"

"I know. But it can be filed off, if it's not too deeply etched in. And there's acids you can use even if that's the case."

I could see he wanted to know how I knew any of this, but he restrained himself. If you ask a man a question like that, it's the same as telling him you don't know the answer yourself.

"What would the serial number tell us?"

"When the gun was manufactured, if it was a legal buy, if it was a registered weapon, if it was bought new. And when it was bought."

"So, if MaryLou bought it herself—"

"Yeah. Who buys a gun without ammo? She didn't reload. She didn't even bring any more bullets with her. A .22 is an assassin's weapon—you have to be a real marksman to make a sure kill. Part of the advantage is that a .22's quiet, but no revolver, especially a snub-nose, is *that* quiet, and a hallway would be a damned echo chamber.

"MaryLou wouldn't know about any of that. She was real close at first, but after she fired that one shot, she just was jerking the trigger blind. But let's get that serial number anyway—who knows, it might be helpful."

"Sure."

"That reminds me: if you get a message that the NRA called, ignore it. If they manage to get you on the phone, just hang up."

"No comment," he repeated, like he was proud he'd learned a lesson.

"That's *not* what we want. 'No comment,' that's a statement. You're not making *any* statements, not to *anybody*."

He nodded as if we had come to an agreement. Better for his

ego than just following orders. But before I could answer the questions I expected, he hit me with one I hadn't.

"Okay, I get it about 'no comment.' But how do you feel about interviews?"

"Are you serious?"

"Not of you. Not MaryLou, either—I understand we can't expose her to the media."

Now it's "we," huh? I thought. "So who, then?" I asked him.

"Me."

"Ah."

"Look, the media shouldn't get all its information from the DA's Office. Granted, the DA *we* have, all he's going to do is read some lame press statement. But it might not be a bad idea to kind of hint that . . . I don't know, maybe something like 'There's two sides to every story. And I caution people against a rush to judgment'?"

"No."

"No to the interviews, or no to my idea of what to tell them?"

"If you're willing to do a couple of things *before* you say anything, it might be a good idea to drop a hint that we've got a sleeve ace."

"A what?"

"Some really heavy stuff that would change everyone's mind about what happened . . . if we decide to go that route."

"Do we have anything like that?"

"Yes."

"Well, what is it? I mean—"

"You don't need to know that now. You might not even want to know. All you have to do is believe it."

"You said if I was willing to do 'a couple of things.' That's only one."

"Yeah. One, don't do any interviews unless you can keep it down to that one answer we just talked about. The sleeve ace. And only if you're sure you can *sell* that answer. If you don't believe what I just told you, it's no-go."

"I do believe it. What's the other thing?"

"Get a haircut," I told him. "And dress serious, like you're going to a funeral. You need to look like an undertaker. One who's getting ready to bury the prosecution."

"Around here—"

"Around here, they don't have school shootings. And they don't have school shootings by star athletes *anywhere*. I'm not arguing about this. This case needs a serious man, on serious business. Serious business he can handle. I think you're the right man for that, but you have to make sure they all get the same message. And that means not dressing like you do now. When the people used to seeing you start to see the change, they'll start to *feel* it, too."

He stood up and extended his hand, like we were sealing a deal. I guess we were.

"Tommy Lyons" was Dolly's greeting when I walked in.

"Who?"

"The boy who drives that purple-and-white-striped truck. And he's not one of the boys MaryLou shot."

"What else do you know about him?"

"He's a three-letter man. Football, basketball, and baseball. All-State quarterback. He only hangs with the fraternity boys. Has all the girls he wants, but he's only interested if you're willing to be nice to his pals, too."

"Any of your girls . . . ?"

"No!"

"Well, they must know *somehow*."

"Everybody knows. It's no secret."

"MaryLou know him?"

"I'm sure. Knows *of* him, anyway. But he wouldn't go near her."

"Because . . . ?"

"One, she might just punch his lights out. Two, she's gay."

"What?"

"You heard me, Dell."

"Other people know that, too?"

"Sure. She doesn't hide it."

Not from the guards, either, I thought. And I flashed on that tunnel between the jail and the courtroom again. But all I said was "Does she have a girlfriend? I mean, did she have a girlfriend who was . . . ?"

"No. Nothing like that. Don't waste your time. Being gay, that's just what MaryLou is—it's not like she went to the prom with a girl, or anything like that."

"Damn!"

"What, honey?"

"That's something I could use. Something I should have thought of. Who did MaryLou go to the senior prom with?"

"I can find out."

"Would you, baby? I'm going to sleep for a while."

"Sleep? It's only—"

"I have work to do tonight."

Dolly nodded her understanding.

Before I dropped onto the cot I keep in the basement, I took Dolly's map and crossed off the Lovers' Lane spot.

I wasn't going back. The video ninja had told me all I needed, and I hadn't asked him any personal questions. I wanted him to believe I'd been watching him for a long time, so I knew everything about him.

It was just getting dark when I came back upstairs. There was something I needed to know. But before I could even ask, Dolly blurted out: "Bluto. Bluto Wayne."

"Who's that?"

"That's who took MaryLou to the senior prom, Dell. Bluto Wayne."

"Bluto?"

"His real name is Franklin, but everyone—everyone with a nasty mouth, I mean—calls him Bluto. He's one of those slow kids. Strong as an ox, not real bright. They moved him here from Brontville. That's not even a town, just a . . . place, I guess you'd call it."

"Go slower, honey."

"Okay." She took a deep breath, let it out. "Football is a big deal in this state. Not so much high school, but college, that's major. Both our state universities always have national rankings."

I fought off the urge to ask her how she knew this stuff.

"Anyway, they don't have a football team in Brontville. They don't even have a school. But, somehow, the coaches found out about this boy. Bluto. Franklin, I mean. He's monster-sized, Dell. Just looking at him, I guarantee you he's at least six six. And probably way over three hundred pounds. But he's not fat."

"Okay."

"No, wait! There's a lot more. They paid his family to move inside the town lines here, and they taught him how to play."

"They?"

"The school. Well, not the school itself. The 'boosters' is what they're called."

"And they paid his family how? With a job or . . ."

"His people don't work. None of the people in Brontville work. At least, not at regular jobs—they wouldn't know what a W-2 looks like. It's only forty-some miles away, but it's another world. All of it's on one side of a hill. None of the roads are paved, and there's no mail delivery.

"There's all kinds of rumors about Brontville, everything from the people who live there all being from the same family—like, incest for generations—to them being cannibals. One of the girls told me that, a long time ago, it used to be the thing to do on Halloween, go quad-running through those back roads. But some of the kids never came back, and nobody knows what happened."

"Ghost stories."

"Sure. Brontville doesn't even have a police department. The County Sheriff is supposed to cover that area, but no one ever heard of anyone getting arrested. I mean, *from* Brontville, sure. But never *in* there."

"Doesn't mean much, what people *didn't* hear."

"I know. But it *is* true that Franklin's family got a nice little house—one of those manufactured homes, so they could get it up and running quick, since they already had the land to put it on. And it *is* true that his father is on the city payroll. As a groundskeeper or something like that, so there's no set hours."

"I thought you said MaryLou didn't hang out with the jocks."

"She didn't. Neither did Franklin. I don't think any of them would try and stop him if he wanted to, but he didn't feel . . . comfortable with people like them. Actually, he didn't feel comfortable, period. He just went to practices and played in games. But, outside of that, he didn't do much of anything. Not in school, anyway."

"He was in remedial classes?"

"I don't think the high school even has those, but I can find out. The impression I got was that Franklin wasn't going to get that kind of help, even if he needed it. Football isn't like other sports. If you're good enough in sports like baseball or basketball, you can turn professional right on your eighteenth birthday. Football, the best you could hope for would be a college scholarship. That wasn't in the cards for Franklin. Not that they couldn't find one to take him; he just wouldn't go. And now that he's already graduated—he was a senior, like MaryLou, but that was only so he could play football for all four years—nobody's interested in him, not for anything."

"His family still have the house?"

"That's a good question. Should I find out?"

"Yeah. Please."

She sat there, like a beautiful bird on a tree branch. Not impatient, but ready to move if she had to.

"Those friends of yours. The ones who we buy the flowers from?"

"Yes . . . ?"

"I need a car, Dolly. It can't be ours. And if I'm stopped driving it, it has to have real papers. Not only that, whoever actually owns it has to tell the cops I'm driving it with their permission. Borrowed it for a few days, or something like that."

"What makes you think they'd—?"

"It feels to me like you're real friends. And there's two of them, so maybe we've got twice the chance of getting lucky. I know they've got some kind of panel truck, but that wouldn't work—their store name is painted all over it."

"I'll ask, Dell. When would you want it?"

I touched one of the red dots on Dolly's map. A little strip of closed-down stores, right off the highway. When I'd asked her why she'd marked that spot, she told me it was a supermarket, but not one you could see. Behind the closed-down stores, you could buy dope—meth and pills, mostly—and other stuff: unregistered guns, bootleg CDs . . . just about anything a burglar could snatch.

Then I put my finger on another red dot, much bigger than all the others. Raised my eyebrows.

"That used to be a fast-food place, but it went out of business. Now it's a day-care center. Fixed up very nicely, and I haven't heard a wrong word about the people who run it.

"But after dark, the parking lot behind it is a different kind of hangout spot than the others. It's run by kids—young men, really—who some of the girls think are so cool that they're willing to pay an admission charge.

"Those . . . the people I'm talking about, they almost live out there. At night, I mean. I don't know what makes them so special, but they have their own thing going. Whatever that is, they don't mix with anyone else. Not the way skinheads don't mix with skateboarders, it's much more than that—nobody in their right mind would just go over to them and ask them to join."

"So why the big red dot?"

"Like I said, that gang has an admission charge. It's sex. No girl would get a second look from them unless they knew she'd be willing to . . . to do whatever. Not like the Lovers' Lane when that striped truck pulls in—I've heard that trick doesn't always work. There's been times when a girl just ran away once she realized what the real deal was.

"But *this* place is different. It's eyes-wide-open. Nobody gets played into coming there. They don't even give girls a ride. And sex isn't enough—the girls would have to be willing to do other things, too.

"Nobody just happens to wander into the back of a parking lot where all the lights have been cut down. There's plenty of parking space right up close to the center during the day. So, if you drive around to the other side, where it's *always* dark, it's the same as . . . well, you know."

"Yeah. That car, I'd want one as soon as I could get it. If they don't want to lend one to you, there's plenty of other ways, but they'd take more time."

"I'll be right back," Dolly said. Meaning, she wanted any call she made to be private. "Why don't you take Rascal out in the yard?"

She came into the backyard in less than ten minutes.

"You can pick up the car tonight."

"That's great. Should I leave something for security, or would I be insulting them?"

"You'd be insulting them. But that won't come up, anyway—I'll drive you over in our Jeep, then just come back home later."

"Do you know which one they'll lend me?"

"No. I didn't ask. And I think they have others, too. Does it matter?"

"Not really. I mean, I wouldn't want something that really stood out, but, outside of that . . ."

"It'll be fine," she said, sounding confident. Then she made a soft whistling sound, and Rascal came bounding over to us. She asked him if he wanted to take a ride, and he went half crazy, like he always does when she asks.

They had three cars in their garage. A charcoal Lexus SUV, a red Mini Cooper, and a faded blue Facel Vega coupé that was mostly in pieces.

"That's a real beauty," I told them.

"You know what it is?"

"A Facel Vega, right? Can't be that many of them left in the world."

"Now you're *never* going to abandon your project," the taller one said to his partner. He turned to me. "Are you some kind of car nut, like Martin?"

"No," I said. "I've just seen a car like this before. It looked new, the one I saw, but one of the guys I was with told me what it was. He said it had to be at least fifteen, twenty years old."

"A fully restored one?" the guy who must be Martin asked me.

"I don't know. I don't know much about them. The guy I was with told us it was a French body with an American engine. Very special, very expensive."

"Where did you see it?"

"Paris."

"Oh. Well, I guess if you were going to find one in original condition, that would be the place to look."

"It was a long time ago."

"I'll just bet," he said. "Did you know that Albert Camus died in a Facel Vega?"

I shook my head. What I did know was that some of my comrades developed that *esprit de corps* so deeply that they loved the whole *idea* of a Facel Vega. To them, it represented the best of an era, that postwar period when gangsters ruled Paris. To a legionnaire, they represented true hard men. They walked their own road, and answered to no authority. The more flamboyantly, the better.

Their idol was Mesrine, probably because he shared some of their early experiences: when he was conscripted, he asked to be sent to Algeria, and won medals for valor in battle. But Mesrine's real specialty was robbing banks, taunting the police, and escaping from prisons. When he was finally killed in a police ambush, he was mourned by many.

Buisson was from an earlier time than Mesrine, but had the same bloodlines. He, too, served in North Africa, in a penal battalion, and also won the honors for bravery in battle. As a gangster, he was known for using Sten guns in holdups, for which they forgave him, because he would drive no car other than a Citroën.

Another critical connection was his breaking his brother out of jail, just as Mesrine had helped comrades escape.

Perhaps the final irony of Buisson's life was to be guillotined at the same "escape-proof" prison from which Mesrine fled, armed with handguns that must have been smuggled in. How the pistols got inside that prison varied with press accounts, but to legionnaires, the aid must have been supplied by members of the OAS, those *vrais guerriers* who had been betrayed by de Gaulle's search for a "political solution" in Algeria. As they saw it, the ground there held too much of their comrades' blood for them to give it up to anyone, ever.

And, to a man, everyone I served with worshiped *la cinéma*. It was accepted that only the actor Alain Delon could "represent" Mesrine, and that only a special car could possibly capture the flamboyance required. Their exemplar was *Le Samouraï*. I never saw that movie, but I knew that *"Delon préfère la Citroën"* was, to them, proof within proof, as if the movie were looping back around Buisson.

Maybe it seems bizarre to you that men trained to kill would glorify movie stars or cry over an Édith Piaf record. To me, it always made perfect sense. Men who have to leave their feelings behind when they go to war would need a way to reclaim them when they returned.

"Which one would you like?" his partner asked, clearly trying to change the subject.

"Would that one be okay?" I asked, pointing to the Lexus. Even though it was really my only option, I was okay with it. Its SUV configuration would look right at home in places I had to go—it could play off as luxury or menace, depending on what I needed.

"Absolutely," he said, handing over a key fob. He gave me a business card with a number written on the back. "If you get stopped, tell the police to give us a call. Either one—it's registered in both our names. The number on the back is my cell. Martin has the same number, but I'm the one who seems to always answer the calls."

"Thank you," I said, extending my hand.

"You are more than welcome," he answered. His grip was a practiced one, under control.

"You're a sweetheart, Johnny," Dolly said, kissing him on the cheek.

"After you explained, how could I say no?"

"I didn't think you would," she said.

"And I'm—what?—not involved?" the other one said.

"Oh, just stop, Martin!" Dolly said. She kissed him, too. "I'm in time for tea, aren't I?"

I took my black duffel out of the truck bed, put it on the floor of the front seat of the Lexus, fired it up. I watched the temp gauge before I put it in gear—I didn't think Martin would appreciate a cold-start move.

I backed slowly out of their garage, turned carefully, and pulled out very gently.

I knew Dolly wouldn't be following behind me, but I kept right near the speed limit anyway. I wasn't in a hurry.

Normally, I'd start fishing where I'd most expect to get a bite. But the place that was marked off limits to Dolly's girls might get more action later on, so I tried the supermarket.

Whoever told Dolly that you could buy "anything" at that place had never spent any time in places where "anything" ranged from counterfeit bills to real children.

I parked the Lexus at the edge and just sat there and watched. As near as I could tell, the cars were like signs at a flea market. The only thing that told them apart was their color—every one seemed to be a big-winged, high-gloss front-driver, with deep-tint windows. What they call "tuner cars" on this coast, probably because they were all powered by tiny engines and huge turbochargers with adjustable boosts—that's how you "tuned" those cars, with a laptop you plugged into the engine.

The car that got the least play was a dull-gray Evo. Same kind of buzz-bomb as the others, but this one was a four-door, with all-wheel drive—a world-class rally racer you could buy right off a showroom floor.

The hand-to-hand marijuana dealers wouldn't need to check out anyone too close—probably only dealt with the people they knew, anyway. But a firearms merchant would be a different story.

If my watching through the windshield of the Lexus spooked

any of them, I couldn't see any sign of it. I didn't see any prowl cars, either.

The small-time dealers had probably reached a détente with the local cops. I guess the lawmen figured they might as well have marijuana traffic all go down in the same place. That way, they could watch it randomly to check the plates of anyone leaving that they might want for something else.

But as I watched, I could see the pattern. It wasn't one car dealing the marijuana, it was a whole crew. Every time I saw a window come down, it would be followed by a quick headlight flash. Then a guy would get out of one of the other cars, and toss a small packet into the open window on the other side of the dealer's car.

I figured the state probably had some "personal use" exception, so getting caught with a half-ounce or so wouldn't draw more than a fine. With enough cars in the chain, they could probably sell off a couple of pounds a night without any real risk.

But "anything" still had to include more than marijuana. And this was an expensive operation, especially in a state where you could buy just about any kind of weapon legally. So either they were moving heavy ordnance, or they were losing money.

Whatever they had going, it was no experiment. Buyers always went to the same car, but the guy with the resupply might come out of any of the others. And that guy would always walk over to the Evo. Sometimes he'd carry a package away, sometimes not.

My night glasses showed me the Evo was slotted between a pair of rust-bucket American sedans. Crash cars. No ATF agent was going to run back to wherever he was parked before the Evo could blast out of there, with the crash cars jamming up the back exit to a dirt road, which split into a dozen others just like it.

On those roads, no federal agent's car was going to catch that Evo.

I'm not good with accents, but I can tune my voice to sound like I'm anything from smart to stupid. Or hard to soft, if that's more useful.

I didn't study this. I didn't even think about it until another legionnaire pointed it out for me. You never asked a man where he was from, but some wore it on their sleeves, like chevrons.

I had picked "Jacques Héron" for my *nom de guerre*. "Jacques" was the most common first name I could think of, so even if I slipped it wouldn't be a long fall.

That's how I figured "Patrice" wasn't such a big jump from "Paddy." He was way older than me—even older than I'd told the recruiter.

"I don't mind," he told me one night. It had cooled down a bit, and we were still far enough away from "engagement" to smoke.

"Don't mind what?"

"This new name I had to pick. Once my time is up, I've got a place to go back to. I just needed to be away for a while. Far away. Can't think of a better place than this one. Not for a man without vast money, anyway."

"They pay us here."

"That's not money, lad. There's a dozen places around the world where a man could earn a hell of a lot more doing just what we're doing right now."

I didn't say anything. I had learned that, if you just nod to show you're listening, that's enough to keep most people talking.

"I miss being home. Like some of the others, maybe. Not all of them, mind. But I left my wife before I even had a bairn of my own. And I left my best mate, too. Mickey, he was like my own blood. We were almost exactly the same age, him and me. We were one and the same—folks called us 'the Twins' even when we were tykes.

"Mickey was no ArmaLite expert; he was a street soldier with nothing but a fire-bottle in his hand when they gunned him down. Then they rolled one of those bloody Saracens over him like he was rubbish standing in their way."

"I'm sorry."

"Ah, don't be slick with me, boyo. I'm trying to help you out. You ain't a Brit. I can smell a Brit at a hundred yards. And you damn sure ain't Irish. Not *raised* there, that much I know. And one thing you can't be is French. What's that leave?"

"I don't know."

"Okay with me, son. I wasn't trying to pull any info out of you. Just tipping you that it wouldn't be all that hard. If a numbskull like me could do it just by listening a little, anybody who *wanted* could do it even easier."

I shrugged.

"You came a long way," he said.

"I don't know," I told him, fighting my envy of all those who *did* know. At least Patrice could mourn the loss of a childhood friend. How could I mourn the loss of a childhood?

Patrice went real quiet when I said that. We were each on our third smoke when he said, "You really *don't* know, do you? Damn! It's sorry I am. Truly sorry."

"Ne signifie rien."

He smiled at that. "You learned their talk quick, huh?" He looked at me for what felt like a long time.

Then he said, "Well, I can tell you two things for sure. One, if you'd come from Ireland, you'd have been a Tinker. Probably you didn't think so at the time, but that broken beak of yours is a blessing now. The whole Gypsy clan has big noses, and yours sticks out a lot less now.

"And, two, no matter what you ever heard, or where you heard it, the curse of the Irish isn't booze, it's revenge. Believe me on that."

"I do."

"Just like that."

"I don't think you would lie to me."

He started to say something, then he stopped himself. "I guess you'll be leaving for the same reason as anyone with half a brain on them would. Like serving a five-year sentence, this is. They're happy enough to use you for their dirty work, but don't fool your-self into believing you'll ever be good enough for them. Men who fight for cause or country, they'll always look down at a man who fights for pay."

"I won't be going to any home."

"Don't ever say things like that to anyone here. Only Gypsies say they don't have homes, and the French hate them almost as much as they hate the Jews."

"Thank you. I will not make such a mistake again."

He crushed the glowing embers of his cigarette between thumb and forefinger—the officers made all the recruits they caught smoking learn to do that; it only hurt the first few times. Even in the dark, I could see his eyes were wet when he said: *"Ah, que le bon Dieu te garde, mon petit."*

I don't know if the saints have been watching over me, as Patrice had asked. He never made it back to where he said he'd always be welcome. I know, because I'd carried his shredded body for more than three kilometers until we were both back with our unit.

The officers praised me for that. And by then, I'd learned enough to say only, *"J'ai fait mon devoir, monsieur."*

Sure, my "duty." In truth, had it been anyone but Patrice, I would have left them where they fell. I didn't understand then, but later it came to me—finally having someone to mourn was more important to me than my own life.

It had been Patrice who had explained to me that this whole *esprit-de-corps* thing was what he called a "user's lie." It was another whispered conversation, under the blanket of darkness, far away from the other men, but still well inside our perimeter. "You look at any operation, I don't care if it's the Legion or the Unione Corse, loyalty only flows in one direction—up. Loyalty from the men who risk their lives, that all belongs to the men at the top. You rarely even get the privilege of meeting the man who owns your life."

"You guys enjoying yourself?" It was a man who called himself Hondo, a big, beefy Rhodesian who never stopped bragging about how his country knew the right way to deal with "original" Africans.

"I always enjoy a conversation with one of my mates," Patrice said, his voice as light as a titanium knife.

"Well, when you get done mating with that kid, I hope you'll let me have a turn."

"I'm done already," Patrice said, as he got to his feet. "Mind your training," he said to me.

Hondo turned to watch Patrice leave. His last mistake. I had my dagger planted in his kidney before he realized that turning his back on me had cost him his life. He never made a sound.

Patrice spun around, flick-knife open in his hand. When we finished slicing up Hondo, Patrice pulled out a pint of rotgut and told me to cut a couple of pieces of cloth from the dead man's uniform.

"Always make sure you clean your steel, boyo," he said, pouring a little bit of the alcohol on one of the rags and wiping down his blade. Then he held his knife pointed upward, poured another few drops into the place where the blade met the hilt, and lit them afire. I copied his every move.

"When they find him in the morning, they'll know it was one of us who did him for. But nobody will have a word to say."

"How can you be sure?"

"The man's been watching us—watching you, especially—for weeks. There's only one way something like that ends, so I took a little precaution."

"Yes?"

"I made sure all the other lads knew he was grassing on us. That's how the bosses always seem to know stuff that's none of their business. Nobody's going to miss an informer. And who ever heard of giving a rat a funeral?

"It's no secret that I don't love the Brits, so you'd think I wouldn't be saying such a thing about a man from another country like mine—one that the Brits refuse to recognize. That gave my talk what they call the ring of truth, see? Remember that always. It's a treasure I was taught as a boy—if you have to lie, make sure the icing on that cake is the truth."

"Aren't they going to put us each in one of the hot boxes until somebody talks?"

"Why do you think I bashed him all over every single wound with that edged piece of rock? I got my knife off a fellow in a pub. He said it was Filipino—they're the best knife-men in the world. That little curve to the blade makes it go in easy and come out hard, so it leaves a real distinctive trail. But now there's no way for them to tell who did it, or even what weapon they used. All we have to do is strip down and carry him a few hundred yards. That way, there won't be a drop of blood on our uniforms to give us away. Hell, they won't even know that sick dog is gone until the count. And even then, they'll probably think he deserted."

"He might have run from enemies he made here, too," I said.

Patrice gave me a long look. "You don't miss much, do you, now? A man stupid enough to say 'kaffir' around Idrissa isn't cured of his disease. Why else would he leave a country that hates the blacks as much as he does unless they wouldn't tolerate the dirty little pederast?"

That was true enough. Idrissa was Senegalese. His English wasn't as good as his French, but he knew what "kaffir" meant. He was a fearless giant who often charged the enemy armed with nothing but the long blade he always carried. He could use it hard or soft. His sentry-kill was a two-handed stroke; his night-kill of sleeping soldiers was a single surgical slice through the larynx, his other dark hand stifling the death rattle.

The night-kills were especially admired, because they were so valuable to all of us. Waking up to find that the man next to you had been dead for hours would plant fear so deep into the enemy that he'd be no good in combat after that.

I hadn't lied to Patrice. I ran away from that hospital in Belgium, where they were trying to fix me. Or cure me. Or . . . I don't know.

They told me I had *"l'amnésie rétrograde."* I didn't understand much French then, but most of the doctors spoke English. Still, "retrograde amnesia" didn't mean anything to me.

But I knew someone had to be paying the bills. It was such a nice, clean place, and the people there were really trying to help. All of that wouldn't have come cheap.

I guess they never expected a little boy to run away. There were no guards or anything. The fence around the grounds was for privacy, not control.

After that, I don't know what would have happened if Luc hadn't found me.

"*Qu'est-ce que tu fais, tu bouffes les restes?*"

By then, I knew enough French to say what I always did: *"Laissez-moi tranquille!"*

"Ça fait combien de temps que tu traînes tout seul dans le coin? C'est dangereux, tu sais."

The only word I understood was *"dangereux."* And an Arab kid who was a little older than me had warned me about old men who are kind to runaway little boys.

So why did I go with Luc? I was cold; I was always cold. I was hungry—I was *always* hungry. And Luc wasn't just old, he was frail. If he turned out to be one of those men I'd been warned about, I was pretty sure I could deal with it. I'd never had a fight in the hospital, but I'd had plenty since I left.

Luc lived in a tiny little dump in the Belleville section, more like a cave with two small windows at street level. And those windows were so blackened with soot that they might as well have been part of the wall itself.

But it was warm, once you got a fire going. And cooking over that fire worked fine.

Luc only went out after dark. I always went with him. He was like a tour guide, pointing out the car-hailing whores, the circling pimps, the hashish dealers, the doors to places I should never go into, the alley gamblers. . . . All the night people were making a living, but none would ever have a job.

I didn't start stealing until Luc was sure I was ready. *"Faire les poubelles, c'est bon pour les animaux. Mais faire les poches ou les serrures, ça, c'est la marque d'un homme qui a reçu de l'éducation."*

By then, I had learned enough to understand what he was saying: "Picking up garbage is for animals. But picking a pocket, or picking a lock, that is work for a man, an educated man."

That's when my "education" started. The war was long over. What the Nazis left behind was a sewer-rat culture, with the criminal class as its rulers.

Membership in La Résistance was a badge of honor, but far more claimed it than deserved it. The old man didn't have to claim it—he hated *les collaborateurs* so fiercely that it was assumed.

I knew he had been a jeweler before the war, and a smuggler

during it. He knew that people fleeing the Gestapo had to travel light, and he could pull apart any kind of jewelry so that only the most valuable parts were left.

Luc went underground just before the Nazis came in and took everything that had been in his shop. He was an old man even then—past seventy. His wife had died a few years before. He had nothing to do except work as he always had. La Résistance had many uses for a man with a jeweler's eyes and hands, be it building bombs or opening safes. But when the war was over, no one had any use for a jeweler without jewels.

Paris was ruled by crime. The old man fit into crime as if born to it. He was careful to live small. Small but proud. *"Une maison, pourquoi faire? Les gens se débrouillent toujours pour te prendre ce que tu posssèdes. Mais qui va venir emmerder un vieux clochard? Ceux que je vais dépouiller, ils me donnent la pièce quand je fais la manche et m'occupe de surveiller leurs maisons."*

I translated in my head, feeling the guile and hate under what was meant to sound like philosophic acceptance of his fate: "What do I need with a house? Whatever people know you have, they will try to take from you. But who bothers with an old beggar? Some of those I plan to steal from put a little coin in my cap as I sit on the sidewalk and watch their houses."

Even then, I knew there was no wisdom to be found in the cafés. Always this pretentious garbage, like *"Le concept de la liberté individuelle chez l'homme est une illusion absolue."*

I didn't need the self-named intellectuals to tell me that individual human freedom was an illusion. For me, I had been free since the moment the old man plucked me from the gutter. To him, I would always listen. And always be obedient.

I never questioned Luc about why he had taken me home with him. And I didn't question him when he told me it was time for me to go. He spoke in English, to make sure I never forgot a word.

"La Légion Étrangère is the only way for you, my son. Listen very carefully, now. You know where their recruiting office is, that place I showed you. I don't know how old you are, and they won't, either. You are a good size, you shave, you tell them you are eighteen, they will not argue.

"But they will ask questions, and you must know the answers. So! Why do you want to enlist? Because you want to be a professional soldier. *'Parlez-vous francais?'* You answer *en anglais:* 'Only a little bit.' Where are your parents? You are an orphan. And you didn't want to stay with the caravan. They will understand from this that you are at least part *gitan,* a Gypsy. Probably a runaway, but that will not concern them.

"Then they will test you. How far can you run before you collapse? Will you get up and run some more if they order it? Physical pain will be your daily diet.

"But the hardest test will be the strength of your mind. That, they will test again and again. You will go without sleep for days at a time. For them, 'adaptability' is all. When they see how easily you can accomplish this, they will not ask where you learned, or who taught you—a stolen knife cuts as sharply as any you buy in a store.

"Whatever name you give them cannot be the truth. For you, this is natural—you don't know your real name. But this you must never admit. So, to the recruiter, your name is Luca Adrian. It is the only version of my name that I can give to you—mine might still call in the hounds.

"If they accept you, they will let you pick a new name. Your *nom de guerre.* When you finish five years, you will be able to claim French citizenship. If you try to leave before that, they will either let you go or not, as they choose. You must never put them to that choice.

"The policy of *anonymat* is a century old, but still in place. Perhaps not as it was originally, but for you good enough. Because this much is still true: no matter who asks about you, no matter their status or their reason, La Légion will ask your permission to disclose. If you do not give it, they will consider the matter closed.

"You come in as a blank slate. So whatever they write on that slate, it will be your truth for five years. After that, then you have a choice: stay or go.

"La Légion exists to fight—if they bring peace to one area, they will be sent to another. The officers will all be French, but those who train with you will not. You will learn all kinds of war, from mountains to deserts to jungles. That may be valuable to you later in your life. Or it may not. But what is beyond value is that any legionnaire may construct his own past.

"I know what is in your mind, my son. You are thinking, after five years you will come back. To this place. To me. But only this place will be here—I will not. It is time for us both to go, you understand? To different destinations. And never again to meet."

I picked up the ragged knapsack that contained all my possessions and climbed up the stone stairs to the street.

I didn't look back. I wanted the last sight the old man had of me to be my complete respect and trust.

I continued to reach for my life before that time with the old man for many more years. I finally just gave up. I accepted that I would never know. Maybe I was never going back to a place where I would be welcomed, but by then I knew I hadn't come from any such place, either.

I got out of the Lexus and walked over to the Evo. I crossed the windshield to let them get a good look, then I stood by the passenger-side front window, hands open at my sides.

The window zipped down. "Do we know you?" a voice said. Young man's voice, trying too hard to sound hard.

"No."

"Then what?"

"I'm a collector. I thought I might be able to add to my collection."

"Who told you to come here to do that?"

"That's a joke, right?"

The voice waited a solid minute. Then it said, "Get in the back."

The back seat held a man sitting behind the driver. Nothing else.

I got in, sat down.

"A collector?" A man's voice. A full-grown man, in his forties.

"That's me."

"You mind a little light pat-down, Mr. Collector?"

"Yeah, I do. I carry. No surprise, right? Anyway, you've got a transmitter-detector running."

"You saw that?"

"No. But if I've come to the right place, you'd have one around somewhere."

"Huh! You collect what?"

"Actually, I collect collections."

"Personal collections."

"Yeah."

"We're talking what?"

"Minimum of fifty full-autos, one-man carry pieces. No MAC-10 conversions, no TEC-9 garbage. And no wire-stock Uzis, either. AK-style, no plastic."

"Hard to find a collection that big."

"That's what I was told. So I came here."

"You're talking about a hundred large."

"No, I'm not. Seventy-five, that's realistic. And a nice markup."

"Not nice enough for the risk."

"I can go eighty. Or I can just go."

"I think you should just go. But tomorrow night—say, two a.m.—you bring the money to an address I'm going to tell you. You wait there while the money gets tested. Checks out okay, you get your stuff."

"Or I get stuck."

"So how do you want to make it work?"

"I come where you say. I bring what you say. I wait like you say. Only you wait with me."

I couldn't see his face, but I could feel him nod. Not saying yes, thinking it over.

"No reason for the money to leave, right? You're testing it right there."

"So?"

"So you're just renting for the night, so you don't have to worry about me coming back. And I don't have to worry about someone going south with my cash."

"You've done this before. And the only people who have experience like that are—"

"That's what you think, call it off. Now, before I waste any more time. You haven't said one word that could get you in trouble."

"Just one question. Why come to a little place like this for such a big buy?"

"I only picked up on you from the word going around. But I was told this is real safe."

"By who?"

"And what you're calling a big buy is nothing but a test run," I said, ignoring his question.

"What's a 'big' buy?"

"Twenty times this. More, if you can get it. And heavier, if you can do that. M4 fifties, armor piercers, surface-to-air, heat-seekers. That kind of load, the farther north you can meet, the better. We'd have to move it all at once. That means one truck, one load. And we don't want it on the road more than a few hours, max."

"So you're based up north? And maybe a bit to the east?"

"Did I say that?"

"No. But I think I'm getting the idea now."

"I think you might be."

"Tomorrow, then?"

"Like I said."

I climbed out of the back seat and walked over to the Lexus, feeling the eyes on my back. If anyone followed me, I'd know. There was a spot I'd already scouted, less than five miles away. That's where I'd stop to put the license plates back on the Lexus.

After I waited awhile.

I didn't have to wait long. Where I was dug in, there was no way to follow me without going off-road. They would have known that, so I expected a jacked-up four-wheel-drive truck. But nothing showed up.

There was another way to leave, and that's what I did. No way to be sure I was the only one who knew that route—I moved very slow. But it was empty all the way through.

That left three possibilities: they were just big talkers, they'd gotten an ATF whiff off me and passed on the deal . . . or they'd been telling the truth.

Since I wasn't ever coming back, that spot wouldn't be worth much to them for months, at minimum; it was *already* worthless to me.

The next spot was almost vibrating with danger. Not the kind of danger most teenage girls would pick up on. But for the kind that would, it wouldn't scare them off; it'd pull them closer. I wasn't sure how any of this could help MaryLou, but I trusted that those red dots of Dolly's would lead to something I could use, if I could just put my hands on it.

I had most of the license plates and car descriptions down when I saw three guys in matching jackets walking over to where I was parked. The jackets were waist-length, black, with dark-red sleeves. As they got closer, I could see some kind of dark-red emblem covering the heart side of each one.

They walked with the kind of swagger only certain people use. I don't know what they think it makes them look like. After I left the Legion, I knew what they looked like to me: if I wasn't being paid, nothing. If I was, targets.

I let the window on my side slide down.

"You one of those old guys who like to watch?" their leader said.

"I'm looking for my daughter," I said. I knew that the stubborn-stupid voice I was using didn't match the Lexus, but it was dark and I didn't think they were looking so much as they were listening. "I need to find out if she's here. I warned her—"

"What's her name?"

"Linda Sue Dickson," I said.

"We know everyone here," the leader said. He turned to his left, asked one of his boys, "You ever hear of a girl named Linda Sue?"

"Nah."

"She's not here, Pop. Maybe you better look somewhere else."

"This is where her friends said she'd be."

All three of them laughed. "That's a guarantee she's not," the leader told me. "Now, why don't you just move on?"

"Not until I know for sure."

"Look, old man, we've been—"

I don't know if any of them had ever seen a sawed-off shotgun before. I was pretty sure they hadn't. Not from the wrong end, anyway. It cut off the leader's words like a butcher knife through a thin slice of cheese.

They all wanted to back away. But they didn't want to move, either. Who knows what a crazy old man might do?

"My name is Larry Tom Dickson. From Brontville. If you know a better place for me to look, tell me. Tell me right now. Or

I'm coming back with some of my kin and going down there to look for myself."

"Rocky's," the leader said, instantly.

"What's that?"

"It's a bar. Just outside the city limits. Right off the highway. You can't miss it—there's always a lot of motorcycles parked outside."

"Uh . . ." I muttered, like I was thinking about what he said. Then, "I'm going over there."

"Sure. Sure, whatever you want."

I stomped the gas, and the Lexus squirted away.

Turned out there *was* a bar named Rocky's. Right where that punk had told me it would be. Even had the motorcycles parked out front.

I took my time getting there, and drove right on past without touching the brakes. I kept going until I found a bridge, then I crossed over and doubled back. As good a way as any to see if I had company.

No.

I didn't expect they'd go driving around Brontville looking for a Larry Tom Dickson, either.

I had the Lexus inside our garage while it was still dark, but only a few minutes before the sky would start to change.

"Dell, are you okay?"

I should have figured that they'd still be up. The two of them, Dolly and Rascal, waiting on me.

Dolly wanted to be sure I was all right. Rascal wanted his rawhide. You can train a dog with food and patience; you can have a dog's love if you give yours. But what makes dogs more reliable than people is that there's no way to make a dog turn traitor.

"I only got three, four hours to sleep, baby. Then I get to go play dress-up again."

"Go," Dolly said, sending me on my way with a kiss.

I went to see the lawyer. He didn't look happy.

"What?" I asked his expression.

"When your own client won't speak to you, how can you be expected to mount a—"

"You went to visit MaryLou? On your own?"

"Yes. Of course I did. After all, I'm her—"

I held up my hand to stop him talking. I had to be sure he could recite his lines when the time came.

"You wanted to tell her about you going on TV," I said.

"Well, I didn't think it would be . . . I mean, like I told you, we have an Ethics Code. Lawyers."

"Let's get all that straight, right now. I don't care about ethics. What we need is a strategy. You don't want to step over certain lines, that's your business. That's what you hired me for, right?"

"A lawyer is responsible for the conduct of all those working under him," he said, pompously. I didn't miss the "under."

"Only if he knows about it," I told him, acting like I knew what I was saying was true. It didn't matter—if he said the wrong thing, he was off the case.

He nodded, as if there was a tape recorder in the room. Okay; that was enough.

"When were you planning to do your interviews?"

"Well . . . they called today. It was on my service."

I guess he didn't want to say "answering machine." If I was dumb enough to believe the cow in the reception area was actually *his* secretary, I'd probably swallow some line about his "service," too.

"You were going to speak to them today. So you went to see MaryLou, get her permission, yes?"

"Well, it would be the—"

"You're not ready."

"What do you mean by that? We already agreed on what I'd say."

"You didn't get a haircut. Or a real suit."

"Look, Mr. Whoever You Are, you think paying the bills turns me into some kind of marionette. Well, you're wrong. I am the lawyer for—"

"No, you're not. The court appointed you, for peanuts. I hired you, for real money. All I have to do is nod my head and MaryLou will change to another lawyer. If you haven't figured that out yet, you're too stupid to be in a courtroom."

He didn't like that. A lot of people don't like the truth, especially when it comes out blunt. But this was battlefield surgery—do it or die. Either this guy got the message or he didn't. And if he was the kind to let his ego get in the way, now was the time to find out.

He let a few seconds pass. Then he said, "Well, it's clear that MaryLou—the client—has placed her trust in you, so, if I want to do the best possible job for her, I have to . . . work with you."

"Done," I told him. "I'm going over to see MaryLou now."

"I'll—"

"—go get a haircut," I finished his sentence for him. Then I got up, turned around, and walked out.

"You okay?"

"I'm fine," she said. "I had one little . . . incident, the guards called it. And that was it."

I didn't need details. Somebody finally forced MaryLou to send out a message that she wasn't going to be pushed. My guess was that the rest of the women she was locked up with wouldn't need another one.

"You're not going to tell me why you shot those boys. But here's what I already know: you went there to kill that guy, and you just picked up whatever tool was at hand."

She cocked her head. "How do you know any of that?"

"I know you're not going to tell me because you haven't said a word. Maybe you'll tell Dolly, I don't know. But you're not going to plead insanity—you already made that clear. As for the decision you made and the tool you used, those are both the same."

She made a "come on with it" gesture.

"You knew who you wanted, but you hadn't planned it out— he would have been easy enough to ambush. And that pistol had to be something that was close at hand. A .22 revolver cut your chances of a kill way down. Only six shots, with small bullets. You're old enough to buy a firearm. With a nine-mil, especially a long-magazine one, you could have hosed down the whole corridor."

She didn't say anything, but she never dropped her eyes. So I went for it:

"You don't know anything about guns. You didn't go shopping, or ask for advice. And there's nobody you'd ask to lend you a pistol—you wouldn't drag anyone into this. So it had to have been in your house already. It's not what you'd call a precision piece, but it's not a Saturday-night special, either. Somebody in your house—I'm guessing your father—got it from somewhere. He might never have shown it to you, but you knew where he kept it."

I could see MaryLou trying to make up her mind. She finally decided on the same "I'm not telling you anything" face. But her eyes stayed on mine.

Dolly isn't going to like this, I remember flashing somewhere in my head, but I was too close to stop.

"Not knowing anything about pistols also means you think one's pretty much the same as another. So it's no accident that the boy you shot first was the only one who died. You had to be real close when you fired, so he was the one you wanted. Once he dropped, you just blasted away until the hammer clicked on 'empty.' Those extra shots, either you didn't care what happened to the others, or you wanted it to look like you had no particular target in mind."

She took a deep breath in through her nose. Let it kind of trickle out, her mouth still closed.

"Maybe they've got a softball team at Coffee Creek" is all she said. Then she stood up, signaling to the guard that the visit was over.

"What's Coffee Creek?" I asked the lawyer.

"It's the only prison for women in the whole state. But they've got different sections, depending on how much time each inmate comes in with. Or if they're considered an escape risk."

"Didn't have many of your clients end up there, did you?"

"No," he said. It didn't come across as boasting; I figured that, even if he caught a woman's case now and then, it would be plea-bargained down to jail time. He'd probably never even seen the place he was talking about.

"MaryLou's ready to go."

"She wants to plead guilty? To murder? That's just . . . wrong. I mean, with her background, with all the community support—you wouldn't believe the calls that have been coming in—we can't just give up like that."

I liked the "we." So I said, "She's not going to plead guilty. She's just ready to take whatever comes."

"She told you this?"

"Yes."

"So there's no point in me—"

"No."

"This 'strategy' thing . . . ?"

"I'm working on it," I told him. "And that haircut, it's just perfect now. You look like a man who people *should* take seriously."

He flushed. I hoped he'd get over that habit quick.

When I got back, Dolly was at the big table, papers scattered all over the place. She looked up, but she didn't say a word.

I took a seat. That was all she needed.

"Dell, where are we?"

"Getting there. What's the name of the boy MaryLou killed again?" I could have asked the lawyer, but I didn't want him to think he knew anything I didn't. Not yet, anyway.

"Cameron Taft. Everyone called him Cam, though. The inside joke was that it was short for 'camshaft.' "

"What's his connection to . . . anything? At the school, I mean."

"He wasn't on any sports team. He wasn't some kind of brainiac. I guess he just . . . went there. I've only got this much. So far, I'm saying," she said, promising more to come. "He was six-one, weighed one seventy-six. Dark-blond hair, medium to long. Blue eyes. No scars. No old injuries. One tattoo on his right arm: a red symbol of some kind. Japanese or Chinese characters, maybe. The symbol was set against a black background. Another on his left pectoral: a large red heart with an ice cube in its center."

"Stomach contents?" I asked, showing Dolly I knew where she'd gotten that info, and how proud of her I was for having built such a place for herself in the community, having won so much respect.

"Not much left. Whatever he ate, it was the night before. No breakfast. But his breath must have been good."

"Because?"

"His teeth were perfect. Not even a cavity. No food particles anywhere. And his oral swab smelled like some serious mouthwash."

"Nails?"

"Pretty much like his mouth, only without the odor. Scalp was clean, too. And if he used drugs, he wasn't injecting them."

"Nice-looking boy, huh?"

"*Very* nice-looking, Dell. Half the girls in the school had a crush on him."

"No kids?"

"Why would a kid—? Oh. You mean, did he have any kids?" I nodded.

"No. I would have heard if he had. By now, I mean."

"Any rectal scarring?"

She gave me a funny look, but all she said was "No. Not even old, healed ones. Nothing."

I sat there, working it all through the filters I had built in my mind. I didn't want to tip my hand to Dolly. And not just because she'd see I wasn't holding much.

"Can you get a photo of that symbol? The one on his arm?"

"Sure. They photograph just about every square inch in a homicide case."

"Homicide."

"Yes, Dell. Homicide. That's what happens when a bullet gets lodged in the brain."

"Why are you being so . . . ?"

"So . . . what?"

"Snippy and sarcastic," I told her, flat-out.

"Maybe because you started it, Dell. You already know it was a homicide. So why ask—?"

"I didn't *ask* anything. I was just thinking out loud. I said one word. 'Homicide.' Now tell me if I'm wrong: when an autopsy report says 'homicide,' all they're really saying is that it wasn't suicide or accident."

"Well . . . of course. It's a standard protocol. Any gunshot wound to the head, you have to rule out suicide. Especially with a teenage kid. But you already knew that this Taft boy didn't shoot himself."

"I knew MaryLou shot him in the head. I knew he died from the shot. That's a homicide, sure. But that doesn't automatically make it a murder."

"I'm not sure where you're going with this."

"Neither am I, honey. Something keeps tugging at me, but I can't see it. Not yet. MaryLou killed him. Okay. But maybe killing him wasn't murder."

"What else could it be, Dell?"

"Self-defense."

Dolly kind of yipped, jumped up, and gave me a kiss. A real one.

"Don't get all worked up, baby. I didn't come up with an answer, just a question."

"But that's so much more than we had."

"Only if it proves out. MaryLou didn't shoot a burglar coming through her window, remember. And she emptied her pistol, too. The only thing we know for sure is that she's not insane. Which means she had a reason. A reason she's not saying. Not telling anyone. Not even you."

"It's *you* she'd tell."

"Why would you say that? I'm not even—"

"I know you, Dell," she interrupted. "I know you better than anyone on earth. I remember every single word you ever said. With you, that's a lot easier than it might be for someone else." She kind of giggled.

"I don't get the joke."

"It's no joke. Didn't you once say that the best way to get someone to tell you what you want to know is to convince them that you already know it?"

I just nodded. She was right. On both counts. "I give up," I said.

That got me another kiss. Dolly usually closes her eyes when she kisses me. This time she didn't. So I asked her, "You ever find out where this kid Bluto—uh, Franklin—ever find out if his parents had to give up the house?"

She gave me the address. I went downstairs to change.

I was glad—again—for that suit Dolly had made me buy. She had called it a "three-season." When I looked blank, she went on: "But, for around here, it's really *all*-season—it's not as if we ever get a real winter. And a silk shirt can look any way you want it to. . . ."

Which is why that cedar closet she insisted on putting in holds a whole mess of them, in different colors.

"His family's name is Wayne," Dolly said. "Spelled like John Wayne," Dolly called out to me just as I was going into the garage.

"Perfect," I said, leaving her to take that any way she wanted.

The Lexus fit perfect for this next job, too. Some things look different in daylight.

The man who answered the door had to be the one Dolly told me about. They couldn't fit more than one of him in that little house, and his face didn't have a line on it.

"Mr. Wayne? Franklin Wayne? My name is Jackson. Dell Jackson. I work for Mr. Swift, the attorney who's representing your friend MaryLou."

When I called MaryLou his friend, the huge kid's face brightened for just a second. Then he remembered why MaryLou would need a lawyer, and his expression went back to dull.

"Would you help me help MaryLou, Franklin?"

"I'd do anything for MaryLou," he said. Maybe he didn't have a wide range of expressions, but I could see that if he'd known Mary-Lou had a problem with Cameron Taft he would have handled it himself. He wouldn't need a gun to get the same result MaryLou had, and he didn't look like a man who'd stop halfway through a job.

"We wouldn't want to disturb your folks with this kind of thing. They don't know anything. And MaryLou is *your* friend, not theirs."

"That's right." Telling me he wouldn't bring a girl like Mary-Lou anywhere near that house or his parents.

"So how about if we take a little ride?" I asked him, kind of nodding toward the Lexus. "I don't know my way around here too well, but I'm sure you know a spot where we could talk without anyone bothering us."

If I hadn't stepped aside quickly, he would have bowled me over on his way to the car. He had the passenger door open before I could get around to my side. Good thing I hadn't locked it. I'd seen plenty of big, powerful men in my life, but Franklin looked as if he could drive rivets with the slabs at the end of his wrists. Or tear a door off its hinges. I was glad I'd remembered to adjust the passenger seat to maximum slide-back and leaned the backrest as far as reasonable.

"Which way?" I asked him.

It took almost twenty minutes of following his finger-pointing, grunting, and "over there" instructions, but he had picked the most logical spot—no Lovers' Lane is going to be occupied in broad daylight.

I slid the windows down before I killed the engine, in case shutting off the A/C would make the kid sweaty.

You don't have to be bright to be patient. I figured this kid was accustomed to responding, not initiating.

"What can you tell me about Cameron Taft, Franklin?"

"He's a jerk. Him and all those others."

"Which others?"

"The ones with the jackets."

"Black ones, with red sleeves?"

"Yes."

"How is Cam a jerk?"

"Huh?"

"I mean, what makes you say Cam is a jerk?"

"Oh. Because he's mean, I guess."

"He does mean things?"

"He always does mean things."

"Like call other kids names?"

"Yeah. All of them do that, but only after Cam says it's okay."

"You mean, after he does it, the others know it's okay for them to do it, too?"

He nodded. His head would have been at home on Easter Island.

"He never called *you* any names, did he?"

"No."

"Because he only called girls names?"

"He called boys names, too."

"Names like . . . ?"

"Just mean names. I don't remember them all."

"Did he ever call MaryLou a name?"

"Nobody called MaryLou a name." I didn't think that could be true, but I didn't think he was lying, either. He could only say what he'd heard. Maybe some gutter-mouth high-school girls called MaryLou a dyke, or made cracks about male hormones turning her into such a great pitcher, but they'd only do that when they were alone, not out in the open. And I didn't think even girls would have let the mammoth sitting next to me hear them slam his to-the-heart friend.

"Do you like the house you live in?" I asked. Sometimes, you throw a man way off subject, his guard drops.

But Franklin didn't have a guard to drop. "It's nice" is all he said.

"Franklin, can you think of any way we could help MaryLou?"

"I . . . I've been trying to do that. If I knew, I would do it."

I believed him.

"So, if I figure out a way, you'd be willing to help me?"

"Yes," he said. But now his tone was even deeper, and his voice came through gritted teeth.

"Tonight's the night, huh?" I said to the lawyer.

"It certainly is, Mr. Jackson."

"Make it 'Dell,' okay, Brad? We're in this together."

He insisted on shaking hands, like we were being introduced all over again.

Then he said, "You were right. About the TV, I mean. The local stations—even the ones way up in Portland—they wanted me to talk right away. And the Court TV people, too. But CNN! I guess it *was* worth waiting."

"Good. Now, remember, they can't *make* you say anything. You give them what we agreed on, and that's all. So either they'll ask the same question over and over, or you won't be on camera too long. And that's just fine for us, either way. Remember, don't let them lead you off the trail. Don't 'speculate.' Don't talk about your own experiences. Don't talk about 'school shooting cases.' Stay on message. Hold your square. Don't let them push you off it, no matter what."

"I won't," he said. Nice and calm—I believed he meant it.

"If the trial goes on for a while, you can start calling some of your own shots."

"What do you mean?"

"Take Court TV, okay? I've watched it a couple of times, but not enough to know who's for real. Not yet, anyway. But the next time that door opens, you'll know the only one who gets to walk through it. Understand? You'll talk to Mr. X. But only to Mr. X. They don't like that, they can do *what,* exactly?"

"Nothing," he said.

"The only thing we have to watch for now is the last-minute-substitute game."

"Now I *really*—"

I cut him off with "They tell you it's CNN, so you naturally think you're getting interviewed by an actual reporter. A journalist. But CNN, it's actually a lot of different channels. When they sit you in a chair in Portland, you can't see who's on the other end. But you'll hear everything. If it turns out to be anything but a straight news show, you just say you were told you would be speaking with a reporter, unhook your mike, and walk off."

"But why would they pull a stunt like that?"

"CNN also has all those stupid 'crime shows.' The ones with the host in the middle, surrounded by little boxes, each one with a different person in it, all kissing ass. Why? Because if they don't their little box gets closed down—the star in the center controls all the mikes. But if you walk off the set when CNN tries to put you in one of those boxes, you're going to be more famous than if you sat in one every night."

"I'm not doing this to be famous."

"Who said you were, Brad? You're using the media to help your client. So, if the media won't keep its word, you won't deal with the media at all. That's strategy, not mugging for the cameras. But it wouldn't be your fault if folks respect you for doing the right thing—going on TV for your client, not for yourself."

"Of course," he said, as if no lawyer would go on TV for any other reason.

I did a quick body-check. His hands were steady; his eyes were good. We'd tape his appearance later that night, and I'd get Dolly to tape Court TV every day, all day. Like Patrice told me so many years ago, before you put down your whole week's packet, you had best study the form.

By accident, I almost walked in on one of Dolly's meetings. But I was able to pull back before any of them knew I'd gotten so close.

"She's not one of us." A girl's voice.

"What's that mean?" Another girl. A girl drawing a line in the sand.

"Oh, not that" was the reply. "I just mean, she doesn't hang out with us, that's all."

"That's not the question," Dolly said. Nice and soft, like she was explaining something. Then the softness turned to iron: "The question is, are *you* one of us?"

"I don't . . . I mean, of course. Right?"

"There's no 'of course' to this," Dolly told her. "We all agreed that we were going to fight for MaryLou. You were there when we made that decision. So it's very simple now: are you with us, or not?"

"Maybe if MaryLou had shot anyone but precious Cam you wouldn't be hemming and hawing," another girl said.

"That's got nothing to do with . . ." the girl who had to make the decision started to say. Then she starting crying.

I faded back to where I'd come from.

"JoAnne, the girl who said MaryLou wasn't one of us? When Cassidy made that crack about 'precious Cam,' it was a vicious shot. Everyone knows JoAnne was with Cameron. For a few hours, I mean. He tossed her out like a used Kleenex when he was finished, but that hasn't stopped her from still crushing on him."

"You got the CD of the lawyer from last night?"

"Sure. But it only went a couple of minutes."

"Good."

I pushed the "play" button. Dolly must have reset the disk so that it started off with the camera coming in on some guy with white hair—he looked too young to have hair that color, but he was good-looking enough to make it into a trademark.

"Can you talk a little about what makes this case so different from all the other school shootings that seem to have infected America ever since Columbine?"

"Other than the obvious—"

"You mean, that the shooting was done by a girl? Or that she had a different motive than the others?"

"All I feel comfortable saying about the case at this time is that it's not over. Not *close* to over."

"Is that a hint that you may be thinking of an insanity defense?"

"No. And it's not a 'hint,' it's nothing more than what I said. By the time this case is finished, the jury is going to learn some things they never even imagined. And what they learn is going to be a game-changer, that you can take to the bank."

"Is that your way of telling us—?"

"That's my way of telling you what I'd tell anyone else. No more, no less."

"Uh, well, on that note, I suppose this is as good a time as any to go to break. When we come back . . ."

When they did, Swift wasn't on the set.

"Nice job," I told him a couple of hours later. I just walked past the harried slob behind the phone bank. She was telling someone she'd take a message. I could tell she'd been saying that all day.

"The phone's been ringing off the hook."

"I expect so," I told him.

"But one of those calls was from the DA's Office. And that one

I returned," he said, speaking from somewhere inside that narrow band between egotistical and self-assured. "The pistol *did* have a serial number. It was purchased about a year ago. By her father. Nothing even remotely illegal about it. He had a license, and the sale was registered."

I made some noise that could have meant anything.

"Does that help or hurt?" he asked.

"Helps. Means the gun was probably just lying around the house, already loaded. No need for questions about who sold it to MaryLou. And now we have confirmation that it wasn't a gun-show buy."

"A what?"

"If you want to buy certain kinds of weapons, you can go to any of those gun shows you see advertised in the paper all the time."

"I'm not following you."

"The guys at those shows, they're all 'collectors.' So they can sell a weapon from their private collection to another collector. Not even illegal. And if you don't want to leave a paper trail, some of them can help you with that, too. But nobody like that would want the pistol MaryLou used."

"Because . . . ?"

"Because it's got nothing going for it. Not a heavy-caliber semi-auto, and even if you were dumb enough to put a silencer on a revolver, that two-inch barrel couldn't be threaded for one."

"They didn't say anything about the barrel. I didn't ask, either. Should I, you think?"

"No. You have to play this like you know a lot more than they do. That was the seed you planted on TV."

"I didn't know you couldn't put a silencer on a revolver."

"When it comes to metal fabrication, you can do just about anything. But an assassin would know that the construction of a wheel gun makes it impossible to quiet it down that much. Besides, why bother with a silencer when you're shooting in front of so many witnesses?"

"Yeah . . ." he said, as if he understood all that. Which was good. For now, at least.

When I got back, Dolly's crew was in full swing. I couldn't tell if the girl who'd had a problem with helping MaryLou was still there; I'd only heard her voice, not seen her face.

"I hacked into his Facebook page and—" one said.

"Posting something on his wall doesn't mean you hacked into it," another cut her off. "Unless you took over control of his account. Is that what you're saying?"

The silence was an answer.

"But Regina could be onto something, anyway," Dolly said. "Everybody here has a Facebook account, right?"

More silence.

"Okay, so you can all log on. Fire up those laptops and get to work."

"On what?" another girl asked.

"See if his account is still open. It was when Regina looked, and that was just last night, yes?"

"Yes," the girl who had to be Regina said.

"So we want to look at all the Facebook pages of anyone who could be involved."

I tilted my head. "I'll be right back," Dolly told them, and followed me down to my den. I closed the heavily baffled door behind us, but we still spoke in whispers.

"Make sure they check one page. One that they may not have thought of. Uh . . . wait a minute. That's too much information for them. If they get to a page for MaryLou's sister on their own, fine. But if not, can you make up an account for yourself, so we can check that one out ourselves?"

She gave me one of her looks. "I already have one, honey."

"But wouldn't that mean anyone could—?"

"No," she said, too impatient to get back to her crew to wait for me to finish. "It's not my name. And I use the Mac laptop for it, not the PC we have upstairs. All the IP would tell anyone is what Wi-Fi zone I was logging on from—there's dozens I can use, and I've got a proxy for e-mail. On top of that, I've only got three 'friends.' I made them up, too—every time I go anywhere away from here, I make a new friend. You have to be my friend to post on my wall, or message me, or . . . Oh, never mind, Dell. I've got this part, okay?"

As I passed by on my way to the basement, I'd heard enough to learn that MaryLou didn't have a Facebook page of her own. That wasn't a surprise. But she did have what they called a "fan page." Another thing to ask Dolly about.

Too many hours until daylight, so I stayed down in the basement, looking through all the paper Dolly had managed to coax out of her computer.

When the place emptied out, we got a chance to talk. Turned out I never had to ask Dolly the question I'd been planning.

"MaryLou doesn't have a personal page, but she sure has fans. You search for 'Mighty Mary McCoy'—or even 'M3'!—and you get a whole bunch of people. Softball fans. Most of them in college. By now, they all probably know she's been arrested. But before that, they were all saying why she'd be going to one school or another.

"Franklin doesn't have a page. Cameron's page is still open. Mostly all kinds of love notes or tributes or similar nonsense. But there were a few I want to see if I can get someone to track down."

"Why?"

"One, they were anonymous. New accounts, set up just to do this."

"What's 'this'?"

"Mostly references to 'karma.' You know, the 'what goes around, comes around' thing. Some were really . . . I don't want to say 'nasty,' considering what side we're on, but stuff like 'I wish I'd thought of that.' I know that's not much. Kids, they say things like that all the time. Especially on the Internet. But maybe one of them actually knows something. . . ."

"Could be."

"Yes. But here's what you wanted, Dell," she said, handing me a few pages of printout. I sat down to read.

MaryLou's little sister did have a page. Her friends called her Danyelle. She had more than three hundred of them. Looked like all of them were male.

I scanned them hard, looking for . . . I don't know what. Whatever it was, it wasn't there.

"Cameron friended her quite a while back," Dolly said. "On this address—Facebook, I mean—that means within the last couple of years or so."

"Friended?"

"You have to ask someone to accept you as a friend. Cameron seems to have accepted a lot of friends. But he doesn't post much on his wall—that's public, anyone could see it. So I think he did all his contacting with IMs—those you can't see."

"Are there pictures? On his page, I mean."

"Oh yes. He's as pretty as a model, but doesn't look a bit effeminate. There's even a close-up of both the tattoos, so I didn't need to burn a favor to get you one. See?"

She handed me a full-page color shot of the red symbol against the black square on his right biceps. I looked at it under a magnifying glass, sector by sector. The closer I looked, the more certain I was that I'd seen it before.

虎神营

But I couldn't be sure. The only mercs who put ink on themselves were the ones dumb enough to show them off in bars. Patrice had warned me to steer clear of those kind of bars. For every lion, there's a lion-hunter. And lion-hunters don't like fair fights.

At least you could keep tattoos like Cameron's covered up. A Russian merc I worked with on a job had all kinds of marks on his hands and fingers. He was real proud of them, said you had to be "entitled" to wear tattoos like his. If you didn't have the credentials, a tattoo on your hand that said you were a killer would get you killed.

A pair of Japanese mercs—twins, I think they were—they had tattoos all over. I didn't know what the tattoos meant, but I saw the ink never went below their wrists.

I didn't see where it mattered much. You might fix things so most people didn't see any tattoo you wore, but that wouldn't last long if you were ever taken captive.

Thinking about how the Japanese had looked down on the Russians didn't narrow the field—they looked down on everyone. But . . .

If I closed my eyes, I could see something like that symbol. It wasn't a unit mark, but I'd seen it before. In Southeast Asia.

That mark couldn't be one of those "Japanese" ones you see in comic books. If you worked Southeast Asia, there was only one foreign language you'd let other people see.

Chinese.

So I knew what language the tattoo was in, but not what it meant. And there was no way a kid Cameron's age had worked as I had. Kids all over the world are conscripted into wars by "legitimate" governments. Or kidnapped, drugged, and terrorized into some warlord's army to defend or depose them, depending on who put up the cash. But Cameron had probably never left home his entire life.

"The school, it would have yearbooks from every graduating class, wouldn't it?"

"Sure," Dolly said. "But we'd never be able to get hold of Cameron's—the police must have it."

"How about a yearbook he signed?"

"He probably signed every girl's in school."

"Probably got asked, anyway."

"I'll get my hands on one."

"I know you will," I told her.

It was dark by the time I woke up. Dolly was still sleeping next to me. We'd never slept together in the basement before.

I padded away, careful not to wake her. But Rascal spoiled that plan. The mutt had planted himself across the threshold, and he wasn't about to move. The instant he sensed me, he yapped like he'd just spotted a squirrel.

"Good boy!" Dolly shouted behind me.

He sure as hell was.

Working alone doesn't bother me. Working any job with part-ners is always a plus-minus: it could make the job easier, but it leaves whoever you worked with too much knowledge. About you, I mean. And that's a card they could play anytime.

I thought about Franklin. I had no doubt he'd help out with what I needed next, but I was afraid he might go too far with it.

And even though I wasn't worried about his talking, I knew he could be recognized by size alone.

I would have bet a lot that he couldn't move as quietly as I'd need him to—that wasn't something any football coach would have trained him to do.

All I wanted was one of their jackets. But I had to make taking one look like it meant something else was going on. A branding iron would do it, but the brand had to at least *look* like it meant something. I decided on a "club," the kind you see on playing cards—a spade or a heart would be too tricky, and a diamond could be mistaken for too many other things. To make a club, I wouldn't need more than a stencil of a circle, a few pieces of iron, a pair of tongs, a small sledgehammer, an anvil . . . and a lot of heat.

Sooner or later, one of them would walk off into the wooded area just past the pool of darkness. They weren't dealing in anything but the chance to hang out with them. But if you're selling "cool," you can't do it in a place that stinks. The shack that someone had slapped together in the woods behind that day-care place didn't have any lines for electricity, and I was betting against plumbing, too. So a visit to the other part of the woods would be mandatory at some point—I just needed to wait until one came out there alone.

From where I was waiting, I could see one move off. But he wasn't going to come anywhere near where I'd been watching from, so I had to parallel him to reach the intersection just before he did.

A .177 air gun makes even the most silenced firearm sound like a cannon. He probably thought the sting in his neck was a mosquito. I'd had to go damn near full-strength on the load.

Even if it wasn't so dark, I'm not good enough with a pistol to take a chance—I had to get him unconscious before he could scream.

I was on top of him while he was still crumpling to the ground. By the numbers: Feel around for the dart, pull it loose, and pocket it in a little plastic bag. Wrap his face with duct tape from just below his nose to the Adam's apple. Stick a couple of cotton wads into his nostrils, loose enough so he could still breathe through them.

Then I started bagging everything he was carrying, from his wristwatch to his wallet. Three gold chains around his neck, three different lengths. Heavy ring on his wedding-band finger. A little squeeze from my tube of a slicker-than-Teflon mix let me slide it away—cutting off the finger would have turned what he'd probably never admit to into something he couldn't deny.

His black slacks were beltless, but I checked the waist anyway. I didn't go too far before I felt a little lump. I tried passing over it, but it was too long. So I moved all the way to the end, then pushed my thumbnail toward where the slacks had been buttoned. Capsules dropped into my hand one at a time, like a dispensing machine.

Finally, the jacket. I wasn't surprised to find a push-button knife inside. A quick wrap with one of the precut duct-tape strips made sure it wouldn't pop open by accident. I'd check it properly once I got it back home. I couldn't risk his cell phone's having a GPS unit, so I just popped out the SIM card and the battery.

He didn't move, even when I used the slicing side of my Tanto to cut off his shirt. He had the same tattoo as Cameron's, and in the same place. But only the one on his arm, nothing on his chest.

I couldn't know when he'd come around, so I pulled out the cotton wads, dipped them in chloroform until they were soaked, then shoved them back in.

I shielded the little gas-fired blowtorch so nobody looking this way could see the glow. Even with the heavy double-mesh gloves,

I could feel the heat from the branding iron as I held it against the arm tattoo.

He slept through it, but his blood was pumping hard, and he'd be conscious soon enough. I sliced off the duct tape from around his face and neck, then wrapped a fentanyl patch around his forefinger, shoved it deep into his mouth, and taped it closed. He wouldn't wake up screaming. Not from pain, anyway.

I pulled the cotton wads out, tossed them into the same bag I'd used for everything else I'd removed, and moved far enough away to smash and abandon the gutted cell phone. Seven minutes, thirteen seconds, start to finish.

Then I was gone.

No reason for the police to pull me over on the drive back, but even if they did, I had all the paper I needed. The plates were from the exact same model car, registered to someone who had left it in a motel parking lot long enough for me to take out a short-term loan.

The reason for branding the man over his arm tattoo was that there *was* no reason. That's all terrorism is: bad things happen to noncombatants; there's nothing special about the victims, they were just in the wrong place when it happened. Not like Idrissa's night-kills—they surely terrorized the enemy, but the enemy were soldiers: they *knew* they were in a war.

I didn't get the feeling that any of the branded man's pals were icy enough to cut his throat and bury him right there, so my money was on an ER dump.

Whatever they told him to say, he'd have to tell the cops that same story. The only thing he really had to lie about was *where* it had happened.

Or maybe he wouldn't wake up until daylight, find himself alone in the woods, and . . .

Whatever was going to happen would shake them all, no matter what they decided to do. And whatever that turned out to be, it might help—the best way to find out who's inside a building is to set it on fire.

An hour after I got the Lexus into our garage, it had the correct plates back on. And I had the branding iron and the stolen plates welded into a single unrecognizable lump, knowing that the little kiln would remove any trace of DNA. While the metal was still pliable, I added some clay and swirled it around until it had the right form. When I pulled that free, Dolly would have a nice flowerpot.

Even held inside my jacket to mask the flash, the digital camera had done a perfect job. The symbol on the jacket I took from the target-of-opportunity in the woods was a perfect match for the dead kid's arm tattoo.

I used the same photo to make a clear scan, then I sent it down a twisted wire of communication lines. It would only take a day or two for me to find out exactly what that symbol meant—provided it meant anything at all.

The next morning, Dolly was still admiring her new planter when I asked her, "How much do you know about softball?"

"A lot, I think. But you're after something a lot more specific than that, Dell. So why don't you just tell me what you're looking for?"

"I don't know what I'm looking for, honey. This is like trying to snatch a moray eel out of an oil barrel. I can't see it, but I know it's there. And I can't just reach in. So I've got to drain the barrel, see?"

"Not . . . really, Dell. Can't you try and just ask narrow questions? If that doesn't work, we can try the long way, okay?"

I thought for a minute or two. Then I asked, "How come you know a lot about girls' softball? Because of all the kids that're always swarming this place?"

"Some of that, sure. But there's a special thing about girls' softball. It took me a while to pick up on it, but it's a sport where you see girls on the field and boys in the stands. Not ogling or anything like that. Supporting. Cheering for their team.

"They start playing when they're kids. Boys have Little League baseball; girls have the same thing, only it's softball. Then there's the juniors—when they're too old for Little League, but still high school age.

"And you know what you see there? A lot? Girls' brothers and boyfriends in the stands, making some serious noise. They hold up signs, wear crazy costumes. . . . Some even have stuff painted on themselves, so they can take off their shirts and make a statement.

"It's not like they're some male version of cheerleaders. They're . . . I know! One time I saw three boys in the stands. All different ages, but you could tell they were brothers. Each one had a word painted on his chest, and they all had their shirts off. Every time this one girl got up to bat, they'd stand up, and you could read the message:

"CRUSH! ONE! TINA!

"I remember thinking that there's something about girls' softball that brings out the best in boys."

"Hmmmm . . ."

"What, Dell?"

"MaryLou didn't have brothers. And she didn't have a boyfriend. I can see Franklin cheering for her, but not holding up a sign or anything like that."

"Sometimes people get, well, not jealous exactly, but crazy to have someone. Obsessed with them. And if they feel rejected, they can turn vicious in a second. But that wouldn't work here. There's no way MaryLou could have been rejected by that boy she shot."

"Because she's gay?"

"And she didn't try and hide it. But, also, why shoot the other boys? It's almost as if they'd all raped her and she was out for revenge. But I can't see any of that. Can't bring it into focus. It's like she just went insane *before* she shot those boys. Even now, she's so calm it's spooky. She has to know she's facing spending the rest of her life in prison, but . . . but that's okay. Okay with her, I mean."

"You always drop into that kind of calm when you know the mission's over. You did a job that never needs doing again. You can go home."

"That's soldiers, Dell. Not—"

"It's not only soldiers, Dolly. You see it every day. A man gets up in the morning, just like usual. Then he kills his wife and kids, drives over to his in-laws', and kills them both. Maybe he's got a few more names on his list—especially if he'd just been fired from his job.

"But when he finally puts the gun to his own head, if you could be there at that moment, you'd see how calm he was about it. The job was done. He was going home."

"That is just crazy."

"To you, sure. Not to him."

She sat down, clasped her hands together in her lap. I knew what that meant.

"I . . . I think I know what you're saying, Dell. Even if what MaryLou did was crazy on the surface, somehow it made sense to *her*."

"She paid what it cost, girl. We just don't know what that 'it' was."

"And she's not going to tell?"

"I don't think so. There's a story to tell here, all right. But I don't think it's her story."

"Then whose?"

"I'm damned if I know. But I'll take another shot at squeezing it out of her tomorrow."

"Thanks" is how she greeted me.

I made a "For what?" gesture.

"The money on the books. Makes it a lot easier to live here."

"Why do you think it was me?"

"They let you use phones here. *Their* phones, I mean. You warned me about not talking about . . . what happened. But I didn't know that even if you're calling five blocks away you have to call collect."

"And you don't like that?"

"I don't. Who would? But who would I call, anyway?"

"Dolly?"

"She's done enough. More than enough. More than I could ever pay her back for."

"She's your friend, yes?"

"I . . . I guess she is."

"So why fuss about paying her back?"

"That's me. That's what everyone knows about me."

Not everyone, shot through my mind, too quick for me to grab it.

"So we're back to 'Why thank me?'"

"Is this a test or something? I know that lawyer wouldn't put money on the books for me. The only person who could do it would be someone who knew he could do it, and how to get it done. None of my friends would know. Dolly wouldn't, either. That leaves you."

"Your family—"

"Forget them," she said. Not like a teenage girl who was annoyed—like a grown woman, giving an order.

"Franklin knows you're in here."

"Franklin? He's a sweetheart. But figuring things out isn't something he's good at."

"You think if he could he'd do it?"

"Yeah, I do. Franklin's like me in a lot of ways. When people look at us, they only see a piece of us. Without Franklin, our football team's a joke. Same as our softball team would have been without me. But that's not all there is, not about either of us."

"I'll keep your commissary on max while you're here."

"I already thanked you for that. And I will find a way to pay you back. I've got a whole life to do that."

"Life at Coffee Creek, is that what you mean?"

"Where else?"

"Don't act like you've already been convicted."

"Are you—? No, that's me being stupid, not you. But I've got no way to beat this one."

"And you knew that going in."

"Yeah. Yeah, I did."

It was time to take that shot I'd told Dolly I'd be doing. "You only wanted one of them."

"I don't know what you're talking about."

"Yeah, you do. You only wanted one of them. Maybe you wanted to send a message, too. But Cameron Taft, he was the target."

"He was just closest, that's all."

"They've got cameras in the hallways, MaryLou," I said, like that settled the argument. It was only a half-bluff—the school did have those cameras, but I hadn't seen the footage.

She bounced back so fast that I knew she'd thought this all the way through. "It might *look* like I passed up a couple of them before I shot him, but that's only because I had a clearer shot if I cut across on an angle."

"I don't understand."

"I think you do, but I'll say it anyway. You know what makes a great pitcher? Not speed—although you have to be able to really bring it if you want to get any mileage out of your change-up—and not a filthy breaking ball, either. You have to be able to hit your spots. Some hitters will murder anything on the outside corner, but going in on them ties them in knots. See?"

"I do. This Cameron boy, he was the spot you had to hit."

"Jeez!" she said, throwing up her hands. For the first time, she looked like a teenage girl—one exasperated beyond endurance at her parents' being so thick.

At that moment, I knew more than I had when I walked into the Visiting Room. But I was still way short of what I needed.

I can make my mind a centrifuge. When it stops spinning, I'm pretty wiped out, but I can read whatever was still sticking to its walls.

The best assassins always have one thing in common—the things they *don't* need. Friends, family, even solace.

Experience can make you better at anything, but only if you learn from it. If you keep doing the same thing the same way, you'll be no better at it than when you started.

There's assassins who might as well sign their names over the bodies they leave. If you read about a man who fell to a barbed-wire garrote in a certain part of Paris, the cops might say something like "Looks like Pierre hasn't lost his touch."

Once the police start saying things like that, you know Pierre might have been working for a long time, but he isn't going to die a free man.

The man who wanted his daughter back found me only by going through a half-dozen networks. I wasn't a member of any of them. Neither was he. But there's a knowledge pool inside them all, and if you have the credentials—and the cash—you can tap into it.

So somebody, somewhere, knew I could kill, and do a clean job of it. But all they'd have is a name, and not the right one. Whatever they'd known about me was all used up—they couldn't find me again, ever.

I'd worked outlaw for a long time, and I never lied to myself about that. The only difference between a mercenary and whoever hires him isn't morality; it's money. A mercenary rents out his own life, and it's not up to him when the lease is up. An assassin is more like a landlord: one that can refuse any tenant he wants to, no explanation required.

But I hadn't worked since Dolly and I came together. And that was a long time. So I'd put a lot of distance between myself and any kind of police.

Besides, I wasn't wanted for anything.

It was the "wasn't wanted" truth of my life that set me on my original path. It was *being* wanted that put me on another.

The hunters in the woods, the little maggot who tortured Alfred Hitchcock to death, none of that had been outlaw work, and not just because I hadn't done it for money. But I still had all my knowledge. Things I'd never forget.

Like:

You don't take a contract to kill unless you know who's offering it. The best way to take out a contract man is give him a job, and then warn the target that he's coming.

If you take a job, you never agree to deadlines. You take a contract; you take your time.

MaryLou is smart, and she's strong, but she's no assassin. If Cameron Taft was her target, why not just wait until she could catch him alone? She could have done the same job with a lead pipe. Probably better—she hadn't even known enough to double-tap him.

The only thing I felt sure of was that, for whatever reason,

MaryLou felt she just couldn't wait. The job had to be done right then.

As soon as I walked in the door, I saw Dolly couldn't wait, either. She was almost jumping up and down with excitement.

"Dell! I made some calls overseas. And you won't believe—"

She caught my look, and her eyes went from glistening to dark in a second, but she rolled right over anything I might want to say. "And, yes, I used those International Calling Cards they sell everywhere, and, yes, I paid cash, and, yes, I—"

I should have known Dolly wouldn't let enthusiasm get in the way of anything I'd taught her. "I'm sorry" is all I could think of to say. I guess it was enough, because all she said was:

"We have to go someplace. It's about a seven-hour drive."

"We, you and me?"

"Yes!"

"When?"

"Now!"

"Can we use the Lexus?"

"Of course! I was planning to have it detailed before we returned it anyway, so it won't matter if Rascal comes with us."

The dog gave me an "Any more stupid questions?" look. I didn't say a word about dogs not being able to retract their claws, and the leather that covered every inch of the back of her friends' car.

We were on the road in another fifteen minutes. A couple of soft-sided bags were already in the empty space behind the back seat—Dolly had packed while waiting for me to come home.

The back seat was all Rascal's, and already covered in horse blankets. I caught his eye in the mirror. He was Dolly's dog, all right.

Dolly was thrilled that the Lexus had two sockets for keeping cell phones charged.

"Now we can both stay on 'full,'" she said, clapping her hands like a happy kid.

I had no doubt whose phone would have stayed on "full" if there had been only one socket. But at least I managed to stop her from playing with the navigation system.

"It wouldn't be fair to your friends," I told her. "I don't know anything about the electronics in this thing, and I've never read the manual—I didn't think we'd have the car this long. It may already have some kind of navigational system installed, but there's no reason to make it easier on anyone who feels like checking where this thing's been the last few days. That's why you have that paper map with you, instead of using MapQuest or something that would stay on your computer."

That last part was a question, but even though she nodded, I could see she wasn't really listening.

"I want to hear . . . well, *everything* about your visit with Mary-Lou, Dell. But if I don't tell you this now, I'm going to burst!"

"I can see that."

She punched me on the arm. Dolly did that whenever she felt like it, but she'd never felt like it when I was behind the wheel before. She was really amped to the gills.

"Oh, you! Just listen for a minute, okay?"

I knew Dolly well enough not to make any comment about her estimates of time, so I just said, "Go."

"We're going to see a SANE nurse. And not just any SANE nurse, but the one in charge of the whole state. She's based in Salem, but she's almost always on the road. Where we're going, it's where she is now."

"SANE?"

"Sexual Assault Nurse Examiner."

"But you said 'sane nurse.'"

"That's just how people say it, 'SANE nurse.' Maybe because it comes out easier that way. Remember, there's all kinds of nurses. I was an R.N. That's a high rank. But a Nurse Practitioner, that's the peak. In this state, they can do all kinds of things that only doctors can do in other places."

"I didn't mean to interrupt you, Dolly. It's just that we've got plenty of time until we get where we're going, and the more I understand, the better, right?"

"Yes." She sighed as dramatically as one of her teenagers.

I shut up after that. It was a good three seconds before Dolly went back to what she wanted to say so badly.

"It all started when I had this . . . I don't know what to call it, but I know to trust it when it comes. Anyway, the more I thought about MaryLou, the more I listened to what the girls went on and on about, the more convinced I was that the key to all this was a kind of controlled violence."

MaryLou's no assassin flicked into my mind. Was Dolly picking up my thoughts now? But I didn't say a word.

"MaryLou beat up her little sister, Danielle, remember?" She didn't wait for an answer. "Like I said, the school thought it was the parents, but nothing ever came of that. After a while, everybody knew the real story. The whole story except for one thing: why?

"So, I thought, well, no way MaryLou lost her temper and took it out on her little sister. She's not like that. She must have done it for a reason. And when she walked into school with that pistol, she did *that* for a reason. So maybe it's not two *different* reasons. See?"

"Yes," I said, thinking of the qualities of a good assassin again. They don't all have to be mercenaries—some only kill for a cause. My old comrade Patrice, he never said it out loud, but I always saw him as an IRA soldier who had to go on the run. If the Brits wanted him bad enough, there was only one place he'd be safe, no matter who asked. Or came looking.

And the only reason they'd want him that bad would be if he'd taken a lot of high-value targets. If Patrice had been a sniper, he sure hid it well—he was the last man you'd pick for that kind of job when we were legionnaires. So I was guessing bomb-building was in his near past. Maybe a bomb that killed a whole mess of people. Or one really important one.

But maybe he was wanted for something he hadn't been ordered to do, something he believed he *had* to do: avenge his mate, Mickey.

"So, like I started to say," Dolly went on, "I made a slew of phone calls. I finally located an old pal, in Switzerland. She said she didn't recognize my voice, even after I switched to French. I couldn't believe she *still* didn't recognize me. So I told her enough stuff that only I could know. Stuff about her, I mean. She still never said my name. That's when I figured she was just playing it safe—maybe trying to tell me she wasn't the only one listening.

"But once I told her what I wanted, you could feel her . . . not relax, exactly, more like she was relieved. She didn't know the woman we're going to see, but she found someone who does, and that's when she agreed to see us."

"Us?"

"Well, just me, actually. But I think I can get around that."

"Or I could just play fetch with Rascal while you talk to her."

"I'd rather you be there, Dell. If I'm right, you'll know better questions to ask than I would."

"I guess we'll see."

"Dell, listen! This woman has a record of all the sexual-assault hospital examinations done statewide. Done by the people she's in charge of. Going back a good seven years, my . . . old friend said. And what that means is that she'll have the names of all the girls who were examined in our area."

"You think . . . what?"

"I think that some of those names are going to be connected.

To this thing with MaryLou. And to each other, even if they don't know it."

"But if all those girls were examined . . . I know they can't put their names in the paper, but when a rapist goes on trial, they could give *his* name."

"There's two 'if's there, Dell. Did the girl know enough to identify the rapist? And did the DA's Office ever bring him to trial?"

I remembered that "soft as warm custard" crack about the DA's Office. Maybe it wasn't the exaggeration I'd thought it was.

"And this SANE woman, she'd know?"

"I'm not sure. But if she has the names of all the girls who were examined, we could find out the rest ourselves."

"That's right. Damn, Dolly! I'm running around in a mineshaft, poking at little seams, and you maybe hit the mother lode."

"We'll see," she said. All the bounciness was gone now. Her lips were set in a hard, grim line.

However Dolly had figured seven hours, she'd miscalculated. I made it in five and change, and never went more than a couple of miles over the limit.

"Cabin Nine" is all Dolly said.

I could see what had to be the car—a pale-green Prius with State plates. "I'm going to park over on the other side," I answered. "Rascal needs some time to himself, anyway. So you can either walk over and knock, or, if you want to try me coming along, I will. But that's no office building, honey—it's a cheap motel court. She may balk if she's expecting one person and—"

"It'll be okay, Dell. We're early, remember? So, while you let Rascal take care of his business, I can call her. That way, she won't be surprised at seeing us both."

Dolly rapped lightly on the flimsy door. It was opened by a slender, coppery-skinned woman with long, straight black hair and high cheekbones. She stepped back, and we both walked in.

"I don't know how to thank you," Dolly said. "Whoever you talked to wouldn't be exaggerating if she told you that this could save a girl's life."

"What I was told is that you could be trusted. And Médecins Sans Frontières was all the proof I needed. I only speak a few words of French, just the little I remember from my elders. *Mwen pa konnen w' mennen yon zanmi.*"

"*C'est mon mari. C'est lui qui s'est occupé de tout pour sauver cette fille.*"

So far, neither of them had used a name, not even their own. This woman's name was no secret, so it had to be a way of protecting each other's contacts.

The woman gave me a no-emotion, measuring look. "You are her husband. And what else, a detective?"

"No," I said, being very careful—what had been a credential for Dolly might be a cross-out for me. "I have certain skills that I've been using, that's all."

"So you wouldn't need to actually *see* anything?"

"*Excusez-moi. Si vous préférez, je peux m'en aller. Je m'appelle Dell.*"

"Mine is Iris," she said. Then she took a pack of cigarettes out of her jacket pocket. If Dolly was shocked at that, she was blown away by the woman's offering one to me.

I knew that to refuse would have been a grave mistake. The woman had made a judgment—not of my character, of my experience. Somehow, she guessed I would know that when an American Indian—I had guessed Creole from the first words she spoke—offers to share tobacco, it goes way beyond a handshake. It is a gesture among warriors of a shared cause. Telling me that she respected Dolly for saving lives, but also that she knew me for what I was.

I didn't make the mistake of offering her a light. We each took a couple of ceremonial puffs before we dropped our cigarettes into a half-filled glass of water. The woman got up with the glass. I could hear the toilet flush. She came back without the glass. Took out a hand-wipe packet and gave one to me. We scrubbed the smoke off ourselves before tossing the wipes into the garbage can.

The woman opened a folder on the little desk that a cheap motel gives "business travelers."

Dolly hunched forward.

"Thirty-nine girls between the ages of twelve and sixteen were examined at your local hospital in the past four years. All clearly had been raped very recently. Sixteen of them said they knew who had raped them. Of the remaining twenty-three, another ten said they would tell only if nobody 'got in trouble' as a result. Every examination result was reported to the local police."

Dolly and I sat quietly. There had to be more.

"Here are some charts I prepared. Unlike the records, you can take this with you. In fact, I want you to—it is work I could not explain if I were asked.

"As you can see, the curve of those reporting rapes who could or would name their attacker has been steadily dropping, year after year. In fact, none such have been reported at all within the past eighteen months.

"It is not even a possible *hypothesis* that so-called acquaintance rape of girls between those ages no longer occurs in your area. Assuming you have not experienced an extraordinary population decrease, the only logical explanation is that reporting rapes is now universally considered to be a futile gesture among those within that age group.

"Girls between those ages continue to be examined, but, as I said, not a single one has acknowledged knowing her attacker. And of those girls who previously *had* named their attacker, not one single prosecution has resulted."

She handed Dolly the folder, as if to say, "I'm done now."

"Some paper cannot be copied," I said, very softly. "But if names on that paper were read aloud, they could be written down in another's hand."

She nodded slowly. Then she said, "But if the paper on which names were written in another's hand were to be found, there could still have been only one single source."

"What you say is not possible," I told her. Before she could respond, I took out another sheet of that flash paper.

When the paper disappeared, the woman picked up another folder. She spoke thirty-nine names in a voice just above a whisper. Her cadence was steady, watching for my nod to indicate I had the names written down.

"You are a true warrior," I said, bending my head slightly forward to show respect, but keeping my eyes up to show I wasn't play-acting. Then I got up and opened the door, to let Dolly know that anything more she might say would be wrong. The time for manners was past, and the quicker we moved away from this spot, the better.

As soon as we hit the highway, Dolly pulled out a laptop from under her seat. She fired it up, impatiently tapping her nails against the machine as she waited.

"It's a good thing I don't need to go out to the Web. Who knows what kind of connection I could get out here. Give me that paper of yours, Dell. I want to write down the names she gave us so I can check them against my own work."

"I can't do that."

"*What?!*"

"I can't do that, Dolly. I gave my word that the names wouldn't leave the paper I used. When we get home, I'll read you the names, and you can put them in your computer. If you don't go online with them—the names, I mean—there's no way to connect them with the SANE boss."

"Why can't you just do that now? This has a partitioned hard drive, with a no-access firewall—it *can't* reach the Net. Read me the names, burn the paper, and it would be just the same."

"No. No, it wouldn't. When we get home, we're safe."

"Safe? From what?"

"From some cop getting a look at your laptop, with those names on it."

"How could that happen? We're not speeding, that pistol you're carrying is legal. Registered and everything."

"Cops love to look in people's computers. Any excuse would do."

"Give me an example," she said. If she hadn't been sitting, her hands would have been on her hips by now.

"Some drunk crosses the median and smashes into us. We're both taken to the hospital, unconscious. The license on this car traces to your friends, not to either of us. So, some cop could claim he looked in your laptop trying to find some medical information."

"That's ridiculous."

"Okay."

"Okay what?"

"Just 'okay.' You said 'ridiculous.' I'm saying, I heard you. That's all."

"But you're not giving me that paper?"

"No."

Dolly crossed her arms over her chest. I always get a kick out of that—she's got a big chest and short arms, so she never quite pulls it off. But I didn't think making one of my usual comments would be a good idea.

She didn't say another word for the next couple of hours. Then she shook off whatever was bothering her the same way a wet dog does as soon as he's inside.

"It's in there, Dell. I know it is."

I knew what "there" meant. But I still didn't see how Dolly could be so damn sure. I didn't ask her, either.

It was past midnight when we rolled into the garage.

Neither of us was sleepy. Rascal wasn't, either, but that was no surprise—he'd slept most of the way home.

As if we'd agreed in advance, we went straight to the basement. I could turn lights on down there without anyone's seeing them from outside.

Dolly plugged in her laptop, turned it on.

"Now can I have that paper?"

I didn't answer her. I closed my eyes. I pushed my thumb against my right nostril, drew in a deep breath, then switched, closing my left nostril and pushing the breath back through the nostril I'd closed. Then I reversed the whole thing, watching the white screen in my head fill with bold black letters.

"Abigail Zimmerman," I said.

"Dell . . ."

"Amber Lang."

"What are you—?"

"Brenda James."

"Oh!" Dolly said. Then her fingers started flying, to catch up. When I said the last of the thirty-nine names, I took one final look at the white screen. Then I opened my eyes.

I was a little dizzy, shaky on my feet. Dolly jumped up, slipped my left arm around her neck, and slowly lowered us both to the floor.

"I'll be okay in a minute," I said.

"I know."

I don't know how much time passed, but Dolly was still right next to me when I came to the surface.

"Those names, the ones you said, they're the same as the ones on that paper, aren't they?"

"Yes." I reached in my breast pocket and handed her the flash paper.

Dolly wiggled just a little. I knew what was going on inside her, so I said, "I'm fine, honey. Go ahead and check the names you typed against the names on the paper."

She came back to where she'd left me. I was sitting in a position I had learned another lifetime ago. I could stay that way for hours if I had to.

"Dell, the names are the same. But they're not in the order she said them."

"Alphabetic. I used the first names, not the last."

"That's why you didn't want me to—"

"Yes."

Dolly held out the paper. Said, "Got a match, soldier?" like she was a B-girl in a cheap bar. But the giggle under her voice was a dead giveaway—I was way past "forgiven," I was back to being her man.

I fired the flash paper.

"You need a nap," Dolly said. Her battlefield nurse's voice. I never argued with it.

When I woke up, it was daylight—I couldn't actually see it, but the big digital clock read 08:29.

I was about to go upstairs, but I stopped. I had to check and see if the info I'd asked for was waiting.

It was. The screen popped to life when I opened the program

that had cost me a titanium rod in my left forearm. The man who designed it was an ace cracker, who knew he still owed me. I hit the sequence to de-encrypt:

|> This was chop of elite unit of the Chinese Imperial Army during Boxer Rebellion (1899). Unit was called Hu Shen Ying, the "Tiger God Battalion," named in opposition to the foreign enemy, who were referred to both as "Lambs" and "Devils." Latter names devised to say that the invaders were both evil and weak. <|

I went back to "encrypt" and typed in:

|> How could it appear on body of a young man today? <|

The punk I'd taken the jacket from had only the one tattoo: that same symbol, in the same place as Cameron had. But, unlike Cameron, he'd had no tattoo on his chest.

I'd work that through later, when the next answer came in. For now, I was drained, and I needed fuel.

Dolly was exactly where I expected her to be—at the butcher-block table. It was half covered with paper, and she had a whole bunch of different-colored markers lined up in a neat row.

I didn't even get a chance to open my mouth. Dolly jumped up and went to work. I was eating an English-muffin sandwich—fried egg with all kinds of green stuff—and sipping at a glass of apple juice before I knew it. And Dolly was back to her work.

I ate slowly. Chewed every bite. Dolly never looked up, but she knew when I was finished. She jumped over to the refrigerator, took out a bottle of something, and shook it hard. When she poured it into a heavy blue glass tumbler, it was hard to tell what color it was, but I knew I was supposed to drink it down, so I did.

"All right?"

"Yeah," I said. Meaning, I was ready to work.

I didn't have to wait long. "Dell, can you think of any reason why these girls . . . No, wait. Not these girls. Not the ones whose names we have, the ones whose names we *don't*. Can you think of why the local SANE nurse hasn't seen a single case prosecuted? Not one single case? Not for years?"

"It's a dropping line."

"I don't understand what you're—"

"Less and less, all the way down to nothing."

"I see that. But I don't see why."

"If you saw a gunfight going on right across the street, would you call 911?"

"Of course."

"What about if the last ten times you'd called 911, nobody answered?"

"You mean . . . You're saying girls stopped reporting because they knew it wouldn't do any good?"

"Why else?"

"I . . . don't know. None of those names were my girls. I don't even remember hearing their names."

"We can't find the ones who didn't report. But the ones who did, they'll have the answer."

"Sure. But I wouldn't even know where to start."

"Take the last one who actually did report, and backtrack from her."

"You?"

"Who else? They can't be hard to find. It's summer; they won't be in school. Some of them could have left town. Or got married and changed their name. It's a small town—I can find them."

"But what could you ask them? How could you even explain where you got their names? And how would any of that help MaryLou?"

"We won't know until I have those conversations, Dolly."

"When are you going to start?"

"I need a shower, a shave, and a change of clothes. Suit and shirt, right? But it's still too early."

"If they have jobs, they'll already be—"

"Dolly, let me do this, okay? There's only one group that we *know* will talk. Talk to you, I mean. Your girls. They'll be here soon enough, I'm thinking. I don't want to be here when they show up."

"But what do I ask them?"

"If one of them ever got raped—no, not that—if any of their *friends* got raped, what would they tell them to do?"

"Climate testing."

"On the nose," I said, kissing her cheek. She stood up, wanting a better one. I tried. It must have done the job, because her eyes got that sweet glow. I patted her bottom, telling her that I was going out. There were other ways to tell her, but I'd used that one so much that it became a signal. There were other ways to pat her bottom, too, but she never got them mixed up.

Sliding around the truth can work sometimes, but an outright lie risks blowing a whole operation. So I didn't even think about telling any of the girls that I was working for the DA's Office.

Swift was worth every penny of his "retainer" just for the paper shield he gave me. Whether he earned another dime past that would be up to him.

No Zimmermans in the local phone book. But there were five Langs—not much easier.

Not much harder, either. The good thing about being in such a small town is that even the most trivial crap makes the papers. So, when I identified myself as "Warren Sims. From the PTA . . . ?" not a single person showed the slightest surprise. Four of them—three males, one female—wanted to know why the PTA would be contacting them; after all, they didn't have any children in school. The woman said she was an "empty-nester"; the men all said they were "retired." None of them complained about being called; all of them sounded sober.

The last number was a cell. It took me right to voice-mail. That one had been listed as "Lang, Teresa." Amber's mother, turning off her cell while she was at work? No way to tell. But her address was in the phone book, too. And it was early enough so her daughter might still be hanging around the house. If she had a summer job, or if a man answered the door, I'd have to catch her alone somewhere else.

The address was a nicely kept little cottage, off-white, with a cedar-shake roof. The girl who answered the door was wearing jeans and a sleeveless purple sweatshirt with "Orcas" in white letters across the chest. Purple and white. The school colors, as per that twisted videographer I'd met in the woods. I guessed she'd cut off the white sleeves.

She wasn't what you'd call fat, but she was well over the weight limit for her height and frame. Bad complexion, which she was battling with some kind of white stuff. Probably saw me through the peephole in the door, checked my age and my suit, and decided it wasn't worth scrubbing it off.

"Ms. Amber Lang?" I said. Like it wasn't a question, just verifying the information I'd been given.

"Who are you?"

I told her my name and got the expected blank look, but I had "I'm a private investigator" out of my mouth too quickly for her to hide the widening of her eyes.

"How come a—?"

"I'm working with Bradley Swift," I said, as if that name would mean anything to her. "He's the defense attorney for MaryLou McCoy."

"The one who . . . ?"

"Yes."

"What do you want with me, then? I mean, I go to Cove, but I'm not even in her— I mean, I'll be a senior when I go back after the summer, but she's already graduated. I've, you know, like, seen her, but I never talked to her. I don't know anything about her except for . . . for what she did. And I wasn't even on the same floor when it happened."

"I know. But I assure you, I wouldn't be coming out here unless I believed you could really be an enormous help."

"Me?"

"Yes. Could I come in and explain? I imagine your neighbors are already wondering what I'm doing here."

"Well . . ."

"If you're concerned about being alone with me, you can call Mr. Swift's office, and he'll verify that I'm working on this case with him. Or I have a letter on his stationery right here in my case," I told her.

I held up the slim black Halliburton I was holding in my right hand; its anodized-aluminum look fit perfectly with the Lexus parked in front, and she couldn't look at the case without seeing past it. I don't know how many "private eye" movies she'd seen, but I was pretty sure I didn't fit the image. Still, nothing reassures some people like the look of money.

She stepped back and held the door open. I crossed the threshold and saw that the front door opened into what must have been their living room. I grabbed the lounger right next to the couch, so she could decide how close she wanted to sit next to me.

Pretty close, as it turned out. She leaned against the arm of the couch, watching as I pulled a legal pad and clipboard out of my black aluminum case. I had a matching pen, too—a black aluminum Halliburton that said more than just "money." It said, "This is serious business."

She had a menthol cigarette all fired up before I could offer her a light. She looked half frightened and half defiant—the cigarette helped her with both.

"Do you prefer 'Ms. Lang' or 'Amber'?"

"Amber's fine."

"Okay. Now, you must have heard all the talk about what happened at school."

"Me and everybody else. It's, like, all some people talk about. I'm, like, who cares? Sure, it's too bad and all, but it didn't have anything to do with me personally."

For a flash second I wished I was younger and better-looking, but I instantly realized that older and harder was actually a better look for this job. If my guess was right, she wasn't a girl who could be charmed into giving up anything. Not again, anyway.

My choice of tactics was narrowed way down. Guerrilla warfare relies on surprise and speed. You become part of the jungle and wait until the enemy relaxes, thinking they're finally in a safe zone. Surprise freezes them, but not for long. That's where the speed part comes in. Hit fast, hit hard, and hit the road.

What the hell, I thought, *she's not the only girl on the list. So . . .*

"How can you say that, Amber? What could be more personal than the death of the liar who raped you?"

Her mouth opened. Her cigarette burned in the ashtray. Her eyes went everywhere but on mine.

"I don't blame you for not naming him when they asked you," I went on, dialing my voice perfectly to the pitch of a professional interrogator—that toneless, no-way-out inexorability that you use only on the target who's not willing to die. The one that says, We both know you're going to tell me eventually, so why make it painful? "Nobody was going to do anything about it, anyway."

"How could you—?"

"That's not important. What's important is that my sources of information are *my* sources. That means I'm the only one they talk to. Nobody knows where I get my information. Nobody ever will."

"But if you know—"

"Amber, listen to me. You know how it works. School, I mean. Do you honestly think a story like yours would be kept a secret? It doesn't matter if anyone believed it or not—if there was any blame to go around, it was all going to be put on you."

She closed her eyes for a couple of seconds. When she opened them, she still wouldn't look at me, but she said, "Not at that school. Not there. You're right."

"So why should MaryLou spend the rest of her life in prison? All she did was what a lot of girls wanted to do."

"They did it to MaryLou?!"

"No. You know they only go after the real young ones."

"I . . . I don't know anything about that."

"Yes, you do, Amber. Because you're one of the ones they threw away when they were finished with you."

"I . . ."

Then she broke down. But her bitter tears stopped as quickly as they'd started.

"You know what? I'm so fucking stupid, I'd probably believe them all over again."

"Stupid?"

"Yeah," she said, turning to look into my eyes. "I had to be stupid, didn't I?"

"I don't see how that fits."

"Really?" she said, her voice turning even more bitter with the sarcasm laced through it. She lit another cigarette. Then she looked at me, as if daring me to deny the truth. "The best-looking boy in school, a boy who runs with the coolest clique, he's going to want some fat pizza-face to hang out with him? Only a really stupid girl would buy any of that. All I had to do was look in the mirror."

"You looked in the mirror plenty," I said.

She was quiet for a few seconds. Then she surprised me. "That's right, I did. And I saw something that wasn't there. Just like I didn't hear what other girls whispered about me."

I used my silence to urge her on.

"Only, I *did* hear. But I told myself they were just jealous. That's a good one, huh?"

"Why are you blaming yourself, Amber? You didn't do anything wrong."

"No? My mother works two jobs just to keep this house. All by herself—my father's idea of child support is to call me on my birthday. She was all the 'role model' any girl could want, but so what? Everything my mother told me to do, I did the opposite. I smoked—not these, you know what I mean—I got drunk, I did lousy in school. You know why?"

"I think so."

"If you're going to give me some 'adolescent rebellion' speech, save it."

"Your father, he's a handsome man, isn't he?"

"I . . . That's right, he is. So what?"

"So you blamed your mother for your looks. For what you *see* as your looks. That all came from her genes, right?"

She shook her head. Not to deny what I said, more like shaking off a punch. "How could you possibly—?"

"Is your mother overweight?"

"Her? No way. She's skinny. Probably from all that work she puts in."

"So get a job."

"What?"

"You heard me, Amber. And you know what I'm saying by it. You don't have any 'fat genes.' That's as good an excuse as any. Because, by the time you really cared about how you looked, you decided it was already too late. Which was still another lie. It wasn't too late then. And it still isn't."

"How could you know all this?"

"I'll tell you. But only if we make a deal, you and me. And stick to it."

"What . . . deal?"

"I want to know what you *didn't* tell. Why you never told. Not at the hospital, not to the police, not to the counselors . . . not to anyone. You tell me, and I'll tell you how I know about the other things. I'll tell you more than that, too."

"Sure. Only, I go first, right?"

"No. But you have to give me your word. You do that, I'll go first."

"For real?"

"First you listen. *Then* you tell me, okay?"

Amber stared at the smoke from her cigarette like it was an Enigma machine. Her way of saying, "Go ahead."

No lies. Just not all the truth. I could do that.

"I don't know who my parents are," I told her. "I grew up with people I don't even remember. But I learned that secret thing all orphans keep inside them. We all make up stories to explain . . . anything that needs explaining. We tell ourselves that our parents really loved us, but they died in a plane crash. Our fathers were all important men. Our mothers were all gorgeous women. Everything was wonderful and perfect.

"Or we tell ourselves our mothers were whores who dumped us in the street. Our fathers, our real fathers, they would have loved us, but they never knew.

"It's like being a writer who can't find a publisher: anyone who shows the slightest interest, we're all over them. We'll do whatever we're told. Why? Because they know the secret words. They just say, 'If you really loved me, you'd—' and they fill in the blanks with whatever they think they can get away with. We have to do what they say, because the only way our stories become the truth is if they believe us.

"I was a soldier once. A long time ago. Some of the men I served with didn't care if they lived or they died. There was nothing for them on earth. No wife, no children, no family, no friends. Nothing to go home to. But they never admitted this, not to any of us.

"In battle, they were the bravest of the brave. You know why? If they lived, all those secret dreams could still come true. A man called Henri, I remember him. All I knew—all *any* of us knew—was that 'Henri' wasn't his real name. Then the fighting. If Henri was brave, if he protected his own comrades, if he risked his own life, that *became* Henri. We knew him by what he did, what we saw with our own eyes. You understand? If we got asked, every one of us would swear that Henri was a brave man. And if Henri died, that's how the rest of us would always remember him, too.

"So, when you think about it for a second, it's easy enough to understand, yes? What did Henri really have to lose?"

Halfway through, I could tell I had misjudged Amber. I could see she fully understood what I was talking about way before I finished the roundabout route I'd chosen.

"So, if someone told Henri they saw something 'special' in him," she said, "Henri would want that to be true so bad that he'd . . ."

"Do anything," I finished for her. "Anything in the world. Even die."

She lit another cigarette. But this time, she was more relaxed about it.

"You already know, don't you?"

"That it was this punk Cameron's crowd, or even Cameron himself? Yeah."

Her eyes filled. "Are you . . . ? Oh God, are you one of the other girls' fathers?"

"And what else do you want to know?" I challenged this girl who had surprised me so much already. Challenged her by letting her think she'd figured out why I was really there.

"I get it. If you'd known, you would have killed him yourself, wouldn't you? That's why you want to protect MaryLou now."

Time to get back to the truth—it would have been too easy for her to check if I went on pretending to be one of the other girls' fathers. "I'm not a father, Amber. Not of anyone. But you're right—if I had a daughter, and I found out what Cameron did, I *would* have killed him myself."

"You could do it, too."

I just nodded, thinking my looks worked a lot better for one role than another. But then it hit me—I'd left out the one part I owed Amber. Really owed her.

"Would you stomp on a cockroach?" I asked her.

"Ugh! Of course."

"How about a butterfly? Would you crush one of those?"

"What's wrong with you? How could you even say—?"

"What's the difference, then?"

"Between a cockroach and a butterfly?"

"Yes."

"A butterfly is beautiful, delicate . . . like a moving flower. But a cockroach is just a filthy insect."

"They're both insects, Amber. One's pretty; one's ugly."

She went stone-silent.

"But that's not the difference. Listen to me. A butterfly spreads pollen. So things can grow. A cockroach carries diseases. So things can die."

"Is this some kind of lesson?"

"If it is, you're not paying attention to it. You have an encyclopedia here?"

"I have my laptop."

"Good enough. Now, look up 'coral snake.'"

She expertly swirled her finger over the mouse pad set just below the keyboard, and the screen sprang to life. She tapped "coral snake" into a box at the top right on her screen. A bunch of underlined sentences filled the screen. She clicked on "images."

"Oh, they're beautiful."

"Yeah. Now look up 'milk snake.'"

It only took her a few seconds: "They're the same."

"Almost. But if you look real close, you'll see a difference in the banding. One's red and black; the other's red and yellow."

"I . . . I see it now," she said, splitting the screen so there were pictures of both snakes on it, side by side.

"The coral is one of the deadliest snakes in the world. The milk snake is completely harmless."

"I don't get it."

"I thought we were going to be honest with each other," I said. "You get it just fine. This isn't some 'don't judge a book by its cover' crap. This is about making mistakes. Some mistakes are harmless. Some mistakes are fatal. You'll never know until you make one."

"What do you want to know?"

"What I asked. What I asked because I promised to tell you that secret I knew. And, Amber, I did that, didn't I? Didn't I trust you?"

"It wasn't Cameron," she said, her voice as dry and painful-sounding as if she had swallowed sandpaper. "I mean, it was Cameron, but he wasn't the one who invited me."

"Invited you . . . ?"

"Gave me the RSVP. That's what they call them. It's just this heavy black card—folded, like a birthday card. On the outside is their sign—like the symbol for something in Japanese. They just walk up and hand it to you. The inside is all white. You're supposed to write 'yes' or 'no' on the blank part. I wrote 'yes,' and he told me 'party of two.'"

"You and Cameron?"

"That's what I thought. Or . . . maybe I didn't think so. Maybe I just didn't care. It was the real thing, I could see that."

"From the symbol?"

"Yes. Nobody else would dare to—"

"Who gave you the card?"

"Bull. His real name is . . . I don't think I even know what his real name is. Everyone just calls him Bull."

"The party was that same night?"

"Yes. There's this old fast-food place."

"What kind of food?"

"I guess it used to be different kinds. Everyone likes the location in the daytime, and it does get a lot of traffic, so different franchises keep trying it. But they always fail. The people who have it now, it's just for kids. Like this huge day-care center. You can leave your kids there all day—my mom says it's open from six in the morning until eight at night. They have rides and swings and a trampoline and . . . it's kind of like an amusement park for kids, even little ones."

"And the other place doesn't open until—*when?*—after dark?"

"Way after dark. Midnight was what Bull told me. I think that was probably when they started."

"Who was there?"

"Everyone," she said again, biting into her lower lip so hard that she drew blood, determined not to cry. Maybe not in front of anyone, maybe never again.

I reached over and took two of her smokes. Lit us each one. She took hers like it was a hit of morphine, stuck into her by a comrade on a battlefield where she'd taken a bullet.

"I don't even know how many there were," she finally said.

"Were where?"

"In . . . Oh, I see what you're saying. Over to the right side, way back in the woods, there's this little cabin. That's where they took me. It was dark, but they have flashlights. And the way was marked with that orange tape—the kind that reflects light. Inside, they have candles."

"And Cameron . . . ?"

"He was there. Bull was, too. But neither of them went first. I mean, neither of them made me do anything. I took . . . whoever it was in my mouth. I kept my eyes closed, so I could think it was Cameron. I told myself it was. But then they all . . . raped me. And did other things. I thought I was going to die."

"How did you get to the hospital?"

"I didn't have a car. They had to hold me up to walk back. To the kiddie place. They had a big sack of something. They put it over my head. Then they drove me to a block or so away from the hospital, and dumped me out on the street. I'm not sure how I got the rest of the way."

"The story around school is if you don't tell, you get . . . moved up, like. On the social ladder. I didn't really believe that, I only *wanted* to. I saw how some girls were just . . . avoided. It wasn't that they couldn't have a boyfriend, they couldn't have any friends at all.

"But when the cops asked me their questions, I could tell they already knew the answers. And they weren't going to do anything about what those people had done to me. All I wanted to do was go home. Just go home and get into bed and never come out."

"Have you ever heard of a girl who *did* report them?"

"A couple of years ago," she said, naming two who were already on the boss SANE nurse's list.

"What happened?"

"Nothing. Nothing ever happened to anyone. It was like that was the way it was *supposed* to be. Like making the pledges for the boys' fraternity dress up like girls and walk around school. Hazing. I mean, if it wasn't supposed to be that way, why didn't the police arrest them? Why didn't any of them go to jail? Why didn't they ever stop?"

It took quite a while to get her to calm down. But when she did, her eyes were clear. Harder, too. I don't know why those two lights always seem to come on at the same time.

"Are you going to kill them?" she asked me.

"No. There would only be more. What has to die is this idea that, like you said, this is the way it's *supposed* to be."

"How could—?"

"That depends on what happens to MaryLou."

"But that's already . . . happened, right?"

"Not even close. The final chapter, that still depends."

"On what?"

"On whether I can find another Henri out there. Only, this time, I won't be looking for a man, I'll be looking for a young woman. A woman willing to do whatever it takes to become a warrior."

I didn't want to go home. I'd have to see Dolly then, and I wanted a quiet place to think. To think about Dolly.

There's a place not far from here where people go to watch whales—the coast is the migratory path for the big ones. The rail was lined with cars. Pickups and RVs, too. Plates from all over. No room for the Lexus to get any privacy, but there was plenty to be had only a couple of blocks away—people around here hate walking, and tourists pick up that habit real quick.

I went as far back as I could go. With Dolly, I mean. I thought about meeting her by accident. Twice. I didn't take that as a sign or anything. I just knew that, for me, it was Dolly or nothing.

A person isn't something you can steal. You might think different, especially if you watch a lot of TV. But you can only steal a body, not a heart.

So, back then, I'd done everything I could to slant Dolly's answer. Things I thought she would like. But until a few minutes ago, I'd never asked myself the hardest part. Not why did she go with me—whatever her reasons, I was too grateful to go poking around. But how come, when I told her she'd have to give up her own past, too, she'd never blinked?

For me, it was nothing. I had nothing to give up except a name that wasn't mine. But for Dolly, she'd had all the stuff regular people came with, hadn't she? A name, a family, friends, a place she could call home. She gave all that up as quick as I told her why she'd have to. I was sure that would have been the deal-breaker, especially when she had to give up those nursing credentials. But it all fell right off her, as naturally as a scab from a healed wound.

She knew I'd tell her the truth about anything she asked, but she never asked. I didn't know what she'd tell me if I asked, and I wasn't going to dig under scar tissue to find out.

What was such a young girl doing in the middle of a tribal war in Africa? Nobody runs to Médecins Sans Frontières to clean up their back-trail. For that group, you'd need papers, real ones. You'd need a background they could check. Credentials. Stuff you couldn't fake.

And Dolly never carried a rape bomb, like some of the nurses did. A "rape bomb" is pretty much what it sounds like. All the women—doctors, nurses, do-whatever-it-takes volunteers—knew what was going to happen if women were ever taken captive, and most of them had a pin they could pull just in case.

Rape is part of the way they fight wars in some parts of the world. When a soldier rapes a woman from another tribe, there's no need to kill her—her own people will do that if she starts showing pregnant. That's how it was in Africa, anyway. I know it happens in other parts of the world, too. There's places where a rapist can call himself a man of honor, even if his victim is his own sister.

Dolly didn't get that. I don't know if she actually believed that nobody would hurt healers who didn't carry weapons. It wasn't that she didn't care what happened to her, either. It was more like she had signed on and she'd either complete the mission or . . . take whatever came.

Not like me, though. Not for life. Dolly must have had a get-out plan for her future, but I never thought there was anything else I *could* do. After a while, I had money, but I still kept on working. As I got better at what I did, I made more money. That was all there was for me—even after I knew I wasn't working for the money anymore.

But when I met Dolly that second time, she'd already escaped one battlefield, and gone on to pick another. And she had plans for another after that.

Dolly hated anything that hurt people, whether it was a crazy boy in a woman's negligee carrying a banana-clipped AK, or a core-killing disease. Me, I didn't really hate anybody, or anything. But I killed people, so . . . why wasn't I one of those things Dolly hated?

Maybe Dolly believed you could change people. Me, I didn't believe that. I only knew you could change what they did. Not because they changed their minds, because they changed their path . . . to avoid places with skulls on stakes. That's what killing was for, to make your village safe. That's how I saw it.

So did MaryLou.

That thought ripped into my thinking like a slice from a ceramic blade—the kind where you don't even know you've been cut until you feel the blood flowing.

What if MaryLou understood rape the same way I did? You are what you do, and rape is what rapists do. She knew she couldn't fix them—the best she could do was stop her little sister from going near them. When that didn't work, she did the only thing she could think of. Maybe she couldn't put Cameron's head on a stake, but she wasn't trying to protect a whole village from invaders. All she wanted was to keep them away from her baby sister.

Maybe this, maybe that. Maybe I was just trying to put off asking the one person who I was sure knew the answer.

I crossed under one of the little bridges they have everywhere here, headed back the way I'd come. Carolyn Kubaw had been one of the names on my list. She wasn't hard to find—the newspaper had followed her life since graduation. Got a degree in hotel management from a community college, then a job with one of the chains. Now she was Carolyn Kubaw MacTiever, married to a guy her age who wasn't from around here. Met him when he was transferred by the same hotel chain. They lived two towns over, a little more than sixty miles away.

I gave up on the idea of trying to make telephone contact. She'd given birth to a child only two months ago, so maybe she was still staying home on "maternity leave" or something. Even in this economy, if she had a job to go back to, she wouldn't be taking any real risk.

About halfway there, I pulled up at one of those little roadside stores. I wanted to stay hydrated in case I got a chance to talk with her. Dolly always says my voice sounds like I'm threatening someone, but I think that's only because folks around where we live now talk much louder than I was used to.

What would I ever have to shout? *"À terre!"* or *"Nord!"* . . . things like that. The first always means what it says: "Get down!" That's when the enemy's still too far away to hear you. A sniper can tap you from a long distance, but he can't hear anything from that far away. The other is the opposite: when they can hear you, but not see you. Not yet, anyway. So you yell, but it's misdirection.

And only the point man would do that. If you're the last man in line, you walk backward, close enough to the man at your back to hear his breath. If you shout *"Nord!"* from that position, it really means "North!"

"Toute erreur est fatale." Yes, every mistake was a fatal mistake. That wasn't some slogan to memorize, it was as if the trainers slipped it into your food during the training. One man, all I knew was his name, Mathieu. I never knew whether he was stupid or just hated doing what he was told. We were working our way up a hill when the point man screamed, *"À terre!"* Mathieu just stood there, like he was frozen.

Just after I heard the sharp *crraack!* of the sniper's weapon, Mathieu kind of floated to the ground. The shooter had to be one of the trainers. Or maybe someone who was being trained. Either way, Mathieu was just as dead. The round he took injected the lesson. None of us moved until we heard *"On laisse rien à l'ennemi!"* from the man on point.

Yes, "Leave nothing for the enemy!" I was right behind the dead man. The man just in front of him tossed down his own harness. I hooked it to Mathieu's belt. Then I hooked up my own harness, secured Mathieu's unfired rifle, crawled around the dead man, and handed the other man his own harness back.

Together we dragged Mathieu all the way up the hill. We didn't speak, but I knew the other man's thoughts, just as he did mine. *Tu n'abandonnes jamais ni tes morts, ni tes blessés, ni tes armes.*

We had been five; now we were four. One man ahead carrying the dead recruit's weapon, two of us hauling his body up the hill, and one man behind, covering us. That was our kind of training—we all knew the sniper was still out there, helping to train us.

When I came out of the store, they were in the parking lot. Five of them. All in their black jackets with the red sleeves. Not making any secret about who they were. They must have all come in the same car, a clumsily repainted Crown Vic that probably came from a police auction. It stood just a few feet away from the Lexus.

For a second, I didn't understand. Whoever had trained them must have been a real . . . Then I realized nobody had *ever* trained them.

One had an aluminum baseball bat—he was taking practice swings with it. Two others had tire irons. I could see the sun glint off the brass knuckles on another's fist. The last one had his hands clasped in front of him—I guessed they were wrapped around some kind of knife.

I could have gone back inside and made a call. And I had a cell phone with me, too. Yeah, they'd never been trained—none of them moved to cut me off from those options. They didn't have me boxed in at all. Maybe they thought I wanted to get into the Lexus bad enough to risk passing right through them.

I kept walking, as if I couldn't see any danger in front of me. I could see their faces tighten.

There's a man who makes water bottles that look exactly like one of those I was carrying—a squeeze bottle that costs around three thousand euros. It was lined with flex-glass, filled with skin-searing acid. You could use the cap to dial it to anything from a mist to a hoselike squirt. Then all you had to do was move so the enemy was downwind, twist the top like you were going to take a drink, and get as close as you could before you sent the acid on its way.

But men like them wouldn't know about such things. Men, not boys—they were older than I expected them to be. I guess I'd thought that, wearing those jackets, doing what they did, they were some kind of high school club.

There wasn't any reason for me to have thought that. A mistake, but not a fatal one.

That's because I knew how to fix it. I stopped analyzing. Why they were there, what they expected—right then, it didn't matter. I kept walking toward the Lexus.

When I got close enough, the man with the brass knuckles said, "What's your problem, man?"

"Huh? I don't have any—"

"What're you, some kind of private eye?"

"Me?"

"What did Amber have to say?"

"Oh! I get it. I'm working for Bradley Swift," I said, as if that name would mean something to them.

"Who?"

"He's a lawyer. Defending MaryLou McCoy. You know, the girl who—"

"Yeah, we know," the man said. "What's that got to do with us?"

"You? I don't even know who you are."

"Then why go see Amber?"

"Huh? Why would I talk to Ms. Lang about the McCoy case? She was in a car accident, and her lawsuit is on for trial in another few weeks. I had to interview her again, go over her deposition, and . . ."

"You just make sure you keep out of our business," he said. I could tell from his voice that he wasn't sure about anything—not anymore, anyway—so I just looked confused.

"Are you threatening me?" I said, trying to sound indignant.

He smiled. I guess whatever I put into my voice worked—he had his confidence back.

"Threatening you? Man, what makes you say such a thing? We're just, you know, hanging out."

"Do you have guns?"

"Guns? Come on, man. Don't make such a big—"

The water bottles were on the ground. They were all staring at them, like they'd just seen a magic trick. Or maybe they wanted to look anywhere but at the pistol I was holding.

"A threat is nothing but a promise. You believe it or you don't. I don't know what you want, and you don't want to tell me. So here's *my* promise: If you don't disappear in another minute, I'll kill you. Then I'll call 911 and tell the cops that you came at me with those bats and things. I was forced to defend myself.

"I'm a licensed private investigator. There's a background check for that, so you know I don't have a criminal record. This is a legally registered weapon. I won't even go to jail. You—some of you, anyway—you'll go to the morgue."

"Look, we made a mistake, that's all."

"Mistake? You think people inside that store behind me haven't been watching us? They can't miss seeing your bats and stuff. But they can't see my pistol. So get in your car and go away. I'm not talking anymore. Get in your car and go away or you start getting dead in the next few seconds. At this distance, I couldn't miss. Especially with you all standing so nice and close together."

Scaring bullies is always a tricky business. If I went back the same way I'd come, there was always the chance one of them could use his cell phone to order up a few firearms. And they knew the Lexus.

If I'd thought they could trace that car to Dolly, they'd already be dead and I'd be making that phone call I'd promised them.

I picked up my water bottles, got back into the Lexus, and drove off in the same direction I'd been heading.

Less than four miles up the highway, I saw a wooded piece of flatland. I pulled over to let the car behind me pass, checked the lanes on both sides until the road was empty, then went off the road. I drove in deep enough to be invisible to passing cars. If a trooper spotted me, I'd say I lost control to avoid hitting a deer.

I scratched the hell out of Dolly's friends' new car by going in so deep. But I knew they carried full-collision and I'd make up the deductible, so I didn't think they'd be too mad . . . especially when I told them how it happened—the "miss a deer" story, I mean.

Only a drug dealer would be stupid enough to use the same throwaway cell twice. I used one to call 911 and say a big greenish car just passed me going in the opposite direction, around mile marker 31—I figured that was a safe estimate, since it would put them about ten miles from that store's parking lot. I said the car was really flying, weaving all over the road. At first, I thought it was an unmarked police car, but as it shot by, I could see it was full of young guys. They had to be drunk or . . .

I lost my connection then. Laying the canvas-wrapped phone across a flat rock and smashing it with the hammer side of my tomahawk made sure of that.

The second throwaway was to call Dolly. On the only throwaway she ever had. She carried it with her everywhere she went, and never used it. Any incoming call would be me.

She opened the channel without saying anything. "It's me," I said. "I had a little accident, but it'd take a fucking winch to pull that little Jap car of yours out of this damn ditch." When she didn't say anything, I was proud of her—anyone can have a good memory, but it takes a soldier's skills to stay calm in crisis. "Yeah, I know it's ten at night," I said, slurring my words even more. "What the hell do you want me to do? I'm still a good fifteen miles from the nearest town, and it's not like I can call fucking Triple-A!"

The second phone broke as easy as the first. The canvas protected the rock from showing signs of the hammer strikes. I bagged the little pieces of the phones inside the canvas. Disposal would depend on what I found after I took a deeper look at the terrain.

I had plenty of time to use the ax blade of the tomahawk to cut cover for the Lexus. There was more than enough foliage to construct a complete blanket, even down to making sure the mirrors wouldn't throw off a glint.

It must have been state-owned land; I couldn't see a thing that resembled a farm, even going in more than a mile deep. I wasn't worried about hunters—much too close to the highway for even the dumbest of them, and it wasn't deer season yet.

But there's no such thing as being perfectly safe. I couldn't predict what might be coming, especially after it got dark. All I could do was deal with whatever showed up.

At 9:45, I DayGlo-taped an "X" on the tree closest to the highway.

At 9:59:25, I heard Dolly pull up. She was behind the wheel of our Jeep. It had plates and registration, but if anyone looked close enough, they'd see that registration was "farm-use limited." The insurance company didn't care that we overpaid every year, and the state didn't care that we had plates for a vehicle that wasn't allowed to leave our property.

I stepped out from the dark, climbed into the Jeep, and told Dolly I'd drive the Lexus back to her friends' place, with her following me.

"Can I?" Dolly asked, holding up her own cell phone.

"Sure."

She called her friends while I cleared the Lexus. Then I just pulled straight out and headed over there, checking every minute or so to be sure I had her headlights in my mirrors.

It wasn't until we were inside their garage that I realized Rascal had come along with Dolly. He watched with great interest as I opened the hatch of the Lexus and removed the set of Velcro'ed plates. I held them out so both Dolly's friends could see them.

"This is my fault," I said to Martin, pointing to the scratched-up paint. "One hundred percent mine. But you don't have to worry about anyone coming around—these plates don't trace back to you."

"We have insur—"

"I apologize for interrupting you," I told Johnny. "But there's no way you can explain all these scratches to any insurance company."

"As if we had to explain anything to those thieves," Martin sneered. "With what we pay them for the bundle, Billy, that's our agent, he would just shoot himself if we ever switched. Fire, theft, on home and business, homeowner's on the house, *plus* the umbrella, never mind the zero deductible on the cars. And we've never made a claim on anything. It's been—what?—fifteen years—"

"Thirteen," Johnny said. I got the impression that they did this all the time.

"It doesn't matter," I told them. "Even if they don't question a word you say, it's still a claim, and you don't want that—especially not with your perfect record. You did a real favor for Dolly, and never asked a question. So there's only two ways to do this: One, you get a complete new paint job, maybe a color you like better? Or I can buy the car from you. It's got less than five thousand miles on it, so it's the same as new."

"Martin's car is just a toy," Johnny said. "This one is a utilitarian vehicle. It's bound to get scratched up one way or another. We're only keeping the car until the warranty runs out, anyway."

"You don't want to sell it to me?"

"Oh, don't act so offended. We don't want to sell it to anyone."

"Then it's the paint job."

"Your husband is a difficult man to deal with," Martin said to Dolly.

"Tell *me*," she said. But her squeezing my arm as she spoke told me all I wanted.

"You know more about cars than I do," I said. "How much is the best paint job going to run?"

"The dealership—"

"Come on. It's getting late. Maybe I don't know cars like you do, but I know any dealership is going to screw you. You'd pay less at a custom shop, and get a much better job, too."

"What do you think we want?" Johnny said. "One of those paints that change color, or something crazy like that?" But I could see Martin didn't think the idea was all *that* crazy.

"Nobody's got money today. They don't have enough work as it is. Five grand would buy you the best there is," I said.

Now they both looked annoyed. Dolly's right—I'm real good at some things, but real bad at others. So I just took out the money—even in hundreds, it was a pretty thick stack—and put it on the still-warm hood of the Lexus.

I saw Martin make a "call me" gesture to Dolly out of the corner of my eye just as we pulled out.

On the way back, I told Dolly everything. She listened patiently until I said, "MaryLou killed the wrong man."

"*What?!*"

"Dolly, I didn't mean—"

That's when she started to cry. All I could do was kind of pat her and wait it out.

"Dell, this town, it looks so beautiful, but there's poison in it. And Cameron, he's just a little piece of it. Those men who threatened you, they were older than him. So this must have been going on for a long time."

"Isn't that what that SANE boss said?"

"I know. But there's no way to change it. I see that. I see that now, anyway."

All I could see was a dream dying. And if I couldn't give Dolly her dream, would she still . . . ? I couldn't allow that question to pollute the pond. Not *our* pond.

"There's a way, Dolly. I swear to you."

"Dell! Don't you even think about—"

"I wasn't. For real, honey."

"Then what?"

"You can't change some people. Once they've become themselves, they're going to keep doing what they do. But you can make them do it somewhere else."

"I know you're not talking about therapy."

"No. I'm talking about raising the stakes."

"Dell . . ."

"I'm sorry, baby. I don't mean to talk in riddles. I wasn't talking about playing poker, I meant—"

"I've been there, too, you know. I've seen those heads on stakes."

"It's no different here. You have to do it in a different way, but you can always deliver that same message."

"But you said—"

"Dolly, listen, okay? Just for a minute. I don't lie to you." *I just don't tell you some things,* I thought. *How was killing the deer-hunters and spraying those green "X" marks on them different from putting their heads on stakes?* "If I thought killing every last one of them would make you happy, if I thought I could pull the poison out of your dream, yeah, I'd do it. But that's not what I meant. We can't change them, or even stop what they do. But we can make them stay away from our village."

She didn't say a word. I knew I had about five seconds to come up with something I could make her believe in. I thought about what I'd found myself saying to Amber. And then I knew.

"Right now, you've got this gang who can do all kinds of things because they're not worried about having to pay for it," I said softly. "There's only one way to change that. And not what you think. The way to change everything is to get MaryLou off."

"But that's—"

"Dolly, listen. This wasn't any Columbine 'kill 'em all' thing—it was an execution. What's the chances of something like that ever happening again? Look, that gang does what they do because they're not worried about their bill coming due. They can rape those girls and nothing happens. But what if that was turned upside down? What if the whole town changed its vote?"

"Dell, you are driving me insane. Nobody votes on . . . rape."

"No? That's *exactly* what they do. This has been going on for years, right? Nobody goes to prison. Nobody even gets arrested. Those girls—the ones like MaryLou's little sister—the town passed judgment on *them,* not on the rapists."

"You mean, like they deserved it?"

"You tell me, Dolly—you're tuned into this place a lot more than I could ever get in a hundred years."

She took a deep breath. Held it a long time. When she let it out, it was like a sigh of surrender. "I'm not plugged in at all, Dell. To the kids, sure. And I know a few of the folks my own age. But nowhere near enough to even take a guess. About what you said, I mean. The voting. If that's what they voted for, goddamn them to hell! Every last one."

By the time we got the Jeep back where it belonged, it was getting close to daylight.

"You don't look tired," I said to Dolly.

"Neither do you. I wish you did."

"I don't—"

"I want to go to bed, Dell. Not to sleep. To be with you. All this . . . filth. I need to get back to what love feels like, if I'm going to help you make this happen."

"I need you to rent a car," I told Swift the next morning.

"Me?"

"You. Use your credit card. I need a car to keep on investigating, and I can't have it traced back to me. I know you guys keep track of expenses, and you can take it out of the next retainer installment if you want to do it that way," I said, putting another five grand on his desk.

"I . . . I understand what you're saying. And it does make sense for all expenses to trace back to me."

And makes you even more of a big shot than you were a few hours ago, I thought. But what I said was "Would you mind taking care of that right now? I have someone I want to interview, and I want to get an early start."

He didn't mind at all.

On the drive over to the rental place, he said, "I don't mind telling you, this case is taking up just about every hour I have."

He must have felt skepticism coming off me. "I know what you must be thinking," he said. "How much work could I be doing, when my own client won't even speak to me without you there?"

I let my silence do my talking.

"Mr. Jackson, I don't mean to come off as condescending, and I know you must be working very hard yourself. But one of the unwritten rules of being a criminal-defense attorney is this: when you don't have the facts on your side, you have to use the law."

"I don't get it," I said. And I wasn't lying.

"Well, let's say, just for argument's sake, that if the DA can't prove premeditation the charge has to be downgraded to—"

"She brought the gun to school. She walked right up to the boy she wanted to kill. She shot him in the head. He died."

"I didn't mean we were going to use that as a line of defense," he said, sounding defensive as all hell himself. "That was just an example."

"All right, I get it now. There might be something in the law that can help MaryLou, no matter what the facts are."

"Exactly! Such as, if MaryLou was a victim of battered-woman syndrome, that could be a complete defense."

I listened to him explain all about this "syndrome" thing. Then I said, "So, if this Cameron Taft was MaryLou's boyfriend, and he was always beating her up . . . Say he was threatening to break her left arm, so he was holding her college scholarship hostage, the same way you just told me, about a man who kept telling his wife that if she ever squealed about beating her he'd kill her dog?"

"That's it. And that's only one of hundreds of possibilities. All I've filed with the DA's Office so far are the usual discovery motions—no point letting them have a peek at our trial strategy."

"You're driving *that* car," I said. Either a gesture of respect or a warning—up to him how he took it.

S wift didn't have any objection to spending my money. "I think a Cadillac would be just the right image," he said. "With that suit

and attaché case of yours, driving around in some econobox would
be the wrong move."

"You're the boss," I told him, taking the letter that said I was
working for him out of my inside jacket pocket, so he'd know I
wasn't mocking him.

Carolyn Kubaw MacTiever was a trim young woman, from her
workout body to a short and bouncy haircut I'd seen before in a
magazine. Dolly told me it was "efficient."

"May I help you?" she said, as if a stranger at her door was standard procedure. Maybe it was all the hotel training.

"I hope you can, Ms. MacTiever." I told her who I was working for, and I wasn't shocked that Swift's name didn't ring any bells
for her. Even when I said who he was representing, her eyes didn't
flicker.

But when I said, "That girl in the school shooting—" she interrupted me by stepping away and motioning me to come inside.
Then she pointed silently at a pale-blue egg-shaped chair. She seated
herself in the chair's mate, separated from me by a small table that
looked like a slab of geode perched on an hourglass formed from
black metal. A high-tech baby monitor stood on the surface of the
geode, as if the whole piece had been designed that way.

"We have to be quiet," she said, holding her finger to her lips.
"I just got Talia down for her nap."

I nodded agreement.

"This is about that crazy girl? The one who brought a gun to
the high school and went wild?"

"The girl's not crazy, but this is about her."

"If she wasn't crazy, why would she—?"

Showing her the photo of the black symbol on the red rect-
angle cut her breath quicker than any stranglehold.

"Them! But they're not . . . I mean, they wouldn't still be in school."

"Yes, they are, ma'am. Not the same ones you remember, but the same gang. Or club, or whatever they call themselves."

"A society," she said, as if I'd been interviewing her about some subject—any subject outside of the rapes. "Tiger Ko Khai."

"Do you know when they started?"

"Started . . . ?"

"The society. When it was formed."

"Oh. I'm pretty sure it was 2001. There was supposed to be some special significance about that, but I never knew what it was."

"You were a sophomore when it happened?"

"A junior," she said, then slapped her hand across her mouth as if to prevent more truth from spilling out.

"And you reported it to the police," I said, as if there could be no question about it.

"That same night. Actually, the next day. After midnight, I mean. But it wasn't me who reported anything—the nurse was the one who called the police."

"But they never ended up arresting anyone."

"No."

"And you knew the name of—"

"Wait! I must have been in a fog when we started talking. The baby kept me up most of the night. She's colicky, so I had to take her into the guest bedroom and lie down with her. My husband needs his sleep. He's working double shifts all the time."

"Ms. MacTiever, I apologize if I upset you."

"You didn't upset me. I . . . I thought I'd put it out of my mind forever," she whispered. "Then you come here and act like you already know all about it. But how could you? Those records are confidential."

"They are."

"Who did you say you work for?" Her voice turned suspicious. Suspicious and scared.

"Bradley Swift, Esquire, ma'am. Please feel free to call him," I said, handing her one of his business cards. "And, please, just to ease your own mind, look him up in the Yellow Pages, satisfy yourself he's an attorney, and that he's representing MaryLou McCoy in the alleged murder of one Cameron Taft."

"This one?!" she hissed, pulling a local paper from some shelf behind her chair.

I glanced at the SCHOOL SHOOTING! headline. "That's the one, yes."

"But . . . she's a star softball player, isn't she? I don't know her. I graduated in 2009. She would still have been in middle school."

"That's not the connection, ma'am. It's Tiger Ko Khai." Slipping in the name to keep her focused.

"The boy she killed—?"

"Yes. And two others that she shot."

"What do you want from me?"

I took that as the red-flare signal: the one that told us to stop working the perimeter and strike at the core. "I want you to help protect the next victims from this gang of rapists."

"Me?"

"You and another forty or so young women, yes."

"I don't understand," she said, glancing around nervously, even though the baby monitor hadn't transmitted anything but the sweet snuffly breathing of a contented infant.

"No one in that gang has ever been prosecuted for rape. You did everything right. Went by the book. But the police never even made an arrest, did they?"

"No."

"And you told them at least one of their names," I said, not spelling out the "their."

"Yes."

"That's happened more times than you could imagine. I mean,

that exact same thing. Why should the police arrest anyone when they know the DA is never going to prosecute?"

"But the nurse—the one who examined me—she told me the doctor had already told them I was . . . And they had those samples, too."

"And every time you tried to ask questions, somebody told you they were working on the case."

"Yes," she said, with a kind of dull bitterness. "After a while, all I wanted to do was get out of there."

"That's why you transferred schools?"

"The school year was nearly over. I got early admission to college, so I skipped my senior year. Nobody did me any favors; I did very well in school."

"I know. I read the papers about when you came back to this area after you graduated."

"Why should that have been in the papers? I never saw it."

"I meant when you got married. You know those society things, 'Mr. and Mrs. So-and-So, the parents of Whoever, are pleased to announce the engagement of their daughter to . . .'"

She nodded dully.

"It probably isn't every day that a hometown girl marries someone with an Ivy League degree. And the chain probably ran something, too, bragging about the caliber of personnel they have. The Cornell School of Hotel Administration is one of the most prestigious in the country, isn't it?"

"It is!"

I guessed she had gone north for college. By the time she graduated, the only job openings were things like working the front desk of a motel chain. Not as far away from a place she'd never call "home" again as she would have liked, but far enough for that "distancing" thing she tried so hard for.

I'm no psychologist, but—*you're asking this woman to open up a wound and you're still playing games with words,* I thought to myself. I didn't like myself much for doing it. So I started over. As a soldier, I'd seen "distancing" plenty of times. The combat zone might only be a klick away, but some people had to move it to another planet in their minds to keep sane.

"You think that's right?" I asked her.

"Do I think *what's* right?"

"Letting them get away with what they did. With what they still do."

"Of course I don't. But . . . I don't know who you are, and you know everything about me, don't you?"

"No, ma'am, I don't. I don't know anything about you personally; I only know that a crime was committed against you."

"My husband doesn't even know. . . ."

"Are you concerned that your name would come out? It wouldn't. That would be illegal," I said, making it up as I went along, and making myself believe it at the same time.

"Sure. Like when they don't use a victim's name in the paper, but they give away enough information that everyone would know, anyway. And the way people down there are always gossiping . . ."

People down there. "You wouldn't be a 'victim' in this case, ma'am. You'd be a witness. And you know they can't give any information about a witness. You wouldn't even be testifying in court," I said, wishing I had asked Swift some of the things I was pretending I knew.

"You don't understand. I would like to help that girl. But if my husband ever found out—"

I cut her off before she could end the sentence with "he'd kill them," or "he'd want a divorce," knowing either answer would carry its own brand of terror for her.

"I understand," I told her. "But I can promise you two things, Ms. MacTiever. One, the only thing your husband will ever know about any of this is whatever *you* decide to tell him. And that includes nothing. Nothing at all. That's not me speaking, that's the law. Two, I don't know your husband, much less how he'd react if you decided to speak with him about it. But I do know this. Your daughter, your baby girl, Talia, when she's old enough to understand, she'll also understand that her mother was a hero. A hero for protecting girls like her."

I barely noticed the single tear tracking down one cheek, but I couldn't miss seeing her jaw clench and her hands ball into fists.

"Do it for her," I said very softly as I rose to my feet and left my card next to the baby monitor—Dolly had printed up a bunch of them for me.

All I could do was hope she'd call the number on the card. Because I know how dangerous any wronged person can be if they ever get a chance to hit back.

The computer screen said:

|> If current, most likely a soldier's tattoo. More info needed.<|

By then, I *had* more info, so I typed in:

|> Outfit called Tiger Ko Khai. Probably started around year 2001. <|

"You have to rent some more office space," I told Swift.

"More space? I didn't even have my own—"

"Short-term. Just for this case. You're going to have all kinds of records and exhibits and stuff like that. You couldn't possibly store them all here."

He gave me a look. Testing the water to see if I was dismissing his work, just using him like a tool, or if I had some reason he could live with.

"I've been looking around places where they don't welcome strangers," I said. "That's why you rented the car. If the plate traces back to you, so what? You're not causing any problem for anyone. And it's appropriate for a lawyer to add on things he needs temporarily, right? I mean, for a particular case."

"That's true. But I'd feel better if I knew exactly what you've been doing."

"No, you wouldn't," I told him. I guess Patrice had been right. About my voice, I mean. The lawyer didn't say another word. He started to get up from his chair, as if he wanted to pace around the little room, but he checked himself.

"I'll get you the address soon," I said, not telling him I'd already rented the place. "And a receipt for a six-month lease."

I found seven more girls on the boss SANE nurse's list. Seven more who would talk to me, I mean. None of them had disappeared, but some were away at school, or staying with relatives, or just told me they didn't know what I was talking about.

I saved the most logical one for last. MaryLou's sister, Danielle. She was real young. Around thirteen. After spending a couple of days watching from a distance, I didn't know how I'd get close to her without sending up a danger flag. She never seemed to go anywhere alone. I guess it was because she didn't have a car—there's no public transportation here. And after what MaryLou said about their parents, I didn't think that either one would help me. Or that I could trust them, even if they said they would.

Before I did something that might backfire, I wanted to make sure MaryLou gave me everything I could possibly use.

They let me in at the jail without any problem. They even seemed apologetic that I had to walk through the metal detector.

There's a dozen ways to get a handgun inside a jail.

The easiest is four pieces of plastic. Through an X-ray, they'd look like side-support bars for my black aluminum case. You open the case, slide them out, snap them together, and just follow procedure: left hand behind the head, right hand drives the spike through the trachea.

It's a quiet death, just a little gurgling sound. Now you have a pistol—the one the dead guard was carrying.

And, if you want, a silencer. The guards all carry the same semi-autos. Even though the barrels aren't extended or threaded, there are silencers that you can push straight in. They won't hold past a single shot, but you couldn't tell that just by looking.

What you want isn't more dead guards; you use the silencer to keep the rest of them silent. That always works—only a gunsmith looks directly into a pistol barrel.

The problem with that move is, you have to run forever after you're done, even if you don't have to kill any more than the one guard. *Like Mesrine,* I thought to myself.

So it wasn't going to be me who pulled off that kind of escape. All I wanted was my Dolly. And the life we used to have. I wasn't going to risk that, even if I had to slip MaryLou enough pills to take herself away from all this . . . if she asked.

"What would I have to say to Danielle to make her trust me?"

"There's nothing you *could* say," MaryLou told me. "You're

too old. That wouldn't stop her from fucking you for money; she's done that before. But *trust* you, not a chance."

"What if your parents asked her?"

"Which one?" she half-sneered. "They're both full-time drunks now. My mother already found one of those lawyers you see on television, so now she's applying for Disability, too. Stress. I guess it's pretty hard on you when your daughter kills someone."

She closed the door on any possibility of their being any help: "That stress, you know, it must be just *so* very terrible." Her voice was venomous enough to French-kiss a cobra and drop it back into its basket, dead.

I know torture only works if you can focus on the target's fear of something that might happen if he didn't tell the truth. Pain is a waste of time. What could I possibly hold over people like Mary-Lou's parents?

But I knew something else: the promise of pleasure works better than the promise of pain.

"Your father, he'd take money to let me talk to your sister, wouldn't he?"

"He'd take the money, all right. But Danielle wouldn't do anything *he* told her to. And he's crazy enough to start whipping on her if there's money in it for him, now that I'm not around."

"He's done that before?"

"Not for a long time. I wasn't even thirteen when I got too big for him to reach for that belt. And, after that, I told him what would happen if he ever touched her again."

"What?"

"I don't—"

"What would happen to him?" I asked her, hoping she wouldn't say she'd shoot him.

"Oh. It could be almost anything. Danielle's a genius, you know. She made up a whole list for me. Wait till he passes out, then open his mouth and pour in a jar of Drano. Or sprinkle cyanide over a pizza and—"

"Where would you get cyanide?"

"Danielle said she could make some. She's the big brain, don't forget." She was whispering so offhandedly that I couldn't tell if she thought the whole idea was silly or she didn't doubt for a second that her little sister had that kind of mind.

"Your mother, then?"

"They're two of a kind, her and my father. She'd take money from anyone, but she wouldn't give you anything for it. Not anything you'd want, I mean."

"What would *Danielle* want?"

"Danielle? There's only one thing in the whole world she wants: to be a movie star. She's smart enough to get into any college, but I know she's going to head straight out to Hollywood the second she's old enough. So, unless you can make her believe you're a talent scout, forget it."

I guess I waited too long. When you interrupt the rhythm, whoever you're milking for information has time to ask questions. The next words out of MaryLou's mouth were "What do you need to speak to Danielle for, anyway?"

Damn! "Uh, we're going to make a motion to have you examined by a specialist."

"What kind of specialist?"

"We're not sure yet. Look, I know you're not going to plead insanity, okay? But if the DA thinks you might be going down that road, we can get a much better deal. The lawyer says the whole office is scared to death of actually trying a case."

"Even with the school's videotape and the gun and—"

"MaryLou, if you pulled out another pistol and shot the judge during the first trial, that office would still be afraid of the *second* trial."

She kind of barked a laugh. Then she looked at my eyes as if staring so hard would burn away everything but the truth. "That makes sense to me, I guess. For me, I'm saying. That's what the other girls in here call this: 'the Game.' There isn't a single one who expects to have a trial. It comes down to what you've got to bargain with. But that's not me. So a fake-out is fine, but I'm not telling anyone I'm crazy."

"Of course not. But that's why we have to interview Danielle, and your parents, too. The more the DA thinks we're building some kind of special defense, the more he'll give away."

Maybe Swift wasn't any great shakes as a lawyer, but he knew all about the local system. And when a guy like him says the whole system is built on not taking cases to trial, I believe it.

I hated myself for the hope I saw spring into MaryLou's eyes. She could do a few years and still have a career as a pitcher. If they let football players off with a warning on a dorm rape, and let basketball players slide on DUIs, why not?

"Would I have to testify?" she asked me.

"I don't think so. But I don't know for sure. Not yet, anyway. You know how these things go, right? If our expert is much stronger than theirs, that'll scare the hell out of them. It's like a softball game—the team could be just average, but a killer pitcher could get them to State."

"I guess that's me, all right." She bitter-laughed. "A killer pitcher."

|> For Chinese, year 2001 is Year of the Snake. Tiger testicles *highly* prized in Japan; China now growing and harvesting its own tigers for such sales. Ko Khai is island in south Thailand close to Malaysia, approx. 460–470 KM from Bangkok. Illegal to stay there overnight, allegedly because it is nature preserve. <|

After that info, the map was easy to draw. Kid enlists at seventeen, takes R&R in Bangkok, just like the older guys tell him. After the "Quick time, okay, soldier?" whore, he walks into one of the little tattoo stalls scattered throughout the red-light district. He's looking for something cool and Japanese, like any kid who quotes comic books the way some do the Dalai Lama.

And the Thai tattoo artist, who knew why any *farang* would wander into *his* shop, must have had that chop displayed on his wall. He'd tell anyone who gave it a second look that it stood for "Tiger Ko Khai" and claim that it meant "Dangerous Dragon" in Japanese.

That same kid had come back to this place, and started the not-really-a-secret society.

If he mustered out somewhere around 2001, he would have been in his early twenties, the perfect time to get teenage punks excited about forming a branch of "Tiger Ko Khai."

That tattoo was the only cred the "combat vet" would need. Even teens would know the biker gangs don't let you ink up unless you're in for real. And for life. Didn't it say so on TV? So the tattoo would be proof enough that he'd been granted authority to form a chapter.

Whoever it was had known exactly the gap to fill: someplace between lightweight skinhead and no-pride whigger. The school had both, and each group had girls. So who better to instruct them in the strategy and tactics of gang rape than a punk who could tell them war stories from a real war?

Still, it was just a theory, so I dipped into my credit again. The cracker once said he owed me his life. I didn't know how to put a value on that, but I figured his poking around various "secure" sites on my behalf wouldn't be stretching it too far.

|> Need list: served in military and returned to this area . . . county, not city . . . discharged somewhere around 2000. Current address, phone, and any other info. <|

I went over to Swift's office to give him a copy of the six-month lease I had signed as his "authorized agent" and a spare key to the place. I'd found just what I wanted: a bare room on the second floor in a cheap-to-build structure, on a main street that had "For Rent" signs in just about every storefront window. Which is probably why the "premium office space" had been vacant for more than a year. And why the number I called got me a promise to meet there in an hour.

I'd told the rental lady—a pinch-faced woman with a lemon-sucking smile—that the three-hundred-square-foot unit at the back of the building would be fine, as long as the parking space behind it was included. She was chicken-necking at every word I said—the place was such an overpriced dump that the prospect of finding a tenant got her all excited.

I told her that I'd left my driver's license at home, adding, "Same place I must have left my head," so she could bend herself into accepting my explanation of why she should make the lease out to "Bradley L. Swift, Attorney at Law."

"That's not me," I told her. "I only work for him. He's got some big case going, so he has to have temporary office space to store all the files and stuff."

The rental lady was saying something about this being an unorthodox situation, when I interrupted her with an explanation that would stroke her soft spot again.

"Your ad said 'temporary,' but Mr. Swift said to tell you that a case like this could go for years, or be over just like *this*!" I said, snapping my fingers and putting three thousand in cash on her desk with the same hand. "That's why he wants to pay six months in advance, provided he can renew on the same terms if he gives you thirty days' notice."

I pulled out a notebook, pretended to be checking it over to see if I had missed something, but that charade was unnecessary—the rental agent hadn't taken her eyes off the cash.

It's a rough market, I thought to myself. *She probably owns the place. A real-estate broker who gambled that the "individual office units" concept would turn that firetrap into a gold mine. For her, the cash was proof that she hadn't tricked herself the way she did her clients.*

A thin blue thread was weaving inside my mind, twisting itself into an empty frame. I knew that frame wouldn't fill until my mind was ready for it.

The first time that happened, the thread frame filled in a split second: a blood-spattered wall, freezing me in place. I calmed myself down and started to scan the area. I didn't see the Claymore until I looked down at my own boots. It was one of the new ones, the kind that shoot steel balls at a preset angle, designed especially for infantry kills. Packed with C4, not the old-style TNT. One more step and six men would have turned into body parts.

The blue thread frame told me that I had something. More than an "idea," a solution of some kind. Concentrating wouldn't help. I knew I couldn't force a solution—the frame would fill in its own good time.

So I went back to work.

"Late afternoon, she'll be hanging out at the skateboard park," Dolly had told me the next morning. "I wouldn't swat a fly, much less a child's bottom, but, Dell, I swear I can understand why Mary-Lou slapped her sister's face that time."

"You don't get raccoon eyes from a slap."

"She didn't use her pitching hand," Dolly said, as if that explained everything.

Something was missing. Something . . . Then it came to me. The more I could get Dolly helping, the more she'd be able to get information from those girls.

"What would I have to do to convince a girl that I was a talent scout from Hollywood?"

"*You?!*" Dolly laughed so hard her eyes got teary.

"Me" is all I said, when she finally stopped.

"Dell . . ."

"MaryLou told me that the only thing in the world Danielle cares about is being a movie star. I'm not thinking about how a talent scout would *look,* but what he'd *know,* okay?"

"You mean, like, names to drop, stuff like that?"

"No. Too easy to check. But I need to *sound* like I know people. And movies, I need to know about them, too."

"Give me a few hours. Some of the girls will be here by then, and I'll dig up a lot before they even show up. You don't have to leave until around four."

The rented Cadillac wasn't as big as I'd expected, and its ground-fog paint job made it look even smaller from the outside. What I also didn't expect was how quick it was, and how well it handled.

I found Danielle right where Dolly said she'd be, wearing a T-shirt long enough to make you wonder if there was anything beneath it. There was still enough sunlight to take any mystery out of the question, and the ridiculous orange spike heels she was prancing around in would get even the girls in the red-light district of Marseilles pointing at her and screaming, *"Salope!"*

Even if Danielle hadn't been putting on such a show, none of the skateboarders would have glanced at me twice. I couldn't guess at their social class. They all seemed to be wearing the same kind of uniform: short-sleeved T-shirts advertising energy drinks, and khaki pants hacked off to make shorts.

I parked the Caddy where they could all see it, and walked down a slight slope of grass. By the time I got close to the configured concrete of the skateboard park, they were all in a bunch, watching the stranger approach.

Three of them broke off from the crowd. I guess I wasn't supposed to see them slip away past a squat brick building—probably public restrooms—and disappear. I didn't care why they were taking off—by then, Danielle had wiggled her way to the front of the pack.

I pointed at her, and made a "come here" gesture. Most girls her age would have backed away, but Danielle swivel-hipped up to me as if I was expected.

When I handed her one of the business cards Dolly had printed up for me, she took it without a word.

The card was a real work of art: a lot of red at the top, a much smaller piece of black at the bottom, with a wide white slash running through them at a sharp angle. Within that slash, in fancy-font black letters:

Patrice Laveque
Arquette Aland Film Productions, Inc.
202 N. Robertson Blvd. · Hollywood, CA 90048

In the red space at the top, phone and fax in the (213) area code, plus the obligatory, can't-be-real-without-one e-mail address: PLaveque@aafpi.com.

And in the little bit of white at the bottom:

www.aafpi.com

Dolly had told me the street address was in the right area, but it didn't actually exist, the phone had the right area code, and the number would be answered by a woman with a French accent— *"Moi, non?"*

And she had found out from one of the girls that Danielle had actually been in a school play. There was even a YouTube video of it.

"But that website, I'm not sure. I checked, and there's no such address owned by anyone, but putting one up—"

"I can get that done," I assured her.

Danielle held on to the heavy-stock card like it was a holy talisman, turning it over and over in her hands. The back replicated the front—no writing, just the colors, making it look as if each band had flowed onto the other side.

"Get the fuck away!" Danielle told one of the boarders who moved closer to us, his fists balled in some kind of sad little protective gesture. "This is business."

When I turned away and walked toward the Cadillac, she followed like an obedient lamb.

I opened the door for her. She slid in and crossed her legs so that her T-shirt pulled up just far enough. The kind of maneuver she must have practiced with the same intensity with which we had learned to field-strip our weapons. For me then, and for her now, our lives depended on learning to do some things with our eyes closed.

"Is there someplace in this . . . town where I might talk with you?" I asked, letting a French accent into my voice. I didn't have to be an actor to do that.

"I'll show you," Danielle said. "Just go straight ahead and turn left at the dead-end."

I did that. We ended up facing the ocean, without even a café in sight.

"This?"

"Yes. It's the only place where we'll have any privacy. You probably don't realize how people in tiny little places like to gossip."

"That may be correct. I have spent my entire life in . . . I am not sure how to say in English, but places like Paris, London, New York, Los Angeles," I replied, making sure I hit "Paris" with a native's pronunciation. "You have my card. My assignment is to get some unenhanced tape of you."

"Tape of me doing what?"

"Essentially, speaking. Acting, that is. You may pick any role you like, from any current film you have seen. In fact, if there is some role in such a film you fancy, we can get you the script easily enough."

"Why me?"

"To be truthful, I do not know. My office was contacted by a director we have engaged on pay-or-play in anticipation of acquiring a certain property. When the owner of the property broke his word and took the material elsewhere, we found another screenplay we rather liked. However, we are, of necessity, on a much tighter schedule now. We were shown footage of you in what appeared to be a school play," I said, spraying the last two words with a light coat of distaste. "Our researchers brought me here. To a place which appears to have no hotels."

"Oh, we do!" she assured me. "It's not like Beverly Hills, but it overlooks the bay, and it's really quite nice."

"I am sure. Ah, it does not matter. Give me the name, please."

She did. I took a wallet-sized cell out of my jacket, hit a speed-dial number.

"I need a suite for tonight at the . . . What was that again?" I asked Danielle. "Did you hear that?" I asked the person on the other end. "*Bon.* Now, I want—Miss Rontempe, this *is* what a personal assistant does—at least one suite, two if I can get them adjoining, and I want to be able to check in within two hours, so we still have some natural light if we need it. Make sure the direct billing covers everything; I have no time to waste with some desk clerk."

I slapped my phone closed in an annoyed gesture. Then I turned to Danielle:

"You are, what, eighteen, nineteen years?"

"Nineteen," she answered, without breaking stride.

"Very well. You will not need parental permission to sign a contract, then. Nevertheless, please feel free to bring a parent or guardian with you. Or any adult you wish. However, I must insist they remain in the adjacent suite while I am getting you on tape."

"I don't need any—"

"I did not ask what you needed," I said, allowing a slight edge of annoyance to surface. "I merely sought to assure you that you are taking no risk. I requested adjoining suites because some young actresses prefer their parents or whoever accompanies them not to be directly present during a screen test, but would want them close by."

"Oh, I'm sorry. I thought a screen test was—"

"Yes, I am sure. That was before all the studios went to digital format. Now all we need is some ten-minute snapshot—you will either be instantly right for the role we have in mind or you will not, *comprenez-vous?*"

She nodded vigorously, truly terrified she might say the wrong thing . . . whatever that might be.

"Do you have a role you feel you could present yourself in?"

"Well, I was thinking of, maybe, *Chocolate Winter.*"

"*Bon.* What role?"

"Rachel Razon?"

I grabbed the phone again and ordered my hapless personal assistant to have a dozen or so pages of that script faxed to the hotel Danielle had told me about. "I will need sides in which Miss Razon had a good number of lines." Then I hung up on her again.

"We do not have much time," I told Danielle, glancing at a

ridiculously oversized bootleg copy of what would have been a very expensive wristwatch. "Would seven be satisfactory to you?"

"Sure!"

"Very well. Where shall I take you now? I know you will want to change your clothes before—"

"For sure! I mean, I just put this on as a joke. There's this guy who has an insane crush on me, and we wanted to gaff him."

I let a slight shadow of disapproval cross my face. "The address, please?"

"Oh, I don't need a ride. I live just down the beach from here. It's easier for me to walk."

While Dolly was printing out some pages from whatever movie Danielle had yammered about, I went downstairs and checked. Either the task had been simple or the cracker had really jumped on the job:

|> 8 probables. 4 still hospitalized or must return to VA daily, 3 physical, 1 psychiatric. 2 KIA. 1 serving a 12-year sentence, manslaughter, imposed 01, but crime occurred 99. Remaining: Ryan Teller. No citations. Discharged OTH. "Personality Disorder," which *could* be PTSD, common military tactic first used for Gulf vets. Driver license shows address that cannot still be correct—entire area burned in a forest fire in 04. 3 arrests, 2 in 05, 1 in 06. Charges dismissed on all but 06. DUI crash. Driver of other car died at scene. Subject sentenced to 5 years probation. Civil suit filed. Not contested by subject; judgment of US$4.5 million remains outstanding. No land-line or cell account under his name. No indication of employment. No bank accounts. Any asset listed in subject's name would be seized by judgment-holder.

Any employment income would be subject to garnishment. No interest by FBI or CIA. Assumed to be living with some woman, all bills in her name, and working off-the-books job. Note: those assumptions from FBI informant files, so accuracy not considered highest quality. <|

"I have to work this alone," I told Dolly. "She's never seen me, but she could have seen you."

"I got all the stuff you asked for. And the reservations have already been made. But you can't run that videocam by yourself, Dell. Even with the tripod."

"Yeah, I can, honey. Don't fuss. I'll be back in a few hours."

"This is just a yes-or-no question, Franklin. Will you do something to help MaryLou?"

"Yes!"

I didn't expect him to ask for details. "Okay," I told him. "All you have to do is listen. You're going to be in a hotel room. Sitting on one side of a wall. Danielle, MaryLou's little sister, she's going to be on the other side of that same wall. She'll be recorded, but she might later lie and claim she never said anything. Then you'd have to go to court and tell what she *actually* said. You wouldn't have to tell anything but the truth. Can you do that?"

"Sure!"

"There's also a bunch of equipment we have to set up. Some of it's pretty heavy. Probably not for you, but it would be for me if I had to do it myself."

"I can move stuff."

"I know you can, Franklin. And MaryLou said she knew I could count on you, too."

He was still beaming when I pulled away, telling him I'd be back in an hour.

The hotel's security system consisted of a peephole in the door. It was only two stories high, with each unit in duplex style, so renting two adjoining "suites" gave us a total of four quadrants of controlled space.

The view from the terrace overlooking the bay was drab. Opening the sliding glass doors cured me of ever doing that again—dead fish don't do any better in intense sunlight than human corpses, and the blazing ball was taking its own sweet time dropping below the Pacific horizon.

We were a little pressed for time—I'd told Danielle the test was at seven, and I figured she'd be early. But Franklin took all the tension away by lifting ridiculous amounts of weight like they were cartons of bubble-wrap. We had all the equipment hooked up, tested, and running, with Franklin installed on his side of the second-story wall, still with a good half-hour to spare.

She was about ten minutes early, her knock confident and assured. It didn't surprise me that she'd come alone.

This time she was dressed in a black jersey V-neck sheath, with a short skirt that was just on the right side of decorous, and matching pumps that she handled a lot better than those stripper-spikes she'd worn to the skateboard park.

By then, she would have checked out www.aafpi.com and been shocked by the truly impressive list of films with which the bogus company had been "associated," as well as the "talent" it had both discovered and developed, never mind the overseas representation of stars whose names Dolly assured me *any* teenage girl would recognize.

Danielle could only access the site by using the "private password" I'd written on the back of my business card. My expert had answered my request with an artist's contempt:

|> If satisfied with template, provide filler. If secure certificate required, 3 minutes after receipt. If not, 2 minutes. <|

Since no one else would know of the site's existence, and it was way too early for it to be picked up on any random search, it would already be either overloaded or one-time-accessed, depending on Danielle's personality.

I ushered Danielle into the suite, asked her to have a seat while I made some final adjustments. If Franklin couldn't hear us both by ten after seven, he would thump on the wall. I hoped that didn't happen, because then I'd have to come up with a good excuse to leave for a few minutes. Besides, I wasn't sure these walls would hold Franklin's idea of a "thump."

I started playing my role immediately, with "I would offer you a drink, but . . ."

"Oh, that's no problem," she assured me.

"Perhaps not for you," I said, with that touch of asperity the French specialize in. *Pour moi, servir de l'alcool à un mineur est inacceptable.*

"Sure. I mean, I party—I mean, drink—sometimes, but I don't, like, *need* one. I just meant I can be sociable if the occasion calls for it."

Remember! I admonished myself. *Don't let the outfit fool you. You're not just dealing with some slutty little girl here—she's got a heavyweight IQ.*

"Bon," I said, handing her the printed-out pages from *Chocolate Winter.* "Now, if you will just—"

The incoming call on my cell came exactly on time.

"No," I told my personal assistant, "that is *not* acceptable. Do you have any idea how difficult it is to run all over the country to these godforsaken places every time A.A. hears some rumor about which actress is going to be the next big thing?"

I listened as my personal assistant whispered something Danielle couldn't pick up even if her ears had been shotgun microphones.

"Ah! Wait, I will ask."

I turned to Danielle. "Your full name is . . . ?"

"Danielle. Only I spell it 'Danyelle.' That way, you can split it into two names if that works better, see?"

"Yes. Your full name, please."

"Danielle Denise McCoy," she said, looking more subdued by the second.

"Oui," I said into the phone. "It is as you say."

"Is anything—?" Danielle started to say, but snapped her jaw closed so quickly I could hear the click when I held up my hand for silence.

"*This* is his latest high-concept?" I said into the phone.

Silence.

"Very well," I said. Then turned to Danielle. "Do you have an agent?"

"I . . . Not now, I don't."

"Oh," I said, pretending I'd been taken in by the implication that her last agent had proved himself unsatisfactory in some way.

I went back to the phone. "I was specifically told that this was not a *vérité* project." Pause. "Yes, I do realize that the company is capable of more than— Ah, never mind. I will present it to *la jeune fille.* If she agrees, I will call back when the test is complete and we have examined the raw footage. If she does not, I will call, and you can book me"—glancing at my silly wristwatch—"on the latest flight to LAX. I am not going to spend a night at some airport hotel ever again."

I slapped the phone closed. Either Danielle was getting more anxious by the second, or she was a better actress than even she thought she was.

"Your sister is MaryLou McCoy?"

"Yes, but—"

"You do understand that she is going to be quite famous. Or, I should say, 'infamous.'"

"I guess so."

"Well, the gifted *artiste* who runs our company is convinced that a documentary of the case, from start to finish, would be very well received. And, more important, we want to be in a position where any fictionalized version would have the same focal point."

When she gave me a doe-eyed look, I changed tone, talking down to her, as if I was disappointed with her lack of knowledge of "the industry."

"You remember *Monster,* yes?" I said, grateful for Dolly's skillful coaching. ("Remember, honey. When it doubt, just act as snotty and superior as you can pull off. The French accent will be a help there.") "It only won Charlize Theron an Oscar. But there were several other so-called docudramas which *preceded* it. One had Park Overall—who, frankly, is a more gifted actress than Ms. Theron—fittingly playing the more difficult role of Wuornos's girlfriend, Tyria Moore. But the sole *actual* documentary provided the impetus for a big-budget effort. I refer to Nick Broomfield's work, *Aileen Wuornos: The Selling of a Serial Killer,* which preceded the film by a good ten years!

"In any event, the concept—the concept as of ten minutes ago"—I half-sneered—"is now to have you star in the docu, and then be the logical candidate for the same role in the more highly stylized 'based on' version. If we move quickly enough, then we won't have to pay some hack writer for the rights to some useless book. And, be assured, *they* will be flocking to your sister's trial like pigs to a trough."

"But I'm not—"

"You don't have to be prepared for *reality,* Ms. McCoy. Of course, you would first have to play your sister in the docu—we can hardly expect access to some prison. Fortunately, I am told they are not allowing cameras in the courtroom, so we could quite easily work with the transcript. That is, unless she simply pleads guilty. Should that happen, we could write our own ending. They do have the death penalty in this state, I believe?"

"I . . . I think so. I never really thought about it. I mean, Mary-Lou . . ." Her voice trailed off as she burst into sobs. Whatever her future held, it wasn't going to be a screen career—porn stars faked orgasms better than this nasty little piece of work faked caring whether her sister lived or died.

"Well, think about it *now,*" I said, sharply. "If Wuornos had not been executed, the film would never have gotten the buzz it did. That 'first female serial killer' nonsense wouldn't have mattered—nobody believed her story, anyway, so it had neither the sympathy factor nor the Hannibal Lecter thing going for it."

"Mr. . . . Laveque."

"What?" I snapped, impatient to get started on the "screen test."

"Age-wise, MaryLou's actually older than me. I'm so much more intelligent than she is that everyone thinks I'm the older one . . . but I'm not."

"How old *are* you?" I asked, dropping the temperature of my voice.

"Fourteen," she practically squeaked out.

"Mon Dieu!" I threw up my hands. "What is next? Surely, you realize you cannot sign a contract without your parents' consent."

"Oh, that'll be no problem. And you have to admit, you thought I was nineteen, like I told you I was."

"I would have believed even older, that is true."

I took a tiny airplane-sized bottle of Cognac from my fancy aluminum case and slugged it down in one gulp. Easy enough to do when it's darkened Gatorade. I hit "speed dial" again, tapping my fingers as it rang at the other end.

"Well, you can tell A.A. that this time I've got a little surprise for *him*. This girl, yes, she is the sister of that MaryLou McCoy. But she is not an *older* sister, she is the younger of the two." (Pause.) "Believe me, she looks old enough to play her sister, and I am assured that full parental consent"—looking hard at Danielle as I spoke—"will be forthcoming, notarized and witnessed."

I paused, as if listening. Then: "*So?* So we would be the only ones with access to the family, the early years, the growing up, the reason why that young lady went berserk that day—everything! What is *that* worth?"

I paused again. Then: "Yes, I thought as much. Very well, we are going ahead now. No matter what the final reason, getting this young woman on tape does not require parental consent—this is hardly some Traci Lords scenario—and if she comes across well, we *must* be first to sign her. Others will have the same idea, and we cannot bind her to an exclusive contract without binding ourselves financially. We must see, and we must see *now*. The camera will either love her, or . . ."

I slapped the phone closed again, and moved behind the tripod.

That last "or . . ." had the girl almost paralyzed with fear. She looked at me as if I was holding a Death Row reprieve in my hands. I didn't even bother to ask if she was ready. Just said, "We start now, yes?"

When she nodded gratefully, I took my shot.

"Danielle, look at the camera, please."
She tried.

"Look *only* at the camera! The lens is the eye. The eye sees only what you show it. The eye is a lie detector. This is why the profession is called 'acting.' You must act in the sense that you are not, in reality, what you are showing the camera. If the director needs you to be a nun, you must be a nun. If a whore, you must be a whore. Do you understand?"

"Yes. I—"

"Je ne veux pas de discours! Essaye encore: est-ce que tu comprends?"

"Oui."

"Parfait. Now, please throw away that useless script you are holding."

She flicked her wrist and the script pages went flying about the room.

"Did I tell you to look at the pages?"

"No. But—"

"There is no 'but.' There *are* no script pages. They are not merely tossed aside, they are gone. They do not exist. *You* do not exist. Only what the eye of the camera sees exists. Nothing else. *Comprenez-vous?"*

"Oui. Je parle français. Pas comme une française, bien sûr, mais j'ai étudié la langue pendant deux ans et j'ai toujours d'excellentes notes. . . ."

I threw up my hands, as if asking the gods to help me with an impossible task. *"Je parle français.* How very nice for you. Perhaps it will help you to win a scholarship someday. Is that what you want?"

"No, no. I'm . . . sorry. I'm just so—"

I glanced at my wristwatch. Not just to tell her that my time was precious, but to remind myself that I had to be as perfectly fake as that watch to make this work. One shot, one kill. Anything less would be leaving the target alive long enough to sound a warning.

"I do not want to hear 'sorry.' I do not want to hear anything. I want you to be what I tell you to be. I tell you; you tell the camera. If you cannot do this, you are useless to me. Do not tell me that you 'understand' again. *Show* me."

I stepped away from the camera. "Do not look at me. The camera is all. The eye of the camera must see truth. It doesn't matter if that truth is a lie—the audience must believe you. If you can do that, you can be all you wish to be. You have the looks, the voice, even the posture of an actress. But the camera is the ultimate judge. Now, look at that eye!"

She did.

"Remember, you are going to be two people. Two different people. You know what method acting is, yes?"

She nodded, but her eyes never left the camera.

"So, then, we start at the end. You start by being you. If you can do that, you can then become your sister. Even if there is no resemblance, even if your sister doesn't look a thing like you, it does not matter. That is acting. The method demands we reach inside ourselves and take out some truth, yes? Then we use that truth to make a beautiful lie. A beautiful lie is a *believable* lie. Acting is no more than that. Great acting, I mean. Not some silly teenager being cute—a *woman,* with the strength, the power, the range of a woman.

"When you are ready to try, take the deepest breath you can. Breathe only through your nose. Hold that breath until you *are* whatever you are supposed to be. When that breath comes out, a tiny red dot will show on the front of the camera. You do not look at this light. You look only to the eye. *Through* the eye.

"Initially, you are going to be yourself. The sister of the girl who went insane in school. I will be asking you questions, as if I am a police officer. Not in a uniform, a detective. When you answer, you answer as you—you, Danielle—would. If you can do this, if you can bring Danielle to life for the camera, then we can try the second test."

She nodded, eyes still glued to the camera.

"I have no time to teach you to be an actress. Either you are one already, or you are not. This is the only direction you will get: be yourself! If you want to move, if you want to cry, if you want to be seductive, that can all still be you. But do *not* be what you yourself are not—it is not yet time for that.

"So! Now you are to forget the camera. You may look wherever you wish to, whatever feels right for the role. When you are ready, you nod. Nothing more. Then you breathe as I told you. When you let that breath out, there is nothing left in you but Danielle."

She nodded so quickly I almost missed it.

I took out my latest-model cell phone, opened it, and pushed a button; a robotic voice said, "Disengaged." That same button activated the tape recorder on Franklin's side of the wall.

Danielle took a breath so deep her breasts threatened the fabric of her dress. When she expelled the lies, all that was left was herself.

I nodded in satisfaction.

"Danielle," I said, all trace of French gone from my voice, "my name is Detective Dautrine. I understand you must still be in shock from what . . . from what you have been told. But we need some answers. The parents of the young men your sister shot need answers. Will you help us?"

She clasped her hands between her breasts, like a whore saying a prayer.

"Yes. I . . . I don't know how this could even be happening."

"All right. Now, tell me, the dead boy was—" I paused and mimed consulting a notebook. "—Cameron Taft. Your sister fired at such close range that our working assumption is he was her intended target. Can you think of any reason why your sister might have wanted to kill him, particularly?"

"It's kind of complicated. I mean, I can think of a reason, but you'd have to understand the whole picture for it to make sense."

"I've got all the time you need, Danielle. Do you want some water?" I said, pointing to the minibar.

She licked her lips as if testing them for dryness. "No," she said, "I'm fine."

I sure am played inside my head. *And I'm making damn sure you see it.*

"Start wherever you feel comfortable," I told her.

She wiggled in her chair, as if getting as comfortable as possible under the circumstances.

What's next, a striptease?

Satisfied that she had called sufficient attention to her assets, Danielle said, "I'm sure you've heard of the Tiger Ko Khai Society?"

"Pretend that I haven't. The more facts we have, the more we can fill in the picture."

"Well, it's like a society. A very exclusive society. Every boy in school wants to be a member, but they only pick a few each year."

"Is it only for athletes, or—"

"No, no. None of that silly school stuff. It's . . . Well, the only way I know how to put it is that it's for the coolest kids. It doesn't matter if you're a football player, or get straight A's, or what kind of car you drive, or how you dress. What you need, it's a special . . . quality, I guess you'd call it."

"Can you think of what that might be?"

"It's different for each boy. And I'm not a boy"—*in case you haven't noticed. Christ!*—"so I couldn't really be more specific. I don't actually know how they pick the boys they do."

"Do they wear any kind of identification? I mean, do they distinguish themselves by the way they appear?"

"Well, except for the jackets . . ."

"Tell me about the jackets."

"They're silk. Fine silk. Black, with dark-red raglan sleeves."

"Raglan?"

"Like those varsity jackets. The sleeves go all the way to the neck."

"So—no collars?"

"No, they do have collars, leather ones. On the left sleeve, there's a patch. A black patch. Inside the patch, there's Japanese writing, in red."

"That sounds expensive."

"Oh, they are."

"So only the rich kids—?"

"No, that doesn't matter. They have boys who don't have a dime to their names. I don't know how they afford their jackets. But I think, maybe, you don't buy your jacket—it's, like, awarded to you."

"That's interesting. Do you know what the writing stands for?"

"I think it's just Japanese for 'tiger.' "

"I didn't think they had tigers in Japan."

"It's not the animal; it's the spirit."

"Like school spirit?"

"No-oh," she said, smirking. "This is an international society. They have chapters all over the world."

"What do they do?"

"Do?"

"Well, any club—"

"Society," she interrupted to correct me.

"All right, society. There must be more to it than wearing fancy jackets."

"There is. But, like I said, I'm not a boy, so I don't know anything about what they do."

"Couldn't one of them tell you?"

"Oh, they wouldn't do that. That would be . . . just wrong. That's something only for members to know."

"All right, we know something about the boy who was killed. But why him in particular? You're saying it couldn't have anything to do with their . . . society, is that correct?"

"I'm *not* saying that. I'm saying I don't know."

"MaryLou is your sister. Your big sister. Sisters are sometimes very close, so perhaps she confided in you?"

"In me? Forget that! MaryLou was this star softball player, but she looks like a lumberjack. And she's gay. So we'd never talk about anything to do with boys. The only one she liked was this retard, Bluto."

"Bluto?"

"Well, his real name is Franklin, I think. He's this huge dummy. The only reason he got through school is that he could play football."

"Athletics are a big thing at your school?"

"Of course. But 'big' and 'cool' aren't exactly synonyms."

I'm not just sexy as hell, I'm smart, too.

"You mean 'cool' in the way this society is?"

"Exactly."

"Are you saying that your sister was one of those . . . uh . . . women who hate men?"

"No. MaryLou only cared about her stupid softball. The reason she killed Cameron is because her jealousy just went all out of control."

"Jealousy?"

"Of me," Danielle said, as though stating the blatantly obvious.

"Well, you're certainly a very pretty young lady. And I know you got top grades in school. I guess I could see your sister being jealous of those things, maybe. But why kill this Cameron boy? What would he have to do with jealousy?"

"Tiger Ko Khai is the most special group in school. And Cam wasn't just a member, he was the leader." She paused for a dramatic couple of seconds. "And he was my boyfriend."

"I didn't know that."

"Nobody would know that. Even in school. That's one of their rules. They don't 'go steady,' or give girls their school rings or letterman's jackets. That's all kid stuff. But MaryLou, she knew."

"Because she was your sister."

"Of course. We have a small house, and it's impossible to hide anything."

"Still . . ."

"Oh, there's no question about it," Danielle said, in a voice that matched her words. "Last year, she even beat me up for seeing him."

"Beat you up . . . ?"

"I mean, beat the crap out of me! I had to go to school with such a messed-up face that they even called CPS on my parents."

"Did CPS find out the reason your sister—"

"CPS didn't find out anything. I didn't tell them, even though I should have. You have no idea how mean MaryLou can be. Why mess up my face unless she wanted me to look as ugly as she is? There's plenty of other places she could have hit me. I mean, where the marks wouldn't show."

"She wanted people at school to see the marks?"

"Absolutely."

"That does sound like jealousy, Danielle. But it's still a long way short of murder."

"Well . . . she wasn't going to kill *me*. And she sure couldn't boss Cameron around. She told me that she was going to break us up—me and Cameron—one way or the other. And . . . and she did just that, didn't she?" Danielle said, bursting into uncontrollable sobbing.

Maybe she was a better actress than I thought.

I held up my hand, palm-out, to signal that the audition was over.

Danielle went into the bathroom, leaving the door open slightly. Probably fixing her face, but wanting to make sure she could hear anything I might say.

I pushed the phone's button, then hit "speed dial" for my personal assistant, cutting out the audio at Franklin's end by doing so.

"Frankly, I think she'd be perfect. I hate to admit it, but when A.A.'s instinct is right, it's *really* right. Even if she can't nail the older sister's part, it really doesn't matter."

Pause, as I pretended to listen. Then: "*Pourquoi?* Well, for one thing, this girl's a real beauty. I mean, *gorgeous*. And her sister is apparently twice her size and . . . well, let's say 'unattractive' would be a compliment to her. If we're going to docudram this one, the two-roles thing might be too much to pull off."

I paused, then said, *"Non, cela ne fonctionnerait pas non plus; elle n'est pas bâtie comme un footballeur, si vous voyez ce que je veux dire. Plutôt que la mettre dans une position absurde, il serait préférable qu'on se préoccupe de son engagement. Je veux dire par là que c'est une actrice. Non, je ne sais pas avec qui elle a étudié, mais c'est clair qu'elle connaît son métier. Je vais prendre le dernier avion comme prévu. Ne dites rien à A.A. Pas un mot! Je veux voir sa tête quand il visionnera les essais."*

Deliberately switching to rapid-fire French, so Danielle supposedly would not understand that I was saying how we *had* to sign this prize. And that I couldn't wait to see the look on A.A.'s face when he saw this footage.

Pause. "That will not be a problem. Yes, she is underage, but her parents are going to sign anything we put in front of them. Yes, yes, I know. But we can always put some financial incentive next to the contract when we ask them to sign."

When Danielle came out, her face was scrubbed all the way down to innocent.

"Did I do okay?"

"You actually . . . well, this is how 'okay' you did, Danielle. If you can manage to keep this secret for another several weeks, you are going to be a very happy young lady. Will you trust me on that?"

"Of course. I've got really good instincts about men, and I can tell you're someone I can trust. I hope we'll be . . . friends, no matter what happens."

"Well, given my position at the studio, I suspect we will be seeing a lot of each other. But not here."

"I guess this hotel isn't anywhere near what you're used to."

"Hotel? No, I mean L.A. Because, as I said, if my instincts are correct, that will be your new address by the time school starts in the fall."

"Really?! But what about the other test? Don't you have to—?"

"The other test would be . . . superfluous. It is now clear to me that you could not play both roles. As you pointed out yourself, in fact."

"Oh."

"May I drive you home? It's rather late, and I didn't see a cab stand anywhere when we checked in."

"Uh . . . well, sure. Can you take me to the same place you did last time? Like I said, walking from there is actually easier."

"Very well," I said, pushing the button on my phone that would send audio to Franklin. "I'll take you home and then come back and load the equipment. It should not take more than a few minutes."

I don't know whether Danielle was eager to get on the phone and tell her friends how she'd just been discovered—which is why we'd decided to leave the website in place for now—or whether she was crafty enough to keep it to herself.

Whichever path she chose, we had it covered.

When I got back to Franklin's suite, the giant was holding his huge head in his meat-hook hands, not ashamed of the tears on his face when he lifted it to respond to my "You okay?"

"She hates her own sister," Franklin said, his voice damaged by the sadness of deep pain. "And she's a big liar, too."

"That's right, Franklin. Now do you see what I meant when I told you that you could help MaryLou?"

"I . . . No." His face flushed. "I know I'm stupid, okay? But I

can't . . . I can't see what . . . I can't see how I can help MaryLou,
like you said I could."

"That's my fault," I assured him. "Look, you heard Danielle
tell lies, right?"

"I sure did."

"So you could swear she's a liar—stand up in court and swear
it—couldn't you?"

"Sure! Sure, I could."

"That's all we need, son. That might be enough to get Mary-
Lou off, right there."

"But . . ."

"What, Franklin?"

"She did . . . I mean, MaryLou shot those guys, right?"

"Yeah. But it's not so much *what* she did as *why* she did it."

"I'm . . . sorry."

I knew what he was really saying. And the need to find a way
to explain what I'd just told Franklin sliced through the mist in my
mind like a surgeon's scalpel seeking a tumor. It hit me so hard I
had to steady my own breathing.

"Danielle's a liar, right?"

"Right."

"And what do liars do? They lie."

"Right."

"She wasn't Cameron's girlfriend—you know that, right?"

"Sure!"

"And Danielle said MaryLou was jealous of her," I said, treading more carefully now. "But that was a lie, too."

"It was all a lie. MaryLou's beautiful. And she's not gay, either.
I took her to the prom."

"You really like her, don't you, Franklin?"

"I think I love her."

"Now, how could you be in love with a lesbian?"

"Right!"

"So that's another lie. Once a person lies about one thing—in court, I mean—the jury can throw out everything else they say."

"But she still shot them." Franklin may have been the size of an ox, but he could give a mule fits in the stubbornness department, too.

"That's exactly right. But Danielle said there was a *reason* she did that. Remember? That she was jealous of—"

"I get it! I get it now. MaryLou, she *wasn't* jealous of Danielle, so that couldn't be why she shot those guys."

"Perfect! Now, listen, Franklin. You have to keep this a total secret."

"Sure. But why? I mean, if I can—"

"It's like football. You need strength, and you need speed. And what else?"

"Timing!"

"That's it. You nailed it, Franklin. We know MaryLou shot those boys for a reason. And we know it wasn't because she was jealous of Danielle. So it has to be for another reason."

"Right."

"We're on the trail of that reason. And we're going to get there. But if we get there too soon . . ."

"Now I understand! It has to be . . . timed just right."

"That's it's, son—you got it perfect. Now, help me get all that damn equipment into my car and I'll run you home."

"What's next?"

"Well, I might have to go talk to some of these 'society' guys. I wouldn't want to do that alone. Will you go with me?"

"You're helping MaryLou. I'll do whatever you say."

The kid wasn't half as dumb as they were taking him for. I'd talk to Dolly about that some other time. But now I had to tell her about how I found the path I'd been looking for . . . by stumbling over the lies I'd told MaryLou's psychopath of a "little sister."

"Dell, are you serious?"

I just nodded.

"You actually think there's some kind of 'syndrome' for what MaryLou did?"

"There is," I said, prepared to match Franklin's stubbornness twice over if I had to. "I've seen it myself. Just listen. What if somebody shot me and I almost died?" I said, watching her face. "What if I was in the hospital, all hooked up to machines, and you were watching over me? And, all of a sudden, you saw the man who shot me walking down the hall. What would *you* do?"

"I . . . know. But Danielle wasn't raped."

"How do you know? That's what those people do. Why else would you have that big red mark at the spot where they hang out? I think everybody knows. The kids, I mean."

"They . . . might. I mean, Iris said that girls don't even report rapes anymore."

"Like Cameron's crew had immunity. Safe passage."

"No. That can't be."

"Why not? You've been in places where certain people would be above the law . . . if there'd *been* any law. If I'm so crazy, then tell me something else that explains what that boss SANE nurse told us."

"I can't," she said.

If I'd been part of this Tiger Ko Khai bunch, and I'd seen my Dolly's face at that moment, I would have gotten as far away as I could, not even saying goodbye to anyone who might know where I was going.

Before I could stop her, Dolly was up and moving, almost knocking Rascal over as she charged to the computer.

"Leave me alone," is all she said.

It was almost four hours before she said another word. When she came down to the basement, she was so sweaty her hair was plastered to her face, and she smelled like she hadn't been near a shower for weeks. But I recognized the smell. It wasn't fear, or even anger—it was Warrior's Perfume.

"Rape Trauma Syndrome" is all she said. Then she slumped forward like there was nothing else in her. I caught her easily, carried her upstairs, laid her down on our bed, and wrote in heavy blue marker, "At lawyer's. All phones turned off."

Then I propped the note up where she couldn't miss it when she opened her eyes.

"You *guard*!" I told Rascal.

"We don't call it 'self-defense,'" Swift said. I had to blink a couple of times to make sure I was looking at the same person. It wasn't his suit or his haircut; it was like he'd been taking self-respect pills. Even the pig at the desk had asked, "You're here for Mr. Swift, aren't you?" as if she really was his receptionist.

"What *do* you call it?"

"Justification."

"That makes more sense," I told him. "I've met plenty of men who should have been killed, no matter what scale you measured them on. Wouldn't matter if you shot them in their sleep or in a firefight, getting them dead was the only thing that mattered."

He gave me a strange look, but not a surprised one. Then he snatched a law book off a shelf behind him. I couldn't help noticing it was already tabbed with several of those little colored sticky notes.

"I'll read you the legal language right out of the statute so we can be sure we're on the same page. Okay . . .

"A person is generally permitted to use physical force for self-defense or to defend a third person from what the person reasonably believes to be the use or imminent use of unlawful physical force.

"Clear enough?"

"Yeah. So, if I thought someone was about to hurt my wife, I could strike first?"

"The key word is 'imminent.' So you could strike first only if you actually believed another party was about to attack."

"A crazy person could 'believe' anything."

"It still has to be a *reasonable* belief, not some delusion. Listen to this:

"The degree of physical force a person may use in self-defense or defense of another is limited to that degree of force reasonably believed to be necessary for the purpose.

"See?"

"So, even if I *reasonably* believed someone was going to slap my wife, I couldn't shoot them in the head."

"No. The law requires this 'reasonable' standard, true, but it is never defined. So what's 'reasonable' under the circumstances, that's up to a jury. What's reasonable to a jury in New York might not seem so reasonable to a jury in Dallas. That's why there's such state-specific case law on the subject. Here . . .

"A jury instruction on self-defense is appropriate when evidence supports that theory. Thus, no matter how unbelievable the trial judge finds the defense testimony, it is an error for the judge to refuse a self-defense instruction on that basis; it is for the jury to assess credibility. Further, the defendant is entitled to an instruction on the state's burden to disprove the defense beyond a reasonable doubt."

"What's the difference?"

"I . . . I don't believe I understand what you're asking."

"That's because I don't know what I'm doing, trying to swim in your pool. I meant, what's the difference between these 'statutes' and 'case law'?"

"Ah, okay. A statute is the law as the legislature wrote it. Those are just words. Case law is how the appellate courts *interpret* those words. And since only the defense can appeal—"

"Wait! So, if a jury was to cut MaryLou loose, no matter how bogus their reason, there's nothing the law could do about it?"

"Ask O.J.," he said. When he saw my blank look, he said, "That's absolutely correct. There's even a concept known as 'jury nullification.' That's when a jury finds a defendant innocent even though there's no way he actually could *be* innocent. This was common in many of the racial murders in the South in the fifties and sixties. In fact, that probably did more to bring about the passage of the Civil Rights Act than any other kind of advocacy could."

"You read this?"

"Yes. How else could I—?"

"I mean, it's written down in the books you studied in school. And nobody argues about it anymore; it's an accepted fact?"

"Absolutely."

Goddamn, this could actually work! But all I said aloud was "Remember what you were telling me? About battered-woman syndrome?"

"Yes. In fact—"

"Have you ever heard of Rape Trauma Syndrome?"

"I have. But I've never tried a case using that defense. And I don't think you'll find anyone around here who has."

"Not a lot of rape cases here?"

"Well, *stranger* rapes, yes, there are some. But if the victim knew the alleged attacker . . . no. And, remember, that defense is only valid if the defendant uses force to defend herself from a person she reasonably believes is about to rape her."

Yeah, because they never get prosecuted. But it wasn't the time for that yet.

"What about if a guy was a known rapist, okay? Let's say he had a record for it, and he just shows up at a girl's trailer, parked out in the woods, in the middle of the night, and starts kicking in her door. Could she shoot him?"

"In Florida, sure. Here, I . . . think she'd have to warn him she was armed, and give him a chance to retreat."

"That's a joke, right? The only edge she has is the gun, and she has to tell him about it? Why? That way *he* gets a chance to start shooting."

"I think that's one of those questions you have to put before a jury."

"I get it. Okay, what if the woman had a baby, and this guy was known for raping babies; would that change things?"

"The law, no. The outcome, absolutely."

"So—this Rape Trauma Syndrome, it plays by the same rules."

"I believe it would. Let me just look. . . ." This time, he went right to his computer. It only took a few seconds.

"No question. In fact, if we went that way . . . Yes. Yes! A justification defense is not *any* form of an 'insanity' defense. So the prosecution isn't entitled to any advance notice."

"You can just spring it on them?"

"Not quite. But you can have the best experts *already* on your side. And the only way you're going to get any of the syndrome defenses before a jury is to have an expert testify that the defendant was suffering from it at the time of the . . . well, in this case, at the time of the homicide."

"I get you them—those experts, I mean—and you're ready to try this case?"

"I'm ready to try it without them, if that's the client's wish. And, as you know—"

"I'll get MaryLou to go along, too," I promised. "The faster the better, right?"

"No question! The DA's Office is sure we're going to want to plead this out, on some kind of temporary-insanity deal. If we start making speedy-trial motions, they'll have a cow."

"Speedy-trial?"

"In this state, if I—the defense, I mean—if *we* don't consent to a delay, either the prosecution has to go forward within whatever the court decides is a reasonable time, or the judge could even dismiss it outright . . . and no judge is going to want to do that in this case."

"Couldn't they just arrest her again and start all over? There's no statute of limitations on murder, is there?"

"No," Swift said, his voice dropping as he spoke, as if we were sharing a secret. "But once jeopardy has attached, if the case is dismissed it's done. They only get one bite at the apple."

That's what Cameron knew, I thought to myself. *That's what all of them knew. No matter what they did, as long as they did it to the right girls, no "jeopardy" was ever going to attach.*

I stopped off to check on Franklin. He was still in the same big chair he'd gone to sit in when I'd dropped him off last night. Didn't look like he'd moved.

"You have to lock your front door, Franklin. One of those guys, the ones who raped Danielle, they're the same ones who got MaryLou locked up for trying to protect her. They could just walk right in."

"I wish" is all he said. "I know what they look like now. That's why I'm staying here. I know if I went out, if I saw anyone in one of those jackets . . ."

Dolly had showered, and the kitchen was full of girls like usual, but most of what they had to say seemed to be focused on Dolly's outfit: camo cargo pants, a sleeveless T-shirt of the same material, and jungle boots, soft-soled, with mesh tops and steel toes.

"No, this is *not* some new thing," Dolly said to one of them, the pug-nosed redhead. "These clothes are older than you are."

"Retro is new," another pronounced, knowingly.

"This never went away," Dolly said quietly. "Maybe someday I'll tell you about it. For now, either get on the plane or stay on the ground."

That sent them back to work quicker than chain-gang slaves who had stretched their smoke break and spotted the Boss Man coming.

"Dell," she said, after following me to my den—the same direction she'd pointed me in when I'd opened the back door—"I went back through the network. Listen to this: Rape Trauma Syndrome seems to actually hit the secondaries harder than the primaries."

I made a gesture she understood to mean "keep going."

"Primaries have actually been raped. In Kosovo, rape was a weapon of war. Worse than death. If you get pregnant from a soldier of another . . . ethnic group, an abortion is your only chance to prevent your child from being an outcast all his life. Like in Africa, but even worse. Because, for many in that area, abortion is a mortal sin. A choice between killing your own child and going to hell, and letting your child live and *sending* him to hell. That's why so many of them went catatonic.

"But for the secondaries, those who either had to watch the rapes happen or even help repair the physical damage from them, it was actually worse. The primaries had already taken the worst that could happen, and they went someplace where nobody could hurt them again—you know what I mean. But the secondaries lived with the fear. As if they themselves had been raped, but they had no place to go . . . not even crazy. Their job was to stand there and deal with the waves and waves of rape victims coming in."

"There's books on this?" I asked, thinking of Swift. If enough people had written it down and it hadn't been challenged, maybe . . .

"You mean, is it accepted within the profession?"

"Yes."

"By anyone who served with Médecins Sans Frontières, there would be no question. But I'm not a psychologist. I'd have to . . . Wait! I know just the perfect person! Debbie Rollo. She is the *best*. Nobody would even *try* to argue with her qualifications. But, Dell, are you sure this could really work?"

"I'm damn sure what happens if it doesn't. Can you get in touch with—"

I looked up, but Dolly was already gone.

Ryan Teller had touched down here less than fifteen years ago. And his '06 conviction would have kept him local for at least five years. Only a few years between then and today. It didn't feel as if he got in the wind. More like he was still hovering somewhere close by, holding on to his status as the founder of a gang that specialized in raping young girls.

I remembered the five men who had braced me outside that convenience store on the highway. They were in their twenties; Teller would be in his mid-thirties.

The same stunt I used before wouldn't work twice. I doubted any of them went off into the woods alone anymore. But maybe they still felt safe inside that permanent pool of darkness behind the day-care center.

This should have been a three-man operation. Like this: One man stands with his back to the field; another off to the side, covering the middle ground from an angle. Only the third man—the shooter—would need a silenced weapon. I already had one of those, but I didn't have anyone I trusted enough to split up the other tasks.

I don't mean "trust" the way you might think. I believed that Franklin would do anything if he thought it could help MaryLou. And that he'd never talk. But you can't use a man's love the way you'd use a tool—that's not only dishonorable, it's way too risky.

Even though darkness was still hours away, I couldn't stop myself from driving past. Just to take a look, make sure I had it down right.

Surveillance was no more difficult than finding higher ground with a decent sight-line. The little monocular was the kind of stuff only the Germans care about making anymore—as clean, efficient, and beautifully engineered as a Minox had been in its day.

There were three of them, standing by their cars in the area that turned into their playpen after dark. Even though I could dial in close enough on their faces to pick up the color of their eyes, and even though they looked too old to be teenagers, I couldn't be sure. Not sure enough for what I'd thought about doing—hell, *wanted* to do—ever since Danielle's "screen test."

But one thing I was sure of—they'd know who Ryan Teller was.

Just as I was pulling back the zoom by touching a button on the side of the focusing ring, I saw the Crown Vic pull in.

I made myself disappear and tried to do the math in my head: (1) That was the same car, unless they had a damn fleet of police-auction Crown Vics. Probability: close to zero. (2) Either my phone call hadn't worked, or they'd been cut loose by the troopers when they couldn't find anything. Probability: high. They weren't drunk, and they'd been following me for miles. They weren't professionals, but they'd know better than to be traveling with any weed, or even an open container. (3) If it *was* the same car, either it was a kind of "corporate vehicle" or it belonged to one of those who got out. That they were all lounging, not working, weighted it in favor of the last. Probability: medium. (4) Americans think terrorism started on 9-11. But it's been around ever since there were enough people to start dividing themselves into tribes, or clans, or whatever. It's always been here. The only thing that changes is how it's inflicted.

But nothing works better than . . . *Damn! That's Rape Trauma Syndrome. An implanted fear that you can't brush off. Because you never feel safe. Now, that's the truest terrorism there is.* Would it work on these punks? If I could really implant that trauma, I could leave this "probability" guessing behind, and get to where I needed to be: utility.

Torture doesn't work if it's designed to extract information. But implanting a feeling deeply enough so that the victim knows something horrible is coming—that form of torture *does.* Some people don't fly anymore. Others don't open their own mail. Some are afraid to start their own cars.

You don't have to be some lunatic predicting the "End of Days" to believe that you're not safe. But you'd have to *be* a lunatic to believe the government has it all under control.

That's how terrorism works. And it's working, one way or another, all over the globe. "Counterterrorism" is a fake. That job shouldn't be to capture-hold-kill terrorists. "Counter" is transferring energy from one side of the table to the other. Like aikido. The only true "counterterrorism" would be to terrorize the terrorists. If our government was willing to hire professionals—not those overpaid, well-connected fools they used in Iraq—that *could* be done.

I couldn't help thinking of the Legion. As professional as they come. Put them here. If I just closed my eyes, I could actually see it on that screen in my mind:

A mob of white-robed terrorists are watching a cross burn on the front lawn of a family that moved into the wrong neighborhood. Suddenly they start dropping like flies under a cloud of DDT. Nobody hears anything; nobody sees anything. They take off, running for their HQ. And when that safe harbor gets blown to hell, each atom from the fallout turns into a Bouncing Betty, spreading the message—they *were the ones in the wrong neighborhood.*

Governments hire mercenaries all the time. But once they step over to that side, they have to trust people whose loyalty is for sale. And the highest bidder isn't necessarily the *first* bidder.

The Cadillac was safely docked almost two miles away, but I had my traveling kit with me.

Because I had some sense of the terrain by then, I had passed the spot, went on for a little bit, then doubled back. I didn't want to cross a highway wearing a balaclava—too good a chance that some cell-phone addict would stop yammering long enough to snap a picture. "OMG!" would be the next thing she texted.

I dressed for my role. Total black, from the toe-weighted boots to the coveralls, gloves, balaclava, and full-wrap sunglasses.

Once I got close enough, all I had to do was wait for a clear chance to send both messages. The hardball .22 round would speak for itself, but only if it was the *second* move in the sequence I'd rehearsed.

I was less than ten meters away from them, just past where the parking-lot asphalt met the woods. That was within the slingshot's range, but not by a lot.

The slingshot wasn't a toy: I didn't know what had been used to construct its frame, but it was heavy enough to be lead. As for the elastic, I couldn't even guess—all I knew was that it wasn't any kind of rubber.

But the real brilliance of the design wasn't that it could fire what looked like way-oversized paintballs; it was the paintballs themselves. They were engineered to burst open on impact and drop a twice-folded three-by-five card to the ground. Result: an impossible-to-remove yellow splatter on the target, together with an impossible-to-forget message on the ground.

I wasn't wearing a watch, and I wasn't counting time. I had guessed that ten in the morning would give me the best chance of finding the far-back parking lot close to empty. So I waited, telling myself, over and over, that there would be other chances if today didn't work out.

It came quicker than I thought. The car I was waiting for pulled in, and three men got out.

N'hésitez pas! I slid sideways into an archer's stance, pulling the slingshot back in the same move. The giant paintball hit the side door of the Crown Vic with an audible *splat!*

"What the fuck?!" one of them shouted as they all jumped out.

All three turned in the direction where I was standing, now right on the borderline of the forest. They were frozen in place, scanning with their eyes, as still as paper targets. I was already braced. I shot the middle one in the head, just above the bridge of his nose. Then I vanished into the woods.

I didn't expect the others to follow me, but making sure of that made me move slower than I wanted to. Even so, I was dressed like a normal person and driving the Cadillac back toward the house within fifteen minutes.

I wasn't worried about being stopped. People who bought a car like this expected an adjustable ride, so the shock settings required plenty of room in the wheel wells. And left plenty of room to Velcro-attach my carryall to the undercarriage. I'd tested the setup over bumpy roads and it hadn't budged.

I couldn't know whether the Tiger Ko Khai maggots would panic and call the cops, or panic and throw the body into the trunk before they took off.

Maybe I couldn't deliver a message to Ryan Teller, but I was sure they could. Both sides of the open-on-impact card had the same message:

TELL RYAN WE'RE COMING FOR HIM

There's no daily news coverage here. There's newspapers, but they only come out twice a week, and usually only print press releases and the owner's "editorials." Dolly keeps the BBC on TV all the time, running mute, but the local news was pretty much statewide, and it would automatically cut in if there was something important enough—college-football rankings weren't international news.

Nothing cut into the BBC, so they must have hit panic button number two. That would have been the only sane move. Trying to tell the local cops that some masked ninja had stepped out of the woods and drilled their friend between the eyes would have gotten them questioned for hours, with more than one detective in the room.

So—what you're telling us is that somebody in a black hood just walked out of the woods and popped your friend in the head? And nobody heard a shot, so he must have been using a silencer? And all this started with a giant paintball hitting your car? How come there's a section of that paintball that looks like somebody pulled something loose? Well, just relax here a bit—we'll have the CSI team go over the car, just in case this guy, this mystery killer, left any evidence behind.

Oh, by the way, this guy, the guy with the hood, was there any symbol on it? You know, like a circle with a cross over it?

And while that was going on, anything that had *ever* been in their car could turn into a serious problem. Never mind the fact that the dead guy and the two of them were all wearing the same jackets.

How about telling us about those jackets? It'll help in our investigation. Maybe somebody has some kind of grudge against your club that you know about? Can you think of any reason why someone would want to kill your friend?

The longer that went on, if any of them had any kind of criminal record anywhere—not only convictions, even arrests—the cops would know about it. That should do it. Even the dumbest cops would know enough to start a roundup. Then they could cut the weakest one out of the herd, and make sure the others heard them do it.

No, you aren't under arrest—that's why we didn't give you any Miranda warnings. But if you want to be under arrest, we can always charge you with obstruction of justice. Then you can call your lawyer, if you have one. Or we'll get someone assigned. Is that what you want? No? That's a smart move, doing the right thing. No reason why you have to go down with the rest of them.

Not giving a damn who you hurt doesn't make you a hard man. Or even a cold one. I knew it wouldn't necessarily be the smartest one who gave the orders. It would be whoever said that an unreported disappearance was better than going anywhere near the cops. In a panic situation, everyone listens to the man who stays calm, even if it's the calmness of a man too stupid to understand that he should be afraid.

Dolly certainly wasn't all that calm when I came back to the house after stashing the Cadillac behind Swift's "extra office space."

The second she got me alone, she starting talking. Talking so fast that I had to ask her to slow down every few seconds.

"She's coming! I called her and she's coming! She's coming here, Dell. And she's going to do all the interviews. And not only that, she got the top forensic psychologist in the whole country to help out. They'll be here tomorrow. Oh God! We have to pick them up at the airport, and . . ."

"Honey . . ."

"I know, I know. It's just that, with experts with *their* credentials on our side, we have a real chance now, Dell."

Good thing, I thought. *This wasn't the kind of case where you could give witnesses an incentive to change their minds.*

D̲ebbie Rollo walked over to me as she stepped through the exit slot at the airport. I don't look like anything special, but wearing a suit and tie and holding up a big white card with her name printed on it was probably enough of a hint.

People who are highly educated sometimes make me feel resentful, although I don't know exactly why—I'd probably have to hire one of them to find out. But she was a sweetheart. "Please call me Debbie. I hate all that formal nonsense."

"Sure," I said, holding out my hand, now that I was no longer a limo driver. "My name's Dell."

"Is that short for Delbert?"

"No."

"Oh, my goodness! I didn't mean to offend you."

"I'm not. I know my name's unusual. It's short for 'Adelbert.' Who wants to get their mouth around that?"

When she chuckled, I could see why Dolly liked her so much. I don't know when they met, but I know it was way before Dolly and I came here. To our home, I mean. So, whoever she was, she was a woman who could keep a friend's secrets.

"Damn it!" she said as I was loading her suitcases into the

Cadillac. "I forgot to tell you. I got an e-mail from Dr. Joel last night. He's still coming, but when I told him it wasn't an emergency, he said he'd just drive up."

"From where?"

"I don't know where exactly. I only reached him on his cell, so he could be anywhere. I can't believe he'd be crazy enough"—she blushed at having just called a psychologist potentially crazy—"to drive from where he lives."

I didn't say anything.

"Tucson," she said. "That has to be over a thousand miles from here! But I know he's some kind of car nut"—it was easier to catch the blush this time; I'd been ready for it—"and he just got some super-special new one."

She didn't say another word for a good twenty minutes, content to look out the window and watch the scenery. Maybe Dolly had told her I wasn't a world-class conversationalist.

"What kind of car does this doctor have, do you know?"

"I can tell you exactly if you give me a minute. I have his e-mail on my phone."

Before I could tell her it wasn't all that important, she was tapping madly on the tiny typewriter keyboard attached to her phone.

"It's a . . . Mercedes-AMG, as if I knew what *that* meant."

"AMG is a special little operation that makes high-performance versions of different kinds of Mercedes," I told her. "Mercedes itself has to approve—it puts its own warranty on anything AMG makes—so they work really close together. This could be anything from a—"

"It's an SLS Roadster," she interrupted. "Does that help?"

"Sure does. 'Roadster' is just fancy-word for 'convertible' today, but the SLS is no car for an amateur—it's so fast it could be dangerous. Probably capable of hitting two hundred–plus on a flat stretch of road."

"My goodness!"

"Yeah. But this doctor, he may *be* nuts. Who keeps a convertible in Tucson?"

She chuckled at that one, too. I hoped she'd tell Dolly I was pretty clever at small talk.

I tried to coax Rascal down to the basement, where I was going to be sleeping. The house really wasn't built for guests, and my den took away the only extra room, so Dolly told me she and Debbie would be sleeping in our bedroom. There's only the one bed. I don't know why it is, but girls are comfortable sleeping in the same bed, the way men never can be.

Anyway, Rascal lived up to his name. Once he had the rawhide treat firmly in his jaws, he ran up the stairs like he was after a bitch in heat. I was good enough for hanging out with, but Dolly, she was his job.

I called him a miserable deserter. In French, to make sure he didn't understand—who knows what words a dog knows? But inside, I was really proud of him.

They were all asleep when I took another look at the video of the little girl who wanted to be called "Danyelle." On zoom, her eyes were the color of steel nailheads. And just as deep. One-way mirrors. A good thing we'd left that website up and rented a 213-area-code answering service. If anyone called, they would just read what we sent them: "Arquette Aland Film Productions." And, depending on what was asked, "No, Mr. Laveque is not available at the moment," or "No, I am not Mr. Laveque's personal assistant. My name is

Trixie. All I do is answer phones in this madhouse." And "Yes, of course, I'll take a message."

No matter what the answer, "Trixie" would be interrupted by a tape of phones ringing, all of which she'd simply answer, "Hold, please." After all, Danielle was an important client. A priority.

I decided to map out the distance from Tucson to where we were. I couldn't get it exact, not knowing where in Tucson this psychologist would be coming from, but it was no less than thirteen hundred miles. I wondered for a second if he knew where he was coming to, but then I let it go—Dolly and Debbie would have worked that one out between them.

The next couple of days turned the kitchen into a phone bank. I didn't know how these girls could all talk into different phones at the same time and not get in each other's way, but they handled it like it had been choreographed.

Dolly didn't even ask me where I was going.

Franklin was home. Sitting on the front step of the house his football skills had bought his parents, glaring at passing cars like he was expecting a drive-by . . . and was wearing a bulletproof vest, with a grenade launcher close to hand.

But he had a smile for me.

"Hey, Franklin. What's going on?"

"I thought you might have some . . . news for me."

"I've got something better, maybe. You got anything inside that's a little more like what I'm wearing?"

"A suit, you mean? Gee, no. I mean, why would I— Wait!" he interrupted himself. "My prom suit. I had to buy it—the rental place didn't have anything in my size. But you can't tell MaryLou. She'd kill me if she thought I'd spent all that money."

"How much are we talking about?"

"The whole prom—I got her an orchid and all—it cost almost a thousand dollars," he said, proudly.

"That's a lot of money . . ." I started to say, before it hit me that Franklin's pride wasn't in how much he'd spent, but in how he'd managed to *earn* that much, so I closed that door quick with ". . . to save up."

"I worked after school. Helping Mr. Spyros. He's an expert horta-something. With trees and all. He knows everything about them. And you know what he paid me? Fifteen dollars an hour! He said that was about twice the minimum wage, and I worked like two men, so he paid me like two men. Isn't that something?"

"Sure as hell is. Especially now."

"Yeah! And I saved every dollar, too. I was supposed to work for him this summer, but now I don't know. I mean, I know I should call him—people who work for Mr. Spyros would do it for nothing, just for what they could learn—but I don't know what to tell him."

"I can help you with that, okay? In the meantime, can you get changed? Not into your prom outfit, just something with a collar on the shirt, and switch those jeans for . . . well, for whatever guys your age wear when they're not wearing jeans."

While Franklin was inside, I sat on his front porch and made a few calls. I figured his father was still inside somewhere, sleeping off his no-show job. I didn't know if his mother worked, but my money was against it.

"You look great," I reassured him for at least the fourth time since we'd driven off.

He never asked where we were going.

I pulled into the parking lot shared by all the various lawyers who rented space in the building. Some of the slots said "Client Parking Only." Only the ones marked "Handicapped" were getting any play. I decided I was "Staff," and wheeled the big gray car into one of those slots.

"Well, good morning, Mr. Jackson. You're here to see Mr. Swift, I'm sure. And who is this good-looking young man?"

"His name is Franklin. With all the threats Mr. Swift has been getting over such a controversial case, I thought it best he have some personal security available."

"Oh, I *understand*," the pig assured me. They're all alike: knock their boots off your neck and those same boots turn into track shoes.

Inside, all I said was "Mr. Swift, this is Franklin Wayne, the young man I told you about."

"My pleasure," Swift said, standing up and holding out his hand. I could see Franklin had a lot of practice shaking hands without breaking them.

"As I explained, Franklin is a very good friend of MaryLou's, so I hope you can use your influence to give him an opportunity to visit with her."

"Consider it done," Swift said. Which meant he'd already taken care of it. His name was packing more weight every day.

"Really?" Franklin asked.

"Sure. Besides, Mr. Jackson says you may play a . . ." He stifled the "critical" he was about to say, replacing it with "highly significant role at the trial."

"Me?"

"All Mr. Swift is saying is that you'd be willing to testify about what you heard her sister, Danielle, say."

"She's no real sister," Franklin half-spit the words out. I started to wonder if he was retarded at *all*, never mind to a lesser extent than I'd been led to believe.

Swift hit a button on his desk. A button that hadn't been there before.

"Yes, Mr. Swift?" the pig's honeyed tones came out of the speaker.

"Can you please tell me if the conference room is available, Jeannine? Oh, and can you call Channel Sixteen back and tell them that I may have a statement later this week, but an exclusive is out of the question?"

"Yes, sir!" she said, answering his last question first—the most important one, in her eyes. "And the conference room *is* available. I'll make sure you aren't disturbed."

"Thank you," he said, tapping a button to switch off the gush.

The conference room was just a bigger version of Swift's office. But it did have eight chairs and a long table. And a sign on the door that you could change from "Vacant" to "Occupied," lending it that special touch of class you find on commercial airplanes.

"Okay, Franklin, here's what we're going to do. Mr. Swift is going to ask you some questions. I want you to remember that he's fighting to keep MaryLou out of prison—"

"Isn't she in prison already?"

"No," Swift said, treading carefully. "That's jail, not prison. It's where they hold people before they go to trial."

"Everybody?"

"Everybody who can't pay the bail the judge sets."

"How much would that cost?" Franklin asked, disarmingly. I revised both my estimates, in opposite directions. Franklin was damn sure not "retarded." I was no longer sure he was even "slow." And I could tell he was more than capable of doing something "wrong" if he believed it would be the right thing to do.

If the Legion had ever gotten hold of this one, he'd be as danger-ous as rocket-powered rat poison . . . especially if you happened to be a rat.

"There's no amount of bail set in this case, Franklin. Even a million dollars wouldn't get her out, not before the trial."

"That's not right."

"No," I said, looking straight at Swift, "it isn't." A few weeks ago, the lawyer would have shrugged his slumped shoulders and said something like "That's the system." Today, what came back was "You're both right. But we only get one chance to ask the court to lower a defendant's bail, and we don't *have* to ask until we've put together every single thing that might help."

Franklin looked down at his clenched fists, as if to say, *What's wrong with these?,* but he didn't say anything.

Swift caught the gesture. "That's why you're so important, Franklin. Now we can tell a judge that we have a witness who will swear that Danielle wouldn't lie *for* her sister, but she certainly would lie *against* her."

"You know what she said—?!"

I shook my head, and Franklin's jaw snapped closed. "When we're in court, we can only answer questions the lawyer asks. I know we're not in court now. But we will be soon. So this is like a test run."

"Like practice?"

"Exactly like practice. You have to be ready to play, right?"

"Yes, sir."

"Okay, Franklin," Swift started. Then he stopped himself and asked, "Or would you prefer to be addressed as Mr. Wayne?" The lawyer was picking up respect by dishing it out. A man capable of learning is one thing; a man *willing* to learn, that's gold.

"Franklin's good enough for Mr. Dell; it's good enough for me."

"All right, then. After they swear you in—you've seen it on TV; 'Do you swear to tell the truth, the whole truth, and nothing but the truth?'—you sit down, just like you're doing now, and I ask you some preliminary questions. I'll just get your name, your address, and ask you how long you've known MaryLou, okay?"

"Sure. I met MaryLou—"

"We don't want to waste time practicing on questions like that, Franklin. We save the practicing for the trickier ones."

"Like what?"

"Like 'Were you present on the night of June 10, 2013, when

Danielle McCoy said that her sister, MaryLou McCoy, murdered Cameron Taft in cold blood because she was jealous of her?'"

"Yes, sir."

"That's a little stiff, Franklin. Just relax. This is a promise: nothing you do here can hurt MaryLou. Fair enough?"

"Yes, sir," Franklin answered again, still polite, but more like he was comfortable in his surroundings.

"Okay, same question. Do you remember it?"

"Yes. And that *is* what Danielle said."

"How do you know?"

"I . . . I don't get it," the giant said, despair suddenly spreading all over his face.

"I don't get it, either," I said, looking hard at Swift. "Franklin knows because he heard Danielle say it. Danielle just didn't know anyone was listening."

"That's right!" Franklin burst out.

"My apologies," Swift said. "My fault, not yours. I put that question poorly. So let's move on, is that okay?"

"Yes, sir," Franklin said. I reached across and tapped fists with him. Not a mistake I'd make again—nobody would call my knuckles soft, but they weren't designed to hit cement.

"Did you hear Danielle say that Tiger Ko Khai was a special group at school?"

"Yes, sir."

"Now, I want you to understand something. The District Attorney's Office, they don't want the truth to come out. So they're going to keep jumping up and screaming *'Objection!'* every chance they get. That won't be because *you* said anything wrong; it'll be because *I* asked the question wrong.

"So, depending on what the judge says, I may not be allowed to ask you yes-or-no questions. You may have to tell the jury what you heard all on your own. Okay? So, if I were to ask you, 'What did you hear Danielle say?' what would your answer be? Remember, you can only repeat what you heard, you're not allowed to give your own opinion. For example, you know Danielle lied about a lot of things, don't you?"

"Yes, sir."

"But *you* can't call her a liar. The *evidence* will call her a liar. So, if Danielle said she was twenty-five years old, her *birth certificate* would prove she was a liar. Okay?"

Franklin nodded, as if satisfying himself that he had it all straight. Then he said, "I heard Danielle say MaryLou killed Cameron because she was jealous. Jealous of Danielle, I mean. Danielle said Cameron was her secret boyfriend, but MaryLou knew about it, and MaryLou wanted him for herself. Danielle said that Cameron was the boss of this special club, Tiger something. She said this was real special. I heard Danielle say that MaryLou was gay. I heard her say that I was a retard-something. I heard her say that MaryLou told her she was going to break up Danielle and Cameron one way or another."

"That's just about *perfect,* Franklin. Just a couple of more questions. Did you actually hear Danielle say these things, or did somebody play a tape recording for you?"

"I was right in the next room. I could hear every word."

"All you have to answer, if they ask that question, is that you actually heard her, Franklin. We don't want to give them any more than they ask for, okay?"

"Okay," he said, nodding slowly, as if to embed the thought.

"Great. Now, do you have an interest in— Withdrawn." Before Franklin could ask what the hell that meant, Swift rolled right on: "Do you like MaryLou?"

"I love her. She's my best friend."

"So, if you thought MaryLou was going to spend the rest of her life in prison unless you told lies, would you tell lies to protect her?"

"Yes, sir, I would. In a minute."

"Now you *are* perfect," Swift said, admiration for the trueness of the young man's love transforming his own face into more of a . . . I don't know, exactly. But I knew it was what we'd need.

I dropped Franklin off at his house, where he could change clothes for his next appointment.

Dolly adored Spyros. They'd gone partners on all kinds of town battles, but the one that brought them the closest was the fight to keep the Animal Shelter open. When I called and told Dolly what I needed, it only took her a couple of minutes to get back to me.

"Spyros says, 'Sure. I wish I had ten more like him.'"

What Franklin had to change clothes for was the first day of his new job. My earlier conversation with Spyros about that couldn't have gone better.

"What!" he answered his cell.

"Spyros, you don't know me. My wife is Dolly Jackson and—"

"Now, there's a girl they named right."

"Yes, sir. But I was calling on behalf of Franklin Wayne. He worked for you—"

"Yeah, he worked for me. And he's going to keep working for me. That young man has a beautiful way with trees. Strong as a bull, but he's got a feather-touch when it's needed. Whatever he'll ever need for this work, he's already got it in him. Once he learns some things, that is."

"So Franklin could start working for you—"

"What do you mean, 'could'? I'm crazy about your wife, buddy, but that doesn't give you license to insult anyone who works for me."

"Insult? When did I do that?"

"Well . . . I guess you didn't. But if one more person tells me Franklin's 'retarded,' it's five across the eyes, you hear me? You want to talk to genuine retards, just go down to City Hall. They've got a whole crew of them there, from the Mayor on down."

"Uh, okay. So I'll bring Franklin over later—"

"What are you, some kind of taxi? That young man has his own truck. Which leads me to a good question: if he's so 'retarded,' how did the state issue him a driver's license? And don't tell me any DMV stories. Here's the answer: maybe Franklin's no rocket scientist, but he ain't no dummy, either.

"My business, it's a craft. You have to have the hands and the soul for it. Franklin's going to take over for me when I finally retire . . . but don't say a word to him about that! I want to be sure he's got some of the nastier parts down before I make that move."

"What could be nasty about horticulture?" I asked, genuinely interested.

"Getting paid," Spyros said, grimly.

"I almost blew that one, didn't I?"

"You skated on the edge," I told Swift, "but you pulled back real smooth—no harm was done."

"Are you sure? I wouldn't want Franklin's feelings hurt. I'll bet, if it wasn't for his size, he'd have been taunted at school. Kids can be merciless, sometimes."

You know all about that, don't you? That blue screen cleared in a finger-snap, and I could see "Sadly 'Not Too' Swift" being poked in the chest by a football player in a varsity jacket.

I got it then. I got all of it. From the first time I spoke to him right up to the man sitting across a desk from me now. A different man. He'd been ready to make the jump for a long time, just waiting for the tiniest push.

"Yeah" is all I said.

"You're probably thinking, how can we use what Franklin heard

Danielle say at the trial? It's hearsay on top of hearsay. But I've been looking into this. And there's an exception to the hearsay rule that we can use like it's never been used before!

"In fact, we *hope* the DA objects. Hearsay is nothing more than an out-of-court statement—which this was—not under oath—which this wasn't—offered for its truth. There's no rule against offering a statement for its *un*truth."

"And Danielle was lying, so . . ."

"That's it. And that's *all* of it. There is no way they can stop Franklin's testimony coming in. And you know what? He'll be the best kind of witness. That young man just exudes credibility. I don't think he'd tell a lie to save his life. So when he said he'd lie in a heartbeat if it would save *MaryLou's* life, that was a knockout punch."

"He convinced me. And I'm not that easy to convince."

"I . . . I think I know that by now, Dell."

He quavered a bit on the last word, so I said, "You're the man for this job, Brad. The right man."

He shoved his nerves back under his skin, replied, "I think maybe, just maybe, this would be the first time any jury around here ever actually *listened* to a justification defense."

"By the time we're ready to roll, I promise you'll be holding a lot more cards, too. And getting Franklin a pass to see MaryLou—"

"Like I said, already handled," he told me, with a half-smile. A confident one.

"*Premièrement, tu dois toujours tenir parole.*" The old man had said that to me when I was still an alley rat. He was teaching me to be a man, one step at a time, switching between French and English so seamlessly that I sometimes got left behind. "*Si les gens savent que tu tiens toujours parole, ils auront toujours peur de toi.*"

"If people knew my word was always good, then they would fear me? *Me?*"

"Of course. No matter what they do, if you walk away with your life, they will fear you for the rest of theirs. Do you know the name 'Adolf Eichmann'? No, why would you? But he lives in fear of every Jew he did not exterminate. All Jews, everywhere, they made a sacred promise."

"I don't understand."

"You will," he promised.

And only a few days passed before that promise came true.

So I picked Franklin up at four that afternoon. "Mr. Spyros said I had to be home by four today," he said, sounding a little puzzled. "I usually work until it gets dark, or even later, but Mr. Spyros said today was different."

"It is, son. Didn't I promise I could get you a visit with Mary-Lou?"

Like everything else the old man had taught me, it worked. I just had never seen it work magic before. Tears sprang into the kid's eyes.

"Thank you" is all he said.

"Franklin!" MaryLou greeted him with a rib-crushing two-handed grab. She was a big, strong girl, but she still looked like a ballerina hugging a bear.

The guard started toward us. Franklin slowly turned his massive head. Something must have required the guard's attention elsewhere.

"We're going to get you out of . . . this place," Franklin said, the moment we sat down.

"Franklin . . ."

"I mean, all legal and everything," he said, stumbling over the words in his excitement.

"For real?" she asked me.

"We've got a decent shot at it," I said, not willing to go beyond that. "But I need to know the answers to certain questions."

"The ones Mr. Swift said when he came around before?"

"I'm not sure. What did he—?"

"It was a lot of them. Questions. But the bottom line was all about what he said was 'saving face.'"

"Whose face?"

"The DA's. He told me not to say anything. And he wasn't going to ask me any questions. All he 'wondered' was, did I care if I had a felony conviction on my record if I could walk away from this place and never come back?"

"What did you tell him?"

"I told him they could change my name to 'Lizzie Borden' for all I cared. I think he's the one who called Coach Taylor."

"Who?"

MaryLou gave me one of those "What are you, stupid?" looks I specialize in acquiring from teenage girls. "Just the coach of one of the best programs in the country."

"Program?"

"Softball program. Coach Taylor said if I was convicted of anything it wouldn't matter so long as going to school could be part of my probation, or whatever. And," she said, clearly communicating that she wished Franklin wasn't there, but making the best of it, "she also said I'd have to have an evaluation. You know."

"I do. And I wouldn't worry about it."

"I'm not. But I'm not sure what one of those is."

"I'm bringing someone here—actually Dolly is—who'll explain everything to you."

"MaryLou," Franklin said, anxious to get back in the conversation, "do you have everything you need? In here, I mean. I have a job. A job where I get paid. So I've got plenty of—"

"No, sweetie," MaryLou said, putting her hand on Franklin's forearm. "I'm fine."

"Did you get a chance to look over that material I sent you?" I said to MaryLou, deliberately watching her hand. And making sure she saw me doing it.

"Yeah."

"It always comes down to a question of trust, doesn't it? There's strategy, too, though. We wouldn't want the other side to hear something they shouldn't."

MaryLou nodded, patting Franklin's forearm. Her gesture was almost absentminded, but I pitied the guard who would even think about telling her to cut it out. Inside my head, I listened to the same two portions of Danielle's tape that I knew MaryLou had played for herself. Over and over and over.

MaryLou was this star softball player, but she looks like a lumberjack. And she's gay. So we'd never talk about anything to do with boys. The only one she liked was this retard, Bluto.

and . . .

Well . . . she wasn't going to kill *me*. And she sure couldn't boss Cameron around. She told me that she was going to break us up—me and Cameron—one way or the other. And . . . and she did just that, didn't she?

I looked down at that picture, thinking that the only way MaryLou's hand would look petite was on a forearm like Franklin's. But there was no way to make her look young and vulnerable for court, not with her size and that "You want some of this?" look she kept on her face.

Franklin turned beet-red. "Uh, okay. Just . . . I mean, can you make calls from here?"

"Collect calls," MaryLou said, her voice heavy with disgust for a system that profits from poverty and increases it in the process.

"You could call me. . . . I mean, if you wanted . . ."

"Franklin, do you have any idea what it costs just to say 'hello' on those pay phones? Even for a local call?"

"I don't care."

"I know you don't. But I'm not playing their game. They can go—" MaryLou halted herself. I had the sense that she never cursed around Franklin. "But there's another reason, a much more important one—they listen in on all the calls. It's just like Mr. Dell told me," she said, sliding into Franklin's name for me as naturally as she would blow a strike past a hapless batter.

Another one they underestimated, I thought. And had the thought confirmed when she told Franklin, "Sweetie, you trust me, don't you?"

"Sure!"

"Then listen. Please listen, okay? I don't want you to talk to my sister."

"Your sister?"

"Yes, Danielle. *I don't want you to say a single word to her, no matter what she says to you.* Okay, Franklin? This is really, really important."

"I don't know her—"

"I know, but—"

"—but I'll never say a single word to anybody who even *says* they're your sister. Or anyone whose name is Danielle," he said, smushing her interruption like he must have pancaked any defensive lineman trying to get at his quarterback.

MaryLou kissed his cheek. "That's my boy! Besides, isn't a visit better than a call? Then there's no chance of the wrong people hearing us."

"Sure! But Mr. Dell can't always be coming here."

"Neither can you," I said to Franklin. "You think Spyros is going to put up with you getting off early every day?"

"Oh, jeez, no! You can't be late if you work for Mr. Spyros. It's funny, though. I'm always on time, and I always have to wait for him. He's probably thinking of a plan. For what we have to do that day. That's why I always get there early—I just do what he tells me to do."

"For now," I said.

"What? Is he going to fire—"

"Franklin, listen, okay? What I was trying to say is that Spyros thinks highly of you. One of these days, you'll be going on jobs by yourself."

"You really think so?"

"He told me himself. But he told me not to tell you; he wanted it to be a surprise. You won't give it away, will you?"

"No, sir."

"If Franklin says it, he means it," MaryLou vouched for the huge, damaged man who was probably the only creature on earth who truly loved her.

"Thirty-nine girls," Dolly said, bitterly, "and we got a grand total of seven willing to get on the stand and tell the truth."

"That's actually a high percentage," Debbie told her.

"You probably couldn't put on any more than that no matter how many you had," I said. "The judge would cut it off."

"How could you possibly know that?" Dolly said, more sharply than I expected from her. But before I could tell her what Swift said, I heard the back door open.

"He's right." I whirled at the man's voice, pulling the left side of my jacket forward to cover the pistol from the girls' sight. *How could anyone just walk in here without Rascal's so much as barking? Especially when the stupid mutt's sitting right next to Dolly?*

"Whoa, hoss! I come in peace," the man said, smiling.

"Dr. Joel!" Debbie half-shouted, she was so excited.

I moved my hand off the pistol to take a look at the man I'd been ready to exterminate a few seconds ago. He was a medium-height, well-built guy about my age. I don't know why, but he reminded me of someone.

"Richard Dreyfuss," he said.

"You're a mind-reader, too?"

"Everybody does that. Usually in airports. I don't know why—I look a hell of a lot more like Richard Gere."

I felt a smile coming to my face, and had to work to keep it from showing up. *Maybe he fucking charms his way past alarms,* I thought, slightly ticked at Dolly's giving him one of her dazzle-smiles.

"My name is T.D.," he said to me, holding out his hand. "T. D. Joel, at your service. I don't know why, but I never spook dogs. I don't have a dog—couldn't do it with my schedule—but it's always been like that with me."

"Couldn't your wife—?" Debbie started to say, then stopped, as if she realized she had just set a new high-bar record for blushing.

"You're not married," Dolly stepped in for her friend. "No wife would let you walk around looking like you slept in your clothes."

"I surrender," he said, shaking my hand and helping himself to a seat so that he was facing Debbie, with me on one side and Dolly on his other.

"How did you know how many witnesses the judge would allow?" I asked him.

"Four hundred and eighty-some trials and still counting, hoss. If they're all going to give the same version of the same thing, the judge is going to stop the parade as soon as the other side claims the evidence is duplicative."

"Oh," I said. My own trial experience was zero. Then he drove another stake in:

"I teach law school, too. The better law schools are all doing that now—offering targeted courses. Most kids leave law school without a clue about trying a case, never mind how to use a psychologist if he's on your side and how to stick him if he's not. And it's not just my field. There's a law school down in Louisiana that offers an L.L.M.—like a graduate degree on top of law—in legislative drafting. Only one in the country so far, but it's got a three-year waiting list, so it won't be long before some others follow suit. It's a shame that—"

"Okay," I said, deliberately cutting him off. The guy was obviously a master narrator. Debbie was already swooning, and Dolly hadn't taken her eyes off him. *Save it for the fucking jury* was my thought, but what I said was "Could I look at your car?"

"Sure," he said.

I gave Dolly a look that said, "Not you!" and walked around to the side of the house. Rascal followed me. I didn't much like that. "Guard!" I snapped at him. He spun in his tracks and went back to Dolly and Debbie.

"Damn, that's a beauty," I blurted out. "What does something like that cost?"

"Well, the dealer offers this easy payment plan. Four hundred grand down, no payments, no interest."

"For a car?"

"I know. But what the hell? I make more money than I can spend. My kids are grown, both with graduate degrees and in professions they chose. I've got no mortgage on my condo, and I don't pay alimony . . . at least, not anymore."

"I get it." And I kind of did. I felt flooded with something a thousand times more powerful than "happiness." This guy was smarter than me. Better-looking, better educated. Respected all throughout his field. Wealthy, but he'd had to work for it.

But me, I had Dolly. I wouldn't trade him if he threw in a billion in platinum, a high-skill harem, and . . . I stopped then, not wanting to think about the one thing I *did* want, no matter how much I tried to never do that.

"I asked you out here so I could tell you a few things. But, mostly, to warn you that those women inside, their hopes are high, and it may take the heaviest weight of your skills to pull them down to reality."

"We'll see," he said, his voice as noncommittal as his expression. "And you don't need the rest of the warnings."

"The rest?"

"That if I hurt your woman—even her feelings—I'm a dead man."

"Ah, that was just for—"

"Spare me, hoss. I've seen men handle guns way too many times. You're a pro. You're way too natural with that piece for you to be anything else."

"Okay," I said, knowing I was caught between two bulldozers: he could out-talk me in his sleep, and he was telling the truth, too.

"Fill me in," he said.

"I have to see some people, make sure they did something they promised to do. How about I tell you on the way over?"

"Done," he said, vaulting over the sill of his roadster like that was his usual way of getting in. Me, I opened the door on my side like a normal person.

I knew Dolly wouldn't worry if I just took off without telling her—she knows I don't talk about my business in front of strangers.

It was like this guy was on a personal campaign to make me jealous. Rascal trusted him on smell—he'd pick up a new scent way before he could see whatever carried it. He was better than me in all the good things. And now he was showing me he could have been a rally driver, too. Not the silly crap they have over here—the hard-core Scandinavian style, where you hit blind corners at speeds that would give a NASCAR ace a heart attack.

Not that he drove all that fast, just so . . . smooth. I found myself playing navigator, like, "About a half-mile down, you'll see a roadside stand selling produce. Maybe a hundred yards past that, a huge tree stump on your left, a Douglas fir that was hit by lightning, so they had to cut it down. Immediately after that there's a hook turn—sharper than ninety degrees—and then you'll be on dirt for another two, three miles before the next move."

He'd just say "Roger!" each time. Drove that car like it didn't have a brake pedal, watching the road, not the instruments—that would have been my job, if this had been a real rally—kicking the rear end out instead of steering when that got him around a corner faster, using the paddles that stalked their way off the steering column to downshift. And when I told him we'd be hitting a clear stretch of asphalt in another minute, he shifted position just slightly. Once we got on that smooth pavement, he shot the car up to *way* over a hundred before I could get a breath.

He kept his hands at nine and three, not the ten and two they teach kids. By the time we blasted sideways into Martin and Johnny's driveway, the paint job on his car would need a lot of touch-up work to return it to its original shade, which was some kind of gunmetal silver mixed with carbon-fiber black.

Martin and Johnny were both on the porch of their house. With that quarter-mile driveway of theirs, they'd probably heard us coming.

I made the introductions.

"This is a friend of mine, Dr. T. D. Joel."

"T.D.?" Martin said. "What does that stand for?"

"Stands for T.D., hoss. I was born and raised in Kentucky. Whole lot of folks from there don't bother with any more first name than one like I got handed."

I made a little twitch of my cheek to remind him we weren't

there to hang out. True, there was no reason for secrecy. But that wasn't why I came.

"Let's see the Lexus," I said.

"You're no candidate for the most trusting man I've ever met," Johnny said waspishly.

"Dolly's always telling me that," I said, smiling to show him I hadn't taken offense.

"Nice!" Joel said, walking around the Lexus, which was standing in the shade outside the garage area, now wearing a coat of what looked like dark green. But the color wasn't stable—it kept shifting as you walked around it, from a kind of black to some sort of blue with a reddish haze over all of it.

Martin glowed under the praise the way he never would have if I'd been the one talking. He reached in the glove compartment and took out a piece of paper and some cash. The paper was a receipt for forty-three hundred from a place I'd never heard of: "B³" with "Buddha's Bad Boys" in a much smaller font beneath it.

"They're the best," Martin said. "But you have to drive through the worst part of Portland to get there. Whoever heard of a custom-fabrication operation built out of cinder block with a barbed-wire fence, and a whole horde of pit bulls running around loose?"

"Apparently you" is all I said. Accepting the money, handing back the receipt.

"I have got to get some of that," T.D. said, walking around the Lexus, running his hand lightly over the surfaces.

"Want to trade?" Martin said, grinning at the very idea of a man who had such a rocket for a car admiring his paint job.

"Don't think so, hoss. Those SUVs really widen our carbon footprint."

It took a second, but then both Martin and Johnny broke out laughing. T.D.'s car probably widened that footprint every time he started the engine.

We strolled back toward the roadster. Martin couldn't stop himself from gaping at it like a virgin walking down one of those streets in Amsterdam where nothing more than glass stands between him and the whores performing in windows.

"Want to give it a run?" T.D. asked him.

"Really?"

"Sure, hoss. Just let me show you a few things. . . ."

It took T.D. a couple of minutes to explain some different settings—things you could turn on or off, depending on what kind of ride you wanted—then he tossed the key fob at Martin, who snatched it out of the air like it was a Patek Philippe watch that wouldn't take well to hitting the concrete.

T.D. just stood there.

"Don't you want to—?"

"Only seats two," T.D. said. "And I know you don't want your partner on my lap."

Johnny vaulted into the passenger seat like he'd been doing it all his life. It was way more showy than when T.D. had done it, but he ended up just where he was supposed to be—next to Martin.

While they were gone, I gave T.D. pretty much all of what I knew, then said: "If I talk to you, is there something like attorney-client privilege?"

"If you talk to me as a patient, no matter what the conversation contains, I couldn't reveal it even if I wanted to. And no court would even try to make me."

"So I've been a patient ever since I opened my mouth, right?"

"Before that, hoss. From the second I saw you do that magic trick with the pistol."

"Why then?"

"Because nobody acts like that unless they've seen some truly ugly stuff in their lives. And anybody who's seen a steady diet of stuff like that probably should be seeing a therapist."

"Because they're, what, crazy?"

"Nothing like that. But PTSD is something you either work through or suffer from—those are the only choices."

"Post-traumatic stress disorder?"

"Yep."

"How did you know that I'd know what 'PTSD' meant?"

"Debbie prepped me. Just over the phone, but more than enough to see the defense strategy. Since you're playing a key role, you'd know."

"I get it."

"But I wouldn't need that," he said. "You're a very angry man. You've learned to put that anger in a box, and you only open it when you want to. So there's something you don't know, something you'll never know. But what you do know is, if you don't keep that question in that same box, you'll go off the rails."

I've been hit. Hit hard. But not like T.D. just did. It took me a while to get my breathing back.

"How could you know that?" I said, knowing I was admitting it just by asking.

"How do you know when a man's about to do something violent?"

"I've seen— No, wait. You mean, it's the same thing? You see enough of something that you . . ."

"Recognize it when you see it again? Yeah, that's it, hoss."

Just then Martin and Johnny pulled up, almost decorously.

"You like it?" T.D. asked, just a shade of sly in his voice.

"It's . . . unbelievable. I've never driven anything like it."

"Tell you what," T.D. said. "That Mini Cooper in there, it's a John Cooper Works, right?"

"It is," Martin said, proud to have common ground with a man who shared his love of cars, never mind one who actually owned a car he could only dream about.

"I'm going to be here a couple of weeks or so. Maybe a little longer. Want to trade?"

"You don't mean—?"

"Sure. I take yours, you take mine. When I'm ready to leave, I'll come back and we'll switch again."

Martin's jaw dropped. It must have taken him a full minute just to get the keys to the Mini out of his pocket.

T.D. took the keys, said, "Let's roll, hoss," to me.

And that's just what we did.

"That was an incredibly fine thing for you to do," I told him. "It'll mean the world to Martin. Johnny, too." *And now I've truly settled my debt to them, thanks to you,* is what I thought to myself.

"I had an ulterior motive," T.D. said. "I've never driven one of these, and I want to see if they can really make a front-driver as sharp as they claim."

I didn't know if they had or not, but after he played with it for a little while, getting the feel of it down, I was back to playing navigator.

And he was back to sliding the car through the turns. One was wild enough that I had to look through his side window to see the road ahead of us.

"Yee-haw!" T.D. yelled, happy as a boozehound watching an "All You Can Drink" sign go up in the window of his favorite bar.

He was still muttering about not being able to fully disable something or other when we slid into the driveway of our house.

"There's no decent hotel close by," Dolly told T.D., "but two good friends of mine have a little cottage they use as a guesthouse, and they said you're welcome to it for as long as you stay."

"Now, that's a generous offer," T.D. said.

"Ah, you don't know them. Nel and Sue are true partners. It goes so deep that you can't even say one name without the other. For them, this is the most natural thing in the world, to help out a friend. Besides, I've told them enough so that they have their own reasons for helping MaryLou."

I guess that was true enough. I'd been there when Dolly had asked them. Right away, Nel started musing about long-term strategy. Sue went on about tiger traps—"you know, the kind with punji sticks"—near where Cameron's gang used to hang out. I told her that they probably wouldn't be using that spot anymore, and she just nodded.

I didn't ask her why she assumed I'd know what punji sticks were. In the Legion, we called those traps *trous de loup,* and feared them greatly. Not just the deep-anchored bamboo spikes, but what the enemy would smear on their tips. And, just like the land mines left behind from every war, some of those tiger traps were still where they were first built—still waiting for the wrong boots to walk those trails.

"Can't say no to that," T.D. told her. "This guesthouse, it wouldn't bother them if they heard a little banjo music late at night?"

"Not a bit," Dolly assured him.

"You play *banjo?*" Debbie said, as if T.D. had just told her he won a Nobel Prize for Perfect Bachelor.

"Only late at night," he said. "When I have to think through a problem, I sometimes just sit back and do some picking. The sound relaxes me."

"Let's go and get you settled, then," I said. Quick, before Debbie got to tell him how she'd love to hear him play. I didn't look at Dolly, but I could feel what she was going to say to me later.

"You can't stage interview times," Debbie said. "One interview could last all day, another could be over in ten minutes."

The camera equipment I'd used on Danielle would be perfect, but we couldn't use the same hotel—which was why Dolly had told T.D. there weren't any decent ones around.

That's where Nel and Sue stepped in again, after T.D. drove over there. Dolly was in the front seat, me in the back—hard to call that little shelf a "seat"—but it wasn't a long ride.

They explained that their guesthouse had two floors, one for living—bedroom, full bath, library, kitchen—on the ground floor, and one upstairs, for working. That floor was already crammed full with computers, fax machine, printer, scanners, work tables, corkboards. They said the downstairs library would be comfortable for just about anyone being interviewed, and they were right. It was certainly private, and easy to wire up like we needed.

"I'd have to drill a couple of holes," I told them.

"I wouldn't mind drilling a couple of holes in any of those scumbags," Sue said. Her eyes said that wasn't a joke. Nel nodded. Case closed.

"She couldn't have been more blunt," T.D. said. We were all watching the tape of Debbie interviewing Victim No. 1—that's how the tapes were going to be labeled, so we could refer to each girl in the presence of others without giving up any information. "But she's so angry that it might look like something else to a jury."

"You really think so?" Dolly said, clearly disappointed.

T.D. just nodded.

I was disappointed myself. When No. 1 said she only wished she could have been there when Cameron cashed in, I thought that was just as good as when Franklin said he'd tell a lie to help Mary-Lou. So I asked T.D. what the difference was.

"Franklin was saying he loves MaryLou enough to lie for her. That underscores the honesty of his other answers, just like you thought. But this girl's coming from the opposite direction: she hates that punk so much that she'd like to watch him die. I believe her. So would a jury. But they might carry that too far, and come up with a 'she'd lie to get MaryLou off, too' scenario. So that doesn't support her earlier testimony; it poisons it."

We all looked at each other. And we all saw the same thing.

Victim No. 4 was the pick of the litter. On paper, she was odds-on to be the runt. Raped by Tiger Ko Khai when she was twelve. Last year, she'd been raped again.

Not by the gang—to them, she was as appealing as a used condom. The perpetrator of the second rape was her mother's boyfriend. Apparently, she'd fought. Hard. Not only did the hospital records find what they called "significant bruising consistent with a prolonged fight or calculated beating," but she had the top of every index for "rape victim." And the aspirated DNA nailed the boyfriend cold. He didn't even know that his DNA had been data-banked years ago, the second time he'd gone to prison.

"'Why should I testify *now*?' That's what I told them. Those little slime."

"The police?" Debbie had asked. Her voice was as gentle as a caress, as comforting as a blanket to a baby.

"No. I mean those two 'girls' from the DA's Office. You could see it was freaking them out. Not me getting raped—them seeing such a sure winner slip out of their greasy hands. You know what else I told them? I said, 'You wouldn't prosecute Jerry Milhouse, so how come you're so hot to trot now?'"

"What did they say to that?"

"Oh, they said that was a different administration. If they'd been working for the DA then, they would have prosecuted him."

"But you didn't believe them?"

"I stopped believing anyone when Jerry and his friends tied me over that sawhorse thing they have."

Debbie made a sound I hadn't heard before. Soft sympathy and red rage, blended together in something you couldn't swallow except as a whole.

"They—those DAs, I mean—they made the same mistake most people do. Just because I'm fat and ugly doesn't mean I'm stupid. Until it . . . happened, I was an honor student. I don't go to school now, but I still read, and I still learn. Over the Internet.

"That's how it started. Thinking back, I can see it so clear. My mother's boyfriend, he said he used to be a teacher before he gave it up to concentrate on his writing. My mother told him I'd been gang-banged."

I never heard her say "Mom" once in the two hundred and twelve minutes of tape.

"And he was so understanding about it. Said he could home-school me so I never had to go back there again.

"I swallowed that hook. So did my mother. By then, she was swallowing everything that came out of his mouth. All he did was play on his computer. His 'writing.' My mother grabbed all the overtime she could, to pay for his toys.

"I guess he figured I was supposed to be one of those. After he raped me, he dared me to go to the cops. 'They didn't believe you the first time, you fat slob. They're sure as hell not going to believe you this time, either.'

"I didn't go to the cops. He was probably right about what he said. But I hurt so much I called my friend—I'm not going to say her name—and she drove me to the hospital. That's when it all started."

"The DAs tried to pressure you—?"

"—into pressing charges. You better believe it. They were the ones who told me about his criminal record. He was a teacher. And he went to prison for burglary, but those DAs told me the *other* DAs, the ones who came before them, let him plead to burglary even though he got caught in the bedroom of a girl. The burglary was more time in prison than what he would have got for attempted rape, and they weren't sure they could convict him of the rape—he never actually touched the girl; she was still sleeping when her dad heard a noise and ran downstairs and grabbed him. So they made this deal. They got a conviction, and he didn't get to be a registered sex offender.

"That was so funny, that part. My stupid mother, she checked him out on the Internet. That was his idea. He *told* her to check the Sex Offender Registry. He said that's what any good mom would do if she was going to let a man move in with her and her kids.

"She really trusted him after that. But, anyway, you know what I told those DAs?"

"What?" Debbie asked, not even trying to calm the girl down, just letting her go with whatever she was feeling.

"I told them it isn't only morons like my mother who can use the Internet. So I'd be glad to press charges against her boyfriend . . . if they prosecuted Panther Wornic and those others for what they did to me. See, I knew they could do that. The statute of limitations doesn't even start to run until I turn eighteen. That's the law. *That's* what I looked up!"

"And . . . ?"

"And they wouldn't do it! They gave me a million lame excuses, but the bottom line was they weren't going to do it. They even tried to tell me that my getting raped before my mother's boyfriend did it was going to make my case—the one against Jerry Milhouse, I mean—harder to prove."

"That's just—"

"—a lie. I know. Either they believed me or they didn't, I said. And if they believed me about Jerry Milhouse, they had to prosecute those others, no matter how 'hard' it would be."

"And they never budged?"

"Why do you think I live in that group home now? That was their worst threat: if I didn't press charges against my mother's boyfriend, well, then, they'd just have to send me back there, wouldn't they? They're even dirtier than he is," she said, more sad than angry, as if resigned to a world where the sun would never shine. "I knew if I was sent back 'home' it was as good as telling that filthy animal he could do whatever he wanted to me."

"Did you have a lawyer?"

"Me? Why would I have a lawyer?"

"I . . . don't know. It just seems as if you should have had one."

"Oh, I had this 'advocacy center.' They were, like, partners with the DA. They told me all the great counseling I could get if I would only press charges. Against my mother's boyfriend. When it came to anyone else, they really didn't see the point."

"You're right," Debbie said firmly.

"About what?"

"About all these agencies that were supposed to be on your side. They were even more foul than your mother's boyfriend. So what did you do?"

"I ran away. I found somebody who wanted me. A pimp. He hurt me sometimes. But sometimes he didn't. I guess I lived for those times.

"Then I got caught. I guess I don't look old enough—or maybe pretty enough—to be flagging down cars in Portland. They sent me all the way back here, and the judge sentenced me to the group home."

"Did you run away again?"

"I thought about it," the girl said, a little surprise in her voice that Debbie would know. "But I didn't do it. I kind of like it there now. I have friends. And the staff is pretty nice."

"And that's when you started a program?"

"To lose weight? That's right. I'm already twenty-five down. Only another fifty to go and I'll be able to stand looking at my body in a mirror. My face, there's nothing anyone can do about that."

"Yes, there is."

"Who?" the girl said, shocked.

"You."

"I don't get it."

"If you have the strength, if you have the will to lose . . . seventy-five pounds! If you have that, I promise your face will change, too. All by itself."

"Easy for you to say. You're pretty. That's something you're born with."

"You think I'm pretty?"

"Oh, come on! You're old enough to be my mother, but you're really cute."

"When I was your age, I thought I was so ugly my face could break a mirror."

"Stop it!" the girl said. But Debbie had managed to tease a little giggle out of her.

"It's the truth," Debbie said. "My counselor helped me understand that the mirror was a reflection of my feelings. I was seeing what *I* saw, not what other people did. And when I lost that weight, I looked in the mirror and, like magic, I liked what I saw. Because my counselor taught me to respect what I'd achieved—losing that weight."

"Hold up!" the girl said. "You're telling me you were fat?"

"Yes."

"And you thought you were ugly, and no man would ever want you?"

"Yes."

"And you went into counseling?"

"Yes."

"And now you're a cute little psychologist?"

"I'm not a psychologist; I'm a clinical social worker. And I guess I'm not all that big. But the other is a judgment. Some might agree; some not."

"I agree."

"Then make the same deal with yourself," Debbie urged her. "And I'll make you another promise: If you're the one who helps MaryLou get found not guilty of killing that filthy rapist, you'll be a lot more than 'cute,' you'll be a warrior. A true warrior for justice. And *that's* what you'll see in the mirror!"

"**Y**ou're really good," T.D. told Debbie. "That is one angry young girl, just like our Number One. But this is anger she can use. It doesn't have to eat her insides out; it can make her into Wonder Woman. Beautiful!"

"Can we all have something to eat before we look at another one?" Dolly said. To save her girlfriend from passing out.

If T.D. knew the effect his praise had on Debbie, he kept it off his face.

But not completely off. Especially if you were looking for it.

I kept thinking of Danielle as an old *Perry Mason* episode, something like "The Case of the Disgusting Diva." But I never let her get even a whiff of that—I made sure Patrice Laveque's personal assistant stayed in contact with her.

But someone like Danielle never trusts anyone. She even tested

Miss Rontempe's accent by firing off a whole paragraph of memorized questions in her schoolbook French. Fortunately, Dolly not only knew how to sound like a haughty bitch, she hadn't forgotten the language she'd had to learn when she served overseas. So all that foul little creature got back was:

"*Arrêtez, s'il vous plaît. Je vais parler très lentement, comme ça vous allez peut-être enfin me comprendre.* Listen! Your silly little attempt to speak my native tongue offends me. When you have mastered French as I have English, do try again, if you wish. In the meantime, understand that I do not appreciate your childish games, especially when Mr. Laveque's schedule is very demanding, which makes him very demanding of *me.* You are not getting the usual 'don't call us, we'll call you,' are you? You are being kept in the loop, are you not?"

Dolly hung up in the middle of Danielle's frightened attempt to assure herself that she hadn't made an enemy, especially when that enemy was a bridge she had to cross to get to everything she wanted in the world.

There's probably no one word that describes that place, only what being there meant: no standing in line to get into the hottest restaurants; the mere mention of her name replacing the need for reservations. Always being able to order off the menu. And *things.* All kinds of things, from fine jewelry to big houses to a staff of servants. Danielle knew she wouldn't need more than a couple of years in L.A. before she landed the only fish she was trolling for: a nice, fat koi.

So, when it came time to see if she could be any more use to us than the tape we already had, plus Franklin's testimony, T.D. stepped in. "I wonder if any of you'd mind me taking a shot at that one?"

I sure didn't. Neither did Dolly. And Debbie took the opportunity to say something you could tell had been nagging at her for years:

"I not only don't mind, I wish you would. Let's face it, my profession isn't self-respecting. It's polluted from the top down. The schools of social work start the prejudgment process, and it doesn't stop until the holy plateau is reached. Any 'doctor' is axiomatically more insightful, more intelligent, more . . . valuable than all the M.S.W.'s in the world, combined."

T.D. nodded encouragement. Dolly squeezed my hand. Meaning: Don't interrupt this!

"Look at social work," Debbie said. "What's the missing demographic?"

"White males," T.D. said instantly.

"Working-class, heterosexual white males," Debbie came back with.

"True" is all T.D. said.

"This isn't about 'role modeling' or any such nonsense," Debbie said, speaking to Dolly and me, as if she and T.D. had already passed that point in their understanding. "When they talk about working with 'at-risk' youth, that's code for 'minority poor.' But poor *whites,* whoever heard of such a thing?

"How are women going to interact with young men who are just beginning to understand that there's nothing for them in the future except the feeling of superiority you get from some 'white pride' group? Never mind black males, who come with their own set of issues and expectations. Everything starts with the premise that it's all 'women's work.'"

"Yeah," T.D. said. "The degree doesn't say a thing about the practitioner. I had a clinical internship, inside what passed for a supermax in those days, not sitting at the feet of some air-pumped 'guru' and absorbing wisdom. But I probably couldn't make a living examining conditions of confinement and testifying about them if whoever hired me couldn't call me 'Dr. Joel' when they put me on the stand."

"Is that why you think you'd get more out of Danielle?" Dolly asked.

"Uh-uh," T.D. said. "Dell already got enough out of her so that I'd bet my car against a detuned minivan that Debbie and I'd agree on a diagnosis from that CD video alone."

Debbie nodded.

"So why me? That one's easy. Debbie's got a lot more experience than I have working with victims. But I've got a lot more than her when it comes to dealing with predators."

It wasn't easy to set up. Danielle's calendar was full. But when a fawning, abject call to Miss Rontempe confirmed that talking with the psychologist the defense was going to be using would be *"un éclairage intéressant"* that might add greater dimension to the planned docudrama, Danielle went from cold and distanced to hot and wet without a second's foreplay.

"We can't use the same hotel," I told Dolly. "And we can't use the cottage, either. Yeah, I know, honey, Nel and Sue might not give a damn, but it's still bad tactics. Right now, nobody on the other side knows about them, and it's better that way."

"Yeah," T.D. echoed. "What's the point of showing your hole card if the other guy hasn't paid to call?"

"What's left, then?" Debbie asked.

It was easy to hide the equipment in Swift's conference room—by now, that's the way the pig at the front desk thought of it. All that extra clutter we added, plus three walls of law books, made it a snap to hide the microphones. And the huge slab of Norwegian oceanic marble that Spyros had borrowed from some landscaping job, the one Franklin had somehow managed to carry in by himself and put down gently over the conference table, changed the look completely.

Everybody played their part to perfection, without rehearsal. By then, the transformation of Receptionist Jeannine from dismissive pig to adoring fan was complete. "Please take the young lady straight to the conference room, Ms. Rollo," she trilled at Debbie. "Mr. Swift is already there, and he'll introduce her to Dr. Joel personally."

Swift made the formal introductions. I'd already told him that, considering who we were working with, *his* credentials would be more impressive than T.D.'s. He didn't understand until he saw Danielle's reaction to a tape of him being interviewed on Court TV by a pretty blond woman with the kind of angry eyes you only get from looking into those of the takers-by-force.

They'd been "reviewing" that tape when Danielle was ushered in. And they turned it off right away. But not before she saw Swift on TV.

By the time he left—after asking if she'd like a beverage and bringing her the Perrier with a slice of lime I'd bet him ten bucks she'd ask for—Danielle was as moist as if she'd been stroked by an expert's mink-gloved hand for an hour.

"I'm just trying to get some background," T.D. assured her. "I've already spoken to a number of your sister's friends. It seems that they all know a lady . . ." He paused to consult his notebook. "A lady named Dolly Jackson. Her house is kind of a clubhouse for teenagers, isn't it?"

"You mean Dolly *Parton,* don't you?" Danielle cracked. "I'm not sure why girls hang out there, but I sure know what the boys come for."

"She's . . . well endowed?"

"Well . . ." Danielle yawned to emphasize her boredom, giving her the opportunity to stretch her shoulders—and her T-shirt. "If you like them cow-size, I guess you could say so. But I'd hate to see her without a bra."

Meaning: Me, I don't need one, I thought, wishing there was a way the tape could be edited before Dolly saw it. I hoped she wasn't enough of a baby to start walking around without a bra herself, but I wouldn't have bet Rascal an extra strip of rawhide on it.

"Okay. Well, that's not important here, but it usually is."

"How well built a girl is?" Danielle asked, frankly curious.

"No. What's truly important always starts with 'Why?' But some 'why's are more important than others. Why teenagers hang out at this lady's house, that's not important. Why your sister went on that shooting spree, *that* is."

"Oh, that again. Do you mind if I smoke?"

T.D. clearly did, and let his disapproval show, but said, "Of course not. I'd like you to be as comfortable as possible."

Danielle smiled. *Another piece of putty,* she was thinking. But when she held the cigarette in her hand for a full minute without T.D. making a move to light it for her, she gave up and used her own pink plastic Bic. A deep inhale gave her another chance to show off the goods. Examining the filter tip of her cigarette to admire the lipstick marks was her deal-closer.

"Well?" she half-demanded.

"Well, what?"

"Well, what comes next?"

"Oh. My apologies. I got the impression you'd been asked that question so many times that answering it again would bore you. But I haven't heard the answer myself, so, if you wouldn't mind . . ."

With a world-weary sigh, Danielle went through her story again. Practically word for word—it was the only script she'd had to study, and she had it down pat. So, when T.D. said, "It's somewhat unusual for an older sister to be jealous of a younger one," Danielle was ready. "I'll bet you never met old Mighty Mary."

"I've not spoken with your sister yet," T.D. told her. "Is 'Mighty Mary' what she called herself? That does sound a bit on the egotistical side."

You could see Danielle was tempted, but she didn't take the bait. Probably realized that T.D. would have many other sources of information, and claiming that MaryLou had saddled herself with that title would be a mistake. "No. I mean, no, she didn't name herself that. But she got it for being such a super-jock, not for winning some wet–T-shirt contest, if you get my meaning."

"I do," T.D. said, with a thin smile.

"Never mind that I got better grades than her by a ton, even with all the play they give jocks."

" 'They'?"

"The teachers. Everybody knows, if you're on a team, that's like adding an extra point to your GPA. More, if you need it."

"Did MaryLou need it?"

"She might have, for all I know. I mean, when your best pal's a retard . . ."

"She was in Special Ed?" T.D. asked, pretending to misunderstand.

"Not her, *him,*" Danielle said, exasperated at the psychologist's slowness.

"Oh."

"Yeah, 'oh' is right. Look, I'll save you the walk around the block. MaryLou was bigger than almost all the guys in school. If she and her boyfriend, Bluto, ever got together, they could probably take on the whole senior class."

"Bluto is . . . ?"

"The retard. Stop interrupting, okay? I'm almost done. Mary-Lou is a big, stupid, lame jock with a retard for a best pal. And she's gay. Gay, and she can't even find a girlfriend, what does that tell you?"

"It doesn't tell me anything, not yet. What does it tell you?"

"It tells me that I'm everything MaryLou isn't. And not only that . . . Oh, I'm not supposed to say anything."

T.D. didn't bite. And Danielle was too smart to expose herself by volunteering the information she wanted to have coaxed out of her.

"There's a bottom line to all this," T.D. finally said.

"Which is?" Danielle asked, lighting another smoke and blowing a jet stream over toward T.D., then making an "Ooh, I'm going to get it now!" face. Very cute.

"MaryLou is facing at least a life sentence, maybe even the death penalty."

"And . . . ?"

"And perhaps, talking with you, I'm thinking there's a way for her to get help instead."

"Help?" You could see Danielle struggle to not say, "For what?"

"Well, for example, if the court finds she was temporarily insane when—"

"Jealousy isn't the same as insanity."

"I understand," T.D. said patiently. "But if you noticed certain . . . cues that MaryLou was mentally ill—and who would be in a better position to notice than you?—that might just save her life."

"I never saw anything."

"I understand. Still, if you were to say that—"

"I'm not lying for her. You just don't get it, do you? She killed my boyfriend!"

"But . . . help me with this, Danielle. It says here that you were . . . a rape victim a couple of years ago. And that you—"

"Now, *that* is crazy. Rape victim? Me?"

"That's the information we have. In a murder case, the District Attorney's Office has to turn over any and all material that could possibly be exculpatory."

"Exculpatory?"

"Ah. I don't know why I keep speaking to you as if you were

a grown woman. I apologize. 'Exculpatory' means anything that would either help the defense prove innocence, or, in your sister's case, mitigate the guilt."

Danielle didn't ask for a definition of "mitigate." She'd fellate a Shetland pony to get a part in a movie, but when it came to saving her sister, she wasn't licking *that* plate. "How could some nonsense story 'mitigate' anything?"

"Well, let's say it wasn't a nonsense story. Let's say what the DA's Office turned over is at least partially true. Let's say you were raped. Not only by this Cameron Taft—the boy who was killed."

"That's a lie!" foamed out of Danielle's mouth as if she'd just caught rabies.

But T.D. just kept talking right through it, as if Danielle hadn't made a sound. "Let's say you were raped, not only by this boy, but by several others. Gang-raped. A jury might go much lighter on a girl who thought she was defending her little sister—"

"You better not try that," Danielle warned, her voice icy enough to hurt your spine. "You try that and I'll just tell the truth. The truth. I wasn't 'gang-raped,' I was *initiated*. Tiger Ko Khai is the most exclusive society. Not just in school, not just in this whole town, but all over the world! They can only have men as members, but anytime a member claims a woman as his own, he has to prove to the others that his woman is for real. If I hadn't had sex with those other boys, it would have shamed Cameron. And he was the leader! Not just of one chapter, of the whole state."

T.D. did no more than shift his weight slightly, and Danielle was already blocking the punch she expected.

"Look, I know sex isn't love. I only loved Cameron, of course. But I had to show the others that I'd do anything for him. I had to do that, don't you understand?"

"I don't think I—"

"They would have excommunicated him!" Danielle said, forgetting all about flirting, putting everything she had into her deadly method acting. "If Cameron's own girlfriend wouldn't do what he asked her to do, he'd lose his whole position. Do you know how they do that? He's got the same tattoo they all have. On his arm. But over his heart, he's got one only a leader can have.

"They'd cut that tattoo right off his body! He could die! And he was willing to risk all that for me. Me! How could I not back up a man who put his own life on the line? What kind of a person would that make me?"

We watched the tape as T.D. carefully talked her down. It was another hour of babble before Danielle was convinced she'd convinced him, and another half-hour before there was any way to end the "interview" organically.

We waited until Debbie got back so we could all watch the tape together. We did that in Swift's new "overflow" office. It wasn't fancy, but there wasn't a chance anyone would overhear. And Rascal was lying down at the top of the staircase, better than any motion sensor.

"All young girls need to individuate from their older sisters, but this is beyond anything I've ever seen," Debbie said.

"The hospital records say she was brought in bruised; with torn tissue, both vaginal and anal; semen from several depositors still in her underclothes," Dolly recited from memory. I'd warned her against carrying any report she wasn't willing to hand over to Swift. If Swift wondered how Dolly had gotten her hands on hospital records, he didn't show it.

"Well, I guess that's one witness we'll never be calling," he said.

T.D. stood up. "Hoss, I don't often make a diagnosis based on a single sentence, but if you don't plan to call that girl to the stand, I'm ready to write you up as clinically insane right this minute."

"But she's only going to exonerate—"

"She can't exonerate anyone," I said. "Even if every word out of that filthy little slut's mouth was true, they'd still all be guilty of statutory rape. And if she's lying—"

"*If?*" Dolly cut me off. "The medical records alone are enough to end that discussion. And there's seven other girls who had a similar . . . experience. Only, *they* all tried to get the perpetrators prosecuted. And they were all slapped across the face for it."

"She's no slut," T.D. said, holding up his hand for silence. "I've spent my life working with the dregs of humanity: serial killers, baby-rapers, torture fans, you name it. And that girl is the most amoral sociopath I've ever met. Utterly relentless. She'll do whatever, to whoever, whenever. All that matters to her is what she wants. You get between her and whatever that is at any given time, you're cooked.

"You put her on the stand, the jury is going to see a horror story worse than any movie. Imagine sacrificing your own life for a person who'd kick you under a falling safe if you were late driving her to an audition. But that's exactly what MaryLou did."

"Danielle can refuse to testify, can't she?" Debbie asked.

"No," Swift said, slowly and thoughtfully. "If we can convince the judge that her testimony is not only relevant but necessary, she could be ordered to testify. The Fifth Amendment only protects her if her own testimony could possibly incriminate her. And her testimony might damn her soul, but it couldn't send her to prison."

"MaryLou should have shot her, too," Dolly said, white blotches of anger on her face.

"No, baby," I said, putting an arm around Dolly, telling her we were in my arena now. "We need her alive. She's MaryLou's best chance now."

When Danielle called Miss Rontempe late that afternoon, she was told that "recent revelations" had caused A.A. to defer the project until after the verdict came in. And that calling back before the verdict would be *very* ill-advised.

I ghosted past the section of parking lot behind the day-care center that Tiger Ko Khai had marked as its own territory years ago—my best guess was a short while after a guy named Ryan Teller had been kicked out of the military and come "home."

It was empty. I made three more passes: one more in daylight, the other two at night. But the place stayed empty. So either Ryan Teller had faded away and wasn't coming back, or he realized he had to make some show of force to keep all his followers from deserting.

But what kind of show of force could he make? He'd built a squad of empty-core nothings: tough guys when they held all the cards, but worse than cowards inside. Cowards just run. You have to be a much lower breed than that to attack only prescreened victims.

If he came back, I'd find out, and I'd kill him. He knew this—I'd sent him the head of one of his tribe on a stake—but he didn't know who I was. If I'd pulled it off, he'd think I was part of a whole gang. *He'll just move on,* I told myself. *Set up shop in some other place. But maybe he's too old for that now. Convincing high school boys is one thing—there'll always be kids who'd listen to the kind of promises he'd make—but men his own age?*

I put it out of my mind, and locked it down. There was no time for that anymore. Ryan Teller couldn't come back quietly. I didn't have my ear to the ground, but I didn't need to; I knew the one person he'd be sure to contact.

Danielle wasn't fat. She wasn't ugly. She wasn't stupid. She'd be a prize for any high school kid, no matter what grade. So she chose

Cameron. Not the captain of the football team, not the kid whose parents had the most money—Cameron.

It hit me then. Hit me in a place I wish I didn't have. That tiny detector that went off every time I was near one of those creatures who'd watch the enemy torture a comrade while keeping *very* quiet in his own safe hiding place.

Danielle was smarter than any of them. They hadn't lured her into that gang rape. Even if they *had* told her some nonsense about an "initiation," she would have laughed in their faces. She couldn't parade Cameron around school, so there was only one place she could really be the kind of "star" she needed to be. Danielle was the Queen Bee of Tiger Ko Khai. And her stinger was pure poison.

If Dr. Joel hadn't made that speech about how valuable she'd be to MaryLou on the stand, I would have had Patrice Laveque give her a call to meet her late one night. And scattered her ashes in the nearest toxic-waste dump I could find.

The lawyer told me how it works in this state. When they start a trial, the prosecution goes first, then the defense. And when they end it, the prosecution gets the last word *twice,* sandwiched around the defense closing.

"So they get the last word, before and after?"

"Yes. But that's not always as good as it sounds."

"You mean it could end up like tossing a grenade around in a circle after the pin's already been pulled."

"I guess so," he said, giving me a funny look. I'd already said too much to this guy. He didn't need to know that they'd made us play that game when we were recruits—it wasn't until even the dumbest of us realized the pulled-pin grenade was a dummy that they all broke out laughing. That is, unless one of us had panicked and screamed or run away when the grenade was tossed in his direction. Then they wouldn't be laughing. And one less man would be around the next morning.

Much later, when we were all legionnaires in the same squad, some played it for real. The same ones who liked playing Russian roulette, to show their courage.

T.D. saw MaryLou. After that, he promised us that if any state psychologist said she wasn't in her right mind T.D. would leave pieces of him all over the wall.

Debbie kept on with her interviewing. All seven of the victims had varying degrees of reluctance, but none of them had pulled out from their promise to testify. Not yet, anyway.

Dolly tightened her team so taut T.D. could have used them for banjo strings.

Danielle kept going back and forth with Miss Rontempe, who explained to her that things always move slowest in the summer months—surely she was aware of this? Besides, had she *not* been told the "project was on hold" until the verdict?

Danielle couldn't have been holding a summer job, not with her making-the-rounds schedule, but she was never at a loss for a new outfit.

Spyros told me Franklin "had the touch." I knew what he meant, even though I'd never heard that term applied to anyone whose skill was in keeping things alive.

I asked Swift to check. He told me Ryan Teller was "off paper." To my look, he answered, "There's no authority holding him. Not parole or probation. He's not on any registry, so he doesn't have to report in. He could be anywhere, doing anything."

"I don't like all this waiting," Dolly said late that night. She'd snuck down to the basement, where I was supposed to be sleeping. She hadn't been any more surprised to find me awake than I'd been to see her show up.

"It's nothing."

"Not for you, I know. I've seen you wait for . . . well, I don't know how long, exactly, but I know you can go hours and hours without even moving."

"It's just my training."

"Your training? No, Dell. That may have helped. It may have taught you some techniques. But this . . . stillness of yours, it's as if you were born with it."

"I don't know."

She burst into tears.

"What, baby?"

"You think I was trying to probe into your . . ."

"'Childhood.' You can say it; I'm all right with hearing it."

"But *I'm* not."

"What's wrong with you, baby? You've got nerves jumping under your skin. That's not you."

"It's me when I think a heroic girl gets paid back for trying to protect her foul little sister with life in prison."

"If she does, it won't be from anything you did. And if she doesn't, it will *only* be because of you. Of what you did."

"What if it was something I *didn't* do?"

"Dolly . . ."

"Listen, Dell. Please. I have to say this. I thought I was so 'with it,' you know? So . . . how do you always say it . . . plugged in? But I never even heard of this Tiger Ko Khai vermin. I must have had hundreds of girls walk in and out of this house, and not a single one ever so much as . . . mentioned it."

"Why would they?"

"Dell!"

"Stop, Dolly. You think you're some kind of geologist, drilling a sample core out of this whole town? You're not. You deal with the girls who come to you. Just those, not more. Your sample wasn't representative, it selected itself. You think any girl could have told you about these *salopards dégénérés* without you doing something about it? You think they don't all *know* that?"

"But—"

"Shut up," I said, pinching her bottom hard. It didn't make her giggle, but it did shut her up. "Be proud of your reputation, Dolly. Not ashamed of it. Remember Médecins Sans Frontières. You're not ashamed of that, are you?"

"Of course not," she said, pinching my biceps harder than I'd pinched her bottom. The difference was, I had to act like I didn't feel it. Which she knew, the little . . . "To have served with them is a badge of honor."

"Will you please let me finish," I said, pinching her harder than she *could* pinch.

She squealed. It was the sweetest sound I'd heard in days.

"A man shows up, unannounced. He tells you that he wants to go in with you on a Médecins Sans Frontières flight. The weapons he carries, they're only to protect your team. What do you do?"

"No weapons," she said firmly.

"But there's more, isn't there? You'd know he wasn't there to protect you; he was there to get info on wherever you set up camp. Then he'd disappear. And the next thing you know, you'd all be captives. Or dead."

"Yes. Yes, that's right."

"Anybody ever try that?"

"Nooo . . ." she said, dragging the word out.

"Because they'd be nailed in a second. Transparent. And that's the same reason none of your girls ever mentioned Tiger Ko Khai—they knew they'd be opening the gates of hell if they did. They weren't protecting Tiger Ko Khai, *précieuse,* they were protecting you."

She snuggled against me. "Dangerous, huh? I've never been called that before," she whispered.

"Maybe if you opened up a little more . . ."

Two days later, Swift called me. I didn't have to burn another cell—this was the same number I'd given out all over the place, in my role as "investigator."

I just said: "Office?"

He said yes. I hit the "off" button.

When I arrived, Jeannine looked as happy as if she'd been entered in a pie-eating contest, installed as the odds-on favorite.

"Go right on inside," she sang out. "He's expecting you."

I closed the door behind me. Swift motioned me to move closer. "I don't trust anything anymore. Do you know a place where we can talk with no chance of being overheard?"

I took Swift to "his" other office. Told him I'd swept it myself that morning, and the motion detectors hadn't registered any intrusion prior to mine.

He made himself comfortable on the carpet, where Debbie had thoughtfully covered a large spot with some Indian-pattern carpet. *Wanted T.D. to feel right at home,* I thought to myself at the time.

"They're in a purple panic," he said.

I made a "Who?" gesture.

"The DA's Office. From the top down."

"You know this because . . . ?"

"They asked me to come in for a conference. That's weird enough, all by itself. It's always the defense attorney who asks for a conference."

"Again, because . . . ?"

"Because 'conference' is a fancy word for 'make a deal.'"

"*They* want to make a deal?"

"They're desperate to," Swift said, unable to keep the smile off his face.

"What kind of deal?"

"Essentially, it boils down to a kind of insanity plea. We agree to have their shrink see MaryLou. If he says she was out of her mind at the time of the shooting—and he will—they'd go for a probation-with-treatment deal."

"*She* wouldn't."

"How do you know?"

"Because I already asked her. She is not going to say she's crazy. Not now, not then."

"You're sure?"

"Hell, yes. I did my best to talk her into it, but she wasn't having any."

"You mind if we go over and see her now?"

"Yeah, I do."

"Why, for God's sake?"

"For *her* sake. I need to hear the whole thing. Why you're so sure they're scared, and whether they actually offered this deal, or you're just confident you can talk them into it."

He nodded. "Okay, you're right. Or your guess was right, maybe. They haven't actually offered that deal. But here's why I'm dead sure they will: they never try cases unless they can't lose. Like the one they just did: a sex offender with a record going back sixty years! They had him on peeping, masturbating in front of little girls, porno on his computer, you name it. And they knew he couldn't even get on the stand to deny anything. His lawyer probably told him, what the hell, if they weren't going to give him a decent deal, he might as well take it to trial. Guess what happened?"

"Don't tell me he got off?"

"No. He was convicted . . . of two misdemeanors! This . . . I don't know what to call someone like that, this person is in his late seventies, but he'll *still* get at least one more chance to keep on attacking kids."

Soft as warm custard rolled through my mind, but I didn't say anything.

"The whole office is like that," Swift said. "Like the DA's personality infected them all. There's a kind of . . . culture to that place. Even if you came in right after law school, wanting to fill up the prisons with people you convicted, you'd be one of the boys soon enough. Some of the prosecutors have been there forever, and they're not going anywhere.

"But there's even more. When you walk into a room and there's four deputies, *and* the DA himself, you know they're terrified. That was supposed to be a show of force, but, to me, it was a show of fear.

"After a while, the others left, and there was just the DA and me. That's when I reminded him that a trial is just like an election. Only, in this one, I just need a couple of votes, and he needs all the rest."

"I thought a jury verdict had to be unanimous."

"Not here," he said, eager to get on with his story. "By 'election,' I was talking about the one coming up. And the DA knew it. That's why he sent the other ones out. So we could talk alone.

"Okay, now here's where it gets tricky. He already knows we're not pleading insanity. You have to file a notice if you're going to do that. That's what scares him to death. If we're not going to try an insanity defense, what does that leave?"

"Justification?"

"Bingo! See, he has to offer the insanity deal. That's the only explanation this town would ever accept—that MaryLou just 'snapped.' But he doesn't get to choose the defense; we do. And if we *don't* go with temp insanity, there's always a chance he's going to lose. That's the one thing people will remember about the trial, that he lost.

"When you lose a big trial like this one, and the jury verdict is the same one the town itself would have brought in, you've made yourself very unpopular. And this DA spends all his time running for office. Making friends."

"Anything else on our side of the table?"

"Oh yes!" he crowed. "They checked out our experts, and now they *really* don't know what to do. No disrespect intended to Ms. Rollo, but Dr. Joel's name scared the holy hell out of them. They'd need a forklift just to carry the transcripts of cases where he's testified—as a witness for the government! He's never exaggerated his résumé. Never changed his testimony under cross-examination. I don't know where you found him, but that's a five-hundred-pound gorilla in a jungle full of spider monkeys."

"Ms. Rollo found him."

"Then you found Ms. Rollo."

"No, Mr. Swift, you did. You found them both."

He sat there for a couple of seconds, then he just nodded.

"Doesn't matter. This was teamwork, any way you slice it. But, bottom line, if Dr. T. D. Joel says MaryLou snapped, she snapped. That's what every single therapist they asked already told them— I could see it right on his face."

"Let's go," I said. "Maybe with this new info, you'll have better luck than I did."

I should have waited, but I couldn't. Even if it meant burning some of my credibility with Swift, I had to risk it—I *wanted* to be wrong.

But I wasn't. "Not a chance," MaryLou told Swift. "That's the one thing that could stop me from the scholarship. And even if it wouldn't, I'm not walking around wearing a psycho jacket for the rest of my life. And come on, okay? If I 'snapped' once, there'll always be people who think I could do it again."

"But, MaryLou—"

"It's no use," she said, no longer bristling at the use of her first name. "Uncle Dell here—that's how he first got in, you know, with my aunt Dolly—he already asked me about all that. Not in so many words, but I knew where he was going. That 'evaluation' thing, he knows I'd pass. I'm not crazy, and I never was. And I'm not *saying* I was."

"So you killed Cameron Taft because . . ."

"Because I had to." She ended the sentence and the conversation with those four words, getting up and smacking the door with her palm to tell the guards she was ready to go back to her cell.

"Is she going to take the stand at all?" he asked, on the short drive back to his office.

"You can't make her, right?"

"No. If I even tried, she could turn around and fire me, right in front of the jury. And she'd be within her rights to do so. That's what the Fifth Amendment is: you can't make anyone testify against their will unless there is no way their testimony could possibly be self-incriminating."

"But you *can* make her sister testify, like you said?"

"Sure."

"Okay. Please trust me on this. I'm not a lawyer, but I know people. Certain kinds of people. And I'm telling you, if Danielle gets up on the stand and tells her story, the second MaryLou realizes what's going on, you won't be able to *keep* her off the stand.

MaryLou is one girl who can take a punch. And hit back a lot harder than she took."

"Justification," he said.

"Justification times seven," I reminded him. "And Danielle doesn't make eight. She's not just one more witness; she's a *multiplier*."

"Oh, they're losing their minds over there," Swift told me later that afternoon. "When I filed that motion for a sealed witness order on the ground that each witness could be in mortal danger if her name was to be revealed, they went bats."

"You think they know?"

"The names? No. How could they—?"

"If the Tiger Ko Khai thing was something they already knew about, why not?"

"I hate to admit this, but, sometimes, not knowing what's going on can make you innocent. Stupid, sure. But innocent—that, too."

"I don't get it. Are you saying—?"

"I'm saying that this DA would think Tiger Ko Khai was a new dish in a Chinese restaurant."

"Doesn't have a clue?"

"Not a chance."

"But with thirty-nine rapes being reported . . ."

"By who, the SANE nurses? We've had six different ones in the past five years. That's an amazing turnover, especially since most people want to live in this part of the state. You know, the sacred coast. That's how our economy can actually live on tourism alone."

"Yeah, so what?"

"They probably left because no amount of nice living could

compensate them for a system where they examine rape victims and report the rapes, and yet nothing ever happens."

"The DA is the one who—?"

"That's not fair, either. Maybe at one time. But, lately, the police don't even bother to ask for warrants, never mind indictments. Why? Maybe they got sick of nothing happening, too. Maybe they were worried about being sued. Maybe the girls refused to name names. I don't know. There's no way *to* know."

"But that one girl, the one who said she'd be glad to report the most recent time she got raped if the DA would just prosecute those scum who raped her *first*. The one they told that they don't make deals with victims."

"That's true. They don't make deals with victims, only with perpetrators. Still, that doesn't say anything about the SANE nurses quitting."

"I think it does," I said, remembering what Dolly had told us. "Rape Trauma Syndrome, it's not just for those who got raped. It probably hits those who have to watch the rapes even harder."

"They didn't—"

"Yeah, they did. Okay, they didn't actually watch rapes take place, but when you enter a profession to do something, and the harder you try, the more you get laughed at, that's pretty much the same thing. Why be a SANE nurse at all if you don't want to do something about sexual assault? Okay, now a victim comes into the hospital where you work. You examine that victim. You say there's no doubt she was raped. None. Not based on what she said, based on medical evidence. Not an opinion, actual medical proof. And *still* nothing happens. The way I understand it is that, after too many of those, they start suffering from Rape Trauma Syndrome themselves."

"This is getting wilder by the minute. If it gets too complicated, no jury is going to follow it."

"It's not fucking complicated," I told him. Quietly.

He looked frightened. I shook my head to get rid of the red haze. "I'm sorry," I told him. "I shouldn't have said that. Look, I'm not any smarter than the average person. I could even be on a jury. I register to vote; isn't that how they pick you?"

"Yes," he said absently. I could see he was thinking about what I said.

"So pretend I *am* on that jury. And the evidence shows me that there's a rape club pouncing on girls barely old enough to bleed."

He gave me a look, but he didn't say anything.

"I didn't mean to be so crude. I'm sorry. I wasn't raised good, and sometimes I say things wrong. Not things that are wrong, like a lie, but wrong the way I say them. What I meant to say was, the girls, they're young. Way young. Too young to have sex with. Legally, I'm saying.

"And *still* nothing ever happens. After a while, that word has to get around. How can MaryLou protect her sister from Cameron Taft and his gang if she's leaving in a couple of days and doesn't plan to ever come back? I'll tell you how. Shoot him in the head. That was the only way left to her."

"But the sister, this Danielle, she wasn't raped at all. She was—"

"So what? We know what Danielle is now. We know she wasn't raped. Or *says* she wasn't, anyway. How was MaryLou supposed to know any of that?"

"It's a huge risk. If we could just persuade—"

"We can't persuade MaryLou to do anything. Dolly might, but she wouldn't even try."

"So . . . ?"

"So we have to take the shot."

"You understand that means—?"

"All or nothing," I cut him off. "And that's what it's meant from the second MaryLou pulled that trigger."

Dolly woke me. It was around noon, but I'd been out all night. And finally found what I'd been looking for: no sign that Tiger Ko Khai had ever existed.

"Dell, the DA got the judge to order a hearing."

"Huh?"

"That sealed witness list that the lawyer asked for? Well, Brad Swift went even further than that—he asked that the witnesses be allowed to testify over closed-circuit TV. Or even from behind a screen, through a microphone. The judge said nothing like that had ever been done before in his court, so . . ."

"When is this hearing thing?"

"Tomorrow morning. And, Dell, Brad said we have to bring the girls in. All of them. I don't quite understand it, but he said we didn't have any choice."

"Let me just take a shower and shave, honey. Then I'll go over to his office."

"You're not going alone."

"Why am I not surprised?" I said. But Dolly was already gone.

"For the girls, he wants an *in-camera* proceeding," Swift told us.

"Bullshit," T.D. said.

"What?"

"You heard me, hoss. The judge can't order an *in-camera* and still keep the case. If he speaks to witnesses to determine if they're really scared of testifying in public, he's hearing evidence that would prejudice him. So either he's a moron, or he wants to dump this case on another judge."

"It's Judge Hurst," Swift said. "I don't know how smart he

is. He doesn't have a reputation for being a good law-man, but no way he's about to give up trying a case that's already national news."

"So, if you just make it clear—"

"I know," Swift told T.D. "I'm just not sure I can."

"*I'm* sure," T.D. said. "All you have to do is get your expert witnesses on the stand before you let him speak to anyone else."

"**C**ounsel, is it your representation, as an officer of this court, not only that your witnesses have a mortal fear of testifying, but that that mortal fear is grounded in actual reality?"

"It is, Your Honor," Swift said, standing taller than I'd ever seen him. I could see the judge blink a few times, maybe wondering if this was the same Bradley L. Swift who had schlubbed his way through these same courts for the past dozen or so years.

"And you have expert witness testimony to support this position."

"I do, judge. The finest in the country."

"So you say. All right, then. Go ahead and call them—I'll decide how 'fine' they are."

T.D. didn't look all that impressive taking the stand. Unless you looked at his eyes, and the judge couldn't do that from where he was sitting.

Swift asked qualification questions, deliberately keeping that part short, as T.D. had told him: "Unless the judge demands more, just tell him my name and how many years I've been practicing, and move on. It's better for the prosecution to put their necks in the noose than to have the judge do it. We want to protect the judge as much as we can. That way, he'll have an even bigger incentive to keep the case."

As it turned out, the judge didn't say a word. Neither did the prosecution. So T.D. was able to get right to the heart of Swift's motion.

"Each and every one of the defense witnesses is suffering from post-traumatic stress disorder," T.D. said. "My colleague Deborah Rollo did the interviewing of all but one of them, and she'll go into specifics to the extent the court requires. However, I've reviewed all the tapes, and I'm prepared to state it is my opinion that you can cover all of the victims with the same blanket. And that blanket is terror. Pure terror."

Ignoring an audible gasp from some of the people sitting behind me, T.D. kept right on rolling:

"The crux of the issue is that these girls are still living in mortal fear. They've been subjected to crimes usually only committed in Third World countries. By that," he said, holding up his hand as if to anticipate some politically correct objection, "I don't mean gang rape. That happens everywhere. What doesn't happen here—at least, I've never heard of such a case, or found one in the literature—is that the victims perceive that the community *approves* of the conduct of the perpetrators, the same way some cultures approve of so-called honor rape. The same way some cultures which practice so-called ethnic cleansing use rape . . . as a weapon of war.

"What all these victims have in common is a shared perception of community approval. As if the victims somehow *deserved* to be raped—that they brought it on themselves. Again, I defer to my colleague on this. But what I can tell this court is, if forced to testify in open court, if forced to reveal their identities to the whole community, the witnesses could opt for several psychological strategies, any one of which could result in permanent hospitalization. At best."

"What 'strategies'?" the judge demanded. With the audience

completely under T.D.'s spell, he wanted to make sure everyone in the place understood whose courtroom this was. But T.D. was more than ready for him.

"Elective mutism, catatonia, decompensation—"

"Doctor, would you mind? Plain English, please," the judge demanded, just short of annoyed.

"My apologies," T.D. said, without a trace of deference, his tone saying, *Excuse me. I thought you'd know what I was talking about, you being a judge and all.* "Elective mutism is a refusal to speak. Not a refusal to answer any particular question, a refusal to speak at all. Very young children often adopt such a strategy when it's the only way to make people stop asking them the same questions, over and over. With teenagers, they may come to believe such silence is all that saved their lives. The most extreme cases never speak again.

"Catatonia means the individual may go beyond a refusal to speak all the way to actual inability to move a muscle. Just . . . freeze. And not all such individuals can ever be 'thawed out.'

"Decompensation generally refers to a state where a patient returns to former behavior that was being kept under control by therapy and/or medication. The classic example is a schizophrenic who, medicated, functions just fine. But if he comes to believe he's doing so well that he doesn't need the medication anymore, he stops taking it. And the result of *that* is quite predictable.

"Now, in the case of these particular girls—I do realize that some have now reached adult age, but each initial trauma occurred prior to that—if they had been referred to therapy, they would have been, to some extent, 'medicated' by individual therapy. But if they're retraumatized—and revealing the hideous details of their prior victimization to the whole community would certainly accomplish that—it could result in a reversion to an earlier state."

"You said 'at best.'" The judge took over again, trying for control over a courtroom where every eye and every ear was tuned to a different station.

"Yes, I did. The most likely outcome of any such event would be suicide."

This time, the gasps were so audible that I wouldn't be surprised if the court reporter put them into the transcript.

"A decompensating schizophrenic may stab an icepick in his own ear to make the voices stop," T.D. continued. "If suicides could talk after death, they would all say some version of the same thing: they wanted to make it *stop*!"

The judge had nothing to say. Swift made a sweeping motion with his hand, as if inviting any of the four people sitting at the prosecution table to take their best shot.

"Let's go over your qualifications, shall we, Doctor?" the fat-faced guy said as he slowly got to his feet.

T.D. said nothing.

"Dr. Joel, I asked you a question."

"No, you didn't. You made some little speech about what you were going to do, but I'm still waiting for you to do it."

I picked up a few muffled chuckles—arrogance isn't popular with most people.

Fat Face opened his mouth and spilled out a string of questions he was reading off a pad he held in his hand. Every question was another strand in the noose he was tightening around his own flabby neck. From "Where did you go to school?" to "How much are you being paid?" it just got worse and worse.

He saved his Sunday punch for last: "Doctor, has any court in the United States ever qualified you as an expert witness in post-traumatic stress disorder?"

"Yes" was all T.D. answered, baiting the trap.

"How many, would you say?"

"To be honest, I'm not sure. I could look it up for you, but I didn't come prepared with a list."

"What did you think you were going to be doing today, Doctor, going to a tea party?" Fat Face asked, doing his best Judge Judy impression. But there's a chasm between "reality TV" and reality—and the silence spoke for itself.

Then T.D. poked back: "I thought I was going to testify in court."

"Well, what do you call this?"

"Up to now, just what I expected. But lame sarcasm, now, that *was* a surprise."

"Your Honor!" Fat Face protested.

Swift was on his feet before the judge could say anything. "Your Honor, if the prosecutor asks a question, he either has to take the witness's answer or rebut it. Counsel's cute little comment wasn't a question at all, it was nothing more than a display of snideness. If he wants an answer, let him ask a question."

"Good idea," the judge said, turning to the prosecutor as if he was waiting for something.

Fat Face flushed. "I ask you again, Doctor. How many courts have qualified you as an expert witness?"

"And I *tell* you, again, that I can't give you an exact number without going back to my hotel and dialing up a list on my laptop."

"Is there any reason why a man of your education and experience cannot remember how many times he has been qualified as an expert witness?"

"Sure. Too many to remember. That's why I keep a list."

"Can you give us a rough approximation, Doctor?"

"Well, it would certainly be more than a hundred."

"One hundred times, you are saying? One hundred courts have qualified you as an expert?"

"At least."

"Can you give us some examples?"

"Let's see, in New York, the Eastern and Southern Districts; in California, the Central and Northern Districts; in Illinois, the Southern District—"

"Wait just a minute, Doctor. Is there some reason why you are only mentioning federal courts?"

"I was trying to keep the list short. In state courts, I'm trying to think of one in which I *haven't* been qualified as an expert witness. Can't think of one offhand, but I can't swear to all fifty. Starting from here, if you go south to—"

"So you've never been certified in Oregon?"

"Oh, sure I have. And those cases held up all the way through the Ninth Circuit. A couple I can think of: *People v. Thompson; Rogers v. Oregon* . . ."

"So you've testified against the state of Oregon?"

"No. Actually, I was hired by the state of Oregon to examine the conditions of confinement in a certain juvenile prison that had resulted in a lawsuit under 42 US 1983."

"Oh" is all Fat Face could come up with.

"Like I said, if you want a list . . . ?"

Fat Face flapped his hand, as if to dismiss the witness. It was about as smart a move as flapping his gums had been.

"Are you saying you are finished with this witness?" the judge asked, clearly annoyed, now that he had a target that the audience disliked.

"Yes, Your Honor."

"Very well. As you asked the witness nothing about his actual experience, the court is forced to assume that role."

The judge stepped very carefully. When he was done collecting answers to his questions, all he said was "This court finds Dr. T. D. Joel to be an expert in the field of post-traumatic stress disorder. For the record, the Court's finding is not intended as a limitation: Dr. Joel is clearly qualified as an expert in forensic psychology. Indeed, this court has never had before it a witness *more* qualified."

Now it was Debbie's turn.

She was dressed in power clothes: a black business suit that was a little too pinched at the waist and just a tad too short at the hemline for what some would call "professional."

T.D. was responsible for that. "What do you want to do, sit up there, swear to tell the truth, and then lie with your appearance? You are one good-looking woman. You follow that lame hyper-feminist script—you know exactly what I mean: don't wash your hair, don't shave your legs, wear a shapeless dress—and you'd *be* lying. I'm not saying dress like you're auditioning for a strip club, but you can't expect them to take you as an expert if you don't dress classy."

Dolly dragged Debbie out of there quick. And had her ready for court in under an hour.

If Debbie was nervous, you couldn't see it. The prosecutor let her put her credentials on the record without any kind of challenge. His fear of looking like a fool again made what the judge said next inevitable: "The vulnerable-witness protection measures are hereby granted."

"Now we have a jury to pick," Swift said, grimly.

"**W**e can play this one of two ways," T.D. said. Swift listened like he was hearing the Word. I guess he was—jury selection is a special skill, and Swift had never seen a case where an expert was brought in just to help the lawyer do his job. Never mind that T.D. was in the absolute elite of that group.

Swift's own prestige thermometer was way past full boil. The media was gobbling up his every word, and the hints that a jury-selection specialist was needed because there were so many "unique aspects" to this case had them ravenous.

T.D. went on one of those bottom-feeder "crime" shows I'd told Swift to stay away from. I couldn't figure out why until he pulled the trigger. A pudgy woman with a voice that could curdle milk while it was still in the refrigerator asked him why, if the client was so innocent, did her lawyer need the services of a jury-selection specialist?

T.D. said, "You think the defendant is guilty?"

"I think the video rather speaks for itself, doesn't it, *Doctor*?"

"There you go. *That's* why I was retained. To help spot people like you and keep them off the jury. The last person you want on a jury is someone who's already made up their mind before they heard all the facts. Even worse would be one who makes sure everyone else knows it."

Not surprisingly, it was a very short interview. But everyone from around here who watched it got the message. And passed it on.

The way they work it is, they bring in a bunch of people and put them in the jury box. Then each lawyer gets to ask them questions. If they show they're prejudiced in either direction, they get thrown out. But if they're not, and either side doesn't want them, they can throw them off themselves without giving a reason. "Pre-empts" is what Swift called them, and each side only gets a certain number.

I'd never heard that word before, but I knew what they were saying: If you're down to your last magazine, you have to make every shot count. If you haven't got enough to take them all out, you want to pick off the most dangerous ones. That's not as simple as it sounds. You don't care about who's the most dangerous shooter, you have to figure out who'd be the most dangerous up close. And you only get seconds to decide.

When they'd discussed it the night before, T.D. kind of took over. "We only got two ways to go. Either we want to hang the jury, or we want them to acquit."

"Of course we want them to acquit," Dolly said.

"You sure? See, if all we want is to hang the jury, we have to make sure the contrarians slip by. But if we want MaryLou to actually walk, we've got to cut those kind off at the knees."

"I'm not sure I'm following you," Debbie said.

"I'm *sure* I'm not following you," Dolly added.

T.D. was ready for both of them. "Some people have a personality disorder where they just have to go against the herd, right or wrong. They're so committed to their own lone-wolf image that . . . Well, put it this way: if the others suddenly came over to their side, they'd *switch* sides. You get one of those on the jury, it's as good as hung.

"But that cuts both ways. We do that, and we're *seriously* dropping the odds that MaryLou gets acquitted. So we have to know what we want, going in."

Everyone in the room looked at Swift. The new Swift. He didn't let us down: "MaryLou did what she had to do. And her belief that she had to act was objectively reasonable. And, therefore, absolutely justified under the law. When we're done, if we don't get the appropriate charge to the jury, I'd bet my license on winning the appeal. The *expedited* appeal."

It took four days to pick a jury. "The longest in the history of this county," Swift told us. Not bragging, just stating a fact.

T.D. and Debbie had split up the assignment between them; T.D. told the lawyer, "If Debbie says no, it means she spotted one of them. Sight, smell, sound, there's no difference. If Debbie feels a wrong one, he's off. If you can't get him to admit he thinks all this 'trauma' stuff is bullshit, or that some girls are 'thirteen going on thirty,' or make him bite on the Polanski question, burn a pre-empt. We can't have anyone like that anywhere near our jury."

We didn't. The DA had four people at his table. Took me a while to figure out that all four were DAs. Or "deputies," like they called themselves. The DA himself couldn't make it—he was giving a speech somewhere.

When the second DA got up and tried to ask a potential juror a question, Swift was ready for it:

"Judge, the prosecution can't have four different people playing the same role."

"Nobody's playing a role—" Fat Face said, before Swift cut him off: "I don't care what they call it, judge. But allowing four separate individuals to question each prospective juror is not only unprecedented, it's giving the prosecution an unfair advantage. And costing the taxpayers a fortune, for no reason at all."

"You've got four people at *your* table," Fat Face whined.

"You mean five, don't you?" Swift answered. "Or aren't you counting the defendant? Add it up: two experts, one investigator, the defendant, and myself. I'm the only lawyer. And I've been the only one asking questions."

"So you have two experts, and we don't have any," Fat Face stated the obvious.

"That's for sure," Swift fired back.

His shot didn't miss. The judge told Fat Face he could have the entire DA's Office sit at his table, but the rule was going to be one lawyer per witness, no exceptions.

What I heard inside my head was *Do not fucking annoy me again, or you'll wish you'd stayed home.* Kind of wasted on Fat Face—he already wished he could have stayed home.

"Opening statements," the judge said.

Fat Face got to his feet, working hard to keep a sleazy smile hidden. "What's that in his hand?" I whispered to Swift. I was on his left, T.D. and Debbie on his right wing, with MaryLou closest to him.

"PowerPoint," Swift whispered.

I didn't want to distract him, so I just shut up. I'd have to wait and watch to get the answer Swift thought he'd already given me.

"Ladies and gentlemen of the jury, this is that rare kind of case where you look at each other and ask, 'Why would they even bother with a trial?' You will hear from the best witness ever devised—the actual crime captured on videotape. You will actually see the defendant shoot and kill one victim, and wound two others. You will see the defendant take out a pistol and execute the victim. Kill him in cold blood, with no more emotion than you might have in stepping on a cockroach."

He clicked whatever he was holding, and the white wall right across from the jurors lit up. Every time Fat Face clicked, another line or two was added. Why he did this, I don't know—it was nothing more than what he was already saying himself. Sure did use up some time, though. As soon as he finished, the judge called a "lunch break." But first he took about half an hour telling the jurors they couldn't talk to each other about the case until both sides had rested and all closing statements were completed.

There was a whole bunch of other stuff I didn't listen to. I was too busy watching the jurors pretend to be hanging on every word. Less than half of them even made a good try of it.

"We got the ones we needed," T.D. said confidently.

"I agree," Swift said. That was important. Not because of what it said, but because of the speaker's voice: a man people listen to. Listen with respect.

"Does the defense wish to make an opening statement?" the judge said, making it clear he'd spent enough time on this case already. And he couldn't be interviewed until after the case was over.

"Yes, Your Honor," Swift said, in a "You're kidding, right?" tone. When he got to his feet, he waited a beat, making sure he had every juror's attention.

"You heard the prosecutor's opening statement. And what you heard was a colossal waste of your time—"

"Objection!" Fat Face half-yelled. "The defense is not permitted to comment on anything except the evidence."

"If the prosecutor had waited another couple of seconds, he would have understood that the defense is speaking directly *to* the evidence," Swift cracked him with a counterpunch, then resumed before the judge could even rule. "You see," he said, facing the jury, "the prosecutor's opening was a waste of time because the defense does not contest a single word that came out of his mouth."

Swift waited a long beat, watching the jurors closely. Then he went on: "The prosecutor repeated what everybody in this town, perhaps everybody in this country, already knows: on Friday, the thirty-first of this past May, MaryLou McCoy shot and killed Cameron Taft. They even made a little wall display out of the exact same thing. And that's why I called it a waste of your time . . . because we do not contest a single factual statement made."

Swift paused, pulling his audience even closer.

"But the prosecutor never answered the one question that you want answered, did he? Why would a young lady who never had so much as a traffic ticket in her life commit such a crime? Was she drunk? Was she on drugs?

"No, you all know she wasn't. MaryLou McCoy is a star athlete, and she trained like one. Others in her age group might be smoking marijuana; MaryLou wouldn't go near a cigarette.

"Who had a brighter future than MaryLou? She was headed to college, on a full scholarship. And she was going to play big-time softball, against the best in the country.

"Was she herself afraid of Cameron Taft? There isn't a doubt in the world that she could have beaten him in a fair fight.

"Why would a young woman who we all expected to bring honor and glory to our town—to say nothing of the recognition we were all going to receive every time she was interviewed after a win—why would she even think she needed a weapon to protect herself?

"Why would a young woman the papers have been calling Mighty Mary since she was a sophomore throw such a bright future away?

"Was she insane? Absolutely not! This is not some kind of 'temporary-insanity defense' case. Get that out of your minds. MaryLou McCoy didn't 'snap.' She did what she did for a reason. And that reason is what we call a 'justification' defense. We're not going to make speeches; we're going to show you why MaryLou did what she did. And why she had no choice *but* to do it.

"The prosecution can't answer *that* question, so you can't get anything from them but more repetitions of the same story they just told you. Telling you the story you all know by heart, and taking a ridiculous amount of time to do it.

"But the defense is going to prove to you that MaryLou McCoy had no choice. And when we're done, you're going to come back and tell this court that you may not approve of what MaryLou did, but you understand why she did it. And that, when she did it, she was *justified*.

"There's only one verdict in this case: not guilty. We are *not* playing for the tie. We don't *want* a hung jury. We *didn't* want a plea bargain. And we don't have any legal technicalities to spring on you.

"No, what we're going to do is put the truth in front of you, and then ask you to do the right thing with that truth.

"We believe you'll do just that. And if we didn't have a deep, abiding faith in that belief, we'd be walking a different road. Listen to the prosecution's case—if you can stay awake—and then we'll answer the question you've all been waiting for: 'Why?'"

Swift was already back in his chair before Fat Face could even get the word "objection" out of his mouth. But, being the toad he was, Fat Face couldn't help himself:

"Your Honor, we ask the court to admonish counsel against *ad-hominem* attacks."

"The defense will withdraw its comment on the banality of the prosecution's presentation, Your Honor. But we do wish Mr. Curtis"—*So that's his name*, I thought; then I decided I liked Fat Face better—"would speak English," Swift slammed back, making the "we" into him and the jurors, and Fat Face into the "them."

"That was sweet, hoss," I could hear T.D. whisper. For Swift, that was the same as permanently increasing his chest size.

The prosecution's supposed to go first, but Swift beat Fat Face to the punch again.

"Your Honor, if it please the court, we are willing to stipulate that on May 31, 2013, the defendant intentionally shot one Cameron Taft. Further, we do not dispute that she wounded two others in that same episode. We submit that, having so agreed, we can dispense with the need to hear those same facts 'proven' again."

"Your Honor, this is outrageous," Fat Face said, struggling to his feet.

"How so?" the judge asked.

"We have a right to put on a case."

"And counsel is already saying he does not contest any aspect of the case you wish to put on."

"That doesn't matter," Fat Face said, not making any friends as he struggled with his desire for whatever moment of glory he expected, but couldn't come up with a real answer.

"'That doesn't matter' may not be the most eloquent argument this court has heard," the judge said. "Nevertheless, I take it that you decline the defense's offer to expedite this trial?"

"Yes, Your Honor," Fat Face said, every square inch of visible skin covered in repellent crimson blotches.

"Then continue," the judge told him, his voice making it clear how interested *he* was in hearing the same stuff again.

Fat Face showed the same videotape that had already been You-Tubed all over the world. He showed the jury the close-up photos taken just before they opened Cameron Taft for the autopsy. Not stunningly effective—a .22 doesn't make a big hole going in, and the slug had never left the dead man's brain.

Swift sat quietly, eyes lidded as if the whole thing was putting him to sleep. But when Fat Face wanted to show the jury a video of the autopsy surgeon sawing off the top of the dead man's skull, Swift got to his feet.

"Your Honor, with all due respect, this so-called evidence is not only well beyond cumulative, it is a blatant attempt to disgust and sicken the jury. We have conceded—and I will not waste either Your Honor's or the jury's time with repeating our proffered stipulation—everything this video could possibly prove. Watching the top of a man's skull being sawed off is such a horrifying sight that any probative value it might conceivably possess is cosmically outweighed by the prejudice such a sight could inflict against the defendant."

"Sustained" was all the judge said. When he saw Fat Face open his mouth, he added, "Unless you intend to offer some other perspective that will show how this videotape is necessary to prove facts which defendant's counsel has already conceded, you will either move on or rest your case, sir."

Robbed of his planned grand presentation, Fat Face said, "Could we have a moment, Your Honor?"

The judge just waved his hand in a "Why not?" gesture.

Fat Face and the three other DAs—I mean, deputies—went into conference. I couldn't hear what they were saying—all I could see was a lot of arm-waving. Finally, Fat Face got up.

"If Your Honor is going to bar—"

"Enough, counsel. This court will not remind you again."

"The state rests," Fat Face said, as majestically as any flop-sweaty swine could manage.

Swift wasted no time. Witness after witness testified—from behind a black mesh screen—that she had been raped by members of Tiger Ko Khai. And that nothing had ever happened as a result.

The prize was the girl who admitted she told the cops that she wasn't even going to look at a lineup of suspects unless they agreed to prosecute a member of Tiger Ko Khai who had raped her a year before. The SANE nurse on duty an hour past midnight—01:03 was the time in the records Swift had marked for entry as evidence—had verified that the girl had been raped "within a couple of hours prior to examination."

That girl wasn't grown yet, but she already had the anger of a person who had been told to "get over it" one too many times. She couldn't have said it more clearly: no promises from them, no testimony from her.

Like I said, the pick of the litter.

But her place as star witness vanished when Swift called a real star to the stand.

Danielle played it to the hilt, giving the blade a final kill-twist after she was sure she'd planted it deep enough.

"I'm not like them," she told the jury, distancing herself from those who lacked her beauty and physical endowments—no black mesh screen for *her*. Making it clear that nobody had raped her. That the train Tiger Ko Khai had pulled was simply an initiation into a special society, run by a special man, who loved her with all his heart. A man named Cameron Taft. "All the girls were after him," she crowed.

"So your sister was jealous of you?" Swift asked, his voice empty of inflection.

"Look at her." Danielle pointed. "And look at me. What do *you* think?"

MaryLou's face was a frozen mask. She looked straight ahead. Not at Danielle. Not at the jury. Not at anything at all. The centers of her eyes were large round dots—they looked like they'd been painted on.

That mask didn't even crack when Swift slapped Danielle with "I think you're the ugliest girl I've ever seen in my life."

Fat Face jumped to his feet, but Swift got off first: "I am done with this witness, Your Honor," the expression on his face telling the jury he was grateful to be relieved of a repulsive but necessary task.

Fat Face had no better luck with Danielle than he'd had with any of the other girls who had testified. Every attempt at getting them to take back what they said only made it worse. And his "I know the last thing you'd ever want to do would be to hurt your sister" had Swift on his feet before Danielle could answer.

"That's not a question, judge. That's the prosecutor's attempt to lead the witness. Or an exhibition of his own delusions."

"I object!"

"To what?" the judge snapped at Fat Face. "Either rephrase your question so that it *is* a question, or move on."

"Danielle," Fat Face coaxed, "would you ever do anything to hurt your big sister?"

"I don't know what you mean."

"Well, for example, would you ever lie to hurt your sister?"

"When did I lie?"

"I'm not saying you have lied, only asking if you *would* lie. To hurt your sister, I mean."

"I don't need to lie," she said scornfully.

Finally, Fat Face gave up. Maybe he didn't realize he'd just injected pus into the same wound he was trying to bandage, but that would make him the only one in the courtroom who didn't.

Danielle stalked off the witness stand, switching her hips on the off-chance that anyone mistook her for anything but what she was.

Franklin told the jury what he'd heard Danielle say. Since the jury had already heard Danielle tell the same obvious lies, none of the deputies even tried to cross-examine him. Or maybe they realized they'd have as much luck getting anything good for their side out of Franklin as they would trying to throw him out of the witness chair.

When Franklin admitted he'd lie under oath if that would do anything to help MaryLou, that had been the killing blow. Even those deputies realized that anyone who'd tell that much truth wasn't someone you wanted to try getting to admit they had just lied.

And the tears on the giant's face when he said that he loved her were more compelling than any testimony could have been.

"You just did more to save MaryLou's life than all the rest of us combined," I told him, after he'd asked me for the tenth time if he did okay.

"You mean that, Mr. Dell?"

"I swear it," I told the giant, putting my hand over my heart. What I didn't say was: *I wonder how many of them still think you're "retarded" now? I wonder how many of the girls wish they had a boyfriend with your kind of love?*

"Is it all right if I tell Mr. Spyros what I told today?"

"Absolutely."

"I know what he's gonna say, too."

"What?"

"Mr. Spyros was in the war, you know. A long time ago."

"And . . . ?" I asked gently. For Franklin, Vietnam would have been a long time ago.

"And he told me once, when you're in a war, it's a lot easier to fight if you know who the enemy is. And when I tell him what I said today, he'll say MaryLou did the right thing."

"Yeah, he will, Franklin. And he'll say you did, too."

"Now comes the fun," Swift told us after court that day. "Tomorrow is the test. But before I put on our experts"—nodding at T.D. and Debbie, who were sitting close together—"I've got a little surprise for everyone. A new witness."

"Another girl who—?"

"No," he said to Dolly, almost busting at the seams to tell us . . . something. "A police officer. A detective who's been on the force almost twenty years."

"How did you—?"

"He volunteered," Swift said to me. "Walked right into my office after he saw me on TV. Or maybe it was T.D., I don't recall. Anyway, what he said was, he'd been waiting for those Tiger Ko Khai rapists to take a fall for years. And even though they weren't on trial yet, he could give us enough dirt on Cameron Taft to shed some light on just who MaryLou shot that day."

"Damn!" is all I said. But I made it clear that I was showing respect. I suspected it was T.D.'s TV appearance that had alerted the cop, but I didn't care—T.D. had enough trophies; this was Swift's first.

"Detective, would you tell the jury your full name and title, and give a brief summary of your career?"

The detective told the jury what we already knew. Nothing for the prosecution to object to, but Fat Face managed to dig one out:

"Your Honor, it would be helpful if we knew what the defense is trying to qualify this officer as an expert in."

Swift acted like he was forcing back a laugh. Then he just said, "If it please the court, the instruction was to call our witness. We have done so. Why the prosecutor believes we are seeking to qualify Detective Lancer as an expert is beyond me."

"Well?" the judge said, looking at what was left of the rapidly melting Fat Face.

Ten seconds passed. Fat Face sat down.

"May I continue?" Swift asked, rubbing it in. All he got from the judge was a curt nod—men who wear comb-overs have to be careful not to go too far with their nods.

"Do I know Cameron Taft?" Lancer answered Swift's first question. "The whole department knows Cameron Taft. I probably arrested him half a dozen times myself. Always on the same charges: sexual assault of a minor."

Fat Face started to rise, but the "Bring it!" look from Swift slammed him back down.

"Not one of those charges was ever prosecuted," the detective continued.

"Do you know why?" Swift asked.

"I don't know as in 'beyond a reasonable doubt' know, but it's common knowledge in the department that the DA's Office won't take a case unless we bring in a notarized confession, or such a mountain of evidence that they know they can't possibly lose."

"I have to object, Your Honor," Fat Face said. "This man is in no position to state what is 'common knowledge'—he's hardly a Gallup Poll."

Swift responded with a simple "My apologies to the court. May I rephrase?"

Another nod from the bench.

"Detective Lancer, in case it is not clear to all, when you say 'common knowledge,' are you speaking of what is common knowledge in this whole community . . . or are you referring to what is common knowledge within the police department?"

"The department."

Swift made a "Well?" gesture . . . and got no takers, not Fat Face, not the judge, either.

"Now, Detective, you can only make an arrest when a crime is committed in your presence or when there's been a complaint, isn't that correct? So, if, say, this Cameron Taft raped a hundred minors, and only seven of them came forward, you would only be able to arrest him on those seven complaints?"

"That's right."

"Your Honor, I must object. Cameron Taft is not here to defend himself against such accusations."

"I believe counsel has confused a hypothetical question—one

which the witness is eminently qualified to answer in his capacity as a veteran police officer—with an accusation," Swift answered.

Once again, the judge endangered his comb-over.

"Did you question Cameron Taft, or did he request an attorney?"

"He never asked for a lawyer, not once. I think he liked playing the game."

"The game?" Swift asked innocently.

"Sociopaths love to taunt, and Taft was a real beauty at it. He actually confessed more than once, but he made sure he only did it with little hints. Gestures, smirks. He'd make sure I knew he'd done the rapes, and that I couldn't do a damn thing about them."

"Your Honor, Detective Lancer may be an expert in police work, but he's hardly qualified to make a psychiatric diagnosis."

"May I inquire further?" Swift asked, politely.

Getting the nod again, he asked, "Detective, if you were to remove the word 'sociopath' from what you just said, is there another word you would substitute?"

"Sure," Lancer said.

"And that word would be?"

" 'Dirtbag,' " Lancer answered, without changing expression.

Fat Face started to rise, then sat down quick, as if the twittering of the jury was a flock of crows headed for his eyes.

"So would it be a fair statement that a local school student familiar with the reputation of Tiger Ko Khai might believe that going to the police would be a futile act?"

"Yes."

For those girls, I thought, *the whole town was nothing but a collection of "les collaborateurs," the kind that Luc had hated with such fierceness. And now my sacred duty is to hate them, too.* But, like so many of my thoughts over so many years, none of that reached my face, or my eyes.

Fat Face was on his feet before Swift sat down.

"Officer, you understand you're under oath?"

"Yes," Lancer said, just short of rolling his eyes.

"Is it your statement, under oath, that this office—that is, the Office of the District Attorney—will not prosecute a case unless assured of a guilty verdict?"

"It's my belief, based on my experience on the force. I've been a cop probably ten times longer than you've been a deputy DA, so I've had plenty of time to develop that belief."

"Ah. So you admit that you can't prove a single word you said during your testimony?"

"Prove? I guess I'll never know, will I? If I make an arrest, and your office doesn't prosecute, I don't have a crystal ball—I can't 'prove' what the outcome of any prosecution would be. But I remember a book we all had to read when we first came on the job. *Sex Crimes*, it was called. About the original Special Victims Bureau in New York. Anyway, one line I remember was something like this: 'Show me a DA with a perfect conviction record, and I'll show you a DA who cherry-picked his cases.'"

"What is that supposed to mean?" Fat Face demanded, determined as always to make things worse for his side.

"To me, it meant that if you want a perfect conviction record you only prosecute the cases you can't lose. Your office must certainly believe that itself. I've testified in God knows how many cases, and the only time I've ever been briefed was in the elevator on the way up to the courtroom."

"Your Honor!"

"What?" the judge snapped.

"I . . . Withdrawn. Officer, do you know anything about this case? The one we are trying right here?"

"No."

"Your Honor, I move to strike the witness's entire testimony on the grounds that it is totally irrelevant to the case at bar."

"Mr. Swift?" the judge said.

"Your Honor, I believe the relevancy of Detective Lancer's testimony is already proven and clearly apparent. However, if the defense fails to show the relevance of Detective Lancer's testimony before we rest our case, I will not oppose the prosecutor's motion. I ask only that this court accept Detective Lancer's testimony on a 'subject to connection' basis. We called him out of order because he has to leave tomorrow for special FBI training in complex sex-crimes investigation. The training will be in Quantico, Virginia, literally on the other side of the country.

"If Your Honor wishes, I can put on a string of witnesses, all of whom will testify that this training is highly coveted, and if a police officer is invited and does not show up, his slot will be filled by an alternate. And that it might be another ten years before this opportunity comes around to *our* police department again. Furthermore—"

"The testimony of this witness is deemed admissible," the judge cut him off. "But only subject to connection."

Fat Face sat down like he'd just won a major victory. His enthusiasm didn't seem contagious—none of the other three prosecutors even acknowledged his existence.

T.D.'s credentials were not challenged—even Fat Face realized how he'd look walking into the same trap twice. But T.D. spun Swift's opening question into a kidney punch Fat Face never saw coming.

"Doctor, have you ever been consulted on a so-called school-shooting case?"

"Yes, I have."

"More than once?"

"Yes."

"Can you give the jury an example?"

"Columbine," T.D. said. The audience suddenly went as quiet as an empty church.

"What was your role in the aftermath of that horror?"

"I was asked to perform what is called a 'psychological autopsy' of the shooters, and to advise on how further such events could be prevented."

"Do you see any similarities between Columbine and the acts we have already conceded that MaryLou McCoy committed?"

"None," Dr. Joel said, absolutely flat.

"Could you elaborate, please?"

"In brief, Columbine was a classic example of *folie à deux*. A kind of negative gestalt."

"Doctor, with all due respect, I'm having a little difficulty following you. I'm not familiar with the terminology of your profession."

None of *us* are, Swift was saying, "us" meaning him and the jurors.

"Columbine was launched by two deeply disaffected and disturbed individuals, who spent endless hours planning and plotting what they intended to do. They sent all kinds of messages, all of which were ignored. They even made videos of what they planned . . . as a school project.

"The killers were marginalized, bullied, and looked upon as freaks by the other students. Each slight, each slur, each humiliation only fueled the fire inside the two of them, two fires which eventually merged into one.

"They entered that school with the sole intent of killing as many people as possible. They never intended to escape; they intended to die. And they wanted to write their suicide note in the blood of those they believed had been their tormentors.

"Compare that fact pattern to MaryLou McCoy, and nothing matches up. MaryLou was never bullied. In fact, she was not only well known throughout her school, but treated as one of its crown jewels. Her athletic achievements were known throughout the state. And beyond. The school was proud of her; the town was proud of her—and they had every reason to be.

"MaryLou had no 'plan' of any kind. She not only acted alone, she acted with the impulsiveness of a very young and immature person who perceived she had no other choice. She did not intend to commit suicide. She did not attempt either concealment or escape. In fact, she literally had no idea of what would happen next. This was no 'school shooting,' as the term is generally used; it was a shooting which took place within a school. That is the extent of any 'similarity.' "

"Your Honor." Fat Face jumped up. "Move to strike all the testimony on Columbine as beyond the scope of this case."

"What?" the judge said, incredulously. "Dr. Joel has been qualified as an expert. His comparison of the events in question to Columbine is certainly not only relevant, not only within the scope of his expertise, but also based on actual, personal knowledge. And, counsel, remember, it was *your* office that introduced the topic of so-called school shootings."

Swift didn't wait for Fat Face to sit down. "Dr. Joel, did you have occasion to speak personally with any of the witnesses who've already testified here?"

"I did more than that. I did a full assessment of Danielle McCoy, including an interview."

"Can you summarize that for us?"

"Danielle is fully as psychopathic as Cameron Taft," he said, and then slid into the rest of his analysis before Fat Face could open his mouth to object. "She is pathologically self-absorbed, utterly without empathy, and capable of assuming whatever persona she believes will get her what she wants. And, for Danielle, what *she* wants is all that matters."

"So that's what a psychopath is, Doctor?"

"Among other things. Danielle has also mastered the dark arts of deceit and manipulation. She is incapable of feeling remorse, no matter what damage she may have done to others. She is so hyper-focused on herself and her needs that, quite literally, nothing else matters.

"Some believe the diagnosis of 'psychopath' cannot be made unless and until the subject is at least eighteen years of age. But, given that Danielle has already skipped two grades, and is highly intelligent, I feel comfortable with that diagnosis in her case."

"Are you saying Danielle is a pathological liar, Doctor?"

"Absolutely not. She is an *expert* liar, not a pathological one. That is, Danielle does not feel a compulsion to lie. For her, lying is simply a tool. If the truth would help her achieve any of her desires, she would tell the truth."

"Well, didn't she testify that MaryLou shot Cameron Taft because MaryLou was jealous of her?"

"She did."

"Do you believe she was telling the truth?"

"I do."

"What?!" Swift stepped back, as if shocked.

"She was telling the truth. But only in the sense that her self-absorption is so overwhelming that she believed what she was saying. Were her statements *actual* truth? Of course not."

"Can you . . . explain that for us, Doctor?"

"Certainly. I have conducted extensive interviewing of Mary-Lou McCoy as well as reviewed—"

"Why would you do that, Doctor? Interview MaryLou, I mean."

"Because you hired me to determine if she was insane at the time she shot and killed Cameron Taft."

"And . . . ?"

"And she was not. MaryLou McCoy was not insane before, during, or after the event."

"Did you learn anything else, Doctor?"

"I did. And all of it was confirmative of my diagnosis of Danielle."

"How so?"

"MaryLou believed Danielle. She not only believed what Danielle told her, she believed in Danielle as a person. When she found out that Danielle was hanging out with Cameron Taft and his gang—"

"Objection! No evidence has been presented that the victim was a member of any gang."

"Subject to connection," the judge said, before Swift could respond.

"The name of the gang to which you refer, Doctor?"

"Tiger Ko Khai."

"You're not from around here, are you?"

"No, sir. Although it's such a beautiful place I sure wouldn't mind retiring here."

"Objection! Where Dr. Joel plans to retire is not—"

"Strike the witness's last statement," the judge said, thereby emphasizing it, just as T.D. had told Swift would happen.

"All right, Doctor, if you're not from around here, how could you know about this gang?"

"Because Danielle told me all about it. She called it a 'special society' which had to be secretive about its inner workings because everyone wanted to be a member, and its exclusivity must be maintained. She described the unique jackets that only the gang could wear, even the tattoos they all must have.

"All this information was delivered in a triumphant, boastful manner. Danielle has converted a gang rape into an 'initiation' because her core personality could not tolerate the thought of her being a 'victim.' In her mind, that was not the role she was born to play."

"But MaryLou was not aware—?"

"MaryLou had no idea that Danielle had been gang-raped. But when she found out that Danielle was spending time with this gang, she knew what was coming, and reacted the only way she knew how."

"Which was?"

"She beat up her younger sister. And warned her if she went near Tiger Ko Khai again she'd get it worse."

"You say 'the only way she knew how,' Doctor. Surely, there were other avenues open to MaryLou."

"Not in her mind. MaryLou is physically gifted, but of only average intelligence. Danielle was much smarter, so it was easy for her to get MaryLou to believe that she was 'hanging out' with that gang . . . instead of being systematically raped by them.

"To MaryLou, hanging out with Tiger Ko Khai meant that gang rape was inevitable. She'd heard the stories, from a great number of sources. So going to social-work agencies, or even to the police, simply never occurred to her. She didn't want anything more than to prevent that gang from doing what she believed it was sure to do.

"MaryLou was undoubtedly in some sort of fugue state when she went to school that day. She knew what she was going to do, and she knew why, but it would have been as if nothing else existed outside that tiny little tunnel in her mind."

"But by that time—"

"By that time, Danielle had already been 'raped into' Tiger Ko Khai. She presented to MaryLou only as a *potential* victim, but she actually viewed herself as a special princess."

"Presented?"

"It's another way of saying how she would appear. To others, and to herself. Those are not always the same. Danielle wasn't fooled into believing she had to be gang-raped as an 'initiation.' That was a story she made up, composed of half-truths she had previously experienced only as rumors, as well as her own need to be that 'star' she was in her own mind.

"To Danielle, being gang-raped was meaningless, just another of a long series of events she had experienced in her life that she had ruthlessly purged from her own mind, or converted into another thing entirely. But being lumped in with those 'ugly' girls, the undesirable ones—that her personality could not tolerate."

"Did MaryLou understand this? Any of this?"

"No. No, she did not. She had neither the training nor the experience to even imagine such a thing. In MaryLou's mind, that fateful Friday was her last chance to protect her baby sister. She—MaryLou, I mean—was leaving the next Monday for summer softball camp.

"She would be gone for a long time, maybe forever. Her home life was a misery, and her only friends were other athletes. She knew she couldn't count on either her mother or her father to protect Danielle. Her conscience would not allow her to tell Franklin—the young man who testified earlier—because she was certain he would respond in such a way as to guarantee his own imprisonment.

"The same conscience told her that she couldn't leave town unless she had permanently protected Danielle from being used as a toy by Cameron Taft."

"Your Honor!"

"Within the province," Swift cut in. "An expert may give opinion evidence. The doctor can certainly testify to the state of mind of an individual he has intensively interviewed."

"Overruled," the judge said, not moving his head.

"Let's say it in plain English, Doctor. Is it your testimony that Danielle was never really 'in danger' from Tiger Ko Khai? Is it your testimony that Cameron Taft was a charming psychopath who thought he had already 'played' one of his own kind? Someone just as empty of human emotion, but not as skilled in using that quality to get what they wanted?"

"Yes. In a few more years, he would have been no match for Danielle. But by that time, Danielle wouldn't have bothered to look in his direction. Cameron Taft may have been a prize for a girl just past puberty, but once she grew to 'legal' age, he would have been dumped on the scrapheap of Danielle's past."

"So it was all a lie? Cameron was no threat to Danielle at any time?"

"No," he said sadly. "If there was an apex predator in this whole disgusting chain of exploitation, it was Danielle, not Cameron Taft."

MaryLou's mask cracked wide open. Her trance broke like a dam giving way. She buried her face in her big hands, but the tears kept oozing through her clenched fingers, the truth finally seeping through the wall she had spent so many years building around her baby sister.

"I have no more questions," Swift said, as if there were no more questions anyone with an ounce of decency in them would ask.

The courtroom was graveyard-silent, except for the horrible sounds of a young woman mourning the betrayal of her own supreme sacrifice.

"Perhaps, then, this is a good time to break for lunch," the judge said.

I didn't despise him for that. I wouldn't have known what to do, either. And Dolly was already up and moving toward MaryLou.

After lunch, a woman got up to do the cross-examination of T.D. Maybe she'd been brought in for that purpose. Or maybe the DA himself heard how his Deputy Fat Face had built his whole case out of translucent Swiss cheese.

"You're not a medical doctor, are you?" the woman closed in on T.D.

"Not unless someone sent me to medical school when I wasn't looking."

The jury laughed. By then, T.D. was one of their own, not some hired-gun outsider.

"Your Honor!" the woman protested.

"The jury is hereby admonished to . . ." The judge let that one trail off. He had to run for office, too.

"What I mean is, you're not a psychiatrist, isn't that true?"

"Sure."

"You seem rather lighthearted about it, Doctor. Are you telling this jury that you are more qualified than a psychiatrist to render a diagnosis?"

"That would depend on the training, background, and experience of the individual psychiatrist."

"And what is that supposed to mean?"

"It means what I just said it does. A lot of psychiatrists spend their career treating wealthy neurotics. Or the rich and famous, for whom a psychiatrist would be a lot better choice than me."

"Because they could afford the higher prices a psychiatrist charges?"

"No, because they can write prescriptions."

The judge started to tell the jury to be quiet, but then snapped his mouth closed like the jaws of the trap he'd almost stepped in.

"Can we stop telling jokes and get back to the question at hand, Doctor?"

"Is that a question?"

"It's . . . Very well, isn't it true that a psychiatrist would have much more training than a psychologist?"

"Maybe yes, maybe no. It's always on a case-by-case basis. Anyway, it's what you have training *in* that matters."

"Can you give the jury one single example of where a psychologist would have more useful experience than a psychiatrist?"

"I could give you hundreds. And that doesn't apply only to psychologists. It's not some food chain, like you're trying to make the jury believe. Some social workers—and, yes, they go to school for even fewer years than we do—have more expertise in any given subject than anyone else might."

"So you're saying that field experience is worth more than academic knowledge?"

"Of course it is," T.D. said, smiling. I'd seen that smile before—on a man facing a straight razor, with a Derringer concealed in his hand.

You could see that the woman wanted to stop T.D.'s train from rolling, but she was stuck on the flypaper. Anyone could see the jury was listening, and if she was the one to rob them of what they all wanted to hear . . .

"Passing a written test doesn't mean you're actually going to be good at whatever you're licensed to do," T.D. went on. "You want a perfect example, think of all those incompetents on the road who passed the same driving test you did."

The woman finally had enough. "That's your opinion," she said, red-faced.

"I don't think much of *any* title—I look at people as individuals, not by whatever membership they hold," T.D. rolled on, as if he was still answering her question. "Sometimes I see things on TV, like those guys who go deep-sea fishing for a living, and I realize they probably don't have a degree in anything, but they must have had one hell of an education."

The prosecutor knew there was nothing more likely to tap the hearts of a jury coming from what was essentially a fishing village, and she just couldn't leave it there.

"Are you trying to tell us—?"

"Your Honor, I have to object." Swift rose wearily to his feet. "Counsel has not asked a single relevant question of this witness for quite some time. And every relevant question she asked has been answered. In depth. Her personal inability to understand what the expert is saying should not be attributed to anyone else in this courtroom."

Before the judge could rule, the woman stalked off in a huff. Walking right past Fat Face, as if this had been all his fault, before taking her seat.

"My goodness!" Debbie said that night. "I was so worried about testifying. As an expert, I mean. But you make it seem so easy."

"It *is* easy, as long as you remember one rule: always tell the truth."

"But if the truth hurts your—"

"That doesn't matter," T.D. insisted. "You don't even bend the truth. You tell it straight out. Everyone who hires me knows that's what they're going to get. I do my work and tell them what I found; and then they either ask me to testify or they don't."

"You mean, sometimes they don't?"

"Oh yeah," T.D. said, smiling. "But when anyone asks me to step off the line, I always tell them I may not know much but I know that trying to ice-skate down a mountain is guaranteed not to work out."

"That's perfect!" Dolly clapped her hands.

I didn't applaud. But I knew he was right.

Qualifying Debbie never got past her saying she had personally interviewed more than one thousand rape victims, and had written several papers and a book on the subject. And her answer to Swift's front question was the "education" T.D. had already told everyone was more valuable than any degree.

"Secondary Rape Trauma Syndrome is what happens when someone has seen too many rape victims, heard too many rapes re-enacted, watched the permanent damage it does no matter what efforts are made to help. In a way, it's worse than primary."

"That doesn't seem logical, Doctor. Could you explain—?"

"I'm not a doctor," Debbie said, rather sternly. "I am a licensed clinical social worker."

"I apologize. But, for now, could you please tell the jury why those who have only seen rape victims *after* they had been raped could possibly be more traumatized than the victims themselves?"

"Yes. Some children who have been raped have also been betrayed. That would be what we call a 'Circle of Trust' sexual assault. Either the perpetrator is trusted by the victim—this is most common in incest cases—or the perpetrator is trusted by the victim's own parents: an athletic coach, a dance instructor, a religious figure. . . . That list is endless.

"And some women learn to *expect* rape. During wartime, in many countries, rape has been the privilege of any soldier on the winning side. That's why so many nurses who volunteer to work in a war zone carry cyanide capsules.

"Despite all this, no matter what was done to them, some victims actually work through the trauma. For them, the victimization happened, but it never hardened into a permanent state of mind. The primary Rape Trauma Syndrome shows all the symptoms we would expect. But it's only recently that we accepted that the secondary syndrome may often be *more* damaging.

"Why? Because, to the individual who works in the field, *the rape never stops*. They see so many victims, one after the other after the other in an endless stream, that they begin to internalize some of the same symptoms."

"Such as?"

"The feeling that rape is inevitable. That it can happen to anyone, at any time. To the wealthy as well as the poor. It doesn't matter where they live, or how careful they are, it can happen. After a while, the 'can' becomes 'will.' And once that terror is implanted, it takes years of intensive counseling to have even a chance against it."

"You examined the defendant in this case, MaryLou McCoy, did you not?"

"I did."

"And your findings?"

"MaryLou is a classic case of Secondary Rape Trauma Syndrome, although the full diagnosis would include a 'by proxy' subcategory."

"By proxy?"

"MaryLou was not a rape victim. But she believed her sister was about to become one. Not only that, but there were definite indications that her sister may have been sexually abused prior to what the defendant believed was inevitable rape by this Cameron Taft and his gang."

"Judge . . ." Fat Face said.

"The court has already ruled on this exact same issue, counsel. If you want me to repeat 'subject to connection,' you've got it."

"Your Honor," Swift said wearily, "it should be obvious by now that the police department itself considers Tiger Ko Khai to be a gang, a gang most recently led by Cameron Taft. At least, we thought it was obvious. If Your Honor requires it, we can adjourn at the end of our case until Detective Lancer returns from training, and ask him to be even more explicit. But given the testimony this court has already heard, we are forced to now ask for a ruling as to whether the term 'gang' may be applied to Tiger Ko Khai by this and other witnesses."

"Your objection is overruled," the judge told Fat Face. His meaning was unmistakable: *If you hadn't opened your big mouth, you wouldn't have forced me into this. But, seeing as you couldn't leave it alone, now you're screwed.*

"You were saying?" Swift said, turning to face Debbie.

"MaryLou feared not only that rape—the rape of her baby sister—was absolutely inevitable, but that it was imminent."

"What is the difference?"

"It's not a linguistic difference; it's a therapeutic one. I mean, those are terms we use in my profession. 'Inevitable' means something that will eventually happen; 'imminent' means that something could happen at any minute."

"Or, perhaps, as soon as the victim drops her guard?"

"Precisely. In Secondary, the victim believes that, the instant she drops her guard over all the victims she's already seen, the trauma will reappear, like a fresh outbreak of a fatal disease."

"And as for MaryLou in particular?"

"MaryLou believed, beyond any doubt, that when Danielle was no longer under her personal protection she would be gang-raped."

"This is a difficult question for me to ask, Ms. Rollo, but I have no choice. Was MaryLou's fear justified?"

"If you're asking if her fear was based on reality, no, it was not, as both Danielle's and Mr. Wayne's testimony proved. As did Dr. Joel's own evaluation. But if you're asking if MaryLou's fear was *justified,* the answer is: 'Absolutely.' On the evidence she had, MaryLou believed she could only protect Danielle if she . . . did what she did."

Swift was already seated before the final words were out of Debbie's mouth.

The third member of the prosecution team was male. Apparently, it was his job to make Fat Face look like a master of the courtroom.

"Are you trying to tell us—?"

"I am not trying to do anything but speak truthfully, in response to whatever questions I am asked and feel competent to answer."

"Fine. Tell us, then, how many rehearsal hours you put in with the defendant's attorney?"

"None."

"You are saying that you did not go over your testimony in

advance? That defense counsel put you on the stand without knowing what you were going to say?"

"I don't know what Mr. Swift thought. He certainly was aware of my findings, and what I was going to testify to. But he never asked me specifically what I was going to say. And he most certainly never attempted to put words in my mouth."

"Oh, really?" the ace cross-examiner asked, putting all his years of practice behind his slimy sarcasm. "So you didn't know that the defense in this case was going to be 'justification,' is that what you're saying? And you didn't know that a justification defense only works if the defendant had a 'reasonable' belief that an attack was 'imminent'? Is all that what you want this jury to believe?"

"What I want the jury to believe is that I told the truth. If your questions were actually questions, instead of nasty little cracks—"

"Objection!" the idiot shouted. "Will the court please instruct this witness to confine her testimony to answering questions, not—"

"Don't call him any more names," the judge told Debbie, risking his comb-over to make sure she could see he was on her side. And to have another look at her legs.

Several members of the jury laughed out loud. The judge didn't seem to have any objection to that, either.

"Well?" the prosecutor demanded, as if the judge had ruled in his favor and the jury was in love with him.

"I did know that the defense was going to be what you call 'justification,' although I suppose anyone in the courtroom would know that, just by listening. I had no idea of the legal significance of words such as 'inevitable' and 'imminent.' They may well have a different meaning in law than they do in counseling."

"I'll just bet," the little snot said.

That was enough for Swift. "Judge, the prosecution has repeatedly requested that expert witnesses refrain from characterizing without a proper foundation. So, unless the prosecution has some actual evidence of these secret 'rehearsals' he wants the jury to believe took place, I think he owes this witness an apology."

"Nobody wants to hear your opinions," the judge told the prosecutor, his voice reflecting the pulse of the room. "If you are ready to make an offer of proof, you and defense counsel may approach the bench. If you are not, you may sit down."

"But, Your Honor, I have not concluded my cross-examination of this witness."

"I think you have," the judge told him.

On redirect, all Swift did was ask Debbie if there would have been *any* way to stop MaryLou once she believed that the rape of her little sister was going to happen, and that it was going to happen as soon as MaryLou had left town.

"Yes," Debbie said, surprising the hell out of me, and making the jury sit up straight in their seats, some of them leaning forward to be sure not to miss a word.

"How could that have been accomplished?"

"If MaryLou had been referred to counseling, and the counselor was familiar with Secondary Rape Trauma Syndrome, then MaryLou could have been given the chance to process her feelings."

"Her feeling that her little sister was about to be raped?"

"Her feeling that her little sister was *certain* to be raped. What is so difficult for those who haven't actually seen the phenomenon to understand is that, to MaryLou, she herself had already been raped. When a person is made to watch or hear accounts of a loved one being raped, it is as if they themselves have been raped. Tortured. Dehumanized."

Swift started to ask another question, then shook his head as if to say, *There! That should be enough for anyone,* and simply said, "Thank you, Ms. Rollo."

A whispered discussion broke out among the four deputies. Finally, Fat Face himself rose to his feet, making sure everyone knew he was in charge.

"Ms. Rollo, you used the word 'dehumanized.' Are you telling this jury that the defendant didn't know right from wrong at the time she shot and killed Cameron Taft?"

"No, I am not."

"Well, then, will you tell us what 'dehumanized' means?"

"In the context I used it, 'dehumanized' refers to a person who feels absolutely powerless. Facing an inhuman situation—being forced to watch the gang rape of a loved one, for example—the victim would feel as if she herself had no human persona. That she had been robbed of the power to do what *any* decent human being should do—"

"Like kill an unarmed man?"

"If that unarmed man was engaged in the rape of a loved one, not to interfere, not to stop the—"

"But there was no gang rape going on when the defendant shot and killed—"

"Your Honor," Swift said, "I have yet to hear of a cross-examination style which consists of constantly interrupting the witness. May I respectfully request that the court instruct counsel for the—"

"Oh, this witness seems to be handling herself just fine," the judge said.

Christ, why doesn't he just ask her for a date? I thought.

"As I was saying," Fat Face continued, the grin on his greasy face showing he was actually stupid enough to think he was winning this round. But before he could go further, Debbie cut him off at the knees:

"There was no gang rape actually in process," she told the jury, "but MaryLou believed one was going to happen. As you said, 'imminently.'"

"I didn't say any such—"

"Does the prosecutor think he's on the stand now?" Swift said.

Before the judge could rule, Debbie started talking again.

"In Secondary Rape Trauma Syndrome, the person who believes they *should* have prevented the rape of another and failed to do so feels as if they had been raped themselves. A person who cannot protect themselves, *especially* a physically gifted individual such as MaryLou, can become so trapped in self-blame that they often act without regard to consequences."

"So the defendant *did* know right from wrong?"

"Those concepts would not have been in her mind at the time of . . . the event."

"Because she was *out* of her mind?"

"No," Debbie said, with just a little exasperation in her tone. "That, again, is *not* what I said. MaryLou wasn't what you seem to be implying. That is, 'crazy' in some way. She knew what she was doing. What you fail to understand is that, in her mind, she *was* doing the right thing. Not only to protect her little sister, but to regain her own humanity."

"Those are some pretty extreme terms, aren't they, Ms. Rollo?"

"They are descriptive terms appropriate to a *more*-than-extreme situation."

"You were present in court when one Franklin Wayne testified, were you not?"

"Yes."

"If MaryLou had asked him for help, what do you think he would have done?"

"Considering that that would have had to happen before anyone knew MaryLou's little sister was a manipulative liar—"

"Objection! Your Honor, is this witness now conferring the status of 'expert' on that . . . on that large young man who testified earlier in the trial?"

"The witness is repeating what another witness has already testified to," Swift shot back.

"Please finish your answer, Ms. Rollo" was all the judge said.

Debbie gave the judge a look he probably took the wrong way . . . which was good for us. She turned to face the jury: "As I was saying, if MaryLou had asked for Franklin Wayne's help, there is not a doubt in my mind that he would have done exactly what MaryLou did. Only he wouldn't have needed a gun."

"Fine. But she *didn't* ask for his help, did she?"

"No. In MaryLou's mind, her baby sister was *her* responsibility. Hers alone."

"Well, let me ask you this. *Hypothetically*, if you had a weapon such as Franklin Wayne at your disposal, a—shall we say—low-IQ man, twice the size of the victim in this case. If that individual would do whatever you asked—wouldn't *you* use him?"

"No, I would not."

"Oh, really? Why is that?"

"It would be morally wrong. MaryLou is a very straightforward, honest young woman. She undoubtedly knew of Franklin Wayne's feelings for her. But she wouldn't, as you put it, *use* someone she cared for in such a matter. Only her sister would be capable of such a foul act of betrayal."

"Objection!"

"To what now?" the judge asked, very wearily.

"The witness refused to answer my question."

"Are you serious, counsel?"

Fat Face sat down like a fighter in his corner. One who knew he wouldn't be coming out for the next round.

"You were beautiful," T.D. said to Debbie. "I mean, you did a beautiful job. . . . I mean, actually, you—"

"Will you stop?" Dolly told him, taking Debbie's hand and pulling her away.

T.D. didn't mistake that for a question.

At least Dolly didn't have to give her girlfriend CPR in front of us all. Even Rascal seemed to get it. He may have slept in that bedroom a million times, but, for now, it was strictly No Males Allowed.

"I have to put her on," Swift told us.

"Yeah, you do," T.D. agreed. "This isn't an insanity defense, where the defendant sits staring into space. No history of mental illness. No 'Trench Coat Mafia' she ran with. No matter what you call it, this is all about self-defense. Or defense of another, actually. And no matter how strong your case, if the jury doesn't hear Mary-Lou's side of the story, they'll hold it against her."

"She's a fucking zombie!" Swift said fiercely. "She wasn't when we started, but now . . ."

"There's no court tomorrow," I said. "There's plenty of time between now and Monday for me to talk to her."

"You?"

"Like T.D. said, now we're in a place where I have an education. A very good one. But I'd want you to come along."

"Me?"

Swift gave T.D. a look. T.D. nodded.

"You don't have to talk, MaryLou," I told her the next morning. "But you *do* have to listen."

"No, I don't."

"You're not going back to your cell until you hear me out," I told her. "And you'll *want* to hear what I've got to tell you. Something you don't know. Something you're going to need."

She didn't move, but I could see a nerve muscle jump in her left cheek. *All the way up from her throwing hand,* I thought.

"Mr. Swift, your lawyer, he's not going to say a word. He's not going to *hear* a word. Him being here protects *me.* I've got some things to say that I wouldn't want the police to hear."

Swift moved as far away as he could, held a soft-cover copy of the *Oregon Rules of Evidence* in front of his face, and made it clear he was tuning us out.

"Cameron Taft was a virus," I told MaryLou, in a half-whisper. "He was a carrier. If he hadn't been stopped, he'd have spread it too far for it to ever be contained."

Her face didn't move, but those hard, pale eyes of hers shifted.

"He didn't start Tiger Ko Khai, but I know who did."

Now her eyes were *locked* on mine. I met her stare with one of my own. Hers was cold, but I'd had way more practice: mine was freezing.

"His name is Ryan Teller. He's gone into hiding now, but I'll find him. And when I do, I'll cut his head off and plant it on a stake, as a warning to anyone who might try to follow his path. I'm trusting you with that."

She made some little noise in her throat. I waited for her to speak, then realized she'd said all she was going to say. For now, anyway.

"I know how to finish what you started. There's no more Tiger Ko Khai anywhere near here. Next year, *nobody's* going to be wearing those jackets at your school. You know why, MaryLou? Because they're scared to death, all of them. They know what's coming. They don't know who, but they sure know what. They're already missing a couple of members. I don't mean the punks you wounded, or that virus-carrier you killed. I mean the ones *I* did."

The nerve stopped jumping in her cheek. She leaned forward, spoke well below a whisper. "Are you saying that you—?"

"Yes. And I'm not finished. But when I am, they'll all be gone."

"Why?"

"You executed that virus-carrier because you thought he was going to rape your little sister. You were wrong about Danielle, MaryLou. But you weren't wrong about Cameron Taft. If you hadn't taken him out, dozens of young girls were going to be gang-raped. Every single year. In fact, they already *would* have been . . . if it wasn't for you."

"Me?"

"You."

"Even if that was true, why would you put yourself in any of this?"

"It was a simple choice, just like yours was. Either you let someone you love get gang-raped, or you shoot the rapist in the head."

"I thought it *was* that simple. I . . . I couldn't just leave her to . . . that. But now—"

"'Now' is Monday, MaryLou. You get on that witness stand and just be yourself. Mighty Mary brought glory to this town. And she couldn't leave it with that virus still alive. Me, I'm not leaving. So I can't let it ever come back."

"You talk like you've done this a lot."

"I've been in a lot of wars."

"This is different."

"No, it isn't. The only difference between you and me is that I'm a lot better at it than you are."

"I killed him."

"You did. And that took out *one* of them. I'm promising you that I'm taking them *all*. I'm promising you that I know how to do it. And then there's the biggest difference of all."

Once she figured out I wasn't going to say anything more until she did, she gave up. "What?"

"I'm going to burn their crops in the field. I'm going to salt the ground so nothing can ever grow there again. I'm going to poison their rivers. Just like I promised you before, I'm going to plant their heads on stakes."

Her mouth opened, but no sound came out.

"And *I* won't get caught," I told her as I got up to leave.

"You sure she's ready for this?" Swift said to me outside the court-house Monday morning. I could feel real nervousness eating at him.

"She's ready. But give her a chance."

"What's that mean?"

"Just put her on the stand, ask her what happened, and get out of the way. You may have to coax her a few times, but I'm not sure she'll even need that much. She wants to do this now. Not for Danielle, not anymore. But, remember, this whole town loved her when she was bringing them to the State Championships. Ask around. Most of them would swear on a stack of Bibles that if they'd let MaryLou pitch *all* the games they would have brought home the trophy."

"That's not love," Swift said, bitterness deeply buried in his voice. But not so deep I couldn't feel it. "These people, they think if some athlete wins a trophy they won it, too. But let that same athlete flop on the field, and watch all the 'love' come raining down."

"MaryLou didn't flop on the softball field. And she won't on the battlefield, either. The one we'll *all* be on today."

"The defense calls MaryLou McCoy" was all Swift said. He was already on his feet, so all MaryLou had to do was push back her chair and walk to the stand. She walked like a soldier. Like so many soldiers I'd served with. A soldier who is going to keep walking until he either gets where he's going or dies where he falls.

Swift skipped all the usual preliminaries. He didn't even so much as ask her name before he launched the rocket everyone had been watching for:

"MaryLou, on Friday, May 31, 2013, did you shoot one Cameron Taft?"

"Yes."

"Did you shoot at other members of a gang known as Tiger Ko Khai?"

"Yes."

"Please tell the jury why you did this."

"The minute I wasn't around to stop him, they were going to rape my baby sister."

"That's a very strong statement, MaryLou. Can you tell us how you knew such a horrible event was going to occur?"

"Objection!" Fat Face screamed out. "She couldn't know any such thing!"

"Goes to the state of mind of the defendant at the time of the events in question," Swift said, as if anyone with half a brain would know that. Making it clear the jury sure as hell did.

"Overruled," the judge said—by now, to nobody's surprise except Fat Face's.

"I apologize for the unnecessary interruption," Swift said, speaking directly to MaryLou. "Unfortunately, I have to ask you *again* how you knew your sister was in immediate danger of such a horrible attack."

"That's what they do."

"And by 'they' you mean . . ."

"Tiger Ko Khai."

"That same gang Detective Lancer described?" Swift asked, looking at the prosecutor's table as if daring them to object again. "Because they had done this before? To your certain knowledge?"

"To *everybody's* certain knowledge," MaryLou said. "The minute I—"

"Objection! Your Honor, how can this witness possibly testify as to what 'everybody' knew?"

Swift pounced. "Anybody who's been in this courtroom certainly knows, Your Honor. The defense has put on several separate young women, *all* of them prior victims, *all* of whom testified to that exact same experience."

"It is not significant whether or not the defendant 'knew' anything," the judge lectured both sides. "The defense here is 'justification.' What is pertinent to any such defense is the defendant's belief—not her factual knowledge, her belief—and the *reasonableness* of that belief. Which is why, the court assumes, the defense witnesses who had undergone a similar experience were put on. The objection is overruled."

"Again, I apologize," Swift said to MaryLou, who sat like a granite-faced statute. "But it was important that the court make it clear what is pertinent to your defense and what is not. So—I am compelled to ask you again. Is it true that you shot Cameron Taft and two others on the date in question?"

"I don't know how many I shot," MaryLou said. "I know I shot him. After that, I just kept pulling the trigger until the gun clicked and clicked. I knew it was empty, then, so I just sat down and waited."

"Waited for what?"

"For whatever. It didn't matter anymore."

"Because . . . ?"

"Because they weren't going to rape my little sister."

"You believed that killing Cameron Taft—?"

"He was the one Danielle was in love with. She had his pictures on her bedroom wall, with kiss marks she made on them. I knew the gang he was leader of, and I knew Danielle had been around them before."

"How did you know that?"

"She told me. Bragging that they thought she was fourteen because she skipped two grades, but she was only twelve and already the best boys in the school wanted her."

"What did you do when she told you?"

"I slapped her all over the room," MaryLou said. "I ripped those pictures off the wall. And I warned her, if I ever heard of her going back around them—the Tiger Ko Khai bunch—I'd punch her silly instead of just slaps. Punch her in the face. Danielle was afraid of that more than anything. So I thought I'd stopped the . . . whole thing from happening."

"And when you found out that Danielle was involved with them again?"

"That's when I knew I couldn't stop her after I left. I knew I could never stop *them*. I was supposed to be going to summer camp. For softball. It's like a showcase. The coaches would all be there. Then, if they liked what they saw, I'd have my pick of scholarships."

"You couldn't stop Danielle, but . . . ?"

"I *could* stop them. I remember thinking that: I could stop them. The next thing I really remember is the police. They probably wouldn't even have grabbed me except there was nobody else. In the hall, I mean."

"Did you intend to kill Cameron Taft?"

"I . . . don't know. I don't know much about guns. But I meant to shoot him, I know I must have. Him and any of the others. Danielle is my sister. My baby sister. She was smarter than me, okay, but she didn't have any . . . experience.

"If you knew my mother and father, you'd understand. She was like my own baby. I knew I had to . . . protect her. And I thought I was. Until the doctor—I mean the doctor that testified here—until he said what Danielle really was, I . . ."

MaryLou started crying then. But she never dropped her eyes, staring at the jury as if challenging them to say a word about it.

Swift sat down.

MaryLou turned slowly and looked over at the prosecution table. Tears were still running down her face, but the eyes they came from were lasers.

The last of the prosecution team must have been saved just for this one job. He was a little older, a little better dressed than Fat Face. All that told me was that he'd been around longer.

"Don't people call you something besides 'MaryLou'?"

"No."

"Oh, come on, now. Are you saying you never heard anyone call you 'Mighty Mary'?"

"Only in the papers. Or, sometimes, people would shout it at games. But nobody ever *called* me that, like a nickname or something."

"I see. Well, let me ask you this, then: were you personally afraid of Cameron Taft?"

"No."

"In fact, if he so much as touched you, there isn't a doubt in your mind that you could have fought him off, is there?"

"No."

"In fact, you could probably beat him to a pulp, isn't that true?"

"I don't know. But . . . yes, I guess so—a coward like him, he'd quit before I would."

"So tell us, why did Mighty Mary need a *pistol* to send a message to Cameron Taft?"

"Message?"

"A message to leave your sister alone."

"Oh. Beating him up, that wouldn't work. He'd never take that kind of humiliation—it would just make him more evil. And he'd take it out on my little sister."

"Why didn't you get your retarded boyfriend to beat him up? He's certainly big enough, isn't he?"

Insulte sa mère! I thought. *Le fils de pute finit enfin par conger!*

You could see MaryLou calling on every vestige of self-control. You could also see the blood-flash in her eyes. *Sure,* I tried to tell the jury with my mind, *MaryLou might snap like a dry twig. Then maybe snap you like a dry twig. But she's a teenage girl, not some icy assassin.*

"I don't have a boyfriend," she finally said.

"You don't know of one Franklin Wayne?"

"Yes, I know him. He's one of my best friends. Probably my best friend."

"Isn't he better known as Bluto throughout your school? And isn't that because he's retarded?"

"I never heard him called that name," MaryLou gambled on the lie. Or maybe nobody ever called him that when *she* was around—now that *would* be retarded.

"And you *don't* know he's retarded?"

"How would I know that? Franklin's the same age as me. If he was so retarded, how did he pass all his courses?"

"Perhaps because he was a star football player?" the prosecution's ace asked.

You just cut your own throat. I felt the pounding in my head. *You're telling this whole town that they looked the other way to get a football player. Why not just go up to the jury box and spit in their faces?*

"I don't understand," MaryLou said, playing it perfectly. Easy to do when telling the truth is the only job you have.

The prosecutor retreated, but it was already too late. The best he could do was "So you *had* to kill Cameron Taft?"

"I don't know."

"What are you crying about?"

MaryLou wiped the tears away with one hand, sweeping them over her prominent nose in the same gesture she might use to brush off a punch to the head. She looked at the prosecutor, as if deciding what to say. Finally she settled on, "I'm not sure."

"Are you crying because, after sitting in this courtroom, you *now* realize that Cameron Taft was completely innocent? In fact, it was Danielle who came to him, not the other way around, wasn't it?"

"Maybe. I don't know. I didn't know any of that when it . . . when it happened."

"You mean, when you murdered Cameron Taft in cold blood?"

"I guess so" was MaryLou's only response.

"So you *thought* that young man was going to rape your sister after you left for this summer-camp thing, and that *thought* made you carry a concealed firearm to school? And that *thought* made you shoot that same young man in the face, killing him instantly—is that about right?"

"I didn't *think* anything."

"Oh, now that you've heard the good Dr. Joel testify that you might have been in a 'fugue state,' you decided to go with that, huh?"

"I don't even know what that is. I said I didn't think anything because that's the truth. I knew something was going to happen. And I knew I couldn't let it."

"Well, you made sure of that, didn't you?"

"I guess so."

"Is that going to be your answer to anything I ask you?"

"I don't know."

"Let's see, then. Why didn't you reload your weapon after it was empty?"

"I didn't have any more bullets."

"So, if you'd had more bullets, you would have shot even more innocent teenagers?"

"I don't know. I don't think so. By the time the thing kept clicking, there was nobody around, anyway. Nobody but me."

"You and the dead body of Cameron Taft."

"I guess so. I didn't look at anyone. I just pulled the trigger over and over again. Then I threw the gun away. And I sat down."

"Why didn't you bring more bullets with you?"

"I didn't know where any more bullets were. I just grabbed the gun from where my father always kept it—under the cushion of his big chair."

"Why didn't you wait?"

"I was already late for school. And I knew Friday was my last chance."

"Your last chance to kill Cameron Taft?"

"My last chance to . . ." The tears came again, but MaryLou ignored them. "My last chance to save my little sister from . . . them."

"But *now* you know—"

"Objection!" Swift cut him off. "What the defendant *now* knows is more than merely irrelevant; it is a blatant attempt to torment her. This is nothing but another attempt by the prosecution to poison the jury!"

"Sustained," the judge said. "I will not tell you again, counsel."

"Then I have no more questions of this witness," the Fat Face substitute said, and sashayed over to his table like he'd just won the case. But before he sat down, he whirled dramatically, said, "With the court's permission?"

The judge made his waving motion again. The deputy took that as encouragement. MaryLou hadn't moved.

"You said before that you couldn't go to your mother or your father?"

MaryLou just stared straight ahead. Not looking at him; not looking away, either. And not going to answer a question that hadn't been asked. I wondered if the jury understood that the question itself was the obvious answer.

"MaryLou, now that you know the truth, do you even *care* that you killed a man?"

"I . . . I don't think so."

"Caring isn't something you *think;* it's something you *feel.* Don't you feel anything?"

"I don't know."

"Do you think, if the court gave you sufficient time, you might come up with an answer?"

"I don't know."

"Is there anything you *do* care about?"

"Now?"

"Yes," the deputy said, making his own disbelief clear. "That's what I'm asking you: what do you care about *now?*"

"Now? Now, I guess I don't care about anything."

"Not even the innocent man you—"

"Judge, can we *please* see *some* offer of proof from the prosecution? A declaration of 'innocence' on behalf of the dead rapist coming out of the mouth of the prosecution's office is not only objectionable as a matter of law, it is objectionable as not being a question for the witness at all. It is an utterly self-serving *excuse* for the failure of their office to prosecute one single perpetrator of the numerous gang rapes Detective Lancer has already testified to.

"It is the heart of our defense that MaryLou McCoy had no idea, no hint, no *concept* of the so-called innocence of the man she shot. All she knew was that he was the leader of a gang who specialized in the rape of young girls. The prosecution is welcome to disprove that, if they can. But they cannot be allowed to foul the record with their weak attempt to defend *themselves.*"

"Your Honor . . ." The deputy stepped in, more to stop the damning accusations coming from Swift than anything else. He wasn't prepared for the dead silence that followed.

Swift stood waiting, his whole stance suggesting he was just waiting to hit back. MaryLou went back into her thousand-yard stare. The judge's stare was a lot shorter, but his was loaded for bear.

The deputy sat down.

"**S**ummations are a little different here," Swift explained again. "The prosecution goes first, then it's our turn, and then they get another shot."

"You knew the job was bad when you took it, hoss," was all T.D. said.

"I knew the rules, sure. But I'll be right up front with you—I've never tried a case like this in my life."

That was too much for Dolly. "I'm sure everyone on this planet who ever accomplished something for the first time would say the same thing before they actually went out and did it."

"The only ones who can't are the ones that never got it done," Debbie backed up her girlfriend.

"I'm not looking for sympathy here," Swift said, nice and calm. "I'm trying to explain criminal-trial procedure, so when you see them getting two bites at the apple you won't think this is something special the judge gave them."

"Oh, I don't think the judge is on their side at all," Debbie said.

"That's the truth," T.D. said. "One look at you, and that old bird was ready to tear up the scarecrow to get at the cornfield."

I was used to Debbie's blushing by now, but this was a beaut.

If there was any argument about who was going to deliver the prosecution's closing, it must have been behind closed doors. The woman whose name I didn't know stood up and addressed the jury in a stiff, formal manner, ticking off the various crimes MaryLou had committed.

In a way, she reminded me of MaryLou herself. She was tall and lean, not a girl who ever got by on her looks. She was absolutely methodical. And she might as well have been talking to a wall. All the jurors had a "tell us something we don't know" expression on their faces.

And that was something she couldn't do.

Swift went right for the carotid. He stood up, looked around the packed courtroom, then walked slowly over to the jury box as if the audience was following right behind him. He began speaking as he closed in. "When this trial began, you heard a lot of promises from the defense. We have kept every single one of those promises. The judge will instruct you on the law of 'Justification.' And you will see that *every single element* of that defense was in play during the commission of *every single act* the prosecution has endlessly repeated.

"We do not deny the truth. We have *never* denied it. MaryLou McCoy did discharge a firearm in school on Friday, the thirty-first of May, 2013. As a result of that act, one individual died, and two others were wounded. Was this conduct wrong? Of course it was. But was this conduct *criminal*? That, ladies and gentlemen of the jury, is not the same question."

Swift closed in on the jury box, as if what he had to say next was just for their ears: a shared confidence.

"Let's say a day-care center is on fire. And when a woman tries to get inside to save her baby, a man bars her way. If the mother shoots him, would that be justified? Sure, it would, and I doubt there's a decent person in America who would deny it.

"Now let's change the scenario a bit. That day-care center is still on fire, but it has already been completely evacuated. And the person barring the mother's way is a fireman, acting in the lawful discharge of his duty. If the mother didn't know any of that, then would that same shooting have been justified?

"The judge is going to explain that the answer lies not in objective fact, but in the mind of the mother. If she thought, if she *believed,* that her baby was still upstairs, the fact that her baby was *actually* safe wouldn't change things. Not one bit.

"Why? Because, even though it was *later* proven wrong, the mother's belief was reasonable, based on her own knowledge of the operation of the day-care center, and not contradicted by any fact actually communicated to her.

"Was that mother 'insane'? Of course not! She might have perished in that same fire, but she was a *mother* protecting her child. She didn't stop to 'analyze,' she didn't do 'research,' she *acted*. And she acted because she believed that if she *didn't* a horrible thing was going to happen to someone she was morally bound to protect . . . no matter what it might cost her.

"So—how does this apply to MaryLou McCoy? In every way possible! She knew, for a *fact,* that the gang known as Tiger Ko Khai specialized in gang rapes of underage girls. She also knew, for a *fact,* that not a single one of them had ever been brought into a courtroom just like this and put on trial.

"How could she be so sure? You heard Detective Lancer. You heard the testimony of all those other girls. You heard them tell you virtually the same set of facts: They were lured to a certain place occupied and controlled by Tiger Ko Khai. And every one of them was gang-raped.

"You saw the hospital records. *You* know all those girls were raped. And *you* know that nothing was ever done about it! You've heard MaryLou state that she herself believed that going to the authorities would be a waste of time. In her position, wouldn't you have believed the same thing?

"MaryLou didn't hide behind some 'insanity' defense. She got up there and told you exactly what was in her mind *at the time this all happened.*

"Why else would MaryLou have done what she did? She didn't

know any of the Tiger Ko Khai gang. Not personally, I mean—she most certainly did know their reputation. A reputation they *earned*.

"Are we looking at a girl who *planned* what happened? I don't think it's necessary for the defense to put on an 'expert' to tell you that a .22 revolver is hardly guaranteed to kill *anything,* not even a squirrel. So why did MaryLou use such a weapon? Because it was there, that's all. If MaryLou's father hadn't let everyone in the house know where he kept his pistol, what would she have done on that fateful morning at school? The truth is that we don't know. And we never will."

Swift spun on his heel, as if allowing the audience to get in on the action.

"I never thought we would have to parade a whole list of school shootings before you to prove that what MaryLou did—and why she did it—had *nothing* whatsoever in common with Columbine. But, even so, we did put on an expert, an expert who had been retained for the specific purpose of evaluating and analyzing the events at Columbine. And he told us what we already knew. Comparing *our* town to Columbine is not merely a dirty trick—it slanders every one of us who lives here."

That brought Fat Face to his feet. "Judge, I have to object. We never made any such comparison."

"The jury heard whatever it heard, counsel," the judge said, making it clear what *he* heard. "And it may draw any inference from what it heard that it chooses. Summations are not evidence. The defense did not interrupt the prosecution's closing; please provide them with the same courtesy . . . especially as you still have a final opportunity to rebut anything you believe was wrongly stated."

"Thank you, Your Honor," Swift said, as if the judge had already personally acquitted MaryLou. "Ladies and gentlemen, the case for the defense is no more complicated than this: MaryLou's belief that her baby sister was in imminent danger of gang rape at the hands of Tiger Ko Khai in general and Cameron Taft in particular was a *realistic* belief. It was based on what MaryLou knew. On what *everybody* at her school seemed to know. All that adds up to just one thing: what MaryLou did was *justified.*

"I said that MaryLou's belief that only the most drastic action could save her baby sister was also a realistic belief, but the word I should have used is 'real.' That is, her beliefs were utterly rational, completely supported by everything she knew from all sources of information available to her.

"That information included the *collaboration* of this very DA's Office in the ongoing acts of vile criminality by Tiger Ko Khai. Am I saying the DA's Office actually participated? Of course not. But I am saying, and I am saying the evidence *proves,* that the failure of the DA's Office to ever prosecute one single case of that gang's *practice* of gang-raping minors makes their office responsible. And, yes, I *am* holding the DA's Office responsible for the reasonableness of MaryLou's belief that the rape of her little sister would be treated no differently. That is, ignored!

"And if you believe that MaryLou's act was an attempt to save her little sister from what she reasonably believed was going to happen, happen imminently, perhaps no later than that very night, then you *must* find that her conduct was justified. Indeed, it was *compelled.*"

Swift's voice was louder, more theatrical, but still well under control.

"This is America. We don't have dictators. We don't have rulers telling us what to do. This is a democracy. And that makes each of us responsible for our own acts. MaryLou has taken responsibility for what she did.

"But MaryLou also had an absolute right to look you in the eye and *explain* what she did. And you have an absolute right to do what Americans have fought and died for since this country was founded—the right to vote, the right to cast a ballot, the right to make your voice be heard. But you don't just have those rights, you have those *responsibilities,* too, don't you? Don't you *all*?"

Swift swept his left hand in a wide arc, sending the message—whatever that jury decided, their verdict was going to be a judgment of the whole town.

"It comes down to this: You can vote that MaryLou McCoy was a cold-blooded killer, like the prosecution claims . . . even though they can't give you one single reason for that claim. Or you can cast a vote for the truth.

"*Now* you know about something very dark and very dangerous lurking in our town. If *you* had known about this gang, and its special immunity, would *you* have tolerated it? You know you wouldn't. You know *none* of you would!

"There's one way to tell the whole world what this town *really* stands for, and now you know what that is. Vote for MaryLou, ladies and gentleman. Vote for a young woman you have always been proud of. For a young woman who has brought nothing but honor to her hometown. Vote for a young woman whose only crime was trying to protect her baby sister.

"MaryLou McCoy sacrificed everything to do that, and now all the prosecution can do is taunt her with the fact that her sacrifice was in vain.

"You know how towns get a reputation? By word of mouth. By what people *say* about them. So we know that some towns are notorious for their speed traps, others are known to be places that look the other way when certain kinds of illegal activity take place . . . and other towns are known to be just the opposite: Places where decent, law-abiding citizens can live decent, law-abiding lives—clean, friendly, beautiful places. Places people want to visit. That's always been *our* reputation, hasn't it? Don't we depend on the tourist trade for much of the business here? We have a *clean* town, and I'm not just talking about the environment when I say that."

Swift's voice dropped, and his tone darkened, covering the whole courtroom with the same blanket.

"But there's been a foul, evil underbelly to this town. One that, before this all happened, none of us even knew about. *But our children did!* And that's wrong. All wrong. Because children always believe that adults know what's going on. Oh, they may not know *where* kids might go to smoke pot, but they know that kids *are* smoking pot. So, from this moment forward, the 'we had no idea' excuse isn't going to fly. The curtain has been pulled back, and we have all seen the depravity behind it. The monsters can't hide from us anymore. They can stay among us only if we *let* them stay.

"MaryLou had every reason in the world to believe she was saving her baby sister from a gang of rapists. She did what any of you would do in the same situation. Am I saying MaryLou was a hero? No. No, I'm not. But I *am* saying she did what she believed was the right thing to do, even at such great cost to herself.

"Remember that mother charging into a burning building? Risking everything? If it turned out that her baby was actually in no danger despite what she believed, are you going to call her a 'criminal'?

"So—what do *you* want others to say about our town? That's up to you, right now. It's time to tell the world who we are. What we stand for. And we can't do that unless we stand *up*.

"What more could MaryLou ask of you?" Swift wrapped it up. "Just do what you know is right. MaryLou can ask for no more than that. And she should *expect* no less. Not from *our* town."

Fat Face must have been consulting a manual on how to be stupid. His entire closing was devoted to pointing out that MaryLou's beliefs were all wrong. She wasn't saving her baby sister from anything. In fact, her baby sister was a psychopathic little monster—"And that's from the mouth of the defense's own witness!"—who wasn't even worth saving. If MaryLou had a brain in her head, she would have known all this, he snidely repeated. Again and again.

Unlike Swift, who kept himself in motion, drawing the jury and the courtroom audience together, making himself one of them, Fat Face was as rooted to a single spot as he was to that single line—MaryLou was a killer.

One of the games the enemy liked to play with captives in the jungle was to make them dig their own graves before they were put in them. If a captive did a very good job, they promised to kill him quickly. Men who'd lived through that were never the same afterward.

Fat Face couldn't have known any of that. But if digging your own grave was a job, he would have been highly qualified for it.

The jurors were sent out right at the lunch break. Apparently, they were all slow eaters—it was almost three hours before they came back in.

And pronounced MaryLou McCoy "not guilty" on all counts.

Dolly ran over from her seat and hugged MaryLou like her own mother never had.

I walked over to Swift. Held out my hand. "You just helped this whole town raise the stakes," I said.

Then I walked away quick, before he could ask me what I meant. Good thing, too—he was getting mobbed by everyone.

Whatever Bradley L. Swift, Esq., had been before this started, he'd never be that again.

Or this town, either.

"I don't know how to thank you," I told Dr. Joel late that night. We'd just returned from reclaiming his car. I saw that Martin had managed to put well over a thousand miles on it since we swapped him for his Mini Cooper. If T.D. noticed, he either didn't care or kept it to himself.

"No thanks necessary, hoss. It's been fun."

"Sure. What I wanted to tell you was—"

"—that if I ever needed something . . . done—something more in line with your own skill set—you'd take care of it."

"Was I that obvious?"

"Just to me, hoss. Just to me. If you've guessed that I heard that same kind of promise a hundred times in my career, you'd be right. But if you guessed that yours is the only one I ever believed, you'd be a hell of a lot smarter than you want folks to know."

"You know how to reach me," I said. I left him standing out there by the garage, alone in the darkness.

I wasn't surprised when Dolly told me that T.D. had decided to make a little detour and drop Debbie off on his way back home. I wasn't even surprised at her sly little grin.

I found Franklin the next morning. He and Spyros were removing dead trees from some waterfront lot.

"I hate doing this," Spyros said. He was a short man, with a big chest, long arms, and a sun-darkened complexion.

"I thought you loved it."

"Saving trees, sure. But the numbskulls who bought this land don't realize it's all going to be out in the ocean the next heavy rainy season we get. And you can't buy mudslide insurance on this part of the coast."

He seemed more upset about the trees dying than about the rich people going broke. It didn't surprise me.

"Does Franklin know about the verdict?" I asked him.

"Sure does."

"It was on the news, huh?"

"MaryLou called him herself. He's going to see her tonight, because she's leaving tomorrow," he said quietly. "But that's tonight, *after* work!" he shouted over to Franklin.

"Quelle est la meilleure façon de dépouiller un rat?" I asked, over the encrypted line.

"*Le brûler. La peau brûle avant les os.*"

The code hadn't changed. Not the best way to skin a cat: the best way to skin a *rat*. Nor the answer: If you want to take all the skin off a rat, the best way is to set it on fire. Then only the charred skeleton would remain.

I thought that through for a split second. Then I told the man I'd never meet the name of the man I was looking for. And added everything else I knew about him.

Ryan Teller could never find a man with such expertise. No professional would even talk to slime like him, not without a better story than any he could concoct. *And* the right introduction, from the right people.

But the man who made seeing-without-being-seen his life's work could find any new set of documents Ryan Teller had bought "*chez un amateur*" as easily as striking a match.

It was late the next spring when "John Norman Wilson" walked down an alley between two bars in Denver, whistling softly to himself, full of blooming optimism.

Both bars were too old for students, too déclassé for yuppies, not hard-core enough for bikers . . . so he was certain they'd become a good hunting ground. All he had to do was make the necessary investment of time.

Besides, they were both close to where the former Ryan Teller now lived. He wouldn't even need a car to reach his new operating table.

He was as free as any man could be. A man who had shed his past as a snake would shed its skin. What lay underneath would be unchanged inside, but it would look brand-new. Fresh and glistening. Ryan Teller was looking forward to his new life.

But he died the way most people live . . . without ever knowing why.